JONATHAN PATRICK

ARCHER'S PARADOX

BOOK TWO

Palmetto Publishing Group, LLC
Charleston, SC

For more information regarding special discounts for bulk purchases, please contact Palmetto Publishing Group at Info@PalmettoPublishingGroup.com.

ISBN-13: 978-1-944313-53-1
ISBN-10: 1-944313-53-2

For David

You are truly missed…

Archer's paradox:

An archer must,

in order to successfully hit his target…

not aim directly at it,

but slightly to one side...

Prologue

Although Palm Beach is technically in South Florida, the onshore breeze working its way between the tall buildings around Palm Beach's famous Worth Avenue sent a chill down Farid's spine. The chill seemed to radiate outward from his chest down his arms and even extended into his hands. Continuing to shiver involuntarily, he began shaking his arms in a vain attempt to make the sensation cease. Considering everything else going on in his life, blaming the cool breeze for shivering seemed almost amusing. Pausing briefly, he took a deep breath of the cool humid air and turned to face the warmth of early morning sun. The warm Florida sun on his face relaxed him and seemed to mitigate his tremors. He walked slowly south toward Worth Avenue occasionally lifting his head, as any tourist would, to look at the beautiful buildings. Perhaps the tremors were just a symptom of stress or a late reaction to his recent surgery. He concentrated on the former self-diagnosis of "stress" and pushed the latter from his thoughts...

It was early to be out and the streets were mostly empty with the exception of a few shopkeepers. They moved like bees in a hive; only they were reloading the windows of their high-end shops with the expensive baubles that drew the well-to-do local shoppers like moths to a flame. Many of the vendors loaded up several decorative racks of black felt covered shelves with watches, diamond broaches or rings then quickly scooted outside to see if it looked good through the thick, smash resistant glass. It was sad that they had to go through this procedure every morning but also an amazing ritual to watch them rebuild the displays.

Farid had wandered the street for a while nonchalantly observing the daily restocking ritual and had even grabbed a large espresso at Starbucks. Even at seven bucks a cup, for coffee, Starbucks couldn't afford to actually be *on* Worth Avenue so it was located in a courtyard just behind the *Tory Burch* store. He had needed to walk into that particular courtyard anyway this morning to make sure nothing had changed since he had last completed the very same ritual being accomplished this morning.

Now, back on the corner of Hibiscus and Worth Avenue, directly across from *Tiffany's*, Farid was again out of the shadows of the buildings and back in the sunshine. Inhaling deeply, he felt a slight pull at the incision site on his chest. He winced slightly. It was frustrating that scar tissue took so long to heal. The sensation was no more than a mere sting and completely harmless.

The espresso now gone, he glanced, without staring, once more at the various security cameras directed toward the popular street. Smiling, his walk continued much like any tourist's, empty cup in hand, gawking at all the sights.

Although confident his future was to be wonderful, in the spaces between confidence and certainty resided a touch of doubt. It was a daily struggle of late and Farid tried hard to erase the nagging doubt and concentrate only on the moment. "The moment" was all that mattered. As he ducked his head and turned away from the bright warmth of the sun, he hoped that what he had been told his entire life was true. If it wasn't, he was certain he would miss this…

CHAPTER 1

—⁂—

The Abyss

As with the previous times, when the IV was adjusted, reducing the flow of the strong sedative Propofol, his patient was suddenly yanked back into a state of first semi-consciousness then, after a few minutes, full consciousness. The patient's respirations switched from long and shallow restive breaths, to deeper full breaths. The man's chest began to rise and fall as he regained what could best be described as normal sinus rhythm. For someone trained to alleviate pain and discomfort, it was very difficult for the doctor to watch, knowing full well what was coming next. With each deep breath, his patient took, it was followed by an increasingly violent coughing spasm...and pain.

Retired Admiral Jiayi Feng could hear loud urgent voices around him and recognized the language being spoken as his own. Where was he? He had obviously survived his ascent to the surface...but the burning pain in his throat and chest was excruciating!

Feng racked his confused mind for a reasonable explanation of his current situation. He clearly remembered leaving the doomed Iranian submarine *Yunes* and feeling the concussive pressure as the submarine exploded beneath him.

JONATHAN PATRICK

He vaguely remembered the air in his rebreather device tasting bitter and then burning. At some point he must have made the conscious decision to hold his breath. Now he was here. What still needed to be determined was where "here" was.

The burning pain in his chest and throat was increasing steadily. He felt as if every subsequent breath was becoming more and more difficult. He attempted to speak but a tube was lodged in his throat making that an impossibility. The admiral was just beginning to panic when his coughing began to subside and his body went slowly limp. He teetered, momentarily, on the razor fine edge of reality and confusion briefly fighting the drugs effect before slowly sliding over the edge into the comfort, blackness, and security of unconsciousness.

He had no sensation of the passage of time other than the sounds of his surroundings changing. It was dark in the room now and with the exception of a muffled voice now and again, eerily quiet. How long had he been here? Admiral Feng tried to get his bearings but felt as if he was mentally in a thick fog. He kept his eyes closed in an effort to concentrate better on his surroundings and not overwhelm his brain with too many sensory inputs at once. At first, he tried to focus on where he was. As familiar as many of the sounds surrounding him felt, he couldn't help but feel strangely disconnected from them. He tried to focus the way he had always been trained by taking a deep breath to sharpen his focus.

One or more people were definitely in the room with him somewhere… just behind his head and out of sight. He could hear people talking but not understand what was being said. For a brief moment, his head felt as if it was clearing but suddenly, instead of sharpening his focus, his chest was racked with a searing pain and he began to cough, violently. Each breath felt as if he was inhaling fire. Feng tried hard not to panic. He took several small breaths in rapid succession. Along with searing pain when he inhaled was a crunchy crackling sound similar to eating puffed rice cakes. Further adding to his confusion, as he coughed, he realized that he had an intubation mask secured to his face. The admiral tried forcing himself to relax and after a few pain filled moments...felt himself slowly drifting away.

4

Commodore Cho, the submarine *Great Wall's* physician gestured for his medical assistant to leave the room. Cho remained behind and watched his patient drift off and shook his head in shear disbelief. He had been practicing ship board medicine for over twenty years, the last ten on submarines, and had never encountered a case such as this. For most people, even one of the symptoms his patient had presented would have terminated their life at this point. This man was not only strong, his will to survive was purely astonishing.

The unidentified man had been brought on board suffering from the bends, or decompression sickness, chemical burns of his lungs and he had technically drowned. Unfortunately, salt water in the lungs was almost always fatal. And just to keep things interesting…he had an air pocket in between his lung and chest wall called a "pneumothorax."

The doctor's original plan had been to keep his patient heavily sedated and parked right on the edge of consciousness, oblivious to the pain, until he succumbed to his injuries. He had only allowed his level of medication to be lifted to assess the condition of his strange patient's lungs. Remarkably, the amount of oxygen detected in his blood without the benefit of the oxygen mask was improving. His O^2 saturation, as it was referred to, had increased from a low of sixty-five percent two weeks ago, to today's reading, only moments ago of eighty-five percent. This was remarkable for several reasons; first and foremost was that this morning's reading had been without additionally supplied oxygen. Secondly, the coughing spasms were a combination of lung irritation from the chemical burns and his lungs were still trying to get rid of excess mucus and potentially residual salt water. The doctor was trying to get rid of the extra fluid by giving him 60 mg of Furosemide in his IV but the onboard supply was down to only two more doses.

When Commodore Cho had originally been consulted about the prognosis of his patient by the *Great Wall's* captain, he had stated rather grimly and definitively that he anticipated his patient to expire within the next 24-36 hours, maximum. Fortunately for his patient and unfortunately for the doctor's professional ego, that expected window had come and gone several days ago.

They had picked the man up off the starboard bow of their submarine almost two weeks ago. The rescue had been in clear weather and calm seas. The crew of the *Great Wall* was well versed in "man-overboard" drills and this man's retrieval from the waters of the South China Sea was performed flawlessly. The man had been recovered less than twenty minutes after the *Great Wall,* according to the captain, had engaged and destroyed a rogue Iranian submarine that had recently threatened an attacked a helpless Vietnamese research ship the *Hoa Biển.* The commodore found several things besides the man's resiliency, curious. For instance, who was he? He wasn't in a uniform and was carrying no identification. How did the captain of the *Great Wall* even know to be specifically looking in the acres of material and corpse debris strewn sea just for him? They had passed by several other survivors and bodies without even slowing down. Silently gliding past men screaming for help as the sea's circle of life process began taking its toll had been more than he could bear and he had gone below deck.

What the doctor had deduced from his patient's condition was that he had exited the stricken submarine, whose identity still remained a mystery to him, at significant depth, had his emergency rebreather malfunction and that he had inhaled a caustic mix of chemicals. He presumed that the man, in order to not continue burning his lungs, had apparently held his breath as he rose from the depths. Somehow in his journey he had also developed a case of the bends. His deduction accounted for all of the man's symptoms to a T.

How the man had actually gotten himself in such a dire predicament was not the doctor's concern. The doctor hadn't stayed alive this long and risen in the ranks of the Chinese Army Navy by asking questions that didn't pertain specifically to him. What had him really quite curious was that this boat's captain never showed compassion to members of his own crew, let alone someone who from all indications was a complete stranger. In addition, his orders concerning this particular patient had been unusual from day one. In the past, the captain would have never said anything explicit regarding patients in his care. For the first time however, the captain of the *Great Wall* had pulled him aside, grasped his arm firmly, made direct eye contact, and said, "This man must live."

That exchange had seemed long ago now when in fact it had only been a week. The doctor signaled for the medic to come to the patient's bedside.

"The captain wants us to remove our patient's intubation tube this morning."

"So soon?" The medic wasn't sure of the decision, but was in no position to question the doctor's authority and quickly apologized.

"Can I at least give him some pain medicine?"

Cho sighed, "Fine…Get me 10 mgs of morphine."

The young medic hurried back and injected it directly into the mystery patient's IV.

After a few moments, the doctor leaned forward and checked the sores that remained in the man's mouth; they too were healing. He mused and reflected on something he heard long ago in medical school: "If you pump enough antibiotics into a man you can save him from anything except himself."

He inserted the laryngoscope and looked as far as he could with the tube still in place. There were still some areas that seemed inflamed, but the risk of his throat collapsing or healing incorrectly had passed.

"His airway is healed sufficiently for its removal and he will make more progress with it removed."

"Yes doctor."

With the tube out, Cho inserted a bronchoscope and took a look all the way down into the man's lungs. It was remarkable. With there being no more existence of open sores it was actually possible that, with time, the patient would make a full recovery.

He stripped his gloves off and washed his hands in the sink near the bed.

"If I practiced medicine in the states or almost anywhere else in the world, I would write a paper and go on a lecture circuit."

The medic laughed quietly. They weren't in the states or anywhere else and from the looks of the way this patient was being handled…no one would ever know he had ever been on this boat. The medic turned off the overhead light and double checked the flow rate on the Propofol before he exited the cramped room.

The doctor walked slowly down the narrow passageway reflecting on the past week or so. In all fairness, as skilled as he was, Commodore Cho still wasn't sure about many things regarding this particular patient. One thing, however, had been made very clear about his instructions from the captain of the *Great Wall* just over a week ago. He shivered slightly remembering the grip on his arm and the stern look in his captain's eyes. The orders to keep his patient alive…hadn't been a request.

CHAPTER 2

—⚹—

Death Spiral

Ever since the "Incident," as it was still referred to inside the beltway and main stream media, the key three letter agencies of power in Washington, DNI, DIA, CIA, NSA, FBI, and the DHS, were still working on several leads to pin down what countries or individuals had taken part in the devastating attack on San Diego. The North Koreans had come forward immediately and confessed that it had been their device. Normally this would have required a straight forward retaliatory strike against the North Koreans. The problem was that according to the North Koreans they hadn't had anything to do with the weapon's delivery to the Port of San Diego, let alone its detonation. Even more frustrating to the Pentagon was that recently, both National Security Agency (NSA) and Department of Energy (DOE) investigators had found enough evidence to corroborate the Korean's version of the horrific event. According to the NSA, the freighter *Shooting Star* had been secretly retrofitted while at dry dock in the Chinese shipyard of Dalian. The work had been completed during the early spring and its identity switched from a North Korean flagged vessel to that of a South Korean.

Despite all the overhead satellite assets and other checks in place to prevent this type of thing from happening, the two sister ships had simply docked next to each other at the Dalian shipyard in southern China, swapped identities and flags, and carried on as if nothing had happened. In addition, they had almost two days of radio intercepts, some rather frantic in nature, from the North Korean's military facility at Pyongyang to the ship. It was NSA's conclusion that at some point in the plan, the ship had indeed been "high jacked" by a third party. No one in their right mind believed that the North Koreans were being completely honest in their level of involvement but enough evidence existed that a retaliatory nuclear strike would be an extreme overreaction and counterproductive to stabilizing the situation.

The personnel over at Broad Ocean Area Transit Smuggling and Surveillance (BOATSS) office which had recently, but not officially, been made a branch of the CIA, had done an amazing job identifying the various actors in the March attack. They knew that it had been an Al Qaeda cell from Canada and Seattle that had planned, attacked, and destroyed both the American's massive COBRA DANE radar facility on Shemya Island and crippled the SBX missile tracking station in the waters off Adak Island, Alaska. By using data from their unique listening array, they also knew the Iranian kilo class submarine *Yunes* had travelled to the Arctic to supply the necessary explosives and logistical support to cripple the SBX. They also knew that despite very public assertions to the contrary, the Chinese submarine *Great Wall* had sunk both the small Vietnamese research ship *Hoa Biển* and the Iranian submarine *Yunes* within moments of each other.

For the past three months, DNI, CIA, NSA, FBI, DOE, DHS and occasionally NCIS, held a teleconference at 5pm to present their own particular SITREP (situation report) to the Pentagon and members of the president's cabinet. Each meeting so far had ended with the understanding that although some progress was in fact being made, far more was still unknown than known. Pressure was mounting for Washington to act and the nation's patience was wearing thin, very thin.

The growing consensus from several key departments was that both Iran and China had been involved with the secret operation up to their necks. The NSA's final report had laid aside any doubt that the signal and software used to control the freighter was the same as the drone software captured by the Iranians several years earlier. The CIA had briefly fought against the conclusions reached by the NSA as it directly conflicted with their original claims that the American drone's software was password protected. They eventually relented when faced with expert testimony from various third party experts, but were still left with the unenviable task and lingering question of what to do next. All this had been done with what the west had considered crippling sanctions. Who or what parties had contrived this plan and put it into motion was still anyone's guess.

China's role in this was an even trickier problem. What Washington did know was that despite China's claims of self-defense, all of the three letter departments agreed that it was much too much of a coincidence to actually be a coincidence that the Chinese submarine *Great Wall* "just happened" to be in the area when the Iranian submarine *Yunes* had, according to both the Iranian and Chinese governments, "gone rogue" and attacked the little Vietnamese research vessel *Hoa Biển*. With some investigating and cooperation from the Vietnamese government, it was learned that the *Hoa Biển* had been using side scanning radar to map the floor of the South China Sea in almost the exact location of the now fully operational Chinese natural gas rigs. Had the *Hoa Biển* seen something, or was it about to see something that would have undermined the final construction of the now fully operational gas platforms?

Regardless of China's involvement in the plot they were, with the obvious exception of San Diego, supplying the West Coast with both raw and finished goods that were still, as of yet, not being supplied by American domestic suppliers and manufactures.

CHAPTER 3

—ɱ—

Circles

"How's our persistent patient today, Major Cho?"

"Doing much better sir! His recovery continues to be quite remarkable."

"Can he speak yet? Would he be able to engage me in a conversation?"

Major Cho looked at the chart and then at his wristwatch.

"Probably another twenty-four hours and we'll try and test those vocal chords."

It had been three weeks now and the captain of the *Great Wall* was becoming impatient on several fronts and was in no mood for yet another aggravation in his day.

"I'll be back tomorrow morning and try his vocal chords myself."

"Sir, with all due respect, it's quite possible that if he overstrains his vocal chords too early he will never get his natural voice back."

"Major Cho you did your job well, as ordered, and the patient is alive, as ordered. Now I must do my job without any interference from you. Are we clear on this point?"

"Yes sir!"

Commander Liú Chung, captain of the nuclear powered ballistic missile submarine *Great Wall*, walked out of the infirmary and back to his quarters.

"I'm running out of time," he quietly mumbled to himself. He sat down at his small desk and gathered his writing materials to write out a list of questions to ask the "patient" tomorrow morning.

He knew exactly who the man two decks down was, and what knowledge he possessed. The trick would be to get this very experienced former submarine commander and intelligence officer to give up the information quickly. It really didn't matter to him if the patient suffered or even died during the questioning. What information he knew for sure was that this man was one of the five remaining architects of the plan to destabilize America and gut their navy. He'd learned through channels that several men had been killed at a meeting Admiral Feng attended last year in Taipei, but not much else. What he didn't know and so desperately needed to find out was the individual's name that actually created and implemented the plan. He had one ace and timing its play would be important to the whole process. He knew the mastermind was Iranian.

The captain of the *Great Wall* didn't see himself as a traitor but rather a skilled opportunist. The Chinese Navy had been good to him but he had no money to speak of and no family. In a nut shell, all he had to show after all these years of service was the promise that he would live out his life, care free, in "New China."

He leaned back in his chair and pictured himself under an umbrella on a sunny beach in Northern California, maybe someplace north of the bay area, perhaps Dillon Beach. He'd Googled it and it looked to be an ideal location. Granted, it would be an expensive lifestyle, but if his questioning went well tomorrow, money would no longer be an issue. Washington had placed a ten-million-dollar bounty on the individuals who had planned and carried out the devastating San Diego attack. Contacts in the states had already set him up with a new identity and he had already located and used the services of a passport forger. The man had done a decent job and been paid well for it.

Although technically at odds with the United States over everything except commerce, the captain actually lamented the destruction of San Diego. If push came to shove he would have to admit that his grief was, for the most part, based in selfishness. San Diego had been his original destination plan in the states, but after last March? That wasn't going to happen. Experts from around the world were in close agreement that it would be close to seventy-three years before anyone could seriously consider moving back to the vicinity of the former thriving city. He liked San Diego very much but had no interest in waiting quite that long.

Exhaling forcefully, the captain sat back straight in his chair and started his list. The first item on the agenda was the man's name. Anything uttered other than a Middle Eastern name would not be an acceptable answer and newly retired Admiral Feng would pay a heavy price.

Currently, the captain's plan lacked a few key components. Primarily, and the one causing him the greatest angst, was how he would actually get the information to the Americans without getting caught. In addition, and perhaps the most difficult, was how he would physically travel to the states. Each version of his plan began with him taking some long overdue leave. The *Great Wall* had gone to sea immediately following the Chinese New Year celebrations in early January. Today marked their third month at sea and they were going to get replenished with food and supplies in the next week or so. Having the *capability* to stay out at sea for six months without fresh fruits and vegetables and *actually* doing it were, fortunately, two different things. They would naturally want to transfer his "guest" at that time as well. Unfortunately, for Admiral Feng, that simply wasn't in the cards.

—⚅—

"Good morning Admiral Feng!"

The medication was wearing off and the retired admiral was looking better than he had been of late but still seemed somewhat unsure of his surroundings.

"I am Commander Liú Chung, captain of the *Great Wall*, and I need to ask you some questions. If you understand, you just need to nod yes or shake your head no, okay?"

Feng nodded slowly.

"You've made some significant headway in your recovery considering what you've been through sir. Do you remember what happened on the *Yunes*?"

Feng lied and slowly shook his head no.

"That's rather understandable. Our doctor said you may have difficulty remembering the specifics of the incident. I'll help by filling you in from what we know at this point."

It was now Commander Chung's turn to lie. "We do know that you were on the Iranian submarine *Yunes* when it attacked the defenseless Vietnamese research vessel *Hoa Biển*."

Feng swung his head around in the direction of Chung and began vigorously shaking his head, "No."

Chung ignored his pathetic animated plea and continued. "It was unfortunate that we were unaware of your mission on the *Yunes*. Perhaps, had we known, we may not have sunk the *Yunes* without warning. To be honest, the world was rather relieved to hear that we had sunk a rouge Iranian submarine. The captain and crew of the *Yunes*, which I'm sorry to say all perished, have been tried in absentia and found guilty of numerous crimes including attacking two United States military targets and sinking two unarmed noncombatant commercial vessels. It goes without saying that they were also linked to the explosion in San Diego…" Chung allowed his voice to trail off for greater affect. "Since they are no longer able to have a penalty levied on them personally, their families are being made to suffer. You know those crazy Muslims when they get their blood worked up!" Chung feigned a chuckle.

Feng was frantically shaking his head from side to side emphatically denying the tone, tenor, and intent of the captain's version of events.

"Listen Admiral," Chung continued, "I've checked out your military record and, like me, you accomplished your duties with distinction and by our records were actually retired at the time of this incident. Our military system cannot protect you anymore and I've been ordered to turn you over when we make port. According to our doctor you have a very short time to explain yourself as the infection in your lungs has unfortunately spread to your heart. Would you care to explain what, exactly, you were doing on the *Yunes* and perhaps we can notify the authorities in Beijing to stop rounding up your family members. It would be a tragedy for them all to perish over a misunderstanding."

Feng lay in his bunk. What good would his money do him if both he and his family were dead? He waved the captain of the *Great Wall* closer. "We were following orders," he said in a voice barely above a whisper.

"I see," nodded the *Great Wall's* captain. "Do you feel well enough to write this all down as a final deposition?"

Feng nodded weakly and signaled for some paper.

Over the next thirty minutes the retired admiral wrote out a chronological report listing names places and events that had transpired over the past year in regard to his current situation. When he was done he handed the pad to the captain.

It was strange, but if someone had asked him how he was feeling today he would have said, "fair," maybe even, "good."

Captain Chung read over the document and saw what he needed to see. He looked up at the clock. It was 10:17 hours. He noted it on the paper. Tearing off the relevant sheets he tossed the pad and pen onto the bedside table.

"Thank you, Admiral Feng. I'll see what I can do for your family."

The captain of the *Great Wall* walked out of the infirmary clutching what amounted to a death bed confession. As he passed through the officer's quarters he cheerfully greeted the boat's doctor.

"Our patient was very cooperative this morning! We had a marvelous chat. Have a good morning doctor!"

At 10:25, the doctor walked into Admiral Feng's section of the infirmary and saw what looked to be a broken man. The man was laying on his side and curled up into the fetal position. He was surprised to say the least. He'd looked well enough during last night's rounds that he had written orders to release him from the infirmary this morning to a regular cabin.

Feng spoke first but was difficult to hear. "The captain said I don't have long to live. How long do you think I have?"

The doctor was at a loss for words. "There must be some type of misunderstanding you have done amazingly well and were to be released today."

His patient suddenly lost what limited color he had remaining in his face.

"I'll go get the captain and we'll straighten out this terrible misunderstanding."

At 10:35 the doctor returned to the infirmary with the captain to find retired Admiral Jiayi Feng hanging from the overhead fire control pipe by his IV lines. On the bed, on half a sheet of neatly folded paper, were three words in very large print:

未了結

(NO LOOSE ENDS)

CHAPTER 4

—◊—

Shell Game

It had now been almost four months since the still unknown terrorists had attacked the formerly thriving city of San Diego with an enormous nuclear device and Washington still seemed paralyzed with indecision. In fact, this wasn't actually the case, but in a town where perception is fact, to the world it appeared they were paralyzed. In reality, the president, his cabinet, and the Department of Defense were bent over the proverbial barrel and both the nation and the world knew it. The death toll in San Diego, as a direct result of the blast, was staggering. To date, over 2.3 million people had died in San Diego County with another 2700 or so people in the Los Angeles area dead as a direct result of the brazen looting and unchecked fires. Estimates were ranging between 475 and 625 people had been killed in the panicked evacuation of both California's southern coast and cities as far east as Phoenix and even Las Vegas. This number included everything reported including vehicle accidents, carjackings, thefts resulting in homicides and looting related fatalities.

The highly radioactive debris cloud had drifted steadily due east, for three days, making it to the Mississippi river before being caught in a fortuitous southern loop of the jet stream. The high level winds drove most of the cloud into the moist air of the Gulf of Mexico where it stuck to the moisture and fell as rain. Radiation sensors and air sampling units stationed along the Florida coast detected minute levels of both alpha and beta radiation from particles they had collected but the levels hadn't been high enough to warrant a public health notice.

Despite the various public service agencies attempted reassurances to remain calm, that the detected levels where just above normal background, the public in South Florida was understandably spooked, very spooked.

Over the course of the past two months, both Hezbollah and a previously unknown faction of Muslim extremists calling themselves "ISIS" or "ISIL," depending on what television network you watched, had slowed their almost daily slaughter of Shiite Muslims and Christians and were now making inroads into neighboring countries such as Syria. The spreading wave of terror had created a massive wave of human misery, most of whom were attempting to get to Europe. Just last week they had made several successful daylight attacks on both the population centers around Tel Aviv and the Israeli port of Haifa. The terrorists knew what the rest of the world knew. For the first time since World War II, the American Navy did not rule the seas and was in no position to help their chief allies in the region and wouldn't be for the foreseeable future. The mess and utter disarray in Syria continued with the migration of immigrants and refugees remaining unabated.

The American Navy was stretched very thin as it was, and not operating as designed, certainly not in any position to back up their own political rhetoric, let alone anyone else's. Within days of the attack on San Diego, the navy had conducted a procedure referred to as force balancing. Several ships from the naval base in Bahrain had been moved out of the waters of the Persian Gulf and out into the open, and presumed safer, waters of the Arabian Sea.

Despite advanced warnings from several reliable sources in the region, as well as the Pentagon brass, two weeks ago an attempted coup in Doha, Qatar had left several key American supporting Qatari's dead and several injured. The joint air base at Al Udeid, in Qatar, one of the most powerful in the region, was positioned less than 300 miles away from several of Iran's surface to surface missile batteries. Several probative terrorist attacks by ISIS along the Qatari coast, although officially denied by the Iranian regime, had served their purpose and rattled the small kingdom and its people. Specially modified high speed ribbed boats had launched a salvo of sixteen surface to surface Qassam rockets at downtown Doha and several had landed in the downtown area near the crowded mall. Although the Qassam rockets had a limited range and accuracy they were excellent at making a psychological impact. Five people had been killed and a few dozen injured. Similar to the missiles launched routinely at Israel, the missiles had not been very accurate, but had done their job scaring both the populous and the Qatari Royal family.

The blame, curiously enough, had been placed squarely on the relocated Gitmo detainees that had been sent to the country the previous year. They had been essentially placed under house arrest with no limitations on their movements in the country, actions or who they could meet with. It didn't really matter who the players where at this point, the royal family was rattled and, that fact, born out by history, was never good. To no one's surprise, the former Gitmo detainees were not at their opulent residences and, as expected, were not currently being "aggressively" pursued by Qatari security forces.

CHAPTER 5

—⟋⟍—

The Big Show

Farid had found his "tailor" through some untraceable back channel communications with the New York Iranian embassy staff. In their case, the term "untraceable" usually meant that they had received the name of the guy they needed...then promptly shot the messenger. The tailor's shop had been located just off the south side of Worth Avenue in a second story walkup. Farid was such a regular in the stores on the block that seeing him walk up a flight of stairs didn't even register as suspicious. He had spent so much time in the area that he had essentially become invisible.

For this particular upcoming visit to New York for work, he had needed some customized alterations done. The tailor had done an amazing job putting together such a beautiful, yet functionally festive, vest. Farid was a large, portly man and buying clothes off the rack wasn't really a viable option. Besides, this particular type of vest wasn't sold in stores. He had designed the vest himself and when he had presented the design to the tailor the man's eyes flew open. It was masterful. The vest had been designed like a garment for the Emmys, Oscars or any other similarly large event. Farid knew that no matter what anyone thought about the vest, no one at his event would have anything like it and he also knew that his tailor would be famous within a week of his attendance of the event. He couldn't wait to wear it, hopefully more than once, on his upcoming trip to Manhattan. He really liked the feel, mentally, physically and emotionally, of wearing something that had been made just for him. Each fitting he had been to an almost giddy feeling came over him. When he thought back in his life to when he had ever felt that way, he recalled the almost surreal feeling the first time he had drawn a deep lungful of hash smoke from a hookah.

The outer front and back of the vest were covered with diamond shaped segments of highly polished titanium steel. The shapes fit together and glistened each time Farid took a breath. The inside of the vest was covered with the same material except Farid had requested it appear to be highly polished gold. To anyone examining the vest it appeared to be just an exquisite reversible vest. It had taken several weeks to order the various components and then three fittings to get the look Farid was after.

Farid had made yet another before-hours appointment to pick the vest up. From the moment he started with his tailor, all of his appointments had been either before the other stores opened or after they had closed for the night. Sometimes it was due to pressing afternoon appointments and sometimes it was to better coordinate with his evening dinner plans. Most importantly, of course, was the absence of security when the majority of the shops were closed. For obvious reasons, he simply told people that parking was somewhat less difficult in the evenings. For what he was paying the tailor for his vest, the man hadn't seemed to mind.

He had gone to pick-up the vest early Monday morning before the other shops had opened to the public. It wasn't raining that morning but Farid had worn one of those cheap $1.99 clear plastic ponchos from the local Walgreens. The tailor had requested, after the last and final fitting, that he have one last go at shining the vest and then coating it with a fine coat of lacquer to keep it from tarnishing.

"Good morning Mr. Thomas! Are you expecting showers this morning?"

Farid smiled, "My friend, you've lived here in Florida long enough to know not to count on the weatherman!"

It was mid-July and showers were always hit or miss. If you *didn't* have an umbrella, the skies never failed to open up and remind you of your transgression.

Abad laughed at that one. His customer was most certainly correct about that. He motioned for Farid to wait while he went into the back of the shop for the vest. When he returned his eyes were gleaming as brightly as the vest he held in front of him.

"You have truly outdone yourself Abad. This vest is magnificent! Box it up please, I'm in a bit of a rush this morning."

"Yes sir. Thank you, sir!"

Abad carefully wrapped the vest in white tissue paper, placed the vest in a nondescript shirt box and extended it to Farid. "I assume you have brought the final payment?"

Farid slowly reached into his left pocket and pulled out a wad of crisp one hundred dollar bills sealed in a small Ziploc bag.

"Count it if you wish," smiled Farid as he placed the boxed vest behind the poncho with his left hand.

With the sight of so much money blurring his senses, Abad didn't even question why the money was sealed in the bag. He bent forward over the counter and began to count. He smiled as he peeled off the last bill and placed it on the counter. Abad grabbed the stack of bills off the counter, shaped them into a neat stack, looked up, smiled and said, "Four thousand dollars."

Abad had glanced up just in time to see the silenced .22 caliber pistol leveled at his forehead. What he saw made no sense. He'd done exactly as he'd been told...The small caliber weapon coughed twice.

The surprised expression on Abad's face lingered for a moment, frozen in time, before what was left of his brain caught up with the reality of what had just happened. He pitched forward briefly, then backwards, landing in a heap on the shop's floor.

Farid's poncho had done its job quite effectively and neither of the two bullets fired by Farid created enough blood splatter to compromise his appearance. He left the blood spattered money where it had fallen, scattered haphazardly on the floor and counter. Farid smiled and picked up the small plastic bag. It had served its purpose well by ensuring that his fingerprints and DNA would not be found on the bills. He paused for a moment. The scene in front of him had no real emotional impact on him, it never did. He'd seen worse in his lifetime and in reality, done far worse. Looking down at the lifeless body, he felt benevolent in a way. He had made sure the man's family would be financially taken care of and in his mind that was far more than most people would do. It was a very dangerous world and the man had taken a dangerous job.

Farid removed his blood splattered poncho and placed it in one of the many shopping bags he knew were kept by the door. From his back pocket he removed and put on another clean poncho. Cameras were everywhere these days. For a few more weeks, caution would be paramount. He walked down the stairs, through the courtyard and back onto Worth Avenue. He spent the next few hours walking in and out of shops. Eventually he made his way to the mounted security camera just above the Polo Ralph Lauren shop. Without looking up, he made a very dramatic show of removing his clean poncho in plain sight of the camera. Glancing down at his newly ac-quired Vacheron Constantin watch, purchased recently from Cartier jew-elers, he yawned and realized it was time for an early lunch. It had been entirely too much excitement for one day.

CHAPTER 6

—⚍—

From The Shadows

Jonah West hadn't been answering his cell phone for several weeks and hearing the device chirping now made him question why it was even on. After a brief week of reconciliation in Anchorage with his dad after the SBX attack, the two were, unfortunately, once again, no longer on speaking terms. Going back to Maine and fishing with his dad just wasn't in the cards at this point and he seriously doubted that it ever would be. Keeping his phone on, he believed, was the responsible thing to do. If there was a family emergency his family would know how to get ahold of him.

For several weeks after the disastrous destruction of the SBX-sea based X-band radar platform by terrorists in the Aleutians, he had been receiving calls from all the major networks, cable and mainstream media wanting him to come on their TV or radio shows and tell his tale of intrigue and danger. Several individuals and groups had offered him good sums of money to come and speak as a motivational speaker and discuss overcoming adversity, etc. They had spun it every way they could think of but his answer had still been, and would continue to be, a polite, "No, thank you."

Maybe it was the fact that he'd been a Navy SEAL for so many years and that he kept the secrets and experiences he had lived through in a special dark place. He was, frankly, rather hesitant to cast a light into who he was and how the events of that tragic week last March had so affected him.

After several weeks the bullet wound on the right side of his neck and his left shoulder had healed quite nicely and he'd regained almost full use of both. The plastic surgeon had offered to clean up his neck a bit but he politely refused. His reflection in the mirror was somewhat different now, after all, what was one more scar to a Navy SEAL?

Following his discharge from Joint Base Elmendorf- Richardson hospital in Anchorage, he had stayed in the local area to get some additional physical therapy and to get his head screwed on straight. Experiencing late spring in Alaska had been cathartic, but he realized after a few weeks of watching the sunsets and beautiful northern lights…it was time to move on.

Jonah knew he was in lousy physical shape and set about fixing that upon his arrival here on Wisteria Island. He had dropped almost twenty-five pounds in the hospital and looked and moved more like a civilian than he had in over twenty-two years. He looked around as he passed through town at men ten years his junior and just shook his head in dismay. Looking better than them wasn't his goal…that bar was far, far too low.

He'd settled in, just over two months ago, and began as close to a SEAL training regimen as he could handle. In the morning, at first light, he ran on the sand until his body begged him to stop, then plunged into the warm gulf waters and swam a few miles. The locals had told him where and when not to swim due to the rather voracious indigenous food chain. So far he'd been bumped hard, once, by a curious Hammerhead shark, but otherwise had been unmolested in his swimming endeavors. It was the infamous Bull Sharks he was most worried about, but so far he'd been lucky. Having the ability to swim in both salt and brackish water wasn't really fair, but Jonah understood that all predatory creatures needed an edge to survive. For that reason alone, he respected the Bull Shark. Jonah knew also that, until he got his own edge back, he would be just like any other person walking the streets…prey.

At times, because of the scenery and the silence, he thought he was on the edge of the world. He would close his eyes and think of all the times he had actually been *on the edge of the world* and it brought joy to him. He would, if the wind was right, catch the smell of local folks grilling on the developed island just south of Wisteria Island. It always seemed to be the same smell of either fish or steaks on the grill. Several times a week he would wander around to the more popular side of the island and share whatever fish he had caught that day with folks cooking on the beach. He would even cook it for the inexperienced grill master, eat his fill and share the rest with the islands visiting diners.

As it turned out, between FedEx and UPS, there was almost no place on earth you could go that they wouldn't deliver. And so it had been that after his first week here, when the running and swimming hadn't killed him, he had ordered two full sets of weights from an online retailer. They had charged him extra because of the weight and location but here he sat with his own little gym behind his natural foliage bungalow. FedEx and UPS had delivered several items to the end of the pier on Trumbo Road. He had re-quested a little leeway from the local navy base commander and had been enjoying virtual seclusion since his arrival.

Twice people had been drawn in close to his camp when his last rep-etition of steel weights had come down with a little harder "clang" than planned. He'd heard them coming, of course, a few men the first time and some lovely, slightly intoxicated ladies the second. It had actually been more difficult convincing the women to go back to their boat than the men. Although in retrospect, Jonah smiled thinking about that night, perhaps he hadn't truly tried as hard as he could have...

Physically, at this point, Jonah was back in the shape of his life. Men-tally would apparently take a bit longer. He lay in his *eno* hammock won-dering if there was anything else he could have done to prevent such a tre-mendous loss of life on the SBX platform. He had run the scenario over and over in his head until he was finally convinced in his own mind there was nothing he could have done. Beating himself up over it wasn't help-ing so he focused on something he knew he could fix, his self-perceived physical weaknesses.

It was eleven a.m. and as he ran in from his morning swim he could, once again, hear his damn phone chirping. He checked the number and it was still the same Washington D.C. area code. The numbers, or at least the last four digits, changed every so often, but it was the specific locality he didn't want to hear from. The ringing stopped, finally, and he ate his lunch and settled in for a quick catnap when the damn thing chirped again. As was now the ritual, he glanced at the phone, saw it wasn't one of the three people in his contact list and began to walk away. Only this time, when he noticed the number, it was local…very local.

—◦◦◦—

"You listen to me!" shouted the very irate Bahamas CIA station chief.

Naval Air Station Key West Deputy Commander Steve Lark cut him off. "What you ass hats don't seem to understand is that I can't order him to answer his phone anymore."

"Is he on government property or not? And before you answer I'll tell you right up front that we've tracked his phone to within three feet of its location on Wisteria Island."

"Mr. Kline, was it? We can make an informal request of him to call you at our very next opportunity."

"And that would be when?" demanded Kline.

His tone made the deputy commander want to punch the man's teeth down his throat two at a time…but he remained civil.

"Let me see, tomorrow's Saturday, let me check his schedule."

"You have the man's daily schedule for god's sake?"

"As I was saying," continued the naval officer. "On Saturdays he runs in the morning from 08:00 to 10:00 then swims a few miles through the channel, that takes about an hour and then he lifts weights for about an hour and a half…So how about two o'clock? After his nap? He might actually be more agreeable after his nap."

Fuming, but in reluctant agreement, the CIA Station Chief of the Bahamas agreed and slammed down his phone purely for effect. The rub, and it was a big one, was that he badly needed retired Navy SEAL Jonah West and Jonah West didn't need him...Or at least he didn't think he did.

CHAPTER 7

—⟋⟋⟍—

Showtime

Farid reviewed the details on his laptop's computer screen, smiled and hit "ENTER." The transaction was complete. Moments later he opened the confirmation email from Delta, he confirmed his departure on a one-way, first class ticket departing from West Palm Beach, Florida on November 19th at 2:15 p.m. and arriving at New York's John F. Kennedy International Airport at 4:45 p.m. With a little luck and light traffic he would arrive just in time for an early dinner. With everything appearing to be in order; he wirelessly printed the email, forwarded a copy to his smart phone and closed the lid of his Dell laptop. He would be in New York City in plenty of time to enjoy the Thanksgiving holiday. He placed his hands behind his head, closed his eyes, leaned back in his office chair and smiled remembering past holiday seasons.

Although he considered himself a devout Muslim, he couldn't help himself but get caught up in the happiness and joy of the large crowds... the sights, sounds, and smells of Manhattan during this important American holiday season. He was, however, often conflicted at this time of the year. In his homeland, there was little joy, ever. Sunnis were always, or so it seemed, angry with the Shias or vice versa. As of late, the ISIS folks had been beheading both Muslims and non-Muslims alike, for no other reason than crossing their paths. Recently, celebrations of any kind, even weddings, were bracketed by beheadings or "honor" killings. Perhaps he'd lived in America too long. He saw no "honor" in killing the innocent.

Being that this would be his last trip to New York, he would need to make a point of going over to Rockefeller Center and seeing the enormous Christmas tree and the ice skating rink. Although it probably wouldn't be lit yet, it was festive enough in its own right. If this trip would be like others in the past, the highlight of this trip would definitely be his outings to the theater district and the fabulous stores on Fifth Avenue. Although he liked to shop, he *loved* ogling the attractive young ladies that seemed to be drawn to the expensive New York stores like moths to a bright flame. Oh my yes; he was definitely looking forward to seeing Manhattan again. As he stood slowly and walked to the waiting steam infused shower he smiled once again, thoroughly enjoying the prospect of mixing his last business trip with an equal amount of pleasure.

Still caught in the throes of what seemed to have been an extraordinarily long hot humid summer in South Florida, he looked forward to the relatively cooler days of fall. They were in the height of the hurricane season and it seemed that a week hadn't gone by without the media warning of a tropical storm. He liked warnings. Warnings were good.

What Farid didn't appreciate were the warnings and hourly updates about storms heading out to sea! He had observed over his years of exposure to Americans that they tended to make decisions based on emotion rather than fact. The news media and big box home repair stores such as Home Depot and Lowe's took complete advantage of that fact every year for the five plus months of the hurricane season. It was one of several traits that he found beneficial. In fact, he loved the fact that two things seemed to be a constant:

1. Americans most often reacted to emotion rather than fact and

2. Americans had very short memories

Farid had been to his surgeon's office this morning and received the all-important clearance to fly. He had been looking forward to his trip at the end of November for three months now. All summer he had done exactly as his surgeon had said and had even seen a dermatologist to treat his rather large abdominal and chest incisions. With special salves and other treatments the scar looked at least six months older than it really was. He had been overweight since his early teens and it had been a tough and often times hurtful way to go through the already awkward time of any young man's life. His peers were much thinner than he was and although culturally he was not encouraged to "date" per se or openly seek female companionship he sensed, perhaps rather astutely, that the women in his life would prefer he not pursue them. Farid had respected their wishes until he felt he couldn't physically take it anymore and eventually he began to pay for his relationships. He had several well used numbers in his little black book of a dozen or so attractive women in Manhattan who would be more than willing, for a price of course, to stroll on his arm to dinners at fabulous restaurants and take in any show of his choosing. Perhaps his connections in New York could get him tickets to the show *Chicago*. Farid had seen the show several times over the years but it was indeed one of his favorites. After all, compared to all the other things they were working on for him for that busy week, tickets to a top Broadway show would be child's play.

He went to his large walk-in closet and removed his new shiny vest from its hanger. Farid had already put it on several times since he had picked it up. He would definitely need, and need was the right word, to wear it more than once. It made him feel powerful, strong and virile. The vest was in a word, exquisite. From a distance of more than a few feet it appeared to be a normal gray herringbone vest. He twisted his portly body back and forth in the full length mirror. Every movement caught the light differently and made his entire chest appear to shimmer. He smiled and sighed softly as he placed the vest carefully back on its special hanger. It made him look, in all honesty, like a Broadway star....

CHAPTER 8

—🐛—

Symmetry

Many changes had taken place in the basement of the BOATSS building over on 9th street. To begin with, the building was now considered a "priority" government address. With this subtle change, came a slew of new upgrades including both additional perimeter and interior security cameras. Both plain clothes and uniformed security personnel patrols were everywhere. The uniformed, clean cut folks had radios, ear buds and a presence at the building's two entrances and exits. The muscle, for lack of a better description, consisted of a plain clothes detail that rotated from interior to exterior patrols on a computer-generated schedule. They carried MP-5s and 40 caliber Glock 35s with laser sights. They were specially trained for urban type "situations" and strictly followed the mantra placed in their heads by their new boss: "Protect this House."

The new head of building security, with some strings pulled here and there, was Ken Shortman. His allegiance to Jewels during the freighter crisis and his leadership abilities had allowed for some normally stringent hiring and time consuming requirements to be waved. Unlike this past spring when none of his friends that worked at other "interesting" three letter offices such as the CIA, FBI, DHS, NSA had never heard of his office, at the time, an obscure office of employment called BOATSS. This summer? Everyone involved in D.C.'s facility security office knew his exact address. The changes to the inside of the building were subtle to the casual visitor, such as a working air conditioning system, some added communication capabilities, and a doubling of the number of linked servers. In many ways, to an outsider, it was the same building as it had been six months ago. In stark contrast to its perceived appearance, in reality, in every way that really mattered, it was all new.

—※—

There had to be a connection. Both Jewels and Gina had looked at the code they had stripped from the drone freighter *Shooting Star's* satellite feed several times now this morning and although something looked familiar, whatever it was, it was for the moment eluding them. What was complicating the problem was that the satellite link that had so successfully controlled the freighter had been a hacked US drone technology, but the actual command codes that had driven the freighter into the western side of San Diego Bay were entirely different. Somehow vaguely familiar...but different.

They'd gotten here at six this morning and although it was just now approaching ten, Jewels was well into her forth cup of coffee for the day and unlike most days, instead of a burst of insight into a particular problem, today it seemed that the only thing that had serious "burst" potential was her bladder. Her recent promotion and new office had come with several perks. To be completely honest, one of her favorites, which she had admitted to only a handful of friends, was her own restroom. She ducked in to freshen up her lipstick, and check her hair, something she'd never done before Mitch Kendrick had entered her life.

Jewels was meeting with the rest of her high level team in five minutes to see if perhaps coming at the problem from a different angle might be a better approach. She fidgeted around the conference table at the far end of her office and hoped that everything went smoothly. She wasn't yet accustomed to the leadership role she had recently been thrust into. Jewels also knew that half of the people coming to this afternoon's meeting, Gina Hughes, Mitch Kendrick and Rick Wagner, all of whom had received both recognition and promotions for their actions surrounding the "incident" in San Diego, were somewhat conflicted in their new positions as well. To further complicate their lives, according to the government contract psychologist, they were all suffering from what the doctor had referred to as "PTSD" or Post Traumatic Stress Disorder. The doctor had felt that it would more than likely be temporary in nature and was more than likely due to repressed feelings of guilt regarding the "incident" in San Diego.

Jewels personally thought the whole PTSD diagnosis was over used. They had been traumatized when the event had happened, so had most of the nation, but nobody on her team was losing sleep over it or having other difficulties. They were far too busy trying to find the bastards responsible to worry about stuff they could no longer do anything about.

Jewels thought it ironic that it seemed to her almost everyone *except* her team called it an "incident" while her team and several other government offices referred to it as the *attack* on San Diego. So who, she often mused, really needed the counseling? Her team, who called it what it was, or the rest of the PC government bureaucracy that continued to call it "The Incident." Fortunately, they had all been cleared to resume their duties which due to the nature of the disaster was a mere formality since none of them had had more than two days off in the past two months. The other members of the meeting were her team's new assistants. They were new hires and some of the brightest minds Jewels had been able to glean from the most recent batch of graduates from the nation's top IT schools. Jewels had conducted the screening interviews herself and worked very hard NOT to fixate entirely on the candidates GPA's or other academic achievements. Her goal had been to hire individuals with extraordinary problem solving skills and imaginations. The general nature of their duties would be to think outside the proverbial box. Of course, it would be an added bonus if they knew how to play well with others, but she hadn't let it be a deal breaker. Somewhat counter intuitively perhaps, Jewels had also directed that the assistants, once selected, not be assigned to the same schools attended by their supervisors.

———ᨆ———

Mitch Kendrick, Jewels' boyfriend of four months, although the term still made him uncomfortable, would have jumped at the chance to move to D.C. just to be closer to Jewels. Their relationship, forged during one of the nation's greatest crises, had not only weathered the tumultuous storm of emotions wrought by the crisis, but in fact had only gotten stronger over the past several weeks. The promotion and a few other perks had just sweetened the pot. It wasn't that Mitch didn't *like* being the boyfriend of one of Washington's prettiest women, it was that he still couldn't believe that *he* was in fact the boyfriend of one of Washington's prettiest women. Everywhere they went, Jewel's appearance turned heads. Jewels stood at 5'11" barefoot, had a knockout body, a gorgeous face, and a Julia Roberts smile, if you didn't look when she walked by...you weren't inclined to look.

Mitch checked his watch, saw he had a few more minutes and tipped back in his chair, closed his eyes and smiled as he cracked his knuckles. Jewels hated that habit. He smiled a thin smile of bemusement. Four months ago he had been a mid-level signals analyst running scans and generating reports on domestic Unmanned Aerial Vehicle (UAV) traffic. He had traveled to D.C. this past March for a three day conference during the Cherry Blossom Festival, technically a boondoggle, and to meet a software designer named of all things "Jewels." He had gotten caught up in both the tracking and pursuit of the monsters that had blown up San Diego and the charms of the smartest woman he had ever met. He had never made it home. He learned rather quickly that when the government needs *you*, there are no obstacles too great that stand in the way of them acquiring your services. Professional (private label) movers had packed up his apartment in Colorado Springs, paid his cleaning deposit, his last month's rent and delivered all his stuff flawlessly to his new address in D.C.

For the past two months, as the NSA's new "golden child," a title he felt he did not rightly deserve, Mitch was hunting for the men, countries, and in some cases, organizations who had detonated an enormous nuclear weapon just outside the port of San Diego. It had been an awkward few months for the small group at BOATSS. Technically, although they had detected and reported the rogue freighter *Shooting Star's* intentions to blow up the port of San Diego, they had unfortunately not been in a position to do anything about it. Mitch glanced at his watch again and with a minute to spare, leaned forward and headed down to his boss' office. He smiled. It was one of the worst kept secrets in Washington that he and Jewels, his boss, were "an item." His smile broadened to a grin as he turned the corner and entered her office. Mitch was the last one in the room and had to take a seat at the far end of the long table. Jewels glanced in his direction just long enough to shoot him "the look." It was exactly ten a.m...and he was already in trouble.

"It's good that everyone could make it this morning." Jewels had masterfully directed the sarcastic remark at Mitch without actually looking directly at Mitch.

One of the many upgrades to the facility since March was that her office had been recently recertified as a Special Compartmentalized Information Facility or SCIF. This was a bonus in that she no longer had to go downstairs to the only other formal SCIF.

She had, of course, met both informally and formally with her new hires and had been impressed enough to hire them. She noticed the smiles after her sarcastic remark and thought to herself that this crew might just accomplish great things. All, with one exception, had received their required clearances and were cleared for today's meeting. The only remaining person had made it through all his interviews and other important clerical requirements only to have his name pop up on the country's newly tightened "no fly list."

The BOATSS security manager or SSO, covered the numerous required security issues, including both what is referred to as their program's specific SCI Indoctrination or "INDOC" earlier in the week. The process essentially involved having the group watch several PowerPoint briefings explaining their personal and professional responsibilities to the program. At the conclusion of the briefing, which to a man appeared to cause their eyes to glaze over, each of the new folks signed documents acknowledging the fact that everything to do with this program would not only be at SCI level security, but also what is referred to as a "Level B" compartmentalized clearance. At this level, the program was to never be discussed outside of the BOATSS' or Langley's secured SCIF facilities. Most of the folks in the room hadn't been with the federal government long enough to know exactly what they were signing. Jewels was very clear and frank in her briefing and even covered the ramifications, personal, organizational, national, and global if their little project was leaked to anyone, even outside the room. When all the required forms had been signed, Jewels suggested they take a break, warm up their coffees, and get ready to hear the framework of *Project Katar.*

"Alright, everyone should pretty much know my meeting format by now." Some chuckles ensued. "Rick will start with what we believe is current as of 0600 this morning. If you notice that he's missed something, speak up immediately. I didn't bring you on board to be church mice. Rick?"

"Thanks Jewels...I mean Ms. Folk."

"Rick, please call me Jewels."

A wink was exchanged between the two. The ice breaking banter had been coordinated in advance so that the new team members would feel more part of the older existing group.

"Sorry, unfortunately what we know as of this morning is sadly not much more than we knew yesterday. We know the signal that controlled the freighter was bounced off a French satellite and that the owner received deposits into a bank account in the Cayman Islands. We had hoped that under more unique questioning techniques, we would have been able to glean more worthwhile intelligence from Monsieur Lebrofe. Unfortunately, that has not been the case and he is, for the most part, just taking up a cot, eating three squares a day and using up oxygen that the rest of us could be using."

Some snickering ensued as everyone knew that even the Supreme

Court had now turned a blind eye to enhanced or, as Jewels had phrased it, "unique" interrogation techniques after the San Diego attack. The word from the top was "whatever it takes." Rick paused; half smiled himself, wishfully thinking of the scenes from the movie *Marathon Man* where Dustin Hoffman is shown getting the nerves of his teeth drilled into in order to extract information. He smiled and started again.

The question in front of the group today and for the past several weeks had been how to quickly and accurately locate where the uplink to the satellite had originated. Whoever had controlled the freighter into the port, detonated what now had been determined to be a 985 kiloton weapon, and destroyed San Diego and the surrounding area was going to pay dearly for their actions. At 985 kilotons, the blast at the port of San Diego had been almost sixty-two times more powerful than the bomb used on Hiroshima, Japan at the end of World War II. The group's core responsibility was going to determine who would be receiving payback. What exactly that "payback" would be, was not in their scope of responsibility.

Jewels fervently hoped to end up with a more decisive conclusion than the FBI had come to after the Sony Company's computer hack several months ago. Since the probable outcome of her report would involve people's lives as opposed to sanctions, her team needed to get it right the first time.

The meeting's format was to hit what they knew first, and then open it up for a round table exchange of ideas. Jewels had hoped that everyone attacking the problem from fresh angles would eventually start narrowing down the paths they could logically follow and the group would coalesce around three to five good ideas.

Sitting in the first chair to her left was Gina Hughes. Since she had been working with Gina all morning, she anticipated her to pass on making a comment, which she did. To Gina's left was one of the new hires. The kid looked like he was maybe twenty. Jewels had hired him and knew he was twenty-seven and brilliant. His name was Chris Sutterfield and he had recently graduated from Clemson University in South Carolina with degrees in both computer software design and systems engineering. He was her chosen "outlier" of the group. First, unlike anyone else in the group, he was former military. A former army ranger, he had been medically retired when a sniper's round found and destroyed his right lung. Chris attended Clemson on the GI bill and found his calling to be computers and engineering. He had played an integral role in almost all the clubs on campus that related to computers or engineering and had even been the president of Clemson's Alpha Sigma Phi fraternity. He had a knack for juggling time and events and multi-tasking capabilities like no man she had ever met. He'd managed all that extra activity while maintaining a 4.4 GPA.

"Chris?" coached Jewels.

"Ma'am?"

"It's your turn."

Chris blushed, "Sorry ma'am, I was counting on Miss Gina to buy me some time."

The other folks at the table had chuckled. Gina smiled and shrugged.

"Ma'am, you said that you would let us all see the code that y'all have stripped from the downlink, right?"

Jewels nodded in the affirmative.

"I'd like to see that a bit later if I could. You've seen it, right?"

Jewels watching him intently, nodded yes.

Chris went on, "On what level, academically speaking, do you think the writer of the code was? I mean writing your own code can be challenging, but essentially hacking into another code as advanced as we've been told this was would take someone with several specialties including computer simulation and modeling experience, and the knowledge of how to simultaneously integrate several high level computer programming languages, would it not?"

There was some murmuring around the table but the general consensus was, yes.

"How many individuals in the world have all of these skill sets?"

Mitch spoke up, "What makes you think it was one guy?"

Gina cleared her throat just loud enough to be obnoxious.

"Or girl," Mitch attempted a quick recovery and failed miserably.

Chris continued, "In my experience, these groups are very tight knit and if they could find one or maybe two people to do it all, they would do whatever it took to make that happen."

Jewels furrowed her brow; she was not entirely sure where his line of thought was going. She was just about to ask where he was heading when another new hire at the far end started to speak.

"Hi, I'm Susan Atwater, sorry, first meeting jitters. Can I speak now?"

Jewels smiled, "The room is yours Susan!"

"Thanks, I think I know where Chris is headed. We are all happy with our jobs right?" She'd paused long enough for the question to sink in. "Let's be honest, who here in this room isn't on LinkedIn or one of the many other job boards?"

Not a hand in the room went up. Not even Mitch's.

"That's what I thought, wouldn't it be safe to assume that whoever wrote this code would also be out on the various computer job networking sites or message boards?"

Jewels smiled as she glanced around the table. There were lots of nodding heads. Jewels knew that the process was working, and she couldn't be more pleased.

Mitch piped in, "Jewels, I'm sorry, I realize it's not really a new idea but remember how we found the Iranian sub *Yunes* by listening for the sound that shouldn't be there?"

Both Jewels and Gina nodded yes.

"I was thinking," started Mitch when his friend Rick Wagner snorted.

"Sorry buddy, that was too easy."

"As I was saying," Mitch continued with a glance toward his friend, "What if we built a list of potential programmers and engineers and then put out requests through various channels saying we were looking for some help in solving a particular problem. I would imagine that anyone on our list who does respond is not our person of interest. It would, if nothing else, significantly shrink our pool of candidates."

It was coming up on eleven and Jewels had another meeting. She glanced at Gina who gave her the "sounds plausible" look. Jewels in turn then gave Mitch the thumbs up. "Mitch, please look into how we can run that to ground and get back to the group tomorrow."

"Alright everyone, get with your former deans and deans from leading schools and build us a list of candidates. We'll pool our lists tomorrow and work on a letter to bait a response from our mystery programmer."

Mitch waited for everyone to leave. "Are you busy for dinner tonight?"

Jewels, head bowed, continued to gather her notes. "Yes, I am," was her rather curt answer.

"Anyone I know?"

Jewels glanced at her door and gave it just enough of a push with her foot that it closed but didn't slam. "As a matter of fact, you do."

With that she spun around dropped the notes on the table and gave him a quick embrace and a kiss that took his breath away. "Now get out of here before someone catches us."

As the door opened and Mitch started to leave Jewels said just loud enough for Maureen the office gossip to hear, "I expect you to be on time for our next meeting." Mitch played along and slouched a bit as he walked past the office gossip's desk.

CHAPTER 9

—〰—

Festering Wounds

Ramón Rodriquez had been out of work for just over four months now. His wife had left him and taken his two kids to St. Petersburg, Florida to live with her mother. His house was in foreclosure and they had come for his prized Lexus last month. He had been living pretty high on the hog running a new intelligence office in Washington called BOATSS until last March when the attack occurred in San Diego. Life had been very good indeed until last February, when two new hires, Gina Hughes and her bitch of a friend Julie Folk had arrived and given him attitude from day one.

Ramón knew full well that he'd been a minority hire and that he never would have achieved his level of authority purely on his own merits. But those two bitches, especially "Jewels" as everyone called her, seemed to relish pointing out his shortcomings whenever possible. There had been some trouble during the March disaster and Jewels had cried to the director that he was impeding their work. He had been summarily escorted from the building, striped of his security clearance and fired before the sun set the following day. In D.C., word travels very quickly in those inner circles and nobody would even return his calls.

He had made the decision to seek revenge after he hadn't even been able to get a job at the local Home Depot. His new career path would be exciting. He was motivated, ambitious, and available. In fact, as he smiled to himself, he could start immediately.

Perhaps he didn't have the grades, aptitude, or scholastic pedigree of the folks he was formally in charge of, but he had something they didn't: street smarts. Inside a stuffy office he may have appeared inept and out of his element, but out here in the streets? He knew how to get things done. His first stop had been to seek out one of the several radical Imams in the Virginia area. It hadn't been his daily routine at BOATSS to read the daily terrorist watch reports, but he had done so anyway. He knew where to find the exact man he was looking for and within a week had set up a meeting to have a little chit chat about three things: His revenge, his money, and his new life.

Although it had been several months since he had physically been in the BOATSS office, he still had a few people he'd kept in contact with who hadn't seen any harm in telling him about the upgraded security and other seemingly trivial things like that. The Imam agreed to meet with him after several others confirmed his story and they were sure he wasn't working a sting to arrest the Imam.

After even more additional vetting, Ramón was granted an audience with the Imam. He had arrived, thankfully, right before the noon call to prayer. After an uncomfortable physical and electronic search for wires and other electronic devices, he was led into a small back room of the mosque to meet the Imam. After what most Americans would have considered a very brief exchange of pleasantries, the older Imam got down to brass tacks.

"What is it you would have us do that would serve both our interests?" inquired the Imam in his somewhat broken English.

Ramón glanced up, he knew that one misstep and they would never find any trace of his body. "I want you to help me blow up a government building," replied Ramón.

The man chuckled softly, "There are too many buildings in this cesspool of a town to choose from, where is this particular building and what is its function?"

Ramón knew the line he was about to cross was a life or death decision. Several of the Imams had turned state's evidence as of late and were helping the government tone down the rhetoric from the more fanatic branches of Islam in the states mosques. He'd last seen the list a few months back and had only his memory to rely on. He paused, "It houses the primary offices and personnel that are trying to track down who is to blame for the attack on San Diego."

The Imam made a motion to a man in the shadows who quickly returned with a small pad and pen. "And what is the address of this mysterious government building?"

Ramón wrote down the address. The Imam read the address, smiled, and reaching behind him, shared the note with his colleague.

"Really?"

Gesturing for the note to be returned, he lit the small folded piece of paper and let it drop to the floor just as the flame reached his fingers. The weathered skin around the Imam's eyes creased with a thousand years of programmed hate and he smiled a wicked smile.

"What you are asking is something we would be delighted to do," the Imam told him with his face now devoid of all expression. "I am curious though, why would you turn on your own people like a hungry jackal?"

Ramón had grinned as he said the word, "revenge." At first, the phrase had seemed awkward; these days the word rolled off his tongue like a smooth, sweet, dessert wine.

"I understand that you wish revenge, an emotion I'm somewhat familiar with, but why?"

Ramón knew where this game was headed and responded with caution, "I was shamed, humiliated, and disrespected by a woman that works in that office."

"Why do we not just kill this particular woman you so obviously despise?"

Ramón pondered that question. He hadn't prepared himself for questions dealing with the morality of the plan. "I want to take everything from her. Her life, her friends, and everything she has built."

The Imam nodded and Ramón continued, "For one million dollars and papers to get out of the states, I will give you all the details you need to be successful in this endeavor."

The Imam bowed his head, spoke briefly to his associate and said the one word Ramón had wanted to hear… "Done."

—◆◆◆—

Over the next several weeks they had worked together on the plan with Ramón gathering intelligence by having a few casual lunches per week with several old friends of friends. He had told them all he was working over at the state department. Everyone bought it. He had always insisted on meeting them at the front of the BOATSS building and they would then walk to lunch. One particular lunch date was inevitably more fun than the rest and often required a full hour of his time. Her name was Maureen Templeton. She had been the BOATSS office manager/secretary when he worked there and she now worked just outside Julie Folk's office.

Regrettably, Maureen wasn't much to look at and the thought of taking her out to a public place actually made him a touch queasy. The perk with Maureen was that she knew she wasn't a looker and as a result brought a certain set of skills to the relationship that Ramón had never been able to enjoy with his former wife.

The first several times he had waited for his friends outside of the BOATSS offices he had been approached by both the D.C. cops and undercover building security and asked why he was standing in front of the building. On three separate occasions, the security had actually called inside and spoken to his lunch date to verify his story. They had certainly upped their game security wise. By the third week he had a pretty good idea who was who and would exchange a quick smile and a head nod sometimes mouthing the word "lunch." By the end of the fourth week Ramón was a part of the lunchtime landscape and doubted whether security even noticed him.

As if he wasn't mad enough at these people, his very presence had now been marginalized *again* by the very same group of people that had put him on his current path!

Maureen Templeton didn't care much for the people here in the BOATSS office. She had watched them go by and used her very best phony smile. They had smiled back like they always did, feigning interest in her day. She seethed inside as Ms. Folk walked past her desk. Now the bitch had not only been promoted, she had even expanded her team. They were too smart, too chummy, and were all destined for greater careers in either the government or private sector. Maureen just knew they all thought they were smarter than she was. She had overheard enough from Jewels' office to know that Jewels and Mitch were becoming more and more an item every day. That had to be against some rule or another. He was tall, muscular, and had "perfect" stamped all over him. It was just one more indignity she had to endure on a daily basis. She knew that a man like that would never be in her future.

Maureen had been a "last call" take home girl for as long as she could go meet men in bars. She'd actually started hitting the bars and clubs before she was of legal age, but the thrill of it was worth the risk and helped her escape the realities of her reality.

Every one of these people would say, "Good morning," or, "Hi," as they passed her desk. She knew deep inside that they didn't really mean it. She had been a GS-5 now for five years and knew that with the current management in place, that's as high as she would ever ascend in the government service. She lived in a crappy little apartment on the wrong side of town, was unattractive, single, and didn't even own a car. Every year at her annual review she had been told her attitude toward her work, the mission, and her coworkers had lots of room for improvement. In short, according to her supervisors over the years, her personality wasn't helping her career. Maureen felt her attitude was just fine. To be completely honest, today she really just didn't care. She had a lunch date with her old boss Ramón Rodriquez. He always made her feel so special. After he had been stabbed in the back by his subordinates here at BOATSS, Ramón had been fired. His ungrateful wife left him a few months after that and in Maureen's opinion it was good riddance. In the darkness of her cramped apartment, Maureen had decided several months back that there wasn't much at all she wouldn't do for a man that made her feel so special.

It was close enough to her lunchtime to leave. She stopped by the ladies room, dropped her hair and freshened up her lip stick. She turned around watching herself in the mirror and adjusted her blouse so her rolls of fat didn't show as much. It actually didn't do much to help her appearance but she smiled all the way upstairs and out into the massive glass atrium at the front of the building. Maureen glanced through the enormous glass windows on the front of the building. He was already there, just outside the large glass doors, waiting...

CHAPTER 10

—*m*—

Iran

KESHEH RESEARCH CENTER SPECIAL PROJECTS FACILITY

It had been four months since he had successfully maneuvered the naive computer scientist Major Fallahi into writing the software for the control of the freighter *Shooting Star* and General ShahAb Tehrani was still basking in his own glory. The Americans had, as expected, done nothing. It was pathetic. He and his little group had expected some kind of response from the supposed most powerful nation on earth.

In General ShahAb Tehrani's mind, the attack on San Diego was only the tip of the iceberg in his personal war on America. Prior to his cold blooded murder of Major Harem Fallahi, the brilliant designer of the drone software, Tehrani made copies of the program and loaded them onto an identical set of computers and servers in the underground Iranian facility at Kesheh and had another idealistic computer geek named Behrouz, working his magic on his next lethal project.

With international shipping of all cargo to the Western Coast of the

United States increased tenfold due to both the destruction of the port of San Diego and elimination of the Panama Canal as a shipping shortcut, the general's particular wing of Hamas had decided that it was only logical that their next "special deliveries" be made by air.

Located in two private aircraft hangars at the Sultan Abdul Aziz Shah Airport in the city of Subang, Malaysia resided two commercial cargo 747-400Fs reconfigured to fly remotely to two yet to be determined targets. With a maximum fuel load of 57,285 gallons and a cargo capacity of 124 tons, the 400F aircraft had a range of just over 7,800 miles. With the added internal 5000 gallon tank the range was extended to almost 9,000 miles. The planes would be flown to their respective targets carrying 20 pallets of "computer equipment and car parts." Of course, even Behrouz knew it wasn't computer equipment but an extraordinarily volatile mix of high explosives. He also knew that 100 tons of the explosive mix would be more than enough to accomplish the task at hand…panic in America.

The general's team had needed to find another satellite to use as a downlink since it was apparent that the Frenchman who had previously been in their association was at a black list detention site somewhere out of the reach of any known legal due process. His instructions had been simple, do this deed, run and hide. Apparently, from what he'd been told, the Frenchman's idea of a good hiding spot was the Baccarat tables of Monte Carlo. Both greed and gambling were sins in the Quran and he had no sympathy whatsoever for distress the man was currently undergoing.

"How's our timeline looking Behrouz?"

Behrouz looked up and announced with some trepidation, "We will be ready to deploy the aircraft in one week's time sir."

"Your voice does not instill a great deal of confidence in the success of your task, Behrouz."

"It is not my piece of the puzzle that has us in limbo, sir. Our contact in South Korea has run into what she is calling 'delays' in acquiring the correct air cargo shipping manifests. She has had to use an alternate method of acquiring the documentation."

"Amateurs!" hissed the General. "Keep me apprised Behrouz, I don't like being disappointed."

Unknown to General Tehrani, Behrouz Yavari was in fact, very aware of his boss's temper. He had, like most computer geeks at this level, been curious in his boredom and begun exploring the computer system's hard drives and connected servers. In his blind search he had stumbled upon the archived video surveillance footage of the room he was currently sitting in. It had aroused his curiosity by both the way it was named and by the unique way the file was formatted. As written, the file could not be deleted. Behrouz knew this because like a dog with a bone he kept chewing on his "new bone." It was more interesting solely because he had never seen anything like it. Out of pure curiosity he had duplicated the file and then subsequently tried to delete it. Although the file would appear to be deleting, it was actually replicating itself and moving to a different location on the server. Whoever wrote this code was both highly skilled at writing code and very paranoid. He had watched the section that had been saved and it correlated to a period 48 hours on either side of his predecessor, Major Fallahi's, apparent brutal murder by his current boss. The Major had seemed very happy at his job and only the few short moments before his murder showed any fear or alarm. The five seconds of the tape that showed his bewildered face looking up into the face of his killer...would forever be etched on Behrouz's mind.

Any kind of death was not in Behrouz's immediate plans. In fact, on his personal list of ways to die, a bullet through his eye socket was not even in the top twenty-five. The 96 hour sequence had been hidden in plain sight and obviously left as a warning to whoever Major Fallahi's replacement would be.

The young man leaned back in his chair and exhaled a long purging breath. It seemed that he hadn't taken a breath for a very long time. He watched the video segment of interest one last time quietly whispering to himself, "Thank you Major Fallahi, warning received."

CHAPTER 11

—w—

Chaos

Jewels and Mitch made a last minute change to their plans and invited Rick and Gina to their dinner outing. At the last possible moment, Gina had cancelled leaving Rick literally standing at the restaurant without an eating companion. Mitch had exchanged a quick glance with Jewels and she had asked him to join them. He had tried to resist, but Jewels had her way, as she usually did and he stayed. It was strange, in a way, although the relationship between Jewels and Mitch had for the most part stayed on course and gotten stronger with each passing week, what had started off to be a potential romance between Rick and Gina had moved forward with at best, fits and starts. Gina was, as Rick confided in Mitch, "very aggressive" in every sense of the word and not one to just be content with a quiet night in.

They had decided to go for pizza and had just sat down when yet another story came across the big screen about the growing discontentment in the ELFs (Emergency Lodging Facilities) FEMA had set up shortly after the attack on San Diego. Most people just called them what they were, FEMA camps. Nine people had actually been shot earlier today trying to leave one of the two largest camps in New Mexico. Publicly it was promoted that they were "guests" at the ELFs or FEMA camps, until they could be successfully re-integrated into society. In truth, however, the only way out was if you had a sponsor and/or a job.

Every once in a while, people were still, even after all these months, finding members of their families who they thought had perished. Dozens of people were still dying every day from radiation poisoning at the camps setup along the borders of Arizona and the western edge of Nevada. Very few folks with elevated radiation readings made it through the National Guard checkpoints. From the air, there were enormous parking lots full of contaminated cars and every mode of transport vehicle imaginable. Enormous trenches had been dug to bury the vehicles and it looked eerie from the air as cars were buried in what looked like mass graves. A few miles to the east were several hundred hospital tents to treat the people afflicted with varying levels of radiation sickness. Large blue panel vans with white stenciled signs of "Mortuary Affairs" on all sides left daily for the temporary crematoriums set up yet another mile to the east. As of last report they were at maximum capacity and running six crematorium units 24/7. The ashes were being buried in groups with a time stamp designator. If the card read: 072020161135, it meant you were "interned" in the month of July on the 20th day in the year 2016 at 11:35 am. The seven by four-foot group casket was marked and an aluminum marker was placed above the spot where the casket was buried. It was down to a science now with the remains of over two hundred people being buried at a time in each container.

As everyone on the inside loop of the Washington beltway knew, these camps were going to be in operation for years to come. Anyone with money had moved on and into communities and reintegrated. Eighty percent of the people in the camps, with some exceptions, had no money, no education and no prospect of finding meaningful employment. Unfortunately, their situations hadn't changed from where they had come from, just their locations. Many were of "unknown legal standing" as it was being called these days. Most had come from a state renowned for its generosity and lucrative public assistance programs were now forced to live in a crowded, very controlled environment where "three hots and a cot" were what the government had deemed appropriate. Every member of congress and senator in the states where the camps were located knew full well that if they opened the gates and let these folks out that their political futures would be over.

The three friends ordered their favorite meat lovers pie with extra cheese and a pitcher of cold beer. They were technically all in the same room and seated at the same table, but even to the untrained eye...they weren't all on the same page. Not even close.

With the exception of ordering the food and beer, no one had said a word for ten minutes. Many of their evenings were like this. It seemed sometimes that the weight of the world was on their shoulders, alone, to solve the crime of the century. It was ludicrous of course to feel that way as dozens of people were not only watching all the moving parts, some were moving the parts themselves.

Jewels was the first to speak, "Do you think Chris' idea will work?"

Mitch shrugged, "In theory it should help narrow the list, but it's a long shot."

Rick had finished his first beer and was in the midst of filling his second, "Alright," he burped loudly and carried on without so much as a pause, "So assuming for a second we figure out the *who*, we'll still need to figure out the *where*. What if *they*," looking at Mitch with a wink, "have moved on from wherever it was that they sent the data stream?"

Jewels finished her beer, nodding to Mitch to fill it again. She leaned forward slightly and looked at Rick across the table. "Rick, yunno we love ya right?"

Rick laughed, "I know one of you does!"

"Here's the thing," Jewels continued, "We're not really looking for 'the guy' we're looking for the computers 'the guy' used. I think I've got something stirring up here," tapping her head gently, "that just might get us across the finish line. We'll need some heavy duty approvals and I'll have to call in some very, very big favors."

More relaxed, after their first beers and with the arrival of food everyone started talking about all the mundane stuff everyday folks talk about. The stresses of tomorrow's challenges would come soon enough.

—⚉—

The morning meeting came and went without Jewels saying anything about her plan. Everyone else had pulled together all the information Karen had requested. Most of the schools had been very cooperative, a few needed some nudging, but all eventually agreed to send out alumni letters with all the results going to a post office box in nearby Silver Spring Maryland. They had been asked to target all graduate and doctoral students that had graduated in the past five years.

The listing they had compiled was massive because, in many cases, a student would get their Masters degree at one school and their Doctorate at another. This caused their names to come up numerous times. Karen had written a program that would hopefully help them trim the list down to mouth size pieces. The hardest and most time-consuming part was entering all the names into the new data base. Many schools had used Excel and still others used Access. Karen hit "run" and the program automatically subtracted duplications and only left the highest level of education on the list. Within minutes the program broke the students out by country of origin and then state or province if applicable.

Jewels had asked Rick early this morning to put in some calls to his supervisors over at CIA to check the availability of the downtown CIA annex for a meeting with the CIA head of operations and some of the legal staff for a secure classified lunch meeting. Jewels wanted her plan at a "need to know" only level. Although convenient to have two SCIFs at the BOATSS building, neither one was large enough to accommodate all of the people involved on this mission. This type of program was on the TS/SCI or Top Secret/Special Compartmentalized Information. Nobody outside a relatively tight forty or so people would know what they were planning to do... and some of them might not know everything.

They left at different times and used different entrances at the annex. Once the usual pleasantries were exchanged, Jewels logged onto the networked TS/SCI server and after opening her account, opened her Power-Point presentation.

"I have named our little plan 'Project Katar' after the ancient Indian punching knife designed to punch through Asian armor."

Mitch's mouth fell open and he whispered to Rick, "Where the hell did she come up with that?"

Jewels either didn't hear or decided to ignore his comment and continued without so much as a glance in Mitch's direction and continued. "The Katar was used for fast punching stabs to opponents, and was very effective due to its speed and penetrating power. I thought the name, all things considered, rather…appropriate."

Jewels turned around and faced her group after someone had whispered just a bit too loudly, "This bitch is crazy." Jewels took it as the compliment she believed it was and whispered back in the direction the comment had originated, "Why yes, yes I am."

"Here's what I'm thinking, feel free to throw the bullshit flag whenever necessary."

From the ensuing laughter it was clear she had struck the correct tone.

"Essentially what I want to do is send out a partial Trojan virus embedded in an "update" from several companies. Here are some of my top choices: Goggle, Apple, Adobe and iTunes. The "update" would not have any code that appeared malicious to any current military or corporate level security software. After the user clicks "accept" which by the way, I've had written into the program as a "strike any key" function, the "update" would then determine the particular base language used on that computer. In this case, by language I mean spoken or written dialect. If it was one of the several languages or various dialects of the countries we expect were involved in the San Diego attack, the "update" would proceed to the next level. If it's determined not to be one of the languages, the update would go dormant and show the user that the update had been completed. If one of the languages that we are looking for resides on the computer, it will then scan the hard drive for programs that dealt with assembly programs, advanced simulations and code compilers. And before you ask, we are putting the finishing touches on a variant that would both detect and scan connected servers.

She paused and looked around the table. As she had anticipated, all the computer folks were leaning forward intently and both Mitch and Rick were sitting back in their respective chairs, mouths agape.

"Come on Intel folks; don't let the geeks have all the fun!"

That at least snapped some of them back to the conversation.

Jewels returned to her presentation, "When it is determined that these parameters have been met, the second half of the "update" will be sent. This portion will essentially act as a key to start the worm in motion."

Now she had everyone's attention.

"Ironically," said Jewels, "the worm will not be malicious in any way. All the worm will be designed to do will be to identify the computer or server's geographic location."

Jewels thought that perhaps she'd inadvertently smirked at that last part. She knew that although what she had told the group was true, she had made the decision to hide the true mastery of her plan from everyone until it would be too late to change.

"Talk it out amongst yourselves, the coffee's hot, help yourselves."

Mitch was the first one out of his chair to get coffee. As he stirred in his creamer he was staring at Jewels with a look Jewels had never seen before… and she shivered.

As they walked, Jewels shouted out a courteous reminder, "Conversations stay in here folks, a restroom break is authorized!"

Mitch walked up still stirring his coffee. It was way past mixed by now, something must be up.

"Hi Ms. Folk."

Now she knew something was up.

"Hi Mr. Kendrick," she said, trying not to sound too awkward. She glanced over Mitch's shoulder and could see that Rick was watching what was transpiring.

Mitch physically maneuvered her so she was facing away from everyone else. Under normal circumstances his brushing against her made her feel warm and tingly inside. This time, she felt something different.

When he was sure no one else could hear, Mitch said, "I love you but you're a very, very bad liar."

Jewels recoiled and tried to pull away but his grasp on her arm was like a vise and he held her in place.

"You're hurting my arm," she hissed.

He released his grip on her arm. He sure hoped it didn't bruise.

"Don't worry, no one on your "council of geeks" noticed…but you lit both Rick and I up like Christmas trees."

Just by the look on her face he knew he was right and that she wanted to know.

"You smirked when you lied about the purpose of the worm."

"I didn't *lie* per say."

Jewels thought she had only subconsciously smirked.

"Babe, either don't lie anymore or think of something to do besides smirking."

He tried to give her a reassuring squeeze but she had inadvertently recoiled at his touch.

With everyone having cycled through the restroom and now armed with a fresh cup of coffee, Jewels continued with the briefing.

Jewels was very aware that many of MIT's graduates had gone to work for several of the companies whose branch offices and or headquarters had been destroyed in the San Diego attack. Others simply knew folks who worked at several of the larger companies such as Semantic Research, Peregrine systems, ViaSat, LRAD. It was a long shot, but after only a few calls that she had already made, she had the feeling that some of the best minds in the computer industry would back her plan. While revenge, as the old adage goes, "is a dish best served cold," the attack had boiled the blood of Americans across the nation. In the world of computers there are computer folks that are either considered to be a "White hat" or a "Black hat." As it was in the old westerns the "White hats" were traditionally the good guys you never hear about and the "Black hats" were what everyone refers to as "hackers." Much like the CIA, which has both divisions for espionage and counterespionage, there are groups and entire companies that are working on developing defenses against hackers. One of these companies is "Symantec." Many of the personnel at Symantec toiled daily creating anti-virus and anti-malware software to protect private sector civilian computers as well as creating and managing defenses against hackers for corporations. In another department, folks would then test the software to see if they could get past the various firewalls and safeguards developed down the hall. Jewels would definitely need their help for her plan to work.

CHAPTER 12

—◊—

Dry Dock – Bremerton, Washington
USS CONNECTICUT

The damage caused by the 985 kiloton blast in San Diego bay had destroyed seventy-nine navy ships and killed every civilian, every sailor, and every member of their families above ground within four miles of the base. The *USS Connecticut* had escaped destruction only by diving at the very last moment before the massive device detonated. Fate proved to be a very sharp double edged sword. Although it had spared the *Connecticut's* crew of 116, the weapon killed all but nine members of their families. Those families were now safely scattered among the states of Indiana, Ohio and Tennessee. Several of his elite crew had asked to temporarily leave the ship and be with those surviving family members. Two were deemed no longer fit to serve and one had needed to be hospitalized in a secure wing. Sadly, to this day, he remained on suicide watch. Seaman's mate first class Dwight Lankins lost twenty three members of his family who had gathered at his home just off base for a family reunion. Family members in Ohio said that they received a text message from one of the men saying that while the ladies had gone onto the base earlier to shop at the PX, he and the boys had gone down to the shore of the Silver Strand Blvd which ran along the coast separating the actual Port of San Diego from the Pacific Ocean to see if they could see the various ships leaving and entering the bay. The very next text had come with a video attachment. The video was of the bow of a very fast moving freighter, sitting very high in the water, heading directly toward the shoreline where they were standing. The bow wave of the freighter was enormous. The caption of the video read simply, "WTF?"

The only structural damage to the *Connecticut* itself was to several ana-lectic (sound deadening) plates that had become super-heated in the boiling water outside San Diego harbor and had actually melted slightly in several places. The submarine would still have been a mighty foe to contend with but would have been significantly noisier as she made her way through the water. The Seawolf class subs had been made tough, but had not been de-signed to survive a nuclear weapon size event at such close range.

Captain Trent Briggs waited for his entire crew to contact or attempt to contact their loved ones before he allowed himself the luxury of doing the same. His wife Stacy and their two children, eight year old Grace and six year old Alex, had made it to Idaho safely after being met by her parents in Lehi, Utah.

She had cried both tears of joy that he was safe, but tempered her joy with the realization of how many thousands of navy personnel had died in that brief instant. In the safety and privacy of his stateroom, Captain Briggs had cried as well.

Several of the top navy brass had come up to Kitsap Naval base in Bremerton, Washington to see him and visit with the *Connecticut's* crew. They all received medals for valor and several of the bridge crew had re-ceived the Navy Cross. It was of small conciliation to those who had lost everything but although the navy had always been part of their families up until this point, for too many of the crew, the navy was their only family now. After consultation with the Pentagon, those that wished to stay and serve on the *Connecticut* were, after a full medical and psychological workup, allowed to remain with the boat.

Briggs was promoted to commander, effective immediately, and was offered a staff job at the Pentagon which he respectfully declined. Although their personal plans and his paperwork for retirement were well in the works, Stacy understood that he needed to stay in the navy. She and the kids, as well as his black Lab Boomer, would be waiting in Idaho when he finished his mission. Stacey was an educated woman. Whoever had done this horrendous act were themselves extremely dangerous or traveled in a very dangerous crowd. Trent had come home for a month of R&R in mid-April. It had been a joyous relaxed time with the kids riding their horses, catching frogs and learning to shoot their new BB guns. They had taken long walks almost every night just holding hands and spending some quality adult only time together. Spring time on a ranch is always a busy time and this year was no different. The daily ranch activities allowed them to shut out the rest of the world. Stacy was many things to her young family but above all things, a realist. She knew both her husband of almost twenty years and the United States Navy had no intention of letting whoever had perpetrated the San Diego disaster quietly slip away into the shadows. Stacy knew that one way or another, this would be her husband's last cruise.

CHAPTER 13

—∭—

Going Dark

It had been another very long day for Jewels and at four p.m. she had been "asked" (which meant see you at 1700) to attend an update on both the National and International economic impact of the San Diego "Incident."

As she sat through the seemingly endless PowerPoint presentations, her mind drifted to a nagging question. What was the US going to do when they, as the president kept saying, "Brought the perpetrators of the heinous act to justice?" She had been paying attention the past several years and knew *that* was bullshit. Something would need to be done that would give these bad actors pause to ever think of doing something like this again. Her mind snapped back to the slide showing Chinese freighters lined up in all of America's working western ports. They seemed to be profiting well from America's situation. A bar chart showing the import export disparity between China and the U.S. went by. Damn, their economy was in hyper drive. And then she tipped her head back as the same information they'd been hearing for weeks was presented. She figured that all they did was change the date of the slide. Her mind drifted to Mitch and the upcoming weekend. He was calling her name, "Ms. Folk!?" "Ms. Folk!?"

That was odd; he never called her that...

Somebody, not so gently, elbowed her.

She jolted back to her real surroundings and realized that the Intelligence officer in charge of the briefing was calling out her name for her assessment.

"Sorry, major, nothing new from our end."

It was a lie, but one she felt comfortable telling. She didn't need to draw any more attention to her plan than absolutely necessary.

"Jewels, where were you?" asked a smiling Gina. She had been "asked" to attend the briefing as well.

"Not here," Jewels whispered.

"Well folks," the voice at the front of the room droned on, "that's all we have for the week, maybe next week we'll have a breakthrough and get something in the works."

The meeting broke up and the two women walked out together.

"Well?" asked an inquisitive and smiling Gina.

"As a matter of fact, I need a drink," said Jewels and the two walked back to their respective offices, grabbed their coats, and headed down the hallway. On the way they passed the new head of security for the building.

"Ms. Folk."

Jewels paused to scold the giant of a man.

"Mr. Shortman."

Jewels placed one hand on her hip and wagged the other hand's index finger in front of the big man's face.

"How many times have I told you to call me Jewels?"

Head of Security Ken Shortman stood well over six foot six and had to weigh in excess of two hundred ninety pounds. He looked eerily similar to the late actor Michael Clarke Duncan from *The Green Mile* and *Armageddon*. The man even had the same deep, sweet as honey voice.

Ken smiled, bent forward, looked her straight in the eye and said, "That ain't gonna happen ma'am."

They both laughed.

"Ms. Folk, would you have time in your schedule next week to have a little meeting with me? It's probably nothing but I just need to show you something."

"My door is always open," quipped Jewels.

"I know ma'am but I..."

Jewels lifted her hand up in front of the man's face, silencing him immediately. She imagined that it must have looked funny from a distance. Jewels was tall, but this man was enormous!

"Here's the way this will work, you come by my office, knock and say "security issue" and you've got my time and attention any time, fair enough?"

"Yes ma'am, have a good weekend!"

Jewels and Gina headed down the hall arm in arm like when they had first met almost fifteen years ago.

Ken shook his head as he watched them leave. He owed them both a lot. Especially Ms. Folk. He sighed heavily and did his end of day walkthrough.

He walked into the "Big Room" as Ms. Folk referred to it. It was essentially the room where everyone had their own new spacious cubicles and computers. She referred to her own office as the "Little Room." He chuckled; he would do anything for her. He paused at each desk, primarily to make sure monitors were off, Top Secret folders were put away, safes were locked and SF 702's were signed off.

—⚉—

Ken walked through the office quickly glancing at everyone's desk. He hadn't been doing security for more than a few years when he realized he had found his niche. He had a knack for it. He noticed things that most people were either too busy to notice or didn't make their threshold of "Give a Shit" list.

He had just passed Maureen's desk when something caught his eye that made him turn and look again. Last week he noticed that her desk was unusually tidy and had a vase of fresh flowers on it. For most women he wouldn't have given it a second thought. For Maureen, it was enough to back him up and turn him around and look at her desk again. She was the person in the office that nobody spoke to and she kept to herself. It must have been tough to be such an introvert in an office with this crazy bunch. He bent over slightly and peeked at her calendar/desk blotter. The blotter had doodles in bright cheery colors all around the margins. That was certainly a new addition. He bent closer and gave them a closer look. There were random swirls and the letters, almost in a monogram style "CR." Somebody's in love big time.

Ken smiled, "Good for her," he mused. On the other side of the blotter were other letters, they were block shaped in black sharpie and had been crossed out in obvious anger, "JF."

As he stood up to leave his eyes perceived a pattern on her planner. Two days every week were the letters "RR" and the word "lunch." Two days ago it said, "OMG FLOWERS!!!"

Ken shook his head. Maybe she was having a change of heart and would start fitting in around the office. Stranger things had happened. He signed the room security form, turned on the room's alarm system, switched off the lights and closed the door. It was six fifteen and he had been here for almost ten hours. Why did these folks always pick Friday afternoons for their damn meetings?

Jewels and Gina had the evening to themselves as the guys had decided they needed to "decompress." Whatever coded activity that referenced, Jewels didn't really care at the moment. They walked to the train without saying very much. At the bottom of the stairs, they turned to each other, and at the same time said, "Donavan's."

Jewels had to speak up as the train was entering the station, "I think we need to decompress don't you?" "Damn right," yelled Gina, flashing an enthusiastic two thumbs up.

They had arrived at Donavan's around seven and the last time that Jewels remembered seeing a clock it had said one fifteen. It wasn't the same being out on the town without Mitch but after the third round of Tequila, Jewels found herself sufficiently "decompressed" from her day to enjoy herself surrounded by fifty plus strangers, and of course…Gina.

It was early Saturday morning and her head hurt, a lot. This is why she didn't drink very often. She made some strong black coffee and flopped back down on her couch. She stared at her toes and big feet for a while.

She called out for Gina before remembering that although she had offered Gina her couch for the night, Gina had passed. After putting Jewels, almost literally, in a cab, Tommy, Gina's latest love interest, had convinced a rather willing Gina to travel across town to his place.

Jewels drifted in and out of thought. It was frustrating having all the technological savvy in her head and not being able to do anything to help America extract some revenge because of the "optics." That was another expression she was getting tired of. She hoped that the phrase would go out of vogue soon, but the overused phrase "overarching" was still hanging around for some twenty years now.

The key she mused was that whatever was to be done couldn't be done overtly or even in the traditional sense covertly. No, whatever she came up with needed to be untraceable and never linked back to the United States government, or anyone else's for that matter, at least until she wanted it to be…

In her many years of study at both University California at San Diego and the Massachusetts Institute of Technology (MIT) and later in the software development industry she had developed a working knowledge of what movies and television referred to as the "Darknet." Darknet isn't so much as a place or destination as it is a series of private network connections used only between trusted peers. Without the proper equipment and knowing someone already active on Darknet, you weren't getting onto their net. Fortunately, Jewels had both.

Jewels had gained the trust of some student's years ago and they had gotten her set up on a network called "GNUnet." GNUnet offered what's referred to as an "F2F topology" option for restricting connections to only the users' trusted friends. The users' friends' own friends (and so on) can then indirectly exchange files with the users' computer, never using its IP address directly.

She began her logon procedure by entering her username: GreenIs! An homage and word play on her own "green eyes" and then her ten character password. Once she had logged into the GNUnet site she logged into her peer. Her specific peer log-on required a 17 character password consisting of both upper and lower case letters, three non-sequential numbers, two different special characters and rolling code phrase known only to the folks operating the particular peer she was accessing.

With her coffee wearing off Jewels was getting a touch impatient.

"Come on already!"

The screen that popped up did not list names and addresses but rather avatars or computer likenesses either real or imagined of a particular user or group. It had been over a year since she had been on the site.

"A watched page never loads," was the geek's take on the old patience saying about a watched pot.

No sooner had she stood up to stretch her legs than the page loaded and filled with characters. She searched the page and found the characters she was looking for, hoping they hadn't changed the site's format.

Jewels scoured the page filled with seemingly random images, smirked, and clicked on the steaming cup of coffee. An email program opened up and she typed in her brief message and hit send. After a few moments, three pictures of Washington landmarks came up. Jewels selected The Jefferson Memorial. A digital clock appeared and she set the time to 13:00. Then a date appeared. Jewels selected tomorrow.

Her computer chirped once as a secure email came in. Only the subject line was filled in. It read "Don't be late." Jewels replied in a similar fashion but stating in her subject line, "Join me for coffee?" It seemed silly but at this point, the less said was better.

Jewels' plan was based on some very sound principles of both computer science and human nature. The key to the plan's success was first and foremost the cooperation of at least five of the largest IT companies in America, and the absolute security and secrecy of what they were doing.

If even one company broke her trust...the entire plan would fail. It was very high stakes and she knew it.

Step one of the "official" plan being launched from U.S. Cyber Command's computers was her plan to send out a Trojan type BOT that would identify if a computer had a particular type of software on it or any of the servers on its network. The programs would arrive over a period of days like any other update from Adobe, Microsoft, PC Matic, Carbonite, Goggle Chrome or even iTunes. The human interfacing with the computer would be given the option of updating or not. Due to heightened security protocols, many people would hit "no" Jewels had written in a "strike any key function" to ensure it was uploaded. If the client selected "YES" the update would run as normal and close when completed. If the client selected "NO" the update would acknowledge the "NO" but upload and run in the background. The architecture of the first "Update" was built on determining what if any high level languages such as ASCEND, Galatea, Python or several others were installed on the machine. With the right programmer, any of these languages could be used or have their code modified to develop the advanced simulation and modeling programs used to control and maneuver the freighter into the coast of San Diego.

Once the first update had narrowed down what computers had the capability to run the software, a second "update" would be sent to determine when the computers had been active. Any that weren't active during the time leading up to the incident could then be eliminated.

When the pool of candidates had been significantly narrowed, a clone of the signal that they had captured during the attack would be sent and the "update" would look for a match.

The final "update" would ask the computer to disclose its location or IP address.

Each piece of the puzzle would be routed surreptitiously back to not only the Cyber Command's designated computer, but to one of hundreds of Darknet servers. At least, that was the officially agreed upon plan...

She dialed Mitch just to be annoying. He picked it up on the second ring.

"Mitch? You're awake?"

"Of course I'm awake! We've been up for hours and are already back from a run."

"Who's we?" Jewels inquired as calmly as she could. Man, did she ever need more coffee.

"Rick."

Mitch sensed the confusion and laughingly announced, "I'm at Rick's place. We grabbed a six pack and came back here to watch the game."

Mitch yawned, "What did you two do last night? You sound a little rough around the edges."

"Tequila," was all she had said. Mitch pulled his phone away and shared that little nugget of information with Rick.

"Sweetie," Mitch was almost wheezing from laughter and she could hear Rick laughing in the background...

"Sweetie," he started again, "You don't drink Tequila remember?"

She held the phone away from her face. She brought the phone back briefly when the laughter had become unbearable. Jewels said, "I hate you Mitch Kendrick!" and pressed "END" on her phone.

Almost immediately she regretted what she'd done. A message marked urgent came in from Mitch. Only it wasn't a message. It was an entire page of laughing emoji's. She smirked.

It was time for a shower and food. Maybe the day would be better after a shower.

An hour passed and when she was feeling human enough she texted Mitch to see if he wanted to grab lunch.

"I need to eat something soon."

"Sushi," was his response.

"I was thinking about a good sandwich and perhaps a little crow," she added several smirk emojis.

"LOL" Mitch replied, "Where and when." He threw in a heart symbol for good measure.

"20 min @ Stachowskis Market."

It was less than a mile away and the walk would do her some good.

"20 min," and thumbs up emoticon was Mitch's last text.

Before the events of this past spring had unfolded, Jewels had normally run several miles a day. With her increased work load and responsibilities came longer less predictable hours. It had become increasingly difficult to find the time to run or much else as of late. Her relationship with Mitch wasn't as easy going as it once had been and although she was unsure of where she wanted the relationship to go, she did know that in its current state, it's survival was unlikely.

It felt good to walk somewhere, anywhere at this point, and the warm breeze on P Street felt good against her skin. She certainly didn't want to arrive hot and sweaty to her lunch date, but she began to lengthen her stride just a bit and see how her legs felt after so many weeks of inactivity.

As her pace increased Jewels noticed that an overdressed man to her left and across the street had increased his pace as well. Jewels may have been just a computer geek, but even she sensed something wasn't quite right. It was at least seventy eight degrees and whoever it was had a hoodie, not only on, but pulled forward obscuring their face. As she crossed 26th Street, Jewels very subtly lengthened her stride a bit more. Two more blocks to go. At five foot ten, increasing the length of your stride significantly increases your speed. The man across the street was definitely having trouble keeping up. Alright, enough of this shit, she thought.

As Jewels simultaneously increased her stride yet again and reached for her phone, the man darted across the street oblivious of oncoming traffic. She raised her phone, activated the Siri function and desperately yelled, "Call Mitch!"

From directly in front of her a voice replied, "Call Mitch what?"

Panicked and out of breath, Jewels grabbed Mitch's arm and turned him quickly to show him the person who had been following her. The street was empty.

CHAPTER 14

—m—

Wasteland

It had now been just over four months since the attack and the Panama Ca-nal was still shut down. Since the Panamanians did not have the required expertise to repair the lock systems, they had ceded control and repair of the locks back to the American's nullifying an agreement signed in 1977 and put in place in 1999.

Unfortunately, the quibbling over the technicalities of who should pay for what, had taken two months to resolve.

The only way goods of any kind were reaching the West coast and ar-eas north of Los Angeles like Washington and Oregon was by rail or truck. Accessing the port of San Diego and the city as a whole was still beyond reasonable safety limits with radiation readings well above safety levels for anyone but protected federal workers and some National Guard units. Even those few individuals were only in specific areas for brief periods of time doing brief area surveys and taking radiological readings.

Most of the people who had survived the initial blast and subsequent fires were literally the walking dead. The amount of radiation had exceed-ed even that of Hiroshima, their bodies had just taken too big a hit to sur-vive. They had all the classic symptoms for each type of radiation they had been hit with. All of the people who had been in direct line of sight had received deadly amounts of gamma radiation and had, as the press put it, "expired." First responders hadn't even gone into the center of the city for five days. Triage, or the staging of patients depending on their injuries, had been more than even the first responders could handle. The burns were by far the most ghastly. After five days exposure to the elements and lack of medical care, the patient's skin had blistered and peeled away and nature had moved in. Flies were everywhere and many of the burn patients were blanketed with maggots. All had been found in shock and many had succumbed to the thermal trauma and shock related injuries.

Occasionally, and it had been rare, a survivor had been found who had no outward signs of injury but was suffering from the ravages of Alpha radiation. Alpha and Beta radiation were by far the most horrific ways to die as the patient died from the inside out.

Most of this group had survived the tremendous initial blast, falling debris and fires, and had tried to walk out of the city. With no protection to cover their mouths and noses, they had ingested the fallout particles from both the initial explosion and the weeks of smoke as San Diego had burned.

The majority of these individuals had been color coded "black" in the triage center and had simply been given strong palliative care such as intravenous Morphine and Fentanyl patches. None of the patients could hold down any oral medications. There just wasn't anything the doctors could do for them and they had died by the thousands from gastric and or respiratory system failure.

To date, with the limited official records available, medics had treated 637 gunshot wounds inflicted on folks that had done everything correctly right after the explosion except trusting their fellow man. Most had told stories of being attacked for their supplies and safety gear on their way out of the city. Many of these individuals had been in rough shape due to exposure but many had survived and were now in various hospitals in Kansas and Oklahoma.

China had stepped up their deliveries of all products that had become staples of life in America. The only way to get freighters to America's West

Coast was an arduous 53 day transit through the Magellan Straights at the southernmost point of South America or the relatively brief transit time of 26 days from most of the ports in China.

Without any competition to speak of, the prices for the very same products that were deals before the disaster were conservatively fifty percent higher. Individuals who had lived on the margins of society or government assistance were starving and the lines at the soup kitchens were long and often violent. The government had been dropping food along the major travel corridors of California and into FEMA controlled aid centers. Much in the same way airdrops don't work in the third world, a percentage of the drops had often been seized by looters and many deaths had been attributed to the food and water situation.

It had been months and martial law was still enforced in all of the western states except Washington and Oregon. Even there, several hundred miles from San Diego, societal tensions were high and patience was waning as panicked hungry people with nowhere else to go had pushed north.

Normally quick to spend other people's money and supply generous perks to its populations, the people of Northern California, Oregon and Washington were closing food centers and shelters to the refugees and had begun centralizing what limited resources they had for their own native population.

CHAPTER 15

—꘠—

Sinclair Inlet - Bremerton, Washington
USS CONNECTICUT

With repairs completed, it was time that the *Connecticut* and her crew take their boat out for an abbreviated shakedown cruise or sea trial. Although the only damage to the boat had been limited to the sound deadening anechoic plates, Captain Briggs wanted to do more than check the seaworthiness of his vessel. Briggs wanted, no needed, to ensure that the crew and several new replacements were still up to the standards he would need to take on his upcoming mission.

Several acoustic tests had been run in port, but nothing would match running full out in the open ocean. With a top speed of over thirty-five knots, the *Connecticut* would need some space to stretch her legs. It would take most of the morning to slowly maneuver through the fifty plus miles of Puget Sound before they reached the Strait of Juan de Fuca. With the depth of most of the Straight being an average of only one hundred and sixty-five feet, they would barely be able to submerge. Briggs planned to exit leisurely allowing his crew to get their sea legs and if they wished, take turns enjoying the magnificent view from the conning tower.

Captain Briggs had already seen his orders and even with the best of fortune his chances of completing his mission and returning to port unscathed were in the low percentiles. Although needing the Chinese to supply the west coast was the politically expedient decision at the moment, secretly, senior staff had been growing more nervous with each passing week with the Chinese buildup of equipment and resources in the South China Sea.

When the world, and even the United Nations, hadn't batted an eye at the secret and unauthorized installation of two massive gas wells in the contested waters surrounding the central Spratly Islands, China took that as a green light to move forward with what had to have been phase two, the building of several landing strips 165 miles south of the two wells on the Fiery Cross Reef. The newest landing strip was already, after only three months, almost 10,000 feet long and roughly 800 feet wide. When completed, it would be large enough to accommodate all manner of military aircraft from Chinese fighters to their heavy bombers. At only 165 miles, Chinese fighter jets and antisubmarine aircraft could be above the drilling platforms in a matter of minutes supplying military air cover and protection. In addition, Chinese dredgers had also created two harbors in the eastern part of two reefs. Satellite imagery found that both harbors were already large enough to host tankers and military personnel transport vessels.

The plan as it stood now was that after their little shakedown cruise they would rendezvous with the only remaining carrier group in the Pacific, The *Reagan Battle Group*. Led by the aircraft carrier *USS Ronald Reagan*, they would meet up, coordinate assets, and take the plan forward from there. The *Reagan Battle Group* was approximately 235 miles north northwest of Hawaii on a training mission and would only move west when the *Connecticut* arrived on station. The transit time for the *Connecticut* would be approximately four days to the rendezvous point and then another nine days depending on sea state for the *Reagan* group to make it to a rendezvous point northeast of the port of Mati in the Philippines. The rendezvous point, now formally referred to as "First Kiss" would be the launching point for "Operation Fiery Kiss."

It had been argued that it would be far easier to pull a group down out of the Mediterranean or even the Gulf but depending on how this whole thing shook out, they may well need the groups to remain on station in their respective AORs (Area Of Responsibility). After crunching the numbers, it actually took less time to move from the east. Tipping their hand in this game of cards would be deadly.

By pure happenstance, the Japanese military was conducting joint drills with the American Navy aircraft stationed at Naval Air Facility Atsugi. The two allies were coordinating P-3C strategies and maneuvers. The itinerary for the visit of two of the Philippine Navy's frigates and escorts to visit Hawaii had been leaked several days ago and had the ships scheduled to arrive in Hawaiian waters in approximately fourteen days.

Of course, there was never any intention of them making it to Hawaii, but it gave them an excuse to leave the port of Subic Bay and Manila in mass and eliminate themselves as potential targets when the Chinese conducted anticipated retaliatory strikes on the surrounding naval bases began. The Philippine Navy wasn't large and currently only operated three frigates, eleven active corvettes, eleven amphibious landing ships and seven auxiliary ships. Dispersing them to open water prior to attack was essential, as they were for the Philippines, irreplaceable.

The goal for this far-flung mission wasn't to start WWIII but to re-level the playing field in the Pacific Rim.

"Well?" said Briggs as he stared through his binoculars at nothing in particular.

"Well what?" replied his first officer never dropping his binoculars.

The Chief Of the Boat, or COB, had followed the two officers to the observation deck on top of the submarine's conning tower or sail. He had watched the men for the past several hours and they seemed to be avoiding eye contact and generally going out of their way to avoid speaking to each other. It was time for this crap to stop. The chief needed to fix the awkwardness of the situation.

Laughter from behind them forced the two most senior ranking officers on the boat to lower their binoculars and turn. Only one man on the boat had the stones to laugh at them and that was the COB, Travis Black. He, as well as Briggs had both been scheduled to retire and had even planned to get some fishing done post retirement out on Brigg's Idaho ranch. Only Lt. Commander Kirkpatrick was really supposed to be here. This was supposed to be his "cherry" cruise after Briggs had retired. This was to be "Capt. Kirk's" boat.

"What is it Travis?" Briggs asked softly.

"Well?" said Kirkpatrick sternly.

Black boomed, "Sir, permission to speak freely?"

Both men nodded.

Briggs spoke first, "What's on your mind COB?"

"If I might be so bold as to share a piece of insight my grandmother used to tell me when I thought I was in an unfair situation?"

"Sure," sighed Kirkpatrick.

"Sir, my grandmother used to tell us that, 'We are all where we are… and where we are, is exactly where we're supposed to be."

There was a long pause and both officers looked off into the distance for a moment.

The first officer of the *Connecticut* turned to his captain and with an outstretched hand said words that Briggs hoped would guide them on the rest of their deadly journey. "We are all where we are, sir."

Briggs repeated the statement and all three men shook hands and carried on with their assigned duties.

Twilight fell as they reached deep water and they dove the boat to 300 feet.

"All ahead flank."

"All ahead flank, aye aye sir."

"Put us on a heading of 270° degrees Mr. Black."

"270° degrees aye."

"37 knots at 270° sir."

"Mr. Kirkpatrick you have the con, I'm turning in. I'll see you at five."

Briggs entered his cabin and honestly couldn't remember a time in recent memory when he'd been this tired. He showered, quickly passed his "library," and picked up some light reading material. Tonight's bed-time story was a few chapters of Walter Borneman's book "The Admirals," which discussed four of America's most successful Admirals: Nimitz, Halsey, Leahy, and King.

He had read for less than thirty minutes when, while turning a page, his eye caught the sight of his newest family photograph on his desk. It wasn't the old one of just Stacy and the kiddos. This one had been taken just over a month ago on his Idaho ranch. It was the four of them, all cozy jammed together with his black Lab Boomer on the steps of his sprawling new house. In the background, you could see the stables and the most perfect sunset imaginable. Briggs closed his book, marking the page with a feather his son Alex had given him, reached out, and placed the book on his desk.

He looked at the photograph one more time before he turned the light off. In the warm glow of his wardroom he remembered the earlier words of his Executive Officer up in the conning tower: "Sir, we are all where we are."

As Captain Trent Briggs slowly closed his eyes and sleep overtook his exhausted body, he sighed heavily and prayed it was true.

CHAPTER 16

—◆—

Wishful Thinking

Behrouz was in a bad spot and he knew it. The thought of being part of this crazy effort to attack America again was so contrary to his personal beliefs it was almost physically painful to work on the project. He'd spent the better part of last evening pouring over Major Fallahi's old files looking for any way possible to communicate with the Americans and give them enough warning to thwart the plan and at the same time give himself the time needed to get out of this crazy secure facility without losing his own life.

He approached the problem in reverse because if he couldn't escape the facility it really wasn't going to matter anyway. Since Major Fallahi had designed the elaborate security features of the facility it was only logical to look in his old files for how the facility was designed to work correctly and then change those operating codes to fill his particular needs.

Fallahi's programs and safeguards were unique to anything the young engineer had ever seen, but had a glaring Achilles' heel in that all of the systems were controlled by the same software program. Fallahi must have been one arrogant programmer to believe that the controls of the entire system could be operated from one program. The password into the system was easy enough, F.A.L.L.A.H.I. Amazing.

Behrouz had waited until General Tehrani had done his morning walk-through/complaining session before he'd started reworking a subroutine for the facility that when he key stroked in the proper code it would globally change all the programmed machinery in the facility including the key pads for the blast doors and elevators, as well as other less essential systems such as security cameras.

It took him several breaks and leg stretching walks to get his timing down, but he'd calculated the average time it took to get to several hallways that eventually led to the outside perimeter blast doors. Of course, although getting the door open was imperative, keeping it closed and locked after he passed through was just as important. Behrouz calculated that it would take at least two days from notification for the Americans to develop a plan and almost that long to get himself out of Iran.

He programmed the clocks and electronic locks on the exterior blast doors to remain locked for forty-eight hours after his departure and then for all the doors of the facility to open and stay open in the locked position for another twelve hours. If the Americans hadn't made it there by then... at least he'd tried. A motion in the small mirror on his desk alerted him that someone was in the gallery above and behind his consoles. With a key stroke his screen faded from what he was really working on to a screen of similar appearance. Only if you knew what you were looking for would you have even noticed this subtle change.

"Behrouz!"

Behrouz swiveled his chair around, and looked upwards into the gallery. "Yes, sir!"

"Where are we in the process?"

"I'm working on the satellite encryption algorithms. I'm adding another layer of encryption so we don't lose communication at a critical part of the mission."

He smiled to himself. What he'd said couldn't have been farther from the truth. In reality, he was about to add another layer to the satellite feed but it wasn't for the general's benefit. It was, he hoped, the Americans best chance of averting another disaster on their soil.

"Carry on."

"Yes, sir!"

Behrouz slowly swiveled his chair back around and looked at the small mirror. He was gone and the gallery was empty. It was obvious that he'd need to be more cautious as he moved forward with his plans.

Behrouz logged into the feed that controls where a particular camera's images were displayed and changed both the gallery camera view as well as the hallway view to be sent not only to the security folks but now to a small window on his computer monitor's screen as well. It wasn't a perfect setup... but it was better than what he had only a few moments earlier.

Looking to the newly created camera feeds and not seeing anyone, he opened the program that controlled what the digital stream to the satellite would contain and started working on two things. The first was to put a backdoor into his aircraft control program. It wouldn't be enough for the American's to know that a pair of 747's were headed their way, they would need at least rudimentary control over the aircraft. This part was definitely the weakest link in the plan. He could only send the code moments before he made his escape from the facility. At this point, he had no idea where in the aircraft's flight that would be; the plan's outcome was as the Americans were fond of saying, a "Hail Mary" at best.

Less tricky, but of critical importance was a fast burst transmission pinpointing the exact location of the Kesheh Research Center.

Finished, Behrouz password protected the files and logged off. He'd missed his supper again, but would try for a piece of fruit or some type of snack. Maybe sleep would come sooner tonight knowing he was only several keystrokes away from stopping a madman and possibly stopping his country from being destroyed.

He entered the elevator and hit the button in the elevator that would take him to the eating level. He smirked when he realized that his whole plan resembled an amateur juggler's act at one of those traveling circuses he'd seen in the states. There was one glaring difference however. The juggler was allowed to drop one of the five balls and still get applause and carry on with the four remaining balls.

His smile faded as he contemplated his fate if even *one* of the balls he was juggling was to drop...he'd be dead.

CHAPTER 17

—⁂—

Ghost

Mitch had contacted both the capital police and notified the security detail from the building but, as was usually the case, nothing definitive had been determined. Several locations along P Street had security cameras but they only pointed out from their store fronts far enough to capture images in a twenty to twenty-five foot arc around the front of their own particular store. One camera, which had been located on P Street, had actually captured more than Jewels' pursuer's feet, but the quality was only good enough to determine that the individual was between five seven and five nine. So, frustratingly, they had only narrowed their search to exclude the cast of *Little People, Big World* and the Washington Wizard's basketball team.

"Jewels, do you think it could have been your imagination?" Mitch regretted saying it the moment it had left his mouth.

"No, Mitch. Damn it guys! I'm telling you I was almost at a dead run. Whoever this person was they either wanted to urgently tell or give me something or do me harm. There's no other explanation."

Ken Shortman looked like someone had stolen his lunch. For the head of security he wasn't radiating confidence.

"All right Ms. Folk, you'll have a shadow for the next couple of days until we can sort this all out. You won't know who it will be but they will be there. All right?"

"Sure, sure. Are you alright Ken?" asked Jewels.

The mountain of a man looked into her eyes "I'm just worried about you that's all."

"I'll be fine. I'm sure I can talk some man into escort me wherever I go..." Her voice trailed off for dramatic effect.

"Yunno, I'm standing right here, right?" Mitch said for some comic relief.

"Jewels, you need to take this seriously considering everything we're working on at the moment."

Rick weighed in with his two cents and launched into his now famous second amendment diatribe.

"You guys know that this would be far less likely to happen if D.C. didn't have such crazy concealed carry laws.

"Yeah Rick, we know," everyone within earshot chuckled.

It was already 10:30 Monday morning and the only headway the group had made was to announce that, as of yet, no one had responded to their online requests for help.

Of course Jewels was making some progress on her own separate front to the problem but she certainly wasn't going to bring that up at this meeting.

The timing of this whole stalker mess really sucked. She checked her watch, 10:45. She had a hair more than two hours to get to the Jefferson Memorial for her meeting with "Kelly" and in that time potentially have to ditch her newly assigned shadow.

Jewels checked her email, reviewed some performance reports and even took a few moments to look at some various interoffice and interagency memos. She had no interest in what they said, but they were an excellent way to kill some time before heading out to lunch. At 11:45 she peeked out her door and, realizing Maureen was gone, scooted down the hall and up two flights of stairs to the lobby level. Going out a side door, she fast walked the one short block east to the Mt. Vernon metro stop and headed south to the L'Enfant Plaza Metro Station. From there it would be just less than a mile to the memorial. She checked her watch again, 12:15. Plenty of time. It had been raining most of the last few days and the puddles were slowly draining. Jewels chuckled to herself, apparently the majority was evaporating and going straight into the air. Everyone wanted the rain to clean the air but nobody likes the humidity in D.C. that resulted from the rain.

Jewels cut west through L' Enfant Plaza and then down Maryland Ave SW, across the pedestrian bridge to the grounds of the memorial. She had arranged to meet "Kelly" under the trees on the east side of the memorial but at this time of day, many people were still here enjoying their lunch hour.

The grass squished beneath her feet as she walked across the short distance from the sidewalk to a more wooded area where the foliage was slightly heavier. A man of medium build passed her by giving her a thorough look over before moving on.

For a moment she felt her heart race with the memory still fresh of the man pursuing her down the street on Saturday. Another man approached and his hoodie was one of those kind that looked more like a hassock than a hoodie. No portion of the person's face was visible from any angle. The person walked straight up to her.

"Would you care to get some coffee?"

Dark sunglasses or not, Jewels was shocked to learn this was not who she suspected at all.

"Kelly" was a woman!

The woman was about to move on when Jewels realized she'd forgotten to say yes.

"Yes."

It hadn't taken too very long for Kelly to get a firm grasp on what Jewels needed her to do. The specific part of the code that needed to be constructed would be metaphorically like the carry-on bag one would take on a trip. The heavy luggage of clothes etc., represented the base code of the particular company or companies helping them, was carried out of sight in the belly of the plane and would be needed for the trip. To make the trip worthwhile, however, you were really going to need that carry-on bag. Once Jewels had received the ISP addresses of the computers responsible for the assault in San Diego, she would launch an all-out assault using the ultimate Trojan horse, the bogus "update" files they had already sent. The way she had written the code was such that the files sent to locate the computers and servers had been written in a manner that they were actually "waiting" for this last hundred or so lines of code. Kelly assured her that the virus she had created would make Stuxnet look like child's play. That would be something indeed because the Stuxnet virus was an almost lethal computer worm that was discovered in June 2010. It was designed to attack industrial programmable logic controllers or PLCs. PLCs allow the automation of electromechanical processes such as those used to control machinery on factory assembly lines, amusement rides, or any other industrial application. Wherever that worm was released would be devastating not only to that specific computer...but for any system connected to it.

With a feigned shake of their hands, the thumb drive with Jewels' program on it was passed from Jewels to Kelly.

If you hadn't known what you were looking for you would have never noticed. Kelly's job was now to connect the virus she had created to the program on the thumb drive.

The woman suddenly threw her arms around Jewels and whispered into her ear.

"Don't let this bug loose anywhere you want to ever use again."

"I won't," replied a startled Jewels.

The woman took a step back and looked Jewels straight in the face and said, "Go Tritons." She turned and walked quickly away to a nearby bike. In five seconds she was just another bike going over the tidal basin bridge towards the FDR Memorial.

Jewels played the exchange back in her mind. Go Tritons? It hit Jewels like a brick. The Tritons were the UC San Diego mascot. That campus, as well as over half a dozen more campuses were now just smoking ruins in the former city of San Diego.

The whole encounter had taken less than a minute. It was time to get back to work. Jewels clenched her fist knowing full well that although she couldn't fix what happened, she'd do what she could to even the score.

Jewels rarely took a cab but today she used that ridiculous app on her phone to hail a cab. It worked! She was on her way in five minutes.

—m—

Jewels arrived back at her office to find that her absence had created a touch of turmoil.

"Where the hell have you been?" hissed a highly agitated Mitch.

"I went to the ladies' room and then to lunch."

Mitch glanced at her suspiciously, but let it drop. "Where was lunch today?"

"I grabbed a Cuban Sandwich at Fredo's, why?"

"You're not supposed to be out alone, remember?"

"It was across the street for God's sake, nag much?"

She turned sharply and walked away. Mitch gazed at the floor where she had just been standing. A subtle twist of mud and grass remained on the carpet. He'd been to Fredo's many times and knew that there was no dirt or grass between where he stood...and there.

—m—

At about 310 miles north-northwest of the Midway Atoll, the carrier group *Ronald Reagan* was participating in scheduled exercises. Although the exercise itself had been scheduled many months ago, the exact location and scope of the exercise was just recently disclosed to the crew. They were running a "dark group" in that there would be no ship to shore communication other than official coded transmissions. They were in an area not historically used for exercises and the navy had disclosed an exclusionary zone to keep other ships out of the area. It was a common practice and hadn't raised any eyebrows as of yet...

The planners had done their best to set up the exercise/practice to reflect as much of the impending operation as realistically as possible they had for the first few days used a scaled distance to work out the tempo and coordinate the plan.

Sitting off to the group's west were two groups of four large oil containment booms that had been anchored to the sea floor. They were attached end to end in a roughly circular shape to represent the two Chinese gas rigs in the South China Sea.

The plan, in its beginning stages, was the sound saturation of the waters around the Chinese submarine *Great Wall*. By flooding the area with all manner of acoustic sounds, the Chinese submarine and its anti-submarine counterparts on the surface would be hard pressed to hear the *Connecticut's* approach. The *Great Wall* had been only out of the immediate area of the gas platforms briefly to resupply food stocks and essential crew and was now on station alternating its deep water positions in the shadows of several of the larger reefs and atolls in the immediate vicinity of the platforms. Thanks in part to the new system that had been implanted on the seabed in the area just before the events of last March; the US Navy knew where the submarine was every time it turned it's screws over for station keeping. Luckily, submarines don't have anchors and because of the tricky currents in the area the *Great Wall* kept its screws turning almost all the time.

The risky plan was to essentially acoustically blind the submarine, and place a new variant of torpedo in the water that would be hidden during its insertion phase by all noise of acoustic jammers. It had been calculated that from the moment their plan was discovered they would have only twenty-five minutes before the Chinese Air Force showed up to defend the rigs.

To avoid an environmental disaster, experts from two DoD (Department of Defense) contractors had been called in to plan and coordinate the strike. They would need to seal the wells to prevent leaks if the automatic systems supposedly installed by the Chinese gas exploration company, "Xīn lìliàng" or "New Strength", failed.

One of the most important aspects to the planning of the strike was to research not so much who had built the two gas rigs. It was well established that they had been constructed in the Dalian shipyard. It was doubtful that it had been a simple coincidence that both the freighter and the drilling rigs had been built at the same shipyard, but had been there at the same time. The former captain of the *Shooting Star*, Captain Kim Lee, had been very clear in his debrief that during his exploration of the Dalian shipyard early last March he had seen the two enormous rigs sitting on the water's edge awaiting final finishing details prior to being towed out to sea.

What they need to find out was who supplied all the various components for the rig. Since the late nineties, most of the various pumps and drills on the rigs were controlled by Programmable Logic Controllers (PLCs) and in early 2001 most had been transferred over to computers. Originally these systems were updated quarterly and used floppy disks. This was not only expensive to mail all the updates out on a specific date, to all users of a particular piece of equipment, it was also incredibly inefficient. The operational problem this created was that if a software update needed to be done a week or so after the last mailing the equipment would not be operating at its optimal level until the next update was mailed. More recently systems were updated via the internet or by satellite downlink.

If it could be determined what company had supplied the parts, the potential existed to download a software update that would implement an emergency stop order. By effectively rendering the rigs inoperable for a specific length of time, they would avoid the potential for an environmental disaster.

After several calls it had been determined that despite having six Blow Out Preventer (B-O-P) manufacturing companies in China, the Chinese government had purchased six American made BOPs from an Indian drilling subsidiary of Marathon Oil. That firm had purchased them from an American firm in Houston Texas named Roberts Oil Manufacturing. Roberts Oil Manufacturing had been more than happy to supply the CIA with the update software. After some work at Cyber Command, the software had been altered to initiate an emergency shut down and well sealing procedure at a specific time of the CIAs choosing. Now, the CIA needed to sit on its hands while the rest of the plan took shape and moved forward.

CHAPTER 18

—⚙—

Gifts From Home

It was late morning when the officers of the *USS Connecticut* finished their staff meeting with the unanimous conclusion that both the boat and the crew of the *Connecticut* were ready for combat operations. For the past several days the crew had been conducting modified sea trials in a 120 mile long, 50 mile wide box shaped area, approximately 250 miles off the coast of Vancouver Island. Their area of operation (AO) included the Cobb Seamount in the southern end of the box to the Endeavor Seamount to the north. The topography of the area allowed them to practice all of the aspects of combat from silent running to emergency surfacing maneuvers.

The support ship *USS Lafayette* had joined their little adventure late last night and had assisted with their shakedown cruise by using a very special acoustic detection system to attempt to *see* the *Connecticut* as it passed at various distances from the *Lafayette*. The crew had escaped detection, at various speeds sixteen out of sixteen times.

After burning a full day transiting back to Sinclair Inlet for weapons loading, inspections, and additional stores and provisions, the *Connecticut* was just passing the 200 mile point on her way to catch up with the *Reagan Battle Group*.

In the *Connecticut's* torpedo room, one of the newest members of the crew was a young torpedo man second class named John Isaacs. He was still taking in the enormity of the torpedo room. It was two decks in height and converted into one large area, if needed, by retracting the walkways.

"Any idea what these are for?" asked Issacs of his new supervisor, Chief Petty Officer Rogers.

"If you dent, scratch or even sweat on my new toys I'll hand your ass over to the chief of the mess to use as he sees fit! Now shut up and do your job! Where are you on your qualification card?"

Rogers grabbed the young man's card from his hand.

"Didn't we just do this step?"

"Yes chief!"

"Then why isn't my signature on your card?"

"Yes, chief!"

It was a touch over the top but the chief needed the young man to focus on his task as if it were his last job on earth.

"Captain on deck!"

"As you were!" bellowed Captain Briggs as quickly as he could. No need to stop progress on his account.

Briggs approached the new torpedoes and grinned as he ran his hand down the smooth surface of one of his boat's new "toys." These six torpedoes were significantly different in appearance than the usual MK-48 ADCAP (advanced capability) torpedoes the *Connecticut* normally carried. These were covered in a new type of sonar absorbent material that made them almost undetectable in open water and rendered them invisible when near or on the ocean's floor. The material looked very much like the neoprene suits that divers wore but it was much firmer to the touch. At a quick glance they appeared smooth but at a slightly offset viewing angle, small almost undetectable ripples could be seen all over the flat black surface.

"Chief Rogers!"

"Sir!"

The captain continued his inspection, "Did they at least come with instructions?"

"No, sir."

Both men caught the look on young Mr. Issacs' face.

Now Briggs was laughing and young Mr. Issacs seemed a touch concerned. He was unfamiliar with this particular submarine crew's sense of humor and wasn't really sure where the jokes started and stopped.

"What about a warranty, chief?"

Rogers worked as he talked and seeing the concern on Issacs' face, dug it in a little harder.

"Sir, no warranty was either expressed or implied and they have a strict no return policy as well."

"Well, chief, it's probably best then that we go somewhere and blow some shit up."

"Aye sir, sounds good to me."

"Sir, I almost forgot. Now that you mention it, they did come with something I've never seen in all my years of service."

"What's that chief?"

"They came with a note card attached."

Now Briggs was close to howling with laughter and it felt wonderful. God he'd missed his crew.

"A card, chief, you're pulling my leg right?"

"I'm not kidding sir, a genuine, looks like it came from Hallmark, card."

"Pray tell from who and what's it say?"

"Well sir," the chief hesitated…"I didn't open it as it was addressed to you, specifically."

Briggs stopped laughing and furrowed his eyebrows in concern. The situation had now taken a more ominous turn. There was a reason weapons or anything else for that matter didn't come with cards attached. It was called chain of custody. These weapons were top secret and access to them had been, or should have been, restricted to the navy onshore weapons folks, and his weapons team crew.

"Where exactly did you find it chief?"

"Sir, it was in the classified pouch that came with the torpedoes."

"Let me see it," Briggs outstretched his hand towards the chief. His tone was no longer jovial.

Chief Rogers handed his captain the envelope. Everyone stopped what they were doing and watched Briggs slowly open the off-white envelope.

Briggs looked at the envelope and it looked, as the chief had said, like a card from Hallmark or any other high end card shop. He noticed right off that someone had taken some time addressing it as it had been done in beautiful calligraphy. He could see immediately that it hadn't been computer printed because of the thickness and richness of the jet black ink. It was very neatly addressed to, Commander Trent Briggs, Captain, USS Connecticut. Briggs opened the card. It had the standard interior card salutation of "Good Luck" followed by a neatly hand written personal note: "We wish you and your crew both continued safety and good hunting." It had been signed: "Your *other* crew at BOATSS." The word "other" had been underlined twice and the sentence had concluded with a smiley face.

"Sir, what's it say?" inquired the chief and several others gathered around.

Briggs felt a knot in his throat the size of a Bartlett pear and it took a moment for him to gather his composure. His "crew at BOATSS" as they had referred to themselves, had saved both the *Connecticut* and its entire crew last March off the waters of San Diego and that was a fact that would never be publically recognized.

Briggs cleared his throat, "A note from a dear friend wishing us a safe mission," was all that Briggs had managed before the tightness in his throat required he move on.

The captain quickly proceeded aft to say hello and pass out "atta boys" to his crew. This type of activity was normally left to his executive officer, but he occasionally did both "inspection" (duty related) walkthroughs and "morale" walkthroughs. This was obviously the latter and his crew was, as usual, respectful but more relaxed as he passed through their duty stations and quarters. They had been through a lot and he felt they all deserved praise for their extraordinary efforts. Maybe it's why his crew would walk through fire for him. Maybe it's why, even after what they had been through last March, 100% of his crew that remained in the navy had requested to stay on the *Connecticut*. Briggs smiled to himself as he continued aft.

Torpedo man second-class John Isaacs watched in sheer wonder at what had transpired before his eyes. He'd never served on or even heard of a ship that operated like this one. Was this really the highest rated and most decorated submarine crew in the history of the United States Navy? He slowly shook his head, smiled at his good fortune, and went back to work.

—⁂—

They'd been working on the logistics of the attack for almost three weeks now and the Imams and Ramón Rodriquez had what they thought to be a pretty good plan. It had not been an accident that Ramón continued to meet his former associates in front of the BOATSS building for lunch or after work. In the past several weeks he had mapped out distance and "selfied" himself in front of the building from almost every angle. He had determined, to the foot, the distances from the street to the various exterior doors of the building. Most importantly, he had convinced Maureen to help him with his plan. The twit was amazingly stupid. Great in the rack, he thought smiling...but really rather stupid.

In Maureen's mind, they would both get away scot-free and live on a beach somewhere in Mexico drinking tequila and making love on the moonlit sand. He really couldn't blame her for coming to that conclusion as he'd cleverly planted it in her mind every time they'd been together. Brochures were pinned and taped all around her apartment about beachside homes in Honduras, Belize, and Mexico.

Half of what she imagined was at least close to the truth. One of them was going to live on a beach, but it wasn't in Mexico or anywhere with an extradition treaty to the United States. No, Ramón rather fancied himself living on the beaches of Vietnam. Last week he had used a computer at the Georgetown University library to research living arrangements on or near the An Bang beach in Hoian province.

This morning he made contact through a friend of a friend, to find some folks in An Bang who, for a modest fee, would facilitate his permanent stay on a lovely beach in An Bang.

—ᵐ—

The Imam was nobody's fool and although he relished the idea of taking down a federal building, he wasn't entirely keen on the agreed upon arrangements. Work had been completed on the weapon of choice and just the fine tuning details remained.

"Send JAveed to me," whispered the Imam to his aide.

Amongst other things, JAveed had proven to be an extraordinary backyard engineer or tinkerer as they called it here in the states. With help, someday he would learn the skills required and become an excellent bomb maker.

JAveed had entered the room silently and waited patiently to be addressed by the Imam.

"Come, sit with me and tell me how we are doing with our plan."

Tea was brought and they both took several swallows of the strongly brewed beverage.

"I am done!" announced JAveed when he had placed his cup on the floor.

"What have you worked out?"

"Once we determined that the human targets we are seeking are below ground it became evident that we needed to somehow get to them. In this case, the weapon of choice will be 93 octane gasoline. I have welded a fifteen foot steel fuel supply boom on a swivel mount that will lock in place behind the truck. This can be done from within the cab. When it is down and locked, it will double as a ram to break through the glass windows on the right side of the front doors. The doors to the right of the glass windows are closest to both the elevators and the stairs leading downstairs. I swapped out the standard distribution pump on the fuel truck to pump all 2800 gallons of its contents out in 90 seconds. At the end of the boom is an electric igniter, with a backup that will operate independently from the truck's power. It is on a timer and will ignite without driver input at the 85 seconds point."

The Imam smiled, "You have done well JAveed, there is no defense against this liquid weapon."

The Imam had frowned for a moment and JAveed grew concerned.

JAveed leaned towards the Imam, "I will drive the truck myself if you wish?"

"No, JAveed, I have a different driver in mind. You are destined for great things and I cannot afford to lose you. "

"Imam?"

"Yes, JAveed."

"As a gift, I built something extra into the truck without discussing it with you because I know how you feel about first responders."

"What special treat do you have in store for the D.C. metro first responders?"

JAveed was beaming from ear to ear. "Exactly five minutes after the truck is put into reverse the remaining 200 gallons of fuel and a 55 gallon drum of ammonium nitrate and diesel fuel will detonate by way of a second charge. This will happen whether the fuel's been pumped out or not."

The Imam smiled. The boy had skills far beyond his years and his talents were not to be wasted on martyrdom. At least, not yet...

USS Connecticut

They had been running at flank speed all day and had come up to communications depth to send and receive any messages. Pearl had a few for them and the *Reagan* battle staff had posted a Situation Report (SITREP) on the "Exercise." They had also received a message from BOATSS wishing to confirm the delivery of his new special "toys."

Routine message traffic wouldn't be brought to the captain's attention but the XO thought this met the threshold of his attention if only for amusement.

Briggs had smiled as he read the note. He didn't know any of these people at BOATSS personally but liked their spunk. If he got through this mission they were all coming out to the ranch for a week of whatever they wanted time.

"XO, send this message back would you?"

"Yes, sir."

"Toys received and look like fun. Can't wait to try them in the pool."

"Sir?"

"Just send it. Hey, address that "eyes only" to Julie Folk!"

"Roger that sir."

"I'll be in the wardroom."

"Captain's off the bridge!" shouted the COB.

Briggs opened the briefing papers that had come with his up scaled Mark 48's and began to read all the pertinent data on their deployment. As it turned out, these torpedoes were actually torpedo-mine hybrids. His orders were that he place five of the six torpedoes, which for good reason, had been code worded "*Sea Dragons*," in the waters around the two gas rigs. They had apparently been modified in several ways, one of which was a variable speed propulsion system that allowed for it to change its forward speed but could also change its acoustic signature to avoid detection. After launch they would proceed to their GPS programmed locations and sink to the bottom. They had enough battery life to remain in a passive state for up to a tested 48 hours. They had all been preprogrammed to the various acoustic signatures of the Chinese submarine *Great Wall* and two other surface ships recently seen in the area and would only target those specific vessels. They had also been sent a disk of other acoustic signatures that could be remotely loaded onto the *Sea Dragons* or by the crew prior to their launch.

Briggs saw the beauty in the system immediately. He didn't even need to be in the strike area when the attack started. Once the *Great Wall* took any other position in the matter other than "standby," he merely needed to send the activation sequence and the *Sea Dragons* would switch to "active" and seek out either the Chinese submarine or whatever ships he deemed a threat. He'd almost closed the binder when he saw a hand written note in the margin. *Briggs, deploy the toys and find a safe place to hide...Call us when it's time and we'll even turn them on for you...we got this. ~ BOATSS*

Briggs chuckled. Although it was great that he didn't have to stay around for all the "fun," he still needed to get the *"Sea Dragons"* where they needed to go. It was time to get with his intelligence and navigation officers. He stretched, yawned, picked up his "directions" as the chief had called them, and glanced at his new favorite picture on his desk. Stacy's eyes seemed to leap off the paper and be looking straight through him. As he closed the door to his stateroom he whispered under his breath, "I miss you guys too."

—w—

The charts of the area, and they were extensive, showed that the best way to accomplish his mission was to enter the South China Sea through a slot just south of Palawan Island called the Northwest Danger Shoals. The debate was what to do from that point. They would need to release the *Sea Dragons* at a point where they would both have enough power left to accomplish their mission when called upon and the *Connecticut* would be in a safe position to maneuver if things went sideways.

Several months ago this plan and the entire operation would have been considered a walk in the park. Unfortunately, since the chaos this past spring, the U.S had sat on its hands AGAIN and the Chinese had taken that for what it was and set about creating artificial islands out of several of the atolls near and around the newly constructed gas rigs.

In addition to the islands themselves, the Chinese had begun a vigorous militarization plan that already had several of the new islands outfitted with anti-ship and anti-aircraft missile batteries as well as artillery. As of the latest imaging, each island also had its own Type 571 acquisition radar, a derivative of the older Soviet P-15 Flat Face, and a Continuous Wave (CW) tracking, and illumination radar. At the ranges that a submarine or approaching surface ship or aircraft were concerned these were of great concern. They weren't the newest tools in the Chinese's box of toys but they were tried and true.

In order to get to a point due south of the rigs, he would need to proceed 195 miles west to an area south of the rigs and drift north through several stretches of relatively shallow water. If that went well, he would then hope to drift north, undetected, straight through the patrol area of the Chinese submarine.

Seawolf class submarines such as the *Connecticut* were dead quiet even under power in deep water. As everyone looked at the plan's projected course, a slight air of unease settled in as the Navigator pointed out the shallower areas. The closer the course of the boat got to the operations area (OA) the more nervous everyone, including the captain, got about Plan A. If a submarine, even one as silent as the one they were on, even scraped a reef for a second it would make a tremendous amount of easily detectable noise. The more they discussed "Plan A," the better "Plan B" looked.

Plan B required that they proceed north using only the minimum power needed to maneuver the boat. Using the prevailing northern current in the Palawan Trough, they would turn west and release the *Sea Dragons* at intervals as they proceeded south to optimize both their range to target and consumption of fuel.

By pre-deploying the weapons, he would affectively be in several places at one time and control hundreds of square miles of ocean from a safe distance. Both options had their supporters and detractors but Briggs erred on the side of caution and decided to ride silently north through the trough and then settle into a deep trench west of *Fiery Cross* atoll. It placed him not only in deep water he could maneuver in but 30 miles southeast of the *Great Wall's* last position and the two gas rigs if anything should go wrong. He and his crew had used up at least eight of their nine cat lives already this year and Briggs was in no mood to push his crew's luck.

Briggs looked at the electronic map again.

"Where is everybody else we need to worry about?"

His targeting officer changed the screen and zoomed into an area just north of the Spratly atolls.

"Well sir, the Chinese destroyers *Kunming* and *Changsha* are here and here respectively."

"Any ideas what they're doing?"

"Sir, the *Changsha* looks to be moving east to support the aircraft carrier *Liaoning*."

Several of the officers chuckled.

"God knows the *Liaoning* needs all the help it can get!"

"The *Kunming* though looks to be heading southwesterly and could cause us some problems if it comes back east at the same time we're still mucking around at the top here."

Lt. Foster pointed to the top three atolls in the Spratly group.

The plan was sound but not without drawbacks. Although they were relatively quiet, the *Connecticut* would hear the older Chinese diesels and avoid them all together. The *Great Wall* was another story all together. It was much newer and far quieter than the others. If only he could somehow think of a way to draw the Chinese submarine out of the area entirely...

"What's this area in here look like Charlie?" Briggs pointed to an area due west of *Fiery Atoll*.

Charlie had been assigned twice to subs and surface ships to navigate these waters for his second and third tours in the navy. If anyone knew how to navigate this area, he would.

"Sir, I can only give you a pre-dredging assessment, but that's a fairly deep area through there."

Briggs looked at the map for a moment in silence. "What if we come over the top and release the *Sea Dragons* down this western side. They'd have deeper water and a shorter distance to their corridors of movement." Briggs looked around the table and saw all smiles. "Gentlemen, I think we have a plan."

CHAPTER 19

—⚊—

Full Circle

Commander Liú Chung, Captain of *The Great Wall*, had been granted leave after two weeks and several awards and celebrations vaunting his exploits in March. His airplane hadn't even been on the ground in Taipei, Taiwan for an hour and he realized he was being watched. Chung knew Taipei well and had been here many times while on leave in the past. This trip was different though as it would be his last time to visit Taiwan.

He had decided several weeks ago, after his interrogation of Admiral Feng, that he would have to try and stay at the Grand Hyatt Taipei. Although it was an impossibility that he could afford the luxurious suite that the admiral had described, even several floors down the view of the Taiwanese skyline was a view to behold. The Penthouse suite was not currently being used and on a whim he'd tipped a bellhop just to let him see the room. If it was as Feng had described, it made his fantastic story just that more plausible. It was.

Chung had used his room for the past two days and nights fulfilling his desires in every way imaginable and was ready for this adventure, however it panned out. He got up early and dressed as nondescriptly as possible and threw everything else he owned into several garbage cans on different floors of the hotel.

He had been to Da An park several times to take his evening "liaisons" for a walk. It was one of the only parks in a sea of concrete where you could stroll and almost forget the stresses of everyday life. Almost, because although the scenery was beautiful in and of itself, the noise of the surrounding city was oftentimes overwhelming. For a man who spent so much of his time in the deepest, quietest parts of the ocean it was oddly stressful.

He picked up his fake American passport from a friend of a friend and also made an appointment at the institute using their required online system. He was certain it was so the government could intervene in situations just like the one he was undertaking today. It had taken three days to get an appointment but he was more than ready to get on his way to a new life.

Of course today, Chung was most interested in the park's one block proximity to the *American Institute in Taiwan*. Although it was just over a tenth of a mile straight up Jianguo South Road, a lot can happen even in that short a distance. He had a friend meeting him with a bike in the woods on the east side of the park and he would simply get on the bike and cross under the highway that separated this part of the city.

The trick would be getting past the guard booth directly opposite the red security door of the institute. He found a black marker and a piece of rice paper and wrote in English "EMERGENCY ACCESS PLEASE". His plan was to simply ride down the street with his fake American passport in one pocket and the note in the other and while acting inexperienced at riding a bicycle, bump into the red pedestrian door leading into the compound. The guard would ask him for his ID and he would present his fake passport. He would state he had an appointment and they would look it up. Timing would be important because if he was being followed the individual would be only moments behind him.

It was 12:45 and lots of people were on the streets...it was time to go. Chung rode with purpose but not so quickly to avoid standing out in the chaotic lunch time mix of pedestrians, other bicycles, and scooters. He could see the red door slightly to his left across the street and the guard shack on the right corner. One hundred feet left to go. The trick would be that no matter what he heard or who called his name, he could *NOT* look right. Even from this distance he could see the slew of cameras facing down all three access points to the institute.

Chung slowed slightly to allow some pedestrians to cross then bolted across the street to the red door.

He put his face to the window and slid his fake passport through the slot.

"I have an appointment at one o'clock." He smiled, perhaps slightly more than he should have.

"Let me check the appointment schedule."

In the reflection of the plate glass he could see all three men staring at his back, one was talking on his radio. He reached in his pocket and was just about to knock on the glass and show his note when the door buzzed and popped open.

"Step in please."

Chung moved quickly, dragging the bicycle inside the small room.

The guard smiled and gestured where he wanted Chung to go, "Across the courtyard and once you're inside, turn to your left. You can leave the bike here if you wish."

Chung looked over, placed his bike alongside the others and hastily walked across the courtyard keeping his head down. The tall building to his left was a Chinese government building that conveniently looked over the entire American compound.

He walked into the building and did not turn to his left, as he'd been directed, but to his right. He walked on until he saw an office, guarded by a non-Asian looking man and addressed the man in a language that attempted to mask his fear. "Hello."

The man said nothing but simply gestured to his left to a door halfway down the short hallway.

Chung smiled politely and approached the large oak door. A sharply dressed western woman just exiting the office almost ran into him as he reached for the door handle. "Excuse me, is this the office that one would go to if one was considering defecting?"

She smiled as if she heard that question on a daily basis. "No, sir, that office is two doors down on this side."

"Thank you."

"You're most welcome," And without so much as a glance over her shoulder, she was gone.

Chung turned and slowly walked down the hall as a man behind him spoke into his lapel microphone. He didn't hear the conversation but the door of the office two doors down flew open rather quickly.

"Can I help you?"

"Yes, I suppose you can. I am Commander Liú Chung of the Chinese Navy and I have some very important information I need to discuss with whoever handles that type of thing."

"Sir, if I can get you to step inside and take a seat we'll be right with you."

Chung smiled. So far, so good. It occurred to him that he may never leave this place but that wouldn't be all that bad.

"Commander, would you step through our security screening equipment?"

"Certainly."

Chung removed his tunic and hat and put them through first then walked through the scanner.

"Alright, sir, follow me please." They entered yet another room down a short hallway.

"Sir, this is Commander Chung and he would like to speak with you."

The man stood, smiled and extended his hand, "Good afternoon, sir."

He seemed sincere enough. Chung shook the man's outstretched hand and returned the pleasantry.

Chung looked for a place to hang his tunic and resorted to just draping it over the back of a wingback chair beside him. He took a seat. "Are you the person I need to speak to about defecting to your country?"

"Sir, it says here that you're already an American citizen."

"Yes, I know. For an additional 150 of your dollars I could have been a Canadian. I needed a way to get in here rapidly and that was the way I came up with."

"You understand that we'll have to keep it, don't you?"

"I don't really care. I'm willing to bet that same 150 dollars that by this time tomorrow, I'll have a real one."

"Fairly confident that you have some information that we need are you?"

"You're beginning to annoy me, Glenn is it? I need to speak to your most senior person who can call the CIA and verify my information."

The man came around from behind his desk and sat on the corner nearest Chung. He smiled. "You must watch a lot of Hollywood movies, commander. That's not the way it works."

Chung returned the phony smile, "It's the way it's going to work today because unless you've caught the individual who blew up the lovely city of San Diego, I'm here for my ten million dollar reward, official documents, and a new life in America."

Glenn's mouth was moving but no recognizable words were actually leaving his mouth. Fortunately, he regained his voice when he managed to grab the phone and dial a number. "Sally, get me Bill Clemons please."

Glenn's face was suddenly turning beet red.

"I don't care where he is I need him in my office five minutes ago! Fine, yes, thank you."

Chung was parched and for whatever reason this man's office thermo-stat thought it was winter.

"Could I get a glass of water or a soft drink?"

"Coca-Cola be okay?"

Glenn returned from a side office with two cold cokes and popped the tops. Both men took large swallows.

"So you were in the navy? What did you do in the navy?"

Chung intentionally hesitated while the man raised the Coke to his lips.

"I'm currently on leave from my position as the commander of the nuclear missile submarine *Great Wall*."

Chung had moved quickly and managed to turn sideways avoiding most but not all of the coke spewing from Glenn's mouth.

He wiped his mouth and was reaching for the phone when a side door opened to his office and three men walked in.

"Commander Chung? Bill Clemons! It would appear that you and I have a great deal to talk about sir! Would you kindly follow me?"

Chung knew he shouldn't do what he was planning to do and actually consciously thought of what he did next. He turned around while Bill Clemons's aide held the door and looked at Glenn Dooley.

"Mr. Dooley, maybe you should watch *more* Hollywood movies."

And with that, Chung bent his left arm up and extended his middle finger giving Glenn Dooley the universal sign of respect and goodwill known around the world...

CHAPTER 20

—ɱ—

Long Shot

With the tap water on, Chris looked in the mirror and the face looking back at him did not appear particularly happy. In fact, it was hardly recognizable. Five days of beard stubble which upon closer examination included several particles of corn chips, what appeared to be a ring of some type of beverage, brownish green guacamole, and a rather telltale dusting of powdered sugar. The BOATSS team had been working long hours and it seemed to several that they were going in circles. Although he had seen very little of his teammates, it was safe to assume that the other members of the team had been doing some heavy lifting on their own specific parts of the puzzle.

He adjusted the temperature of the water to begin shaving and stopped. His mom had always warned him that he should stay in school and study hard or he'd look like a street person. Although he'd stayed in high school and graduated near the top of his class his next stop had been the army where he had served in both Iraq and several other hotspot locations in the region referred to as "special duty assignments." The last time he'd looked this rough around the edges was after a four day patrol that had gone sideways on the first day and only gotten progressively worse.

On the first day, the helicopter dropping them off had been so badly shot up attempting to put them in a LZ (landing zone) that in a panic the pilot abruptly left too soon with his wounded co-pilot bleeding profusely in the seat beside him and his loadmaster barely hanging on to life in the back of the helicopter. Unfortunately, they were missing some of the "extras" that would have been handy on a mission such as this like the extra water, extra food, extra ammunition, and the spare radio.

Day two had generated more suspicion of the three Iraqi troops imbedded with them. That suspicion had only grown stronger when their interpreter, who the squad had been working with for several months, had been found on the morning of the third day with his throat slit. With a strong feeling they had been compromised and the body of their friend and interpreter, they had called for an evacuation only to be told the weather was too sketchy to risk the extraction and they would need to hold for clearer weather. As night fell the Americans slept back to back with one man on watch as the other man slept. It had been a very long, cold night.

At daybreak, they awakened to find that their three imbedded Iraqi troops had deserted them and taken one of the radios with them. By lunchtime, they were taking some small arms fire and by late afternoon the mortars arrived. Although wildly inaccurate to start, they had found their range at sunset and it looked grim for about thirty minutes. An A-10 on sector patrol literally stumbled across their position and making a single pass had thinned the mortar positions out like no other plane in the Air Force inventory could. The men had gone from listening to approaching mortar explosions every minute or so as the enemy found their range to the sudden sound of one long BURRRRRRRRRRP and then complete silence.

They received the radio call shortly thereafter that help would be inbound at daybreak but their position was not conducive to a successful extraction. Overnight they used the cover of darkness to move approximately three quarters of a mile due east through a series of wadis and ravines to grid coordinate supplied by their headquarters.

Chris paused in his thoughts and glanced at his watch. It was right about this time of the morning when they heard the helicopters and moved at a dead run from their covered positions to load onto the chopper. Looking back he would tell people that the round that struck him felt as if he'd been punched. It hadn't hurt at first, so he kept running. Each of his last few steps had seemed very difficult, almost as if he were running in wet cement.

It was almost three days later when he'd finally been allowed to hear what happened. The snipers 7.62x39 bullet had entered his chest from behind and just below his right shoulder as he was trotting to the helicopter. The wound cavity destroyed his right lung and completed its downward trajectory into his stomach. The medics and surgeons used twenty-three units of blood to save him but the surgeons, as hard as they'd tried, had been unable to save his lung.

He had mornings like this every once in a while and usually when he was under stress or exhausted. In his current physical and mental state it was of no surprise that his mind drifted back to that fateful day almost five years ago next month.

Chris lathered his face and started to shave. Almost twenty minutes, a second razor and a second shower later, he was dressed and heading across town to the BOATSS building. He hoped that Ms. Folk would be able to use what he'd found. They could really use a break...and soon.

—⧖—

"Good morning everyone!"

It was ten o'clock Friday morning. As Jewels looked around, many of the normally happy, smiling faces were dark and had a weary look to them. All but one...

She knew to the minute how long each of the team members had been working this week and it had been astounding. Due to the sensitive nature of the project, no work could be taken home, so for most of the group they practically lived at the BOATSS building fourteen to sixteen hours a day.

Grumbled responses of "good morning" was probably the best she was going to get so Jewels didn't press them.

"Did everyone get some sleep?"

No response...

"Top off your coffees and put on your big boy and big girl pants because we've got a bunch to cover this morning."

"Chris, since you're the only one who looks as if they are prepared for this morning, would you care to lead out with what you've been working on and any progress you've made this week?"

Chris had already uploaded his files over to the *Project Katar* folder on the server so it was just a matter of opening the *Project Katar* file and then the tab with his name on it.

"Ready ma'am."

"Chris?"

"I'm sorry, but calling you Jewels is gonna take some time, ma'am."

Jewels laughed, "Alright Chris what have you got for us?"

Chris opened the file and the entire screen was filled with almost a thousand lines of code. That woke everyone up except the only two guys in the room whose knowledge of computers was limited to word processing, a little PowerPoint, and searching Google or Amazon for deals on the latest headphones or designer beers.

Mitch and Rick's mouths literally were hanging open in shear wonder. Not so much at what was on the huge LED screen at the front of the room, but that anyone knew what it was. From all around were chattering voices discussing what, to them, looked like meaningless letters, hash tags, asterisks and backslashes.

"Jewels," said Chris with a grin, "I was able to strip all of the code of the original Northrop Grumman drone program out of the data stream NSA captured in the downlink as the freighter approached the West coast last March. Everything remaining on the screen was written after the drone was disassembled by the Iranians. As you can see, whoever this guy is, he knows his stuff. I was hoping that one of us might be able to identify not only the various software he or she used but maybe the individual's particular style of code writing."

"Jewels?"

Chris tried again, "Ms. Folk?"

Jewels held up a finger in Chris' general direction requesting he not speak. She'd seen something and now it was gone.

One by one the team members said, "Nope," or, "I got nothing," and put their exhausted heads down on the conference table in surrender.

"Did you see it?" asked Gina.

"Uh huh," was all Jewels could manage to utter.

They had both moved to within feet of the screen and were fixated on several lines of code halfway down the page.

5R3507 07734

"It can't be," said Jewels in disbelief.

"No way," was Gina's echoed sentiment.

The heads around the table began to rise to the vertical.

"In plain sight and yet not."

"Jewels, for the rest of the confused brains in the room what the hell are you two going on about?" asked Mitch, partially annoyed at the whole situation.

"Hey everyone, sorry about that, Jewels and I had a professor at MIT who hated the fact that one of his doctoral requirements was he had to teach for a semester. He thought rather highly of himself and he was indeed a genius with both languages and hardware. He would bury the line 5R3507 07734 on all our projects just to remind us of his superiority."

"Gina, please, what's the point of the numbers?" asked Mitch, not seeing the humor whatsoever.

One by one the other eggheads around the table chuckled.

"Guys," said Jewels as she walked to the white board. "If you take the sequence 5R3507 07734, she was writing in large block letters, and the letters 5R and flip them over you have, "heLL0 L0seRS."

"Doctor Fallahi!" said both girls at the same time.

"Now we know who and probably why as well," Gina shook her head.

"Doctor Harem Fallahi was born poor in the slums of Iran and was mentored through school and finally sent to the university system in the states for his college degrees. We met him at MIT when he was our reluctant professor for one semester."

"Was he troubled?" asked Rick, relieved they were once again discussing something he could understand.

"He had trouble assimilating into our culture for starters. He considered our lifestyles opulent and wasteful. Where he was from, his entire family wouldn't eat as much as we consumed in one sitting."

"What did he do to relax?" asked Chris. "It would be hard to be in such a stressful existence for so long."

"He dreamed a lot or so he said. He would always say stuff like, 'Someday I'll build something magnificent and all the world will be in awe,' goofy shit like that."

"Well, whatever happened to the good doctor?"

"Unknown, we took his course, figured out how to ace it, and never heard from or thought of him again until now."

"Rick, you're gonna want to get your folks at Langley on this pretty quick. This is the biggest break we've had in months."

"Roger that, I'll step out and give them a call."

"Downstairs SCIF Rick," reminded Jewels as he stood up to leave.

"Got it," was his reply as he left the room with Mitch in tow.

"High fives everyone, and Chris? I owe you lunch!"

"We'll pick this up later at two o'clock. I'm kicking you all out of here at three today. Go home or wherever and take some deep breaths, recharge, and we'll hit it again on Monday. Lunch!"

—⁊ℳ⁊—

Rick wasn't going back after lunch like the others and had settled into his desk at Langley. He looked around at his various knick-knacks, mementos, and guy crap and felt a calm he hadn't felt in several months. It was almost strange sitting here at his desk after so many months of working over at BOATSS. Sure, he had a desk over there, but it was different. Here he was surrounded by his memories and could close his eyes and remember where a particular photo was taken or what he'd done for a particular award. Rick reached over and picked up the picture they'd taken the first night they'd all gone out last March. Mitch grinning ear to ear with the most beautiful blind date any man could imagine, Jewels hugging Gina and actually smiling and himself, also smiling, at the prospects that Gina presented. He laughed. It seemed like an eternity ago. So much had changed for them personally and professionally since then. The last thing he picked up was a picture of his father and himself in their little eighteen foot whaler fishing boat fishing for something in the estuaries of the Chesapeake. It was in a sterling silver frame and stood out from everything else on his desk, as it should have. His father had expressed the hope before he had passed away that someday Rick would find a calling that he enjoyed and be successful at it. Rick got a knot in his throat and felt his eyes watering up. He gazed into the picture and thought of all the petty arguments and joys they had shared over the years. His dad had been taken too soon. He stared at the picture and thought: "Hi Dad, I catch really bad guys in the world and not only that, I'm actually pretty good at it, it's a blast." Rick coughed twice, and blew his nose.

"You all right Rick?" asked his co-worker from across the partition. "Are you allergic to hard work?"

"That's it!" exclaimed Rick, "Gotta be."

They both shared a quick laugh and got back to work.

Today's news was greeted as the true double-edged sword that it was. Although it was with a great sense of relief that they had at least narrowed down the "who" in the investigation, the preliminary stuff coming back on Harem Fallahi wasn't encouraging news. According to several reports in front of him regarding Harem Fallahi he'd just received from the analysts at Langley, Harem was potentially a very dangerous fellow. The analysts who did this kind of work were thorough and were trained to find out things as obtuse as the name of the girl who sat next to you in second grades sister's boyfriend's name. According to them, using numerous sources many of them redacted with a wide tip black Sharpie, Mr. Fallahi became Dr. Fallahi in the spring of 2008 and Dr. Fallahi became Captain Fallahi in the Iranian Army's "Special Projects Group" in the fall of the same year. That was potentially very troubling news.

He dialed slowly, but then set the receiver back down and took a swallow of his now warm Dr. Pepper. He needed to call her. She would be mad but not as mad as if he went around behind her back. He hit redial.

"Jewels? It's Rick."

"Hi Rick, good lunch?"

"I didn't eat, and now I've lost my appetite."

"What's wrong?"

Jewels had known Rick long enough to sense when he was concerned about something.

"We need to go secure."

Now Jewels was worried. Rick had only just left the office an hour ago. What had changed? Going secure on the new phones was much faster than it used to be and in just a few seconds Jewels was back on the now encrypted line.

"I show us secure."

"Here as well."

"Hey, we've got a problem. Your former professor left MIT with his PhD in Advanced Computer Languages and Electrical Engineering, went back to Iran and joined the dark side."

"No way," was Jewels' immediate response.

"He hated violence and always talked about how tired he was of all the fighting and the drama involved. He wanted to build stuff."

"Well, he apparently got his wish Jewels. At last report Dr. Harem Fallahi is now Major Harem Fallahi in the Special Projects Branch of the Iranian Army. They're involved in everything from nukes to missiles and drones. Jewels, I know you like keeping everything in-house but I need to bring the rest of the team off the bench."

He could hear her exasperated sigh over the phone.

"Who?" asked an obviously depressed Jewels.

"Well, the Office of the Director of National Intelligence and the National Counterterrorism Center for starters and probably the folks over at Cyber Command as well."

"Cyber Command! Those folks are such, such..." Her voice faded..."Fine," said Jewels eventually.

"I just wanted you to know, Jewels. Jewels?"

The line was dead, she'd already hung up.

It was time to increase their pool of talent. He dialed them in no particular order and having gone secure briefed them all and suggested they all get together in the same room and discuss a plan of action. Monday at nine here at Langley was the tentative time until he checked with everyone over at BOATSS. He called over and let Jewels know about the time and have the chief of security send whatever was needed to get everyone into the building. He called his security office and told them to get badges ready for at least five visitors with full access and that the names and information would be coming their way shortly.

He leaned back in his chair and called Mitch.

"Is she throwing darts at my picture yet?"

"Not yet," laughed Mitch, "but she's pretty pissed off at the situation."

"Would beer help?" asked Rick cautiously and then quickly added, "I'm buying."

"I'll ask her, we're out of here at three today. I'll call you back around five."

He straightened his desk, secured his crypto key, and locked up his classified briefs in the safe.

Mitch called back in less than one minute.

"Jewels says she hopes you've got deep pockets because she's real thirsty."

Rick looked at his watch. "O'Malley's at four?"

Mitch relayed Rick's suggestion. "She's nodding, so I guess we'll see you there at four."

Rick hung up the phone and peeked in his wallet. Staring up at him from the crease of his wallet were three badly wrinkled Washington's and a newly printed Hamilton. "Damn." He thought briefly about running to the ATM but then thought about what the team had accomplished this week and started grinning from ear to ear. Tonight he would do something his cheap ass never did. Tonight, Rick Wagner would actually run a bar tab!

Most of the BOATSS crew had eventually made it to O'Malley's Bar and Grill around four fifteen with the rest filtering in soon after. Rick, as promised, opened a tab and bought the first round. Four pitchers of cheap beer in D.C. and he was already down eighty dollars.

"A toast to our new crew! We work too hard and get paid too little!"

Everyone raised their glasses in unison and, for a change, they were in complete agreement.

CHAPTER 21

—ɯ—

Reflections

Last night's decompression at O'Malley's had been just what the doctor ordered and despite having a touch of a headache, Jewels needed to get up earlier than she had wanted. With Rick's unanticipated move to bring the other big Intel offices into play, she was now down to two days to launch her bogus update program and she hadn't heard back from her contact in over two weeks. She had just started to log on to GNUnet when someone buzzed her from the lobby. Damn! It was only eight fifteen!

Jewels gathered her robe and walked to the intercom box on the wall.

"Hello"

"Morning babe."

Damn, he showed little to no interest in her last night when she had time and now with a full day planned on her little project, Mitch was literally at her door!

"Good morning to you too. This is an unexpected pleasure. What's up?"

"Can you buzz me up?"

"Mitch, I was just getting in the shower. Did you need me or can we get together for lunch maybe?"

"Sure, lunch would be great. Is everything okay up there?"

"Everything's fine, I'm just behind in my day and have some things to take care of this morning."

Mitch just stared at the speaker. Something wasn't right.

"Call me when you're ready for lunch?"

"Sure thing."

He heard some static on the line and she was gone.

Mitch took a minute to gather his thoughts. Something definitely wasn't right. She had been acting differently for just over a week and even more so after her stalker episode. He left her building and walked slowly east on 20th towards DuPont Circle.

He headed across the plaza with the intention of burning an hour or so at the book store when he found himself sitting on a bench by DuPont fountain instead. It had all started here at this very spot back in early March. Now, almost five months later, he was no farther along in their relationship than he had been months ago. It was as if an invisible barrier existed between the two of them. Was it a trust issue? Jewels had flat out lied in the meeting the other day. That was way off what he would have ever considered "normal" for her. Maybe he didn't really know what "normal" was for her after all. The country, after all, had literally been turned on its ear since they met. Was any part of their relationship "normal?"

Mitch got up to leave and grinned as he remembered the first moment he saw her here at the fountain with her fabulous legs and beautiful smile. He wanted to make this work out, but she was going to have to meet him somewhere in the middle.

—⟋⟍—

Jewels grabbed another cup of coffee, her third, and got back to work. She quickly logged on to the GNUnet and left a message for her "friends" requesting a status update. Due to her official position at the CIA, Jewels couldn't have very well contacted the various software companies that she needed for her rather elaborate plan directly through normal channels.

Today she hoped she would find out whose software had been collected voluntarily and whose had needed to be "borrowed."

This business with Mitch was nagging her to distraction. At what point was he going to move this thing forward? Most guys would have made some kind of move by now. For the number of heads she turned on a daily basis it was apparent that she had that part of the package taken care of. In four months they had held hands and kissed. She thought for a moment. Yes, they had kissed seventeen times and if she had the time she could write down all the times and locations. Granted, she wasn't all that experienced in the relationship department, but come on. In fairness, all of their dates had been either fun, entertaining, or both. Maybe when things calmed down she would put a little more effort into the relationship. As for now, Jewels was hesitating to get in the shower because she was hoping to read the response to her message.

Jewels dropped her robe and looked at herself in the mirror. She wasn't getting any younger but still looked damn good. Mr. Mitch Kendrick better get his game on if he wanted any part of this.

Today was what men refer to as a long shower as it involved shaving the legs, etcetera, as well as washing her hair and adding conditioner. All in all, twenty-five minutes had elapsed from dropping the robe to grabbing the towel. Still dripping wet, Jewels tip-toed out to her computer. After ensuring that at least her arms were dry, she logged back in to check on her requested status update.

One message dropped into her box just as she opened up the mail function.

"Seven companies are on board. You have five days from launch before they will send out a real update and delete all of your 'unique' code." The bottom of the message gave addresses in the system to where she could find the base code that she would attach her code to. Jackpot!

Jewels squealed with delight and headed back to the bathroom to finish getting ready. If she could at least get one section done before lunch and the rest after lunch she could still have that lunch date with Mitch!

CHAPTER 22

—⟋⟍—

Shadows

It was Saturday morning and Jonah had reversed his routine in order to swim across the channel before too many pleasure boaters had ventured out for the morning. He was halfway across when he heard the unmistakable high pitched sound of a very fast moving cigarette class racing boat. Jonah glanced up to see that the pilot of the craft was not paying attention to his task at hand and was bearing down directly on his position. He dove deeply and was scant four feet below and slightly to the left of the propellers when the boat had passed overhead. He surfaced, fist first, in time to catch the sight of the name on the stern of the boat: "Could Care Less."

The boats were built for speed and if his eyes and ears hadn't deceived him the boat that just passed overhead had five engines. The newer boats were outfitted with five 350HP Mercury Verados. They were the ultimate go-fast boat and with speeds in calm water approaching eighty knots and speeds even in rough waters approaching fifty knots, nothing on the water could come close to matching their speed.

He quickly finished the short remaining distance across the channel and grabbed the ladder that extended down from the navy pier. He removed his flippers and climbed high enough out of the water not to become a curious snack for a passing Bull Shark and looked off into the direction the boat had disappeared. He was both shaking mad and smiling at the same time. Although not wild about the situation that could have potentially caused him injury, he had enjoyed the rush of adrenaline the experience had dumped into his system. He missed it.

In what had now become routine, he shucked his wetsuit down to the half way point, connected his flippers and mask with a piece of Velcro, at his waist, fashioned for this exact purpose and walked the two hundred or so feet to the pier office near the middle of the pier. Jonah swam over from the island every two days or so to get his mail and to chat with the older gentleman who ran the pier.

Clarence Peabody was the old navy vet's name. He and Jonah had hit it off right from the start. Jonah had asked him several weeks ago if he could use the pier office as a mailing address and Clarence graciously agreed. He had also agreed to deal with the FedEx and UPS people when they showed up with a delivery. Clarence was a man deeply tanned with the wrinkles and skin of a man who just didn't give a damn about the sun. Ernest Hemingway would have immediately cast him to play the fisherman, Santiago, the lead character in "The Old Man and the Sea."

According to Clarence, he apparently had a soft spot in his heart for SEALs stemming from his days in "Nam" as he called it. Apparently, he and what was left of his squad were trapped up a river and cut off. Darkness was falling and hope was fading when a Swift Boat with some SEALs had come up the river and retrieved him and three of his buddies. The SEAL team had stayed when the Swift Boat departed and he'd never had a chance to thank the men who'd saved him. From that day forward he had carried the weight of what he called "an unpaid debt" to those men. It was a good story and well told, but Jonah had no way of ever checking it out.

"Mr. Peabody!" hollered Jonah as loudly as he possibly could.

"Mr. West!" croaked the old man. Jonah could tell the old man's health was failing him these past few weeks but was respectful of the older man's wishes and had never mentioned it but once in the brief few months they had known each other.

"Anything for me?" asked Jonah, his voice now back to a more respectable level for indoors.

"You're dripping water on my floor again, SEAL," was the man's amusing reply.

Jonah looked down at the puddle forming on the old plank floor. "Sorry."

"Geez, are you guys ever dry?"

Both men laughed until Clarence started coughing. The old man was clearly working hard to keep up appearances and Jonah could see the pain on his face as they spoke.

"Two letters, one's from Maine, probably your Pop, a USPS two-day envelope and, just because I know you hate them, a chance to enter a sweepstakes from your friends at the Publishers Clearing House."

Jonah laughed. "Well, yunno what they say?"

Both men mimed the announcer on the famous TV commercial for Publishers Clearing House.

"You can't win if you don't enter!"

Clarence laughed briefly, handed Jonah his mail, then took Jonah's arm and led him outside. "Can't talk in there anymore Jonah."

Jonah's guard went up. He had heard that line way too many times in his career not to fully understand the implications. He feigned a robust laugh and followed Clarence outside. When they were about fifty feet away from the office, Clarence stopped and sat gingerly down on a large wooden spool wrapped with heavy cable.

"Jonah, I don't have very long my friend and I'm rather glad you came ashore today. When you didn't pick up the other day I feared the worst, but I guess I should have known."

Now Jonah was truly puzzled. What was he talking about?

"Jonah, there are people watching you."

"What are you talking about?"

Clarence continued a bit softer now. "I know it might be hard looking at this old hollow shell of a man, but let me tell you, I did enough recon in my day to spot an advance team."

Jonah saw the old man's pain and realized the seriousness in the old man's body language.

"What did you see?" Jonah gave the man his utmost attention.

"Three men and a woman with ear pieces, radios, and the biggest pair of hand held binoculars I've ever seen looking off towards Wisteria Island. They were here several times this past week at different times."

"Maybe they were a repo team scouting out a foreclosed boat?"

"I would almost buy that, but twice last week the wind had shifted while they were here and I heard them say *Mr. West.*"

"No shit!"

"No shit, my young friend. Coincidences, which I don't believe in by the way, might happen once, but not twice."

"Hey, Mr. Peabody, I've got to go. Can I borrow your boat?"

"Son, it's yours."

"I'll bring it back tomorrow."

"No need son...It's yours if you want it."

Jonah looked into the old man's pain filled eyes and realized that today was literally his *last* day. He seemed to have aged before Jonah's very eyes. He had hung on long enough to warn Jonah about the perceived threat and now he was finished.

"Can I help you inside?"

"Yes," the man's voice was now a whisper.

Jonah half-carried Clarence back to his office and placed him carefully in his decrepit old leather chair.

"The boat keys and the registration paperwork are in the top drawer," Clarence whispered weakly as he pointed toward his old peeling laminated desk.

The man tapped his ears and pointed around the room. He motioned Jonah closer and very deliberately whispered in his ear.

"I don't know what you're about to get into son, but you've grown in here, tapping Jonah's heart, in the past few months and I respect you for it. God speed and kick some ass for me!"

He was completely spent and had seemingly no breath left to speak. He put his hands to his lips begging Jonah to light him a cigarette. Jonah did as he'd asked and grabbed the paper work out of the desk.

Clarence's breathing was slowing and his chin was resting on his chest now. Jonah removed the cigarette from the old man's stained fingers.

Jonah bent low and whispered in his ear, "Hey Clarence, you do know you're not supposed to smoke in here?"

"Screw em," were more than likely his last words. They had come with a brief, but very practiced, arthritic one finger salute. They were the last words Jonah heard before he dialed 911, left the phone off the hook, wiped it for prints and hurried down to Clarence's little Boston Whaler tied to a piling just behind and below the office. Clarence had even left it full of gas. Jonah needed to get back to his place and think of what had just transpired. He left the pier slowly, toting an old fishing hat, the kind with the sides to block the sun and headed south. He could hear the sirens as police and paramedics responded to his 911 call.

Jonah was being stalked. He could feel the adrenaline welling up in his body. Jonah didn't like being stalked. He was used to being the hunter not the hunted. The good news was that for now, although perhaps just briefly, he had a small advantage. Having the boat now meant he could control how and when he could get off Wisteria Island.

It was time to plan his first op in almost three years and he felt he was already a day behind the time curve of this mission. He glanced briefly at his watch. It was time to play catch up and he had a pretty good idea what he needed to do.

—◊◊—

"God damn it, Commander Lark, you had one job! Call Jonah West and request a meeting! Now you tell me he's no longer on the island!"

Naval Air Station Key West Deputy Commander Steve Lark gazed casually at the large digital clock on the wall. It read 15:23 in bright red numbers.

"Mr. Kline, it is very unusual for Jonah to break his routine."

"You're damn right it's unusual commander, we've been watching him all week and he varies no more than five minutes in his routine. It's so very unusual that my supervisors in D.C. think that maybe you tipped him off."

"Mr. Kline, just for clarification, you say you had 'eyes on' Mr. West several times this past week?"

"Yes, that's correct."

"I'm going to go out on a limb and assume you've never served in our armed forces?

"That's correct. What's your point?"

"Mr. Kline, have you ever heard of the term 'hyper vigilance?'"

"No," responded Kline in his first non-screaming word of the conversation.

"Hyper vigilance is what Hollywood would refer to as "Spidey sense" or sixth sense depending on your preferred genre of movies. SEALs are trained to move into an area and make friends with the indigenous population, develop contacts and overall, learn who belongs and who doesn't. Is it safe to assume that your team consisted of the same people each day?"

"Yes, again, what's your point?"

"My point is that our boy, or more accurately former boy, spotted your people. He may have even had someone watching your people watch him! He's gone Mr. Kline, "in the wind" as law enforcement likes to say."

"How far can the man go without transportation?"

"Mr. Kline, I don't know why you are so desperately, and I might add sloppily, looking for Mr. West, but I'll give you some words of helpful advice. Jonah West will have what he needs when he needs it."

"What makes you so damn smug about Mr. West's capabilities? He's a forty something retired Navy SEAL."

"Mr. Kline, with all due respect, your image of retired Navy Lt. Commander Jonah West is way off the mark. Being active with the SEAL teams for over twenty years is an extraordinary accomplishment, being referred to by his teams as the 'SEAL's SEAL' is the honor of honors."

"Any other witty and otherwise useless remarks Commander Lark?" replied the Station Chief.

"Just one, and probably the most important, now that he knows you're looking for him..." A leering smile crept over the naval officer's face.

"What's that?"

"Watch your six Mr. Kline, watch your six." replied the commander as he slowly let the phone slip from his fingers into the phone's cradle.

It was Saturday and he'd already been at work way too long. He'd personally gone over to Wisteria Island in a ribbed boat with a few volunteers on shore leave from the USS Farragut to see if they could find the former commander but although his camp remained, at the moment, all traces of the man were gone. To make his afternoon even better, he'd stepped right into a wave as they were getting back in the boat when someone had lit off some fireworks. No one in their little landing party would ever say anything about him jumping as they all had. None of them liked the idea of looking for a Navy SEAL, particularly one that didn't want to be found.

Cathy was going to ride his ass if he wasn't home soon. He gathered his wet shoes and socks, pulled on his cover and made his way to the golf cart he used to get to and from work here on base. He grinned at nobody in particular. Although he had absolutely no idea what Mr. Kline's next task was this afternoon, Lark knew exactly what he was doing. In less than ten minutes time he would be lighting a perfectly stacked pile of charcoal in his Weber grill and begin an evening with a very pretty lady and a half filled cooler of ice cold beer.

CHAPTER 23

—◊—

Zig Zag

Jonah drove the little boat slowly and carefully to the southwest and turned to the west once he had cleared Tank Island. It was busy on the water now and the waves from the Fort Myers-Key West ferry were definitely something to watch out for in a small fifteen foot boat. As he cleared the western edge of the island, he could see an enormous roster tail of water coming up from behind a very fast moving boat.

Was it really going to be this easy? Jonah thought as he gazed to the north. The boat had slowed and was making its way into a luxurious boathouse. The boathouse was large enough to accommodate two large pleasure craft and a pontoon boat. Sure enough the "Could Care Less" was on its lift being washed off with fresh water as he rounded the corner. The boathouse was part of the Sunset Key pier and included one hundred and thirty-five feet of covered dock area where people could walk out and enjoy the view without being brutalized by the hot summer sun. He made some notes on what was where and continued his journey to the western side of his island where he would be out of sight from anyone back on the pier. Knowing that this boat, if needed, was only a short swim away from Wisteria Island was somehow reassuring. If his plans suddenly changed and he needed access to a fast boat to escape by water, Jonah couldn't think of anyone else who deserved to have their boat go *missing* than this clown.

It didn't take long to gather his stuff together. It had been a minimalist living situation on the island and he'd known this day would come. It had served its purpose well. He dug up his cache of documents and the two bundles of ten thousand dollars and placed everything in water proof dive bags. He changed out of his wetsuit and put on a pair of jeans and a very loose fitting long sleeved white silk shirt. Into his waist band he tucked his Beretta 96 and into his left front pocket a spare magazine. On his right calf, hidden from view by his jeans was his combat knife. He buried his weight sets under a tarp and lots of sand and debris. Using several small trees, he dragged the sand around his former home, obscuring all evidence that he had lived there for almost four months. When he was done he tossed the small trees onto the other pile of debris. The whole procedure had taken forty-five minutes and he needed to go.

Jonah backed his way down to the deserted beach, dragging a branch, obscuring his footsteps as he went. When his footsteps began to blend with a larger group of foot prints from today's visitor's to the island, Jonah suspended his efforts and cast the branch aside. He looked back in the general direction of his former residence and couldn't see any evidence that he'd been there. Jonah placed everything under the front seat of the Whaler and with one shove was drifting backwards away from Wisteria Island.

The small fifteen horse power motor rumbled to life on the first pull and he slowly headed north. Two miles later he had skirted the northern most point of Fleming Key. Turning the boat again, Jonah navigated back to the east and to a mooring site he had found off a small bay on Dredgers Key. Not a soul was in sight as he pulled his little boat ashore. Jonah grabbed the mail and a bag from the Whaler and dragged the small boat into some tall scrub brush near the boat ramp. His 1990K5 Blazer was right where he'd left it and on inspection, appeared that nothing except perhaps the seagulls had caused any damage. He popped the hood, connected the battery and replaced the two fuses he had removed to deter theft. The Blazer turned over and purred like a kitten. It should. Other than the way the Blazer *looked*, it was all new. An old navy friend from years ago had an auto customizing shop just outside of Charlotte and for fifteen grand had made him a brand new Blazer and hung an empty rusty shell on it. From the exterior it looked like the side windows had been busted out but that was by design. It was water tight and the interior was immaculate. Mechanically it had a new engine, transmission and a reworked suspension and frame. It would do whatever Jonah needed it to do. Jonah left slowly on the marina road until he was sure nobody could see him and lit the tires up to give the fuel injection system a little workout.

Jonah smiled and drove a short distance to a familiar Quick Mart just on the outskirts of Key West and approached two young marines at the pumps.

"Marines!"

"Yes, Sir!" was their immediate programmed response.

"I need three burn phones and an ice cold six-pack of beer. I'm paying twenty bucks for you to get them for me."

These two were E-3's and twenty dollars was a bunch of money for the requested task. They only asked him what kind of beer as they trotted away with six twenty dollar bills.

After about five minutes Jonah could see the young men returning. He had been careful to keep his back to the store and avoid any chance of being photographed by the store's three security cameras.

The young marines trotted back his way and handed him a bag which held three burner phones and a six pack of cold beer.

"Kinda trusting aren't you mister?" asked the younger Marine.

Jonah smiled, he slowly, casually rolled his shirt sleeves up just enough to allow the two Marines to see his forearms. "No, not really." Jonah smiled.

Jonah's SEAL tattoo and other ink caught their eyes immediately. The older of the two men said "SHIT" at least three times in rapid succession.

"Here's your money gentlemen." Jonah peeled a twenty off his small stack.

"Spend it wisely."

As Jonah drove away he could see the young men high five each other and head back into the mini-mart. Beer would help sufficiently dull their memories if anyone came looking for him.

The drive north to Marathon would take about an hour and would get him into a no-tell motel around five o'clock. He turned on the Blazer's radio to 103.1 classic rock, set the cruise control, and watched the South Florida scenery pass him by.

—ᴍ—

One of the best things about being involved with such a small group of people for such a long period of time was that you made lots of contacts. One of Jonah's oldest friends that he still kept in touch with was Jimmy "Patch" Bicksford. Jimmy had a reputation for fixing things and had been the medical component of many a SEAL mission in the early days of the Iraq and Afghanistan conflict. Most members of the teams had nicknames and "Patch" seemed to fit him perfectly. He now owned and operated a truck stop in Florida City, Florida. He had said that if Jonah was ever in the neighborhood he should drop on by. Jonah had just finished his Blackened Sea Bass and first Corona when he called Patch at the truck stop.

"Bicksford's truck stop!"

"How many Navy SEALs does it take to screw in a light bulb?" asked Jonah.

"Nobody cares! SEALs see in the dark! Jonah West, you son-of-a-bitch! How the hell are you? What's this phone number?"

Jonah laughed. Same old Patch.

"Geez, if you shut-up a second I'll fill you in!"

"Sorry man, like a church mouse, like a church mouse."

"Will you have some time tomorrow morning to catch up? I know it's Sunday, but I need to see you."

"Sounds serious."

"I don't know yet, but I could use a little group think on this one."

"Where are you now?"

Jonah ignored the question completely…and Patch got the message.

"I'll see you at nine then?"

"I'll call you when I'm on property."

"Roger that," and Patch hung up.

CHAPTER 24

—⚏—

Sleight of Hand

It was Sunday morning and Jonah was well on his way at 0830. The trip would normally take two hours but the combination of it being Sunday morning and the fact that he was traveling during the off season meant he would be getting to Patch's place just before 0900. The truck stop had been left to "Patch" by his grandfather who had bought a bunch of property in the early sixties when south Florida land was still a bargain. The location was perfect in that all traffic coming off the Keys drove right past the truck stop. The large commercial trucks had their own side with a restaurant, showers, and a food mart type of setup with many items catering specifically to a trucker's needs while on the road. Passenger vehicles and smaller trucks were segregated from the big trucks for both safety and convenience for all parties concerned.

Old habits die hard and Jonah had scoped out the entire place figuring out where to park and which way to go if his little meeting went unexpectedly sideways. He picked up the burn phone and dialed his old team member.

"Have you seen enough of the place yet?" was how Patch had answered the phone. "I'm starting to feel like an overpriced whore!"

"The backside of your place smells like one too!" was all Jonah could come up with.

"Well, come on in!"

"Can't do, Patch, can you come out to my ride?"

"Sure, give me two shakes."

Jonah watched his old friend come out to the Blazer. Every few steps you could tell something was a bit off in his gait but his prosthetic leg was doing its job. Patch had come a long way since their first encounter.

They'd almost finished their mission in Ramadi back in mid-05 when an RPG had skittered and bounced into the passenger side door of a marine Humvee and detonated. It had been a horrific scene but Jonah and the other team members had thrown a tourniquet on Patch's right leg just below his knee and saved his life.

Jonah had gotten everyone out of the vehicle, returned and directed fire on the enemy position, called in an airstrike and, when the area was secure, an Army medevac chopper flight. Jonah had taken two grazing rounds across his back and one through and through in his left thigh but he hadn't quit on the Marines. One of the Marines, a Roger something, had a horrific shrapnel wound in his chest. Jonah had tried to see the kid's name, but had been unable due to the severity of the wound. The medics and surgeons had worked very hard to save him, but Jonah learned later that he succumbed to his wounds. He remembered the other Marines screaming at the kid, "Skip hold on, come on Skip! If you die we'll kick your ass." It was to no avail and the young man had never regained consciousness. His fellow marines had taken it very hard and kept saying, "he was the best!" over and over again. He had seen so much death, both meted out by the enemy and himself and his team that the names didn't even register anymore. Maybe someday he would remember. He wasn't looking forward to it.

Although he personally hadn't thought he was worthy, he received the Navy Cross for his actions that day and the respect of not only the teams he was responsible for, but everyone he came across for the rest of his time with the teams.

Patch walked up to the Blazer and walked around it twice just to make a point.

"Get in here!" bellowed Jonah.

Patch was laughing as he entered the Blazer.

"Is this the best you can do on retired officer money? It looks like shit!" laughed Patch.

"You don't like my ride?"

Patch dropped into the passenger seat and Jonah turned on his sound system and dropped the Blazer into gear.

Patch looked around the interior of Jonah's ride. Although from the outside it appeared that the old Blazer was way past its due date at the local salvage yard, the inside was amazing. What appeared to have been plywood covered over windows on the rear of the vehicle were in reality just a way to make the vehicle appear to be junk. The interior was covered with either leather or brand new upholstery and the sound system and tech package was all high end new gear. The main attraction was the Pioneer AVH-X7700BT seven inch flip-out display DVD player that came equipped with Bluetooth®, Siri® eyes free, Spotify®, and AppRadio One®.

Jonah leaned toward Patch, "A piece of shit, really?" He tapped the screen of the sound system and hit the gas at the same time. The Blazer seemingly flew out of the parking lot. Jonah kept his foot in it for a good six seconds and lifted his foot as the "Old" Blazer hit 110 mph.

"Weee Haaaaw!" hollered Patch over the blaring beautiful sounds of AC/DC. "What the hell's under the hood of this beast?"

Jonah pulled over, popped the hood and walked Patch through the more salient upgrades and refinements of his Blazer.

"Well to start, my buddy in Charlotte dropped in a crate 350 horse power motor then added a four barrel Demon carburetor. He also said I needed a non OEM transmission and a new suspension package."

"Hot damn man, that's awesome."

Jonah smiled, "Yes, yes it is..."

Jonah checked his watch.

"Not why you're here though is it?" asked Patch.

"Unfortunately, no. Jump back in and I'll fill you in."

As they drove back, Jonah turned down the music enough so he could bring Patch as up to speed as he felt he could and then waited for Patch's response. He'd inadvertently pulled up on the trucker's side and was receiving the appropriate glares.

"I'm pretty busted up man," Patch patted his prosthetic leg, "But I'll do whatever you need me to do."

Jonah popped open the glove box and showed his friend his iPhone.

"Do you know of anyone heading cross country today or tomorrow that would be willing to turn that on and off every few hours? If they're tracking me, I need them to think I've panicked and headed west."

"Where will you really be going?" Patch sounded concerned.

"Best we just leave it at that buddy. Can you help me out?"

"Hang on a second." Patch dialed a number on his phone.

"Kathy, is Ronnie still eating?"

"Yea, Patch do you need him?"

"Ask him if he's still headed to Seattle?"

"Hang on."

Patch covered his phone.

"Ex-Marine, Good guy, Afghani sniper gut shot him and now his pecker don't work so he drives his truck back and forth across the country to get rid of his demons."

"Patch?"

"Yea baby?" Patch put them on speaker.

"Ronnie's only going as far as Eugene, Oregon."

Jonah gave the thumbs up.

"That'll do fine, can you ask him to wait for me Kathy?"

"Where are you by the way? We had a report of a fast moving Blazer tearing up U.S. 1. Did you see it?"

"See it?" Patch laughed. "Baby, I was in it!"

Jonah tapped his watch and looped his finger twice through the air. He needed to get going.

"I'll explain in a minute."

Patch looked at Jonah. "Whatever you're into…fair winds and following seas."

They fist bumped and Jonah gave him the phone.

"Remember, Patch, tell him not to turn it on before Tennessee!"

Patch gave Jonah a thumbs up and slammed the door of the Blazer. Looking back at the Blazer he was somewhat surprised the door hadn't fallen off.

As he watched Jonah drive away Patch pondered why after all these years they still had never talked about that fateful day in Iraq. Now he honestly wondered if they ever would.

—⚏—

It had taken the *Connecticut* just over three and a half days to meet up with the *Reagan Battle Group*. With the seas almost flat the crew took advantage and was up on deck for a vitamin D break. It was highly unusual for a submarine to be on the surface, but Briggs was trying to keep everyone's marbles in the game. The submarine assigned to the group was still submerged and on patrol keeping them safe from any threats real or imagined.

Captain Briggs and several officers and crew were taking turns trying to fish. They caught several in the fifteen minutes he'd allotted but not enough to feed the crew of 118 supper, at least not yet. Briggs surrendered his pole and went below decks to get ready for his Seahawk helicopter transfer to the *USS Reagan*. For all his efforts at fishing, he was "dining out" this evening on the *USS Reagan*. It would be a working dinner in that, as planned, after several ship and mission status reports and the obligatory PowerPoint presentations, the senior staff of several of the ships would break bread together in the wardroom. His crew was the only one in today's navy to have experienced a nuclear blast and it was, even after four months, a topic that always seemed to come up at gatherings.

Most people didn't like the horse collar hoist but Briggs thought it totally exhilarating. They hauled him into the Seahawk which then climbed and banked hard to port in the direction of the *Reagan*. He had always been impressed by carriers and could have chosen that path several years ago, but he enjoyed the thrill of the hunt too much to leave his sub. The *Reagan* was massive in comparison to the *Connecticut*. At just over one thousand feet long and a two hundred fifty plus feet wide flight deck the *Reagan* looked like an odd looking building had been set adrift.

They touched down just to the left of the enormous super structure and after several handshakes and Briggs giving the seaman who'd hoisted him up a *USS Connecticut* challenge coin, he was escorted to the bridge.

CHAPTER 25

—⚛—

Shifting Sands

The imported Saltillo tile felt cool beneath his darkly tanned feet and the breeze from the oversize ceiling fan high above him felt amazing. The renovations and security upgrades to the main house had been done for three weeks now and the exorbitant amount of money he'd spent on, not just the upgrades but getting it done quickly, had been well worth the additional expense.

Atash sat here often, staring out the enormous new bullet proof window as the deep blue ocean stretched out before him changed from its deep dark blue of the early morning to the lighter brighter more subtle hues of bluish green as the hours approached noon.

He had quickly learned the rhythm of the tides and could almost predict what sea life he would see on a given day, just by glancing at the height of the waterline on the sparkling white sand glistening no more than a hundred feet away. He mused that it was good that he had grown comfortable with this view because, unless by pure happenstance something out of his control changed, this would probably be his view for many years to come.

It struck him funny that such a strong childhood dream and all the efforts taken to achieve it came down to his being trapped in a paradise of his own making.

Atash Rahbar was growing weary of his existence on the small tranquil Caribbean island of Martinique. Living on the edge of the ocean on a beautiful tropical island had been his lifelong dream. It was that very dream of forever escaping his home country of Iran and the seemingly thousands of square miles of hot sand and barren land that had driven he and his now dead partners to hatch the plan of blowing up San Diego, eliminating the threat of three entire carrier strike groups in the Pacific, and the financially successful well-drilling venture now underway in the South China Sea.

For their part, the Chinese had held up their part of the bargain and he was receiving his "commission" deposits directly into his secret Cayman Island account on the first of every month. Even with his lavish and, at times, quirky tastes and a full entourage of security staff, the average monthly commission checks of just over five million dollars amply covered his monthly expenses.

The problem, as he saw it, was that he hadn't thought he'd be so very alone in his little version of paradise. He missed his childhood friend and coconspirator, Mehrak, and to this very day wished that the secretive Chinese men in Taipei had given them some type of warning before putting a bullet through his friend's forehead.

Surrounded at all times by his security team, he had only made it into town a dozen or so times in four months. He was surrounded by women that he paid to dote on his every need and desire, but even that had become old and he'd eventually sent most of them away.

His home, and the several he had purchased recently to act as a barrier to his primary residence, was located on a small bay on the most eastern peninsula on the island of Martinique. The sunrises were spectacular and the evenings, although absent a view of the setting sun, spectacular in their own right.

Despite rigorous screenings of personnel and precautions to keep his presence secretive, individuals or perhaps an organized group had tried on two occasions to snatch him from his new island home. The first attempt was amateurish and lacked the polish of a skilled assault team. The three men had literally run into the compound with their weapons drawn trying to kick down the doors of the houses in the compound. They never even reached the main house and had been eliminated by his security team. Unfortunately, they had all been immediately shot dead. Although very efficient in dispatching the threat, it would have perhaps been better to wound one of them to find out the basics of who they were and perhaps even who sent them. They opted to not involve the French police, who governed the island. His team checked ID's and determined that they were just local thugs hoping for a fast score. The French police on Martinique had a tendency to either look where they were not supposed to...or required some type of financial compensation to look the other way. Sufficed to say, he imagined that the Tiger and Reef sharks, as well as several species of bottom feeding sea creatures in the cove to the West of his residence had eaten well for several days after that particular fiasco.

The second group arrived after dark just over two weeks ago and had been far better trained. Subsequently the entire experience had been significantly more terrifying. His team's insistence on the new safe room paid off and he hadn't been injured in the physical sense. Atash had been far more fortunate than his detail. Three of his men had been mortally wounded by incredibly accurate rapid firing automatic weapons. This group had completely ignored the guest houses and came straight at the main house. This had actually been their undoing as they were flanked by his detail and once again shot dead. One of them even killed himself as his security team closed on his position. That was a little too professional for everyone's liking and he hadn't been willing to leave the compound since.

These past few weeks since the second attempt, his only true solace was his afternoon raft floats just off his little section of beach. Every day, weather permitting, he would float out thirty to fifty feet from the shoreline, soak up the tropical rays and let the waves calm his nerves. His security team basically locked down the compound and cordoned off the beach for thirty to forty-five minutes while he floated undisturbed. They'd insisted that he use a tether to hold his position off shore. It was a small 1/4 inch polyester line that kept him in the current a set distance from shore and not affected by the almost steady breezes. They said it was so he didn't drift away. Atash suspected that it was because they didn't feel like swimming after his little one man raft in waters that contained sharks with a newly acquired taste for human flesh.

In reality? Atash didn't really care. For a brief part of his otherwise boring day he could pretend he was floating in the warm waters of the tropics surrounded by his departed friends.

CHAPTER 26

—⚍—

Northbound

Jonah had driven almost all night and was mentally exhausted. I-95 was a challenge on a good day and for whatever reason last night was, or seemed to be, amateur hour at the Billy Bob Trucking Academy. He thought about the driver who graciously agreed to transport his phone to Oregon and felt a twinge of guilt. Jonah had given some serious thought to his next move and decided to confront his antagonists on their territory. He checked in at a Silver Spring Maryland Motel 6 just on the outskirts of D.C. just before ten. Jonah had noticed it before in his travels but still found that motel managers always looked at you in that funny way when you check in at ten in the morning. As it turned out, they didn't have a room ready and he was asked to come back at eleven. So, at just after eleven o'clock on a Monday morning, Jonah found himself drinking strong black coffee at a Burger King across the parking lot from a cheap motel.

He had memorized the phone numbers of whoever called him repeatedly the week before and twice had entered the digits into his burn phone this morning only to cancel the call. He was about eight miles out of downtown D.C. and calculated that it would take him, with parking, about fifteen minutes to get to the Silver Spring metro stop, ten minutes on the orange

143

line after transferring and he would be on the National Mall proper in approximately thirty minutes from start to finish. Jonah figured he would need another fifteen minutes to get into the rhythm of his planned location at the mall so whoever wanted to meet with him could do so in an hour.

Jonah's thoughts were interrupted by the ringing of his second burn phone. It was the motel letting him know his room was ready. He crossed the hot parking lot and retrieved his key from the front desk. Opening the door to his second floor room, Jonah threw his duffle bag on the bed and quickly used the bathroom. It was now eleven thirty and for his plan to work, as planned, taking advantage of the lunch crowds on the mall, he needed to be moving towards the D.C. Metroplex in the next fifteen minutes.

After a quick shower Jonah examined his limited wardrobe choices. The weather was clear and sunny so he was wearing his finest Florida tourist attire with some modifications. He was wearing a garishly patterned, bright green *Tommy Bahama* shirt over a pastel colored dress shirt. His hair was up and neatly tucked into a hemp colored beanie cap like skateboarders tended to wear and he wasn't wearing his favorite Chaco's sandals. Today, depending on how the conversation went, might develop into a foot race. With that in mind, his brand new ASICS running shoes would serve him well getting out of any mess he might encounter at the National Mall.

Jonah learned in his many years in the teams that it was far better to be paranoid and prepared for no reason and laugh about it later than to enter into an unknown situation and deal with those consequences. In reality, Jonah had no reason to be alarmed over some phone calls from D.C. What was somewhat disconcerting is that almost no one had his iPhone number and several of the calls were seemingly from different locations in D.C.

After convincing himself that he had all angles covered, Jonah entered the first set of memorized numbers again. Busy. Seriously! All that buildup for a busy signal!! Even the busy signal was helpful though, in that whoever had called, from that particular number, wasn't calling from a large organization with numerous lines and a switchboard.

He dialed the second set of numbers. The phone was picked up in two rings by a very pleasant sounding, and by Jonah's guesstimation, lady in her late thirties.

"Mr. Batsly's office."

Jonah hesitated, he didn't recognize the name.

"This is Jonah West. I keep getting calls from this number and have no idea who is trying to contact me."

"Good morning, Mr. West! Mr. Batsly has been expecting your call! Can you hold for a minute?"

Expecting his call? Jonah knew this game, if in fact it was one, and politely declined to play. "I'll call him back."

"Sir, it will just be a moment."

"No, thank you."

Jonah hung up his burn phone and downed the now tepid bottle of water he'd picked up at the motel's front desk earlier.

"Apparently we're going with plan B," mumbled Jonah to his empty room.

Jonah made the run into the city with no incident except stepping onto some asshole's discarded wad of gum.

"Damn it! Brand new shoes!"

As Jonah predicted, forty-five minutes later he was settled into position on the northern edge of the mall near the National History Museum. He purchased a disposable camera inside the museum and now looked like any other tackily dressed visitor to our nation's capital.

He used a different burner phone for this call than he used previously. The first phone he had used was back at the motel in the "on" position and charging. Anyone tracing his previous call would now find an empty room and an erased phone.

Jonah dialed the number he had committed to memory again. He noticed it only rang once this time.

"Good afternoon, Mr. Batsly's office."

"Hi, it's Jonah West calling back."

"I'll put you straight through, Mr. West."

"Commander West!"

Jonah thought quickly, the man had a Midwestern accent and was someone who was very confident in their position.

"It's just Mr. West now."

"Of course sir, of course, my apologies."

"Accepted," said Jonah in a controlled tone.

"Have you been trying to get in touch with me?"

"Yes, Mr. West, we have."

"Who's 'we,'" asked an attentive Jonah.

"Mr. West, I'd rather not say over the phone."

"Well, sir, here are your options. You can tell me now, let me play twenty questions or meet me and discuss this apparently urgent matter, face to face.

Silence greeted his suggested proposition.

"I understand you've been out west and now you're back in Florida?"

Well, that answered that. They had already traced both his iPhone, that at this point was somewhere west of the Mississippi, and the number of the phone he was currently using back to the place where he had purchased it in Florida. Somebody was obviously trying to make a point because if they knew one phone was out west…they damn well knew he was in D.C.

"Here's the thing, Mr. Batsly, I haven't been calling you, you've been calling me. If you want to talk, go to the front door of the Freer Art Gallery. I'll assume you or someone you know is aware of the location?"

"Yes, Mr. West, I do."

"Wear a scarf, I'll find you."

Jonah glanced at his watch and at the thinning lunch crowd.

"Oh, and Mr. Batsly? You've got twenty minutes."

Jonah placed his phone in his insulated and specially modified lunchbox. From all appearances it looked like a normal insulated lunchbox but several weeks back he had lined the inside with copper mesh creating a Faraday cage that no cell signal could penetrate. It was overkill but why risk being tracked when preventing it was so easy. He could have taken the SIMM card out but in a running situation; removing the card was usually a onetime deal.

At exactly one-thirty, Jonah noticed a somewhat winded older gentleman heading up the stairs of the Freer Gallery. As he watched the man, who appeared more than a little annoyed, he started pulling a rather large and bulky scarf out of a shopping bag. Although humorous to watch, Jonah decided he'd seen enough and walked up the stairs.

"Mr. Batsly?"

"Mr. West," the man extended his hand in greeting.

"Are we all done with the cloak and dagger crap?" asked Jonah in the most sarcastic tone he could muster.

"Well, Mr. West, or may I call you Jonah?"

"Jonah's fine and you're…"

The man met Jonah's gaze, "Roger works for now."

"Ending that cloak and dagger crap, as you call it, depends a lot on you. Do you have time for a walk?"

Jonah had to hand it to the man, he had a disarming character.

Jonah thought he'd seen at least one man paying an inordinate amount of attention to them as they moved off down the path that ran parallel to the grassy green center of the mall. The man had skills but Jonah's were better.

"Will your buddies be walking with us the entire way down the mall?"

Roger paused and shook his head and chuckled softly. "Some people were worried your skills may have started to fade."

Roger reached up and tapped his head twice. Immediately, the two men Jonah had spotted turned on a dime and headed off to Jonah's six o'clock position.

"And the third one?" inquired Jonah.

"Sorry, he'll hang back, but regulations say that one of them has to keep me in sight at all times."

"Alright Roger, you called this meeting, what can I do for the CIA?"

"CIA? Who said anything about the CIA?"

Jonah laughed, "You just did!"

This time it was Roger's turn to laugh, "All right then, now that that's out of the way."

They walked on for a ways before Roger broke the silence.

"Jonah how would you like to kill the bastard that started this whole mess out west? If your answer is *yes* we'll grab a bite to eat and head to my office for more details. If your answer is *no*, we'll still grab lunch and you can head back to the Motel Six in Silver Spring."

Jonah just smiled. He actually was impressed, but he damn well wasn't going to let Roger know.

They had lunch at a place that wouldn't have let Jonah in if he hadn't had the dress shirt available under his rather garish Tommy Bahama shirt. They stuffed his shirt and hat into the shopping bag with the scarf and brought the bag to the table.

They both ordered Rueben sandwiches and settled into some guarded small talk.

"We've actually been involved with your exploits since last March."

"And what exactly do you mean by that?" asked an inquisitive Jonah.

"Well, for now, all I can say is that my people are looking for some redemption and some payback as well.

"I know that five minutes doesn't seem like a very long time, but for the difference of five additional minutes my folks could have stopped that ship before it got to San Diego."

"No shit?"

"No shit."

Roger let Jonah chew on that for a bit.

"What happened? What was the delay?"

"A couple of factors really but one of them, sadly, was a lack of trust and a credibility gap at the DoD. Sufficed to say, that was rectified the moment the crab boat detonated."

"Hey Jonah, I've got some meetings to wrap up back at my office if you're not interested. On the other hand, my calendar belongs to you if your answer is, yes."

The men sat there in silence, hands folded on the table staring at each other, sizing each other up. The men's looks were more curious than threatening in nature.

Jonah slowly finished up his half of the potato fries and thought of all the work he had put into getting his life back on track. Here was something he could do that would make a difference. Jonah finished his drink, wiped his mouth with the cloth napkin and looked back at Roger. He could feel his lips turning up into a smile.

"So that's a yes?" asked Roger.

"Yes, sir, it would be an honor."

Roger reached above his head and made the okay signal.

The waiter walked over and smiled.

"Your check has been taken care of, sir. Would you gentleman care for some drinks to go?"

As they walked out of the restaurant a black Lincoln town car pulled up and a man jumped out and opened the rear door for the men. As the car pulled away from the curb Jonah's curiosity got the better of him.

"So where are we headed to Roger? Off to meet your boss?"

The driver of the town car chuckled.

"What's the joke?" asked a slightly embarrassed Jonah.

"My apologies, Jonah, I haven't been very forthcoming with you as to who I am. It was refreshing to have lunch with someone in this town that didn't know who I was. As I said when we met, my name is Roger Batsly and I do work at the CIA. What I wasn't candid about was my position at the CIA."

"And that is…?"

"Jonah, I'm currently the Deputy Director of the CIA and as of this point forward, you work for me."

—✺—

Jewels had been working diligently over the past several weeks making sure her standalone hard drive would be the only drive that could possibly get infected from her little virus attack. It was still much too early to determine who or what country would be the actual recipient of her little plan, but this kind of cyber-attack took planning. She peeked at the program twice just to see how it was set-up. It was considered "safe" until a particular sequence of keys was entered. It was, as she liked to think, as safe as casting your eyes on Pandora's Box, without actually opening the box. One of the key components of the program, she insisted on, was an activation timer. If the situation warranted, Jewels needed to be able to set the virus' activation time to however many hours after its release as she needed.

If anything were to go wrong, Jewels wanted to make sure she had done everything possible to interfere and complicate an investigator's progress. It had been a bit of a chore to make sure all evidence of the standalone drive ever being connected to her personal laptop was erased from the hard drives of both machines. She would, of course, physically disassemble the standalone drive and destroy it. But since nobody in their right mind would believe that a person of her education had a clean hard drive, she needed to erase all evidence that one drive had ever been connected to the other.

Jewels poured herself a tall glass of Merlot and reviewed her plan. As far as she could tell she was ready. Ninety-five percent of the virus had been sent out and infected about two percent of the world's computers that met the specific parameters for "infection." On the remaining computers, the virus had not self-destructed, as she had lead everyone else to believe, but had simply gone dormant. That's *not* what she had told anyone else but... oh well.

From her two peeks at the program, she knew she would need to select a country, enter a password, initiate the transmission and then cut the cord back to her standalone drive.

She had already looked online for a high-level science project on the construction of a powerful electromagnet to electronically wipe the drive in question immediately after the transfer of the file. Jewels had even gone so far as to write a sticky note reminding her to get her good computer out of the room before turning on the electromagnet.

In the top drawer of her credenza she had collected all the necessary tools to physically take apart the drive and had even mapped out where in town to distribute the various pieces.

Jewels sat back on her couch, took three large swallows of her wine and looked at everything she had set out before her. She had probably gone overboard on the plan but...better to be safe than in solitary.

CHAPTER 27

—⚍—

Heroes

The trip to Langley seemed to take no time at all, and with Roger's credentials, they flowed through the various security checkpoints with relative ease. They were greeted in an annex off the main hall just before actually entering the main building and Jonah was given his visitor badge and lanyard. It was a restricted access badge but he imagined that as long as he was with Mr. Batsly he wouldn't be challenged.

"Have a seat, Jonah. Something to drink?"

"No, sir, I'm good."

"Jonah, we've started the reactivation process for your clearance but you will need to go back through some CIA specific ENDOC training. Are you okay with that?"

"Sure."

There was a knock at the door and Mr. Batsly nodded to an associate who opened the door.

"Rick!"

"Hi, sir."

"Jonah, this is Rick Wagner. He is one of the people I was telling you about earlier."

Rick's face looked puzzled.

"Sir, I received a message that you wanted me involved in a briefing?"

"That is correct, Rick. Do you recall the name Jonah West?"

"The guy on the crab boat right? Saved the crew?"

"The same." exclaimed Roger as he gestured in Jonah's direction.

"No way!"

Rick tried very hard not to act as if he was in the presence of a rock star, but…

Jonah reached out and shook Rick's hand. "Well, now, I don't know about saving the crew, everyone on the boat got shot at least once!" Slightly embarrassed, Jonah forced a laugh. "I even took two rounds myself," Jonah chuckled pointing to his still slightly pink throat.

"Ouch," Rick looked at Jonah's neck and suddenly realized he was staring.

"Jonah, why don't you talk to Rick for a bit about what you've been doing the past few months and we'll check back with you in a while."

Jonah wasn't entirely sure what was going on, but felt safe where he was and, in reality, he wasn't going anywhere they didn't want him to go. He had noticed the security increasing exponentially as they had made their way from the garage. Although the tone in the room had been both casual and cordial the rather conspicuous cameras in the corners let him know that he wasn't here for afternoon tea.

Roger left the room and proceeded directly to a non-descript set of elevators that would take him upstairs. The ride was short and he was greeted on the second floor by one of his covert mission liaison/team leaders, Bill Carson.

"What do you think sir?"

"His skills are still sharp but he doesn't know why he's here yet. I can't risk telling him until everything's official."

"Yea, yea, whatever," Both men laughed.

Roger patted Bill on the shoulder as they walked down the long hall toward Roger's office.

"He has the skills, is highly motivated and apparently has some time on his hands."

"Perfect!"

"Almost."

"Why almost?"

Bill thought that perhaps he'd missed something.

"We were chatting and he mentioned he thought he was being watched last week, actually, he said 'stalked.' Can you check out who was down in Florida last week?"

"DHS maybe? Why?"

"Well, according to former Navy SEAL commander Mr. Jonah West, in his own eloquent words, 'they sucked.'"

"I'll be sure to pass that on."

The two men had stopped in the hall a short distance from the director's office.

"How much time do you want him in there with Rick?"

"As long as it takes the folks downstairs to get him cleared. I want him briefed and either in a go, or no go, position before close of business today."

"Five o'clock today?" asked Bill.

"Put it to everyone this way, Bill, nobody's going home until Mr. West is onboard with the program. Is that clear enough?"

Bill looked at his boss's face.

"You want him don't you?"

"You have no idea."

The two men exchanged a look and parted ways.

—◊◊◊—

Roger Batsly grimaced slightly and walked the remaining distance down the hall. As he entered his office he suddenly felt it necessary to loosen his tie and sit down. He opened his bottom desk drawer and pulled out a bottle of Glen Fiddich single malt whisky and quickly poured out three fingers worth into the cut crystal lowball glass he kept for just this type of situation.

It was a waste of excellent whisky but he drained half the golden liquid in two gulps.

On the far right side of his desk was a framed picture of a group of Marines sitting on the hood of a Humvee, all of them in various silly positions hamming it up as if they hadn't a care in the world. Roger picked up the framed picture and felt the all too familiar knot tightening in his throat.

"A promise made is a promise kept, son."

He turned the picture over and read the black sharpie note on the back of the photo."Hi Dad, we're on our way to Ramadi this week to extract some SEALS!! 10/18/05 Love you! Skip."

Roger let the picture slide to his desk blotter as his eyes, now filling with tears of pent up grief, attempted to focus on the other picture on his desk. It was a tombstone in Arlington Cemetery. The epitaph simply read:

Roger "Skip" Batsly II
Loving Son
Outstanding Marine
2/1/1980 - 10/24/05

He'd never thanked Lt. Commander West for all his efforts to save his son and as the years passed it had become more awkward. The fact the he had never been able to extract revenge against the men that had killed his son had eaten him up over the years. He truly hoped that by giving Jonah the opportunity to extract revenge on behalf of the nation it would help with any demons Jonah was harboring deep below in his sub consciousness.

—⁂—

"Where are you staying tonight, sir?"

The men had made about as much small talk as two strangers could possibly make before the situation became awkward.

"No plans really. I should probably head back to my motel and grab the few things I have before I make any decisions on where I'm spending the night. Why?"

"Well, I've got a pull out bed at my place and since we'll need to be in here early tomorrow maybe you could crash at my place?"

Jonah looked at his watch. "Well, it's coming up on 1730 now, I don't suppose you have a car?"

"No, sir, I don't, but we could get to the motel and get back here fairly quickly using the metro...But you already know that don't you."

Rick smiled, "Can you hold on a second while I make a call?"

"Do I have a choice?"

"Mr. West, you can leave at your discretion. I just thought you might want to unwind a bit this evening instead of sitting over at the Motel Six. I just need to step out for a moment and touch base with a buddy of mine. I just need to find a phone."

Jonah gave him a thumbs up and Rick left the room to find a landline. Although they weren't currently using the room for interrogations today, the room's other purpose was just that. For that very reason, the room had no phones, computers or cell service.

Rick found the office down the hall still open and used their phone to call Mitch.

"Mitch Kendrick."

"Hey."

"Hey, yourself, did you fall off the edge of the planet today? Where've you been?"

"Mitch, I've been up to my ass in processing a new guy. Are we still grabbing pizza tonight?"

"As far as I know, why?"

"Well, the new guy is from out of town and I thought he could come out with us."

"Sounds good to me, what time?"

"How about seven? We still need to run out to Silver Spring and get his stuff then we'll be back in town."

"Sounds good. Stay in touch."

"Hey, are the girls coming?"

"That I'm not sure about. Jewels has been acting a bit off. I could ask her though."

"Who's the new guy?"

"Jonah West."

"That name sounds really familiar."

"It should! Hey, I'll call you when we're back in town."

Rick hung up the phone slowly. The more he thought about it the more he realized that Mitch was absolutely right. Something had been, as Mitch had put it, "off" with Jewels for a few weeks now. Probably hormone related. Rick walked back down the hall and reentered an empty room.

—◊◊◊—

"Damn it!" yelled an irritated Rick Wagner to anyone who was in ear shot. He slammed the door to express his anger and was even denied the pleasure of a good slam by the piston controlled door actuator that prohibited the door from slamming. "Seriously?" He was fuming mad. He could hear the jokes now, "Wagner, you had one damn job!"

Rick walked down the hall and entered the men's room. He should have taken care of this about an hour ago and stood staring at the tile wall momentarily lost in his own little world.

"What's going on out there?" asked a familiar voice.

Rick was so startled he almost zipped himself up in his zipper. "Geeez, Jonah! You scared the shit out of me!"

"Well, at least you're in the right place," Jonah laughed.

Rick shook his head, maybe after a few beers tonight it would be more humorous. "I'll be back in the room."

Five minutes later a smirking Jonah entered the room.

"You okay, Rick?"

"Yea, I just thought you'd bolted and I was deep in thought racking my brain on how I was going to explain your absence when they come downstairs."

"Hey, can we call upstairs and see where we are on my status? I'm not sure what the urgency is, but I'm starving and thirsty. What did your friend say about tonight?"

"We're on for whenever. I told him we needed to pop out to Silver Springs and he said we'd shoot for a soft target of seven back at our pizza place. Hey, I didn't ask you before but do you mind if a couple young ladies join us?

"No problem, I'm just a tag along tonight."

Rick smiled to himself. "You say that now, but you haven't met Jewels."

"Who's Jewels?"

"Well, until a few weeks ago I would have said my buddy's girlfriend, but I think they are on the outs."

"Hey, if it's going to be awkward, maybe I should just stay at your place instead of going out with you guys."

Rick looked at Jonah. The man looked like that dude, what's his name, Hemsworth that played *Thor* for God's sake. No, actually Jonah appeared to be more muscular. This was either going to be a great idea, in that this might be the push Mitch needed to move forward with his relationship with Jewels...or an unmitigated disaster.

"Sorry it's taking so long. I'll go check if you promise to stay here this time."

Jonah flashed his "Scouts Honor" sign and Rick left to go see what was taking so long.

CHAPTER 28

—∞—

Illusions

Jewels had literally just sent the last file to her GNUnet server instructing her semi-malicious update program to launch at midnight Greenwich Mean Time which was Eastern Standard Time minus five hours, when the phone rang. Coffee going in one direction, various papers and notes going in the other Jewels grabbed for the falling phone. "Damn it," she took several breaths and grabbed her phone on the forth ring.

"Hello!"

"Hi Jewels! Hey are you okay? You sound out of breath?"

"I'm fine Mitch, what's up?"

"Rick called and wanted to know if you wished to join us for pizza and beer tonight around seven. He's processing in a new guy at his office and thought that it would be nice if we included him."

"What time were you thinking?" Jewels looked at the mess beside her.

"That's still up in the air, but probably around seven-ish. Do you want me to come by and we could go together?"

"No, I'll walk over. Fire House Bakery right?"

"Uh, yea."

Mitch was shocked. Jewels *ALWAYS* wanted him to come by and walk with her wherever they went.

"Hey, if tonight's not good we could do it some other time..."

"It's fine. I'll see you guys there. Should I call Gina?"

"Sure, if you want to. I'll call you if there's any significant change in plans."

"Bye, Mitch."

The phone felt heavy in her hands as she placed it back in its charging base. Jewels looked at her watch. Five forty. She had plenty of time to both get ready and get started on what promised to be an interesting evening.

Jewels turned on the water of the tub, adjusted the temperature and threw in some bubble bath beads. She had just started to undress when she stopped. She looked at herself in the mirror. Black lace panties and a blue Brooks Brothers dress shirt. She sighed deeply. Today, with the unauthorized launching of the update malware, she had crossed the preverbal *Rubicon*. There was no turning back. Failing at having anyone handy to celebrate with she decided she wasn't quite ready for the bath...yet. She walked back out to her refrigerator, opened the door, selected the open bottle of Robert Mondavi Merlot and a chilled glass. She giggled to herself as she walked back to the bathroom and closed the door. Someday, perhaps soon, she hoped to be able to share days like today with someone.

The first glass was finished before the tub was even full. Jewels refilled her glass and slipped beneath the warm water and the scented foaming bubbles. Something was different. It was then that she noticed her face felt different. Not bad or painful, just different. She reached up to feel the area around her mouth and quickly discovered what was different. She was smiling. It had been so long since she had actually relaxed and been happy.

It was six o'clock and there was no way she would be ready at seven. Jewels closed her eyes. For the first time in over six months...she just flat out didn't give a damn.

—❦—

Rick double knocked on Roger's door.

"Sir, Mr. West is inquiring where we are in the process. He's hungry, thirsty and growing impatient."

Roger looked up and leaned backed in his high-backed chair. "I was just going to send someone down to get you guys. We're good to go and I'll see you both here tomorrow morning at eight!"

"Sir, I don't see a problem with eight, but Mr. West might."

"How about nine due to the lateness of the hour tonight? What are his plans for the evening? He's not seriously considering staying out at that dump in Silver Springs is he?"

"I offered him the pull out bed at my place until he can get settled."

"Are you guys grabbing dinner?"

"I thought I'd introduce him to some of the BOATSS group over at the pizza place."

"Have fun and tell the lovely lady I said hello if she decides to grace your grizzled group with her presence."

They'd grabbed a cab and it was six thirty by the time they made it out to Jonah's motel in Silver Springs. Under Roger's instructions Rick paid for the room while Jonah got his stuff together.

"Rick, do you have parking at your apartment?"

"Yea, but I only use one of the spots. It's kind of a waste but it was part of the rental agreement."

"Well," Jonah hit the remote door unlock on the Blazer. "Tonight's your lucky night."

Rick looked over towards the Blazer with the flashing lights. "You can't be serious!"

"Don't judge this book by its cover," laughed Jonah. "Come on, city boy, let me take you to downtown D.C. like you've never done before."

Rick warily opened the passenger side door and his jaw dropped open. "Dude this thing is, is...off the hook!"

Jonah laughed. "Yes, it is."

Jonah turned the key and the customized engine roared to life. The exhaust roared as Jonah pumped the gas twice.

"Oh My God!" Rick, always the tech nut looked at the gauge package in amazement. He then turned his attention to the sound system and immediately noticed the DVD player, MP3/iPhone interface, GPS with touch screen, fully digital instrument package and Corbeau bucket seats.

Jonah West left the parking lot of the motel without so much as chirping a tire. He saved that for the first green light he came to. Traffic was a bit heavy, but he got his foot into it just long enough to hear Rick Wagner, CIA dude, scream like a little girl.

CHAPTER 29

—◆—

Superman

After brief introductions, the first pitcher of beer had come and gone as had the first pepperoni pizza. Looking around at the crowd, Jonah was relieved they'd been able to stop at a clothing store over on Wisconsin Avenue on the way back into town. It felt good to throw on some clean clothes, but the much needed shower would have to wait. Parking was tight at that hour, but the short length of the Blazer made it somewhat easier. Jonah hated shopping, but he needed something besides what he had worn earlier. He grabbed a few dress shirts and a pair of khakis. They weren't clean or ironed but still smelled and looked better than the clothes he had worn all day. Five minutes after they'd left the store they were walking into the pizza joint Rick had recommended.

Since he'd been living on the island for several months, Jonah had grown unaccustomed to the sounds of crowds and the closeness of so many people. After only a few minutes, he excused himself and stepped out in front of the restaurant to grab some air and momentary peace and quiet. His initial intentions were to walk to the end of the block and back just to stretch his legs.

Jonah was just returning from his stretch and approaching the restaurant when two men emerged from a brick stairway and walked purposefully in the direction of one of the most beautiful women Jonah had ever seen. He'd heard the distinctive sounds of the two men talking. Hearing the Farsi language alone stirred some emotion, but the appearance of the large kitchen knife brought the whole situation to a new level. The woman's face dramatically changed when she saw the two men, from what was relative ease, to terror. Although the woman was close to six feet tall, had an amazing body, she was unfortunately in high heels. Running away simply wasn't going to work.

In six long strides, Jonah set upon the two men. The confrontation was brief but violent and left one man hanging on to life and the other with a knee that would never work the same again.

"Are you okay?" asked Jonah of the terrified woman.

"I'm fine!" responded the frightened woman.

"Who, or rather what, are you? You look and move like a super hero action figure!"

Jonah offered his arm to steady the woman as they moved away from the two men still writhing on the ground. He could tell that she had consumed at least one glass of wine this evening.

"My name's Jonah and you are?"

"Julie Folk," she smiled and shook Jonah's hand. Her hand was literally swallowed up by his much larger hand.

"Wow." Jonah inadvertently said out loud. She was amazingly attractive.

"Wow what?"

Jonah recovered his wits quickly. Taking two guys out had barely raised his pulse rate but holding the hand of this woman had his heart racing. "That was a pretty close call. Did you know those two men?"

"The shorter one with the hoodie looks very similar to a man that was following me a few weeks back, but I don't recall ever seeing the larger man."

Jonah wanted to get her off the street as soon as possible. This wasn't a robbery gone bad, this had been an attempted cold blooded murder and it might not be over yet. He paused just long enough to drag both men into a store entranceway before he turned his attention back to the young lady.

"Are you on your way home?" asked a concerned Jonah

"No, I'm on my way to meet some friends at that restaurant." She gestured in the general direction of the pizza restaurant.

"Well, I was just coming out to stretch my legs from that very restaurant and would be happy to walk with you the remainder of the way."

She'd already given Jonah the once over and liked what she saw. She knew it was the wine talking, but the words left her mouth faster than she could put thought behind them. "I'd like that."

She pulled herself a little closer to the large man and entered the restaurant hanging on his arm.

Mitch was just in the process of draining the last drop of beer from his glass and his eyes focused on the scene at the front of the restaurant. The enormous man who had left to stretch his legs was walking in with a gorgeous woman on his arm. Normally he wouldn't have minded, but, although he didn't know the man, he knew the woman, or so he thought, very well.

"Rick, what the hell is this all about?"

Rick twisted around in time to see Jewels walking in on the arm of Jonah, who for all to see was grinning ear to ear.

"Jewels," Rick shouted.

Jonah's smile left his face immediately. "You're Jewels? You said your name was Julie!"

"It's Jewels to my friends and since you apparently just saved my life, you can call me Jewels as well."

Mitch was still trying to absorb the entire scene playing out before him and was still trying to find words. "You two know each other?" was the best he could come up with.

Jewels gave Jonah's arm a squeeze and smiled. "We do now! In fact he just saved my life!"

Jonah eased her down in the vacant chair by Mitch.

"Oh, do tell," replied Mitch perhaps a bit more obnoxiously than he should have.

"Seriously, you guys, two middle eastern guys just tried to kill me out in front of the restaurant. Thor here went through them like some Hollywood action hero and now I'm safe in here with you."

"For now," sighed Jonah as he continued to watch the door. "Let me go peek if the police showed up. I'll be right back."

"So, he's the new guy at your office? Did you guys put an ad out for a good looking bouncer?" quipped Jewels.

"Jewels, I realize that since you've had a glass or three of wine, I'll temper my response. Do you recognize the name Jonah West?"

"Sounds vaguely familiar," she was lying through her teeth. She knew the name of the mountain of a man was, but wasn't going to let on for a second.

"How about the guy who saved the crew of the crabbing boat that crashed into the SBX platform?"

"No way! He's *that* Jonah!"

"You're acting smitten Jewels. Do you guys want to get your own table?"

Rick jumped in, "Mitch, you're being an ass. The guy just saved Jewels' life!"

"So she says."

"Oh my God! You're jealous!" exclaimed Jewels.

"I am not jealous. If you want to walk around town on someone else's arm, that's fine by me."

"What are you tonight, Mitch, nine years old?" Jewels was getting herself worked up and that usually didn't go well.

"Mitch, the guy just got to D.C. today, give her a break."

"Et tu Brute?"

"Mitch, why don't you call it a night. You haven't said anything stupid yet and we'll all laugh about this tomorrow."

"Screw you, Rick," hissed Mitch as he left the table. He made a wide berth around the returning Jonah.

Jonah winced, "Well that could have gone better. Can I get the next round?"

"Sure, Jonah, then we should probably call it a night."

Jewels scooched her chair a little closer to the table and looked into her new found friend's eyes. "Maybe we will...and maybe we won't."

Jonah smiled and attempted the honorable route as was his nature. "Jewels, your friend's upset. You have to admit it must have looked a bit off when you came in on my arm?"

"Maybe my *friend*, as you call him, should grow a pair and act like he wants me at least as much as anyone else in the restaurant."

The second round of beer arrived as did the pizza. Jonah did most of the eating and Rick and Jewels drank all but one glass of the beer.

Rick pulled Jewels a bit closer and whispered in her ear as gently as possible, "We should get you home Jewels." Unfortunately, Jewels blurted out, "Fine," loud enough to get the attention of several surrounding tables.

Jonah picked up the check and they walked Jewels around the corner to her apartment. Just as they thought the whole evening would blow over, Jewels reached up unexpectedly, and getting as close to Jonah's face without touching it, said, "Thank you very, very, much for saving my life tonight. I hope to see you again...soon. "With that she turned on a dime and went into her apartment building's lobby.

"Jonah?" Rick asked slurring his speech slightly.

"Yeah?"

"How about we agree to never speak of that particularly awkward exchange ever again?"

Jonah laughed for the first time in quite some time. "Sounds good to me, Rick, sounds very good to me." The two men shook hands and Jonah gave Rick a well-meaning slap on his shoulder. The impact sent Rick forward a few steps.

Catching his breath for a moment, Rick reflected on the evening's events. Jonah had to be at least ten years older than he was and yet could still disarm bad guys and charm the ladies without even trying. It was at that point he decided it was a far better position to be friends with the big man...than not.

CHAPTER 30

—⚡—

No Secrets

Nine o'clock came early and Rick and Jonah were at the visitor's desk getting Jonah's credentials straightened out. The paper work had been done last night, but the badge wasn't ready until this morning.

All things considered Jonah looked, excluding a jacket, like most of the other folks he'd seen so far.

"What's next Rick?"

"Let's see when Mr. Batsly's secretary wants us to go up to his floor. Here's my office. Coffee's over on the left wall and there's usually some type of donut or something on the credenza down from the coffee. The coffee and the mystery pastry du jour are both fifty cents."

"I'll grab a cup while you call. Do you want one?"

Rick nodded his head and mouthed, "sweet."

"Nancy, Rick Wagner, Good morning."

"Is Mr. West with you?"

"Yes, he's with me. When would you like us to come up?"

"Rick, are you aware of an incident involving Mr. West last night?"

"Yes, ma'am."

"Be here at nine thirty sharp."

"Yes, ma'am." Rick hung up the phone slowly. That certainly wasn't a good start.

He rounded the corner to find the women of the office gawking at Jonah. He was like ice in response and they got the message.

"What did she say?"

"Nine thirty."

"Jonah, we've got a problem."

"What's that?"

"Somehow they know about last night."

Jonah laughed, "Well, it's not the best way to start a new job. On the other hand, I guess there's nowhere but up from here."

—m—

It was nine thirty sharp and Rick was in Nancy's alcove of an office.

"Good morning, Mr. Wagner, Mr. West."

Jonah gently shook her outstretched hand.

Not a bad start all things considered.

Rick parted the heavy drapes and pretended to look out the window. "So he heard about last night, huh?"

"Mr. Wagner, how long have you worked at this agency? What Mr. Batsly wants to know about, he knows about."

Nancy's phone buzzed twice.

"Mr. Batsly will see you now. Good luck."

The two men entered his office and Rick closed the door behind them.

"Good morning guys." Roger Batsly directed them to take a seat. "I understand you had an eventful evening. Who would like to start?"

Jonah couldn't help but laugh. "My first day at work and I'm in the principal's office already. Well, sir, since Rick wasn't there I'll tell you what happened."

"Mr. West, let me stop you right there. I know exactly what happened from someone who was not twenty feet away from Ms. Folk."

"Well, sir, what can I contribute then to this conversation?"

"I guess I want to know how you knew Ms. Folk was in danger. What led you to attack those two men and quite possibly save Ms. Folk's life?"

"Well, sir, I heard the Farsi language and heard one of the men say, 'That's her,' and immediately after that, is when I saw the knife drop down into the larger man's hand. At that point, I knew I had to act."

"I see." Roger leaned back in his chair and stared at Jonah.

"If I might ask, sir, what happened to the two men? I know for a fact that one couldn't breathe very well and the left knee of the other one will never work properly again. I didn't hear any sirens."

"They were picked up by two other men in a car whose plates we ran this morning...stolen as you would expect."

"You had a man there, sir?" asked Rick from a distant corner of the office.

"Yes, we've had Ms. Folk followed since the curious incident the weekend before last. Those two men, despite their injuries, are lucky to be alive today. Our man was just about to drop them both in a much more permanent fashion about one second after Mr. West here removed the threat himself."

"At this point, Rick, I'm going to need you to leave as you won't be directly involved with Jonah's project."

"Yes, sir."

"Jonah? Call me when you're done and maybe we can grab lunch."

"Sure thing."

Jonah waited for Rick to close the door before he spoke. "Sir, it would appear you have put a tremendous amount of effort in fast tracking my hiring. I'm not a management or Human Resources expert, but I'll bet all the money in my wallet you don't personally hire everyone who the agency needs."

"Right you are Jonah. Give me a second, will you?" Roger Batsly hit the intercom function on his phone. "Nancy is Bill here?"

"Yes, sir, he just arrived."

"Send him in please."

The door opened and a fierce looking man of about forty-five walked through the door.

Roger casually introduced the two men. "Bill Carson, Jonah West."

The two men exchanged handshakes and sat down when Roger gestured them to the two high back leather chairs opposite his desk.

"Jonah, Bill is what we would like to call your "handler" or "project manager" for your first endeavor for the agency. Bill has extensive field experience and will probably be able to answer any questions you have far better than I. Bill, why don't you tell Jonah what we need him to do."

"Jonah, Mr. Batsly told me he has already told you about the opportunity to balance the spreadsheet just a little by killing the man who started the whole chain of events that led to the device detonating in San Diego. To be clear this is not the way we normally would do this, but Mr. Batsly has his reasons. I understand you lost a good deal of friends at the SEAL training center?"

"Yes, sir, I did."

"You did an excellent job for the conditions you were under to save the crew of that crab boat. Does it bother you that you weren't able to thwart the destruction of the SBX?"

"Yes, sir."

"Well, as I've alluded to we have located the mastermind of the whole disaster and we need someone with your particular skills to go and kill him."

"Kill or capture?"

"Kill! We sure as hell don't want any more prisoners at GITMO."

"You said you know where he is?" Jonah was leaning forward in his chair now.

"We sure do. He is on the farthest most eastern tip of the island of Martinique. He has a security detail of eight or nine men and never leaves his property. Is this something you think you could get your head wrapped around?"

"Yes, sir."

Bill looked over at Roger Batsly and waited.

Jonah followed his queue and looked toward Mr. Batsly as well. He was met by a long penetrating look. Not angry or cruel but one of determination maybe? Resolve?

Roger Batsly nodded once, never breaking his gaze on Jonah.

From the ceiling above the credenza a screen dropped down and stopped. At the same time a projector descended from the ceiling and after two slides of security classifications and notifications a map of Martinique appeared. The next slides were high definition satellite pictures of a compound of sorts. Someone had drawn a red line encircling the boundaries of the compound.

"We have it on excellent authority that the man we're looking for is one Atash Rahbar and several other men shown here." Bill Carson advanced the briefing to the next slide showing what Jonah imagined were Interpol mug shots of the original conspirators. There were five Iranian names, but only three pictures. One picture was Atash Rahbar, the second was, according to their source, the mastermind Mehrak Kazemi now deceased, and three names of Chinese generals but only one old grainy picture.

The next slide was a stock photo of the Grand Hyatt Taipei. "Apparently, just over one year ago all of these men met in the penthouse suite of the Hyatt and hatched a plan to both cripple the US financially and at the same time line their pockets, as well as some Chinese general's pockets, with money from both the increase in trade to our west coast and profits generated from these two new gas wells in the South China Sea. As an interesting side note, since we've received this information, and with the cooperation of the Brits and their sources in Taipei, the local police there have closed four open homicides from the week of that very meeting. One of the deceased was the supposed mastermind, Mr. Kazemi. Why he was killed is still being investigated, but our source mentioned greed or some sort of disrespect issue with the Chinese gentlemen at the meeting." The slides now changed to the two gas platforms in the South China Sea and then to a beach in Martinique.

"Sir, these images are amazing. It's like you're standing right there!"

"Drones can do more than drop bombs, Mr. West," said Roger dryly.

"Looking back at your target for a moment. He never goes to town and other than a small unit assault on his compound we only see one opportunity to get the guy and that's while he's on the beach. He goes out with his security detail everyday between one and three for a stroll then a dip in the ocean. Here's the video footage we received a few days ago. We have a fairly good handle on his cash flow and we've pegged it at almost two million dollars per month. Apparently, he spends a good deal of it on his security detail. Our experts in these matters say that by watching them move they can tell he's hired some of the best mercenaries money can buy.

Jonah left his chair and approached the screen.

"Can you run that loop on the beach again please?"

"Sure thing. Did you see something?"

"When do you want this done?"

"Well, Jonah, we have a tremendous amount of planning to do and these things will take some time."

"Sir, I have my plan already done and just need a laundry list of items to accomplish the mission."

Bill looked at Roger and laughed.

"He's got a plan. That's rich! Twenty seconds of video and he's got a plan."

Roger smiled, "Let's hear it."

"I'll take him from the ocean side," said Jonah quietly, almost as if he was working on the plan while they were talking.

"The ocean side? That's your plan?" Bill was almost shouting.

"Yes, sir."

"Would you care to elaborate?"

"Sure thing. I'll simply lay in wait for him in the surf and take him when he enters the water. No one will see me and his body will never be found. I assume you don't want the body?"

Bill Carson now sat in his chair with his mouth slightly agape.

Roger leaned forward and smiled, "Just tell Bill what you'll need?"

"I'll draft up a list of items for you today. I can tell you now though that I'm going to need some serious bucks for some dive equipment and cash for renting some items. I'll get the important things on a list by this afternoon.

Do you know when the IT folks are going to get me set up somewhere?"

Roger looked at Bill and then they both looked at Jonah. Bill was the first to speak. "Don't you think you're being a little too confident?"

"No, sir, I don't. If Mr. Batsly didn't think I could do the job I doubt he would have recruited me so aggressively."

"He's right on that account," laughed Roger.

"Anything else, sir, before I get started?"

"Sure, Jonah, ask Nancy to give HR a call and at least get you squared away in that department."

"Yes, sir."

Jonah hadn't been out of the room five seconds when Bill and Roger cracked up.

Roger slid Jonah's dossier over to Bill. After a few minutes of reading, Bill closed the cover. "Kind of a waste to send a guy like that all that way just to kill *one* guy!"

Roger Batsly, Deputy Director of the CIA, smiled a mischievous smile, opened the bottom drawer of his large wooden desk and pulled out two glasses.

—⚇—

Jonah looked at his watch. Too late to get buried in what he needed to do and too early for lunch.

He placed a call to the guy in HR to see what he needed to get everything going from the financial side.

They had his social security information from last night's paperwork shuffle. What they didn't have was a residential address.

"Can we leave that blank and just use my office address?"

"They tend to frown on that, but from what I understand your case is somewhat unique..."

"Sure, unique would be one way of putting it."

"I've got everything I need, Mr. West. Did you have any questions for me?"

"Sure, and it will definitely affect my residential address question. How much am I getting paid in this position?"

"Mr. West, you took a job with us and didn't know what your compensation package was?"

"Yes, sir."

"Let me see…ah, here it is…$115,000. Now that doesn't include bonuses for your particular job."

"Do I get time off to apartment hunt?"

"We have a service to help you with that; would you like their extension?"

"Yes, please."

"It's extension 5413, Mr. West. Is there anything else I can help you with?"

"No, thank you."

"Okay, Mr. West, I'll have someone run your W-2 up to you shortly. Have a nice day."

Jonah did some quick math in his head, $115,000 plus the $30,000 from his navy pension? $145,000? That was out frickin standing! Jonah looked at his watch again. That had only eaten up ten minutes. He called Rick.

"Wagner," Rick answered the phone like he thought a CIA guy should.

"It's Jonah."

Rick laughed, "Start using just your last name when you answer the phone. Hey, how'd it go in there this morning?"

"Super, hey is it too soon to grab lunch?"

"Too early? No. Options are fairly slim though unless we drive into McLean. That's about ten minutes. We should beat the lunch crowd if we leave now. Do you have any idea how to get back to my office?"

Jonah looked toward the numerous doorways out of the room. "No, I do not."

Rick laughed. "Fine, I'll see you in five."

Jonah made some notes while he waited. He could easily spend between $1800 and $2800 a month on rent.

Maybe Rick could give him the nickel tour of the area at lunch.

For the next hour and a half, in between almost peeing his pants while Jonah drove his beast of a vehicle through the streets of Langley, Virginia and laughing like a little kid, Rick had actually managed to give Jonah a fairly decent nickel tour of the surrounding areas of the more well-liked and reputable apartment complexes. Many were rather lavish in nature with more amenities than Jonah could ever imagine using. He simply need-ed a gated complex with surveillance and a two-bedroom apartment...with a good view of the parking lot.

CHAPTER 31

—◊—

Razor's Edge

Dinner on the *USS Ronald Reagan* was served after an abbreviated hors d'oeuvre hour interspersed with war stories and scuttlebutt on what was going on in the San Diego area and California in general. Unfortunately, as had been the case for several of these get-togethers, the conversation always seemed to drift back to the moment the device had gone off in San Diego.

"What did it look like?"

"What did it feel like?"

"Was the crew frightened?"

Trent was ready for the questions this time and not only answered them as factually as possible, but had thrown in a comment or two about a pretty girl from an outfit called "BOATSS." He made a big show of how Jewels had stunned the crew with her beauty before she even opened her mouth. Trent went on to say that if anyone in his midst at the moment gets a call from her it would bode well for them to heed what information she was passing on.

"CHOW!" Hollered someone on the other side of the room.

"Saved by the bell!" said Trent feigning a choke hold on his own throat.

The admiral gestured for Trent to join him at his end of the table. Trent knew his protocol inside out and it dictated that he sit farther down the table. Knowing that fact was one thing, but when the admiral tells you where to sit, that's where you sit.

Admiral Boozeman nodded to the captain of the USS *Reagan* and the captain rapped the lip of his water glass three times with his spoon.

"Gentlemen and ladies, a toast, to the good luck charm of the fifth fleet!"

All around the ward room he could hear spoons rapping on the tables.

"All right everyone, let's eat."

The admiral leaned closer towards Briggs. "I understand you have arrived on station with some new 'toys' for us to use in our endeavor?"

"Yes, sir, they're called '*Sea Dragons*' and they were put together by several groups of very smart people."

"How are they different from our tried and true Mark 48's, Trent? Heading into a conflict with a unique and marginally tested weapon system? It honestly gives me shivers up the small of my back, but for all the wrong reasons. You're going to need to convince me they work, Trent, before I can count on them. Hell man, we could accidentally start WWIII in a few days. Can you at least tell me how they work?"

"Well, sir, from what I've read, and honestly I've yet to read everything, the seven *Sea Dragons* we have on board have been preloaded with a set of particular acoustic algorithms that will only allow them to seek out the specific acoustic targets such as the Chinese missile sub *Great Wall*, which is, as of last report, still guarding the two gas rigs in the South China Sea. They are designed as a fire and forget weapon and will only arm when they receive a coded message to do so. They have the standard self-destruct measures, but if push came to shove and we needed them, I don't see aborting them as realistic."

The admiral sat quietly looking at Briggs as if they were the only two men in the room. His face seemed to wear both the mantle of experience and foreboding. He had, as of this moment, over 7,500 men and women under his command and knew for a fact that he would be losing at least a few, possibly hundreds over the next several days. At his disposal and within arm's reach if needed, were the combined might of his aircraft carrier and flag ship the *USS Ronald Reagan* and its sixty-five aircraft, a guided missile cruiser, two destroyers, a fast attack sub, two logistics ships, and somewhere in the nearby depths both a ballistic missile sub and a fast attack sub like the *Connecticut*. Although the admiral honestly viewed having the *Connecticut* along as an added benefit, he wasn't completely sold on the idea of staying as far away from the action as the current plan called for.

All of that would be worked out in the next few days. Tomorrow would be the full scale brief and all the stress and angst that would accompany it. Tonight, they would relax, tell lies about their pasts, and share their dreams of the future.

—⚏—

Jewels glanced at her watch. It had been almost eight hours since her "update" malware hit the servers of the world and she was jumping every time the phone rang. The emails started coming in about a half hour ago from various friends in the industry that she hadn't heard from in years. For the most part, there were two kinds. One was a thumbs up and the other was a smiling emojis. One stood out, however, and it was from an old classmate, and dear friend, business partner and colleague at work. This note said:

Help wanted.
High level analyst position suddenly available.
Please call 305-589-2355
Ask for Gina

Well, that answered that. Gina had somehow figured it out. Jewels picked up her phone to call her best friend when Gina walked in the door, and closed it.

Jewels didn't say a word and neither did Gina. Instead, Gina walked over to the coffee urn and poured herself a cup. She sat down in front of Jewels and blew the steam off the scalding hot brew. They just looked at each other for a moment.

Jewels spoke first, "I'm sorry."

"You're *sorry*."

Gina set the coffee down on the front edge of her friend's desk, leaned forward and hissed, "Are you out of your cotton pickin damn mind!?"

"Yes, probably so," replied Jewels.

Gina continued, "What were you thinking doing something like this? Do you have any idea what the repercussions are?"

"Gina, I'm sorry, I didn't want to involve you because of that very reason."

"Sweetie, I think you're failing to grasp the situation. I don't give a damn about the 'legal ramifications,' I'm pissed off that you kept the most fun project we've come across in years...a secret!" Gina was still hissing at her.

Jewels eyes grew large and her heart raced. "That's what you're upset about?"

"Of course! What did you think I was upset about?"

"How did you find out?"

Gina drummed her fingers against themselves trying to appear devious.

"Do you recall who helped you set up your GNUnet system? Did you not think I'd set up the same system?"

"I didn't contact you though."

"No, but Glen Asperson over at the *Symantec Corporation* did and so did Karen Tuttle at *Adobe*. They both thought I should keep an eye on you."

"Now you mention it!" Jewels was relived, but cautious of her friend's news. "I could have used your help coding last weekend."

Gina sat back in her chair and threw her hands up in the air. "Not my fault."

"Alright, we got the chicken shit stuff out of the way. How about the more serious stuff at hand like your failing love life?"

Jewels got up and walked around the desk and gave her friend a hug. "Will you visit me in prison?"

"Absolutely," responded Gina with a smile. "I'll even bring cool stuff for all 'yo cell bitches' too!"

That had taken the edge off and they both laughed together for a few moments with Jewels walking through her office doing her best 'Gangsta' impression.

"Let's talk about my failed love life over dinner at my place. Just the two of us, like old times before the world went crazy!"

"Seven o'clock, okay? I've got the wine, you just need to bring the food."

"Chinese?" Gina whispered as the door slowly closed.

Jewels gave her the thumbs up and a wink.

Gina walked past Maureen Templeton and attempted to engage her with a courteous "Hello."

She was greeted with an icy stare and thin lipped smile.

Gina walked on a few feet and looked back. What the hell was her deal today?

Maureen looked up as Gina had approached. The mere sight of her so enraged Maureen that her body actually shook. Her perfect smile, her perfect tight little ass, and her perfect group of friends.

Maureen had acknowledged her presence as she had passed by. Nothing more and nothing less. She held her smile until Gina had rounded the corner and disappeared from sight. In a second, her face turned to a cement hard look of pure hatred. She felt her blood begin to pound in her veins and her face get warm.

"Smile now bitch because one day soon, real soon, you'll have no face to smile with."

—∽—

Work on the modified fuel tanker was now complete and JAveed wanted to test the system's timing circuits and everything else just short of detonation. They filled the tank with 2800 gallons of water and pumped 2600 gallons of that out just five seconds faster than they'd estimated. Both timing circuits, the one to the igniter at the end of the boom and the circuit to the internal "bomb" worked flawlessly. JAveed adjusted the timing on the boom igniter back a full minute to compensate for the slightly faster than anticipated pumping speed and had adjusted the signal to the "bomb" to only three minutes after the truck was placed in reverse. They were ready. All they needed now was a date, time, real fuel for the tank, and they would be ready when the word came down.

The Imam approached nodding and smiling at JAveed, "I am very impressed JAveed. You have done well in your efforts!"

"Thank you. We do have one small dilemma still facing us and that is we still have not decided on a driver."

The older man chuckled. "If you can make the doors lock the moment the truck is placed in reverse...we have our driver."

JAveed looked at his Imam as if he had been scalded with hot water. "I will not need you to lock the doors! It is both my honor and duty to fulfill this task."

The older man placed his arm over the shoulder of his bomb maker. "We have discussed this previously JAveed. I know that to be true and if you were to be the driver of the truck, we would not even need doors. But you are not to be the driver. We cannot afford to have the infidel survive this attack. He will be a danger to us for all eternity. Just think JAveed, with the current climate in this pathetic country and his status as a disgruntled former employee, it will more than likely be written off as work place violence."

Both men laughed together as three other men pulled an enormous tarp over the tank portion of the truck.

"JAveed? One other item. Do we have anyone who can either position cameras or be nearby to film this? I want to be sure the Americans and our brothers around the world see this spectacle over and over again."

"I've already positioned two cameras on the truck itself and we have two volunteers to help with HD digital cameras from across the street."

The Imam rubbed his weathered hand through his beard of thirty years and smiled at the prospect of seeing this event over and over on the news. He could almost hear the news people chattering for days on who, what, and why this was done. "Excellent."

CHAPTER 32

—m—

House Rules

It was Tuesday evening and for the first time in several weeks, or so it seemed, everyone had left either early, or at least on time. Ken didn't mind staying late, it was part of the job, but getting home before seven was a nice break. For two weeks now he had another reason to get home early, a girlfriend. He had not even tried to establish a relationship of any kind when he knew he couldn't afford to ever do anything about it. With his recent promotion, and the education package the girls had put together for him, he knew he had a bright future and he wasn't going to squander the opportunity. His mind drifted back to the events that cascaded them all to where they found themselves today. He chuckled to himself when he recalled taking Ramón Rodriquez out of the building. Boy that man had been pissed off.

Computer screens off, folders picked up and lights off. It was the same routine every day, but he took it seriously. He had just pulled the door closed to Ms. Folk's office when he found himself staring at Maureen's blotter. He'd noticed all of the entries a few weeks earlier and had been surprised and even a touch curious when he thought she was involved with someone. Tonight when he looked at the blotter almost every day of the week had something on it up until Tuesday, the fourteenth. On that day, all that covered the date were little drawings of smoke, fires, and lightning bolts. He worked his way backward through the weeks and saw the same initials as he had seen the weeks before, "RR." This time, though, he remembered whose initials they were and he felt sick to his stomach. *Ramón Rodríguez.* The pieces were coming together and the picture didn't look very good. Maureen was having meetings, or at a minimum making contact with her former boss, at least twice a week, sometimes more.

Ken picked up the calendar from Maureen's desk. What concerned Ken the most, as he reached up and toggled the light switch above her desk, was that Maureen's calendar was completely devoid of all appointments *after* the fourteenth. What was happening in two weeks?

Ken reached up to his collar and keyed his mike.

"Tony, are you still in the building?"

"No, Mr. Shortman," laughed Tony, obviously impressed with his own sense of humor.

"Very funny! Hey, I need you to meet me at the ground floor security desk in about five minutes."

"Problem boss?"

"I hope not. You might want to call your wife and tell her you might be late."

"Shit! I was just thinking how nice it was that we were actually getting out of here on time!" Tony laughed, "This better be a matter of life and death."

Ken hadn't laughed back but had instead keyed his mike twice. His silence to something said in jest immediately made Tony uneasy.

"Boss?"

"I hope not," was all Ken had replied.

—⚏—

As Tony came around the corner he could see his boss holding up the large desk calendar.

"Need a calendar at home boss? There's a whole stack of new ones in the third floor supply room."

"It's not funny, Tony."

"Sorry boss."

They walked over to a small room off the main entrance foyer, unlocked the door and stepped in. It was setup as a mini command center when they did a lot of the new wiring with the rest of the renovations a few months back. They'd yet to use it for that purpose, but when visitors came, it was a good way to check clearance paperwork and more secure than having the former laptop setup.

"I need you to bring up a photo for me."

Tony entered his password and opened the employee data base system. "Alright, what's their name?"

"Ramón Rodriquez."

"Hey, I remember that asshole!"

Tony finished typing which was, and he agreed, not his strongest of skill sets. "There you go boss!"

"Super! Now the thousand dollar question, have you seen him recently?"

Tony looked at the picture on the screen and racked his brain for an idea of when he'd seen him last. "Sure that guy comes here a couple times a week. Hey, I'm sorry boss he looks nothing like the picture in the file. What's up?"

"I don't know what's up, Tony, but I'm going to find out right now. You can view a history of security footage from here right?"

"Yeah. Are you going to tell me what's going on?"

"Go to..." Ken looked at the calendar entries from the week before. He pointed at the date in question. "Go to this date at 11:45 and show me camera one."

The image that played before him was somewhat unnerving. It showed Ramón walking up to the glass, peering in and then walking back to the curb. He then either wrote something down or texted someone something. He waited by the curb until he was joined by Maureen a few moments later. He turned her ever so slightly to the left and took a selfie. He could tell because the flash made a bright white dot.

"Tony, do you see anything unusual about that picture?"

Tony played it again in slow motion. "He takes crappy pictures, that's for sure."

"What makes you say that?"

"At that angle of the phone there's no way either of them are in the picture."

Ken had noticed the same thing but wanted to see if his preconceived idea of what he thought was going on was perceived by someone else.

"Geez, boss, it looks to me like he's casing our building!"

"I agree, let's check out these other dates and see what we can see."

Over the next half hour the two men looked at every date Maureen had on her calendar and in each instance Ramón greeted her in a slightly different spot and took a goofy angled selfie.

"Who's off tomorrow?"

"Stan starts his weekend tomorrow."

"Call Stan and tell him I need him to come in at least in the morning. You and I are going to have a very busy day."

The two men locked the system, the door to the room and even double checked the side doors on the way out. Ken set the final alarm code and walked away from the building. He made it about a block when his anger welled up inside. "No son of a bitch is gonna screw with MY house."

Ken reached into his pocket and pulled out his cell phone and dialed the number and the name that was in all capital letters. The phone rang several times before a woman answered.

"Hello."

"Ms. Folk, I'm sorry to disturb you. This is Ken Shortman down at the building."

"Hi Ken, remember to call me Jewels," she laughed.

"Not tonight, ma'am, I think we have a really big problem here at the building and we need to get the senior staff together first thing tomorrow morning."

"Who were you thinking Ken?"

"Everyone."

—〰—

Last night Jewels had called Gina first and then Mitch. Mitch had called his FBI contact who had in turn called the local LEO's. They all arrived at different times and used different entrances to access the building. It was no longer a question of if they were being watched, but more of who and how many.

Everyone had been told to report directly to the downstairs conference room and not to tell anyone about the meeting. Jewels greeted everyone, offered coffee, and got down to business.

"I'm going to hit the low points first and get some feedback from the folks who do this stuff for a living before I make any comments. Ken Short-man made a discovery yesterday and being the professional that he is, stayed late with another member of his team to run his hunch to ground. What he has discovered is a pattern of clandestine meetings with one of our current employees and a former supervisor that this office had the pleasure of firing earlier this year. Ken can you show everyone what you found?"

"Good morning. I'm not used to public speaking so if I trip over my words..."

Several people chuckled.

"I noticed some unusual annotations on Maureen Templeton's desk calendar a few weeks ago, but didn't understand what the initials and abbreviations in the margins meant until last night. This is a copy of her calendar. I put her calendar back on her desk early this morning so she wouldn't get suspicious. Over the past several weeks, or longer, Miss Templeton has been meeting with this man, Ramón Rodriquez, several times a week."

Tony played a compilation of the various meeting times on the big screen TV.

"As you can see in these recordings he is clearly taking pictures, from various angles, of the front of this building. The most worrisome part is that Miss Templeton's calendar is meticulously filled out until this day.

"What are those, drawings?"

"From what we could decipher it's doodlings of fires, smoke and either lightning bolts or explosions."

"So what, everyone doodles on their calendar."

Ken was respectful, but abrupt. "Sir, it's my job to keep everyone in this building safe. If I see something that looks like a threat I'm duty bound to report it."

An eerie silence griped the room.

Ken attempted eye contact as he scanned the room. "Am I the only person who thinks it's a touch creepy that there is nothing on this woman's calendar after the date covered with the drawings?"

Jewels stepped forward, "Thank you, Ken. No, you're not and it is my opinion that we run this potential threat to ground. What say you Mr. FBI?"

"I think we need to get some more FBI folks onboard as well as the counterterrorism task force. It's not a lot to go on, but we'll, as you say, run it to ground."

"Alright folks, thanks for coming and remember not a word to anyone inside or outside this building that you aren't sure isn't involved."

As everyone filed out Jewels sidled up to Ken. "So you've never spoken in public before, huh? That was pretty darn good for a newbie."

"Thank you, ma'am."

"Thoughts?"

"Yes, ma'am, but I didn't want to tell everyone in the group."

"Well they're all gone. What's on your mind?"

"Well, ma'am, it occurs to me that whatever they are planning to do obviously involves the front side of our building."

"Go ahead."

Ken walked over to a whiteboard that was leaning in the corner and turned it around. On the whiteboard was one of the most detailed drawings Jewels had ever seen on a whiteboard. It was almost a work of art.

"Oh my God Ken, where did you find that?"

"I drew it this morning."

"*THIS* morning?" Jewels was incredulous at the detail of the drawing. "Where did you learn to draw like that?"

"I've always been able to draw. I just never had any resources to take it to the next level, ma'am."

"I'm still in shock but carry on."

"In several of the videos I noticed that it seemed like Mr. Rodriquez walked differently toward the building than away."

"So?"

"So, I think he was measuring for something. I think whatever they are doing involves a precise distance to the front doors of our building."

"So, what do you propose?"

The big man clasped his hands behind his head. "Yunno the contract that we had to put in those pneumatic posts for traffic control?"

"The bollards, yes, I remember. It was delayed for some reason or another."

"Do you think we could put those in over several nights and not tell anyone? Maybe they could pretend it's a water main break or something and cordon the front of the building off for a few days?"

"Why don't we just arrest the two of them and be done with it?"

"Because you know as well as I do, and I'm not the smartest tool in the shed, that whoever is in charge of this attack, and it's most certainly not Mr. Rodriquez, will just move on to somewhere else that's less prepared."

Jewels sat back in her chair and looked at the giant of a man in front of her. How many people had walked past this man over the course of his life and probably dismissed him for one reason or another? Jewels realized in that flash of a moment that although she worked with some of the brightest minds around, Ken Shortman had just said the smartest thing she had heard anyone say in a long, long time.

CHAPTER 33

—m—

Logistics

Jonah met with Stan Williams, from operations support, early the next morning and explained what he would need as far as equipment and the basic logistics of the operation.

Although many of the items on Jonah's list caused Stan to ask, "What the hell is that for?" Jonah got the okay for his rather exotic list of tools and toys for his upcoming mission. His list looked legit to any high end diver, but the specific pairings of some of the items would lead an experienced diver to recognize this was equipment far better suited to a "hunt" than a dive. Jonah carefully researched the shallow waters around Martinique and selected his full body Lycra wetsuit to be a camouflage pattern that would render him invisible from the surface and almost invisible against the bottom. He'd even gone so far as to research the amount of shadows at the probable time of his mission and determined what level and combination of colors and contrasts would be most effective for his wetsuit. Every part of his body would be covered with the same blue and gray pattern including his gloves. Nothing in Jonah's silhouette would stand out more than any other part of his ensemble.

His spear gun was top of the line and packed an incredible wallop. At close range, the spear, and the two tips he selected, would have a more devastating effect on his target than most conventional large caliber hand guns. If he moved fast enough, he would be able to take two shots. Perhaps one for his intended target and one for defensive purposes. His ace in the hole, and the largest ticket item by far, was his rebreather device. Online, the rebreather booked out at close to $10,000. The rebreather would allow him to stay submerged and leave no trace of bubbles on the surface. He had it ordered in the same camouflage pattern as the Lycra wetsuit.

The several other items on the list paled by comparison and Stan just scribbled his name next to the item listed on the requisition form.

Although he hadn't done the travel arrangements himself, he knew that traveling to the Island of Dominica by air wasn't as easy as it sounded. His actual arrival on the island required he take a flight to San Juan Puerto Rico, stay overnight and leave on a flight to Dominica at seven thirty the following morning. Jonah would be dragging a bunch of dive gear and was happy that he was in such excellent shape. Arrival to the country wouldn't be all that difficult but he needed a couple different ways to get off the island if things didn't go according to plan. The "travel offices" downstairs arranged everything to appear as if he was a tourist coming in for a few days of diving. Arranging for the fast dive boat on Dominica had proven even more challenging, but when it needs to get done, the folks downstairs got it done.

The trip had been set up for a round trip to the Island of Dominica with flexible tickets in both his real name and alias of "Eric Dawson." Essentially he would spend the next two weeks analyzing the information they had on his target and learning the lay of the land around the beach compound on the neighboring island of Martinique.

Due to the priority of the mission, dynamic tasking of overhead assets such as satellites wasn't foreseen as a problem during the mission, if necessary, but the current plan was to have a Global Hawk drone loitering overhead on mission day.

The meeting with Stan Williams had taken less than an hour and he felt comfortable leaving the ordering of all the gear in Stan's experienced hands.

Jonah went down to find Rick to see if he could bust loose for an hour and do a walkthrough with him on an apartment he'd found just over two miles up the road from the CIA headquarters building. At $2350 a month, the rent was a little more than he wanted to spend, but less than his maximum budget.

Jonah walked past where he thought Rick's cubicle was and found the desk in two tries, but he wasn't there. Jonah walked up toward the front of the room where the administration personnel assigned to the section had their desks. Only one young lady was at her desk. Her brass name plate said "Elizabeth."

"Hi, Elizabeth."

"Hi, Mr. West."

Jonah was slightly taken aback.

"I'm sorry, Elizabeth, have we met?"

"Please, call me 'Lizzy' if you want."

Elizabeth leaned forward exposing far more of her assets than Jonah had expected and with a smile and a look that could melt cold steel said, "Everybody knows who you are, Mr. West. Have you found a place to live yet?"

In a unique combination of body language and vocal tone, Jonah suspected she seemed far more than just curious...

"Well, Elizabeth, I think so. I'm on my way to take a peek at a place in a bit and dropped by to see if Rick was in."

Elizabeth smiled her very best dreamy smile up at him and he found himself smiling back.

Silence...

"Is Rick available? I went past his cube and he's in the wind."

"Hold on, Mr. West, I'll buzz his cube."

She moved to call Rick's extension.

"Elizabeth, he's not there, I checked remember?"

"Oh, how silly of me of course you did. Let me see what his calendar has marked for this morning. Oh, he's due out of a meeting in about five minutes. Would you like to wait over there?"

Elizabeth gestured to a row of high back leather chairs to her left.

"Sure, I'll wait for him."

Jonah sat in the chairs that, to the apparent delight of "Lizzy," gave her an unobstructed view of her new favorite eye candy. Jonah reached for a magazine and found last month's issue of *Golf Digest*. Jonah couldn't stand the game, but it was easier to pretend to read *Golf Digest* than watch Lizzy's attempts to flirt.

In the five minutes it took Rick to get out of his meeting, Lizzy had managed to "accidently" drop both a pencil set and dish of paper clips off the front of her desk. Jonah wasn't sure if there was a Guinness World Record for slowest retrieval of dropped office items category, but if there was? Lizzy was definitely in contention for the award.

When Rick walked up a few minutes later, Jonah could have told him the style, make and cut of her underwear, the pattern on her pantyhose, and the location of both a mole and birth mark not normally seen during normal business hours.

Jonah was out of his chair the moment he heard Rick's voice.

"Hey, Rick!"

"Hey, Mr. West."

"Can you bust loose for an hour and check out an apartment with me? Two sets of eyes on the place before I sign the lease."

"Sure thing! Let me just check my messages and we'll get out of here."

Rick pushed some buttons and after listening for a few minutes walked over to Jonah with a slight perturbed look on his face. "Ready?"

"Yeah, is everything okay?"

"I think so...but it's going to be a busy afternoon."

"Hey, I could go on my own."

"No, it's not a problem. After *that* meeting it's probably best I get some air and clear my head anyway."

"Hey, what's the deal with the admin gal?"

Rick laughed. "Oh, you met Elizabeth? She's been waiting for you to come by since your picture floated through the secretarial pool a few days ago."

Jonah cringed. "Seriously?"

Rick laughed again. "Sorry man, she's definitely got the hots for you!"

"That sucks!"

"Probably."

Jonah got the joke and feigned hitting his new friend in the head.

—⚇—

The apartment was on the twenty-fourth floor and offered an amazing view of the surrounding Virginia countryside. It was everything Jonah had been looking for.

"Nice place."

"Thanks, Rick."

The manager gave Jonah a disapproving once over and handed him the lease as they walked toward the elevators.

Jonah skipped to the bottom of the lease form where it stipulated payments, terms, etcetera. "First month, last months and a maintenance deposit equal to half a month's rent?"

"Yes, sir, that's pretty standard for this area. Will that be a problem?"

Jonah glanced at Rick for confirmation and received an affirmative nod.

"I assume you'll take a personal check?"

"Well, yes, but I'd prefer a credit card."

"I'm sure you would...but that wasn't the question, was it George?"

The man hesitated and looked at Rick. Rick just looked at the man and slowly shook his head.

"Do you even have a job here in town yet? The residents have high standards and pay a premium to maintain those standards."

Jonah smiled at the man whose attitude was in severe need of adjustment and smiled a razor thin smile. "Yes, I do, just up the road about 1.8 miles on the left."

Jonah held his smile while the man did the math...

They'd reached the lobby and had taken a few steps when then the light clicked in the man's head. "Yes, sir, a check would be just fine, just fine indeed."

Jonah wrote him a check and signed the lease, got his keys and bar code sticker for the security gate.

He smiled and took the check from Jonah's outstretched hand. "Thank you, Jonah. Welcome to Magnolia Towers."

"George, is it?"

"Yes."

Jonah drew himself up to his full height and leaned forward for affect. "George my name's 'Mr. West,' are we clear?"

"But I thought..."

"Obviously not your greatest strength, George..."

With that, the two men had turned in unison and walked out through the fancy doors into the bright sunshine of a pleasant Virginia morning.

—⁂—

It had only taken three days for his wetsuit and other dive gear to be delivered to the mail address he'd been supplied by Stan. They called him when it had come in and said the smaller items would be brought over to his office at some point this morning. It was agreed that the larger items would remain down on the first floor in the logistics office. Apparently, the CIA often had equipment and other items delivered to an offsite address to alleviate any eyebrows being raised on unique deliveries. Jonah was relieved that the agency even had a pool that he could use for dry runs with his equipment. They scheduled his practice times not to conflict with normal pool hours for rather obvious reasons. He also had been assigned a diving buddy/safety observer while he practiced. He was glad they had the time to practice. His first plan was to shoot the bastard as he lay on his raft, but after burning through three rafts Jonah found he couldn't get the damn thing to deflate fast enough to get away clean. The new plan, was to simply grab the man by the hand and pull him off his raft. Once submerged, Jonah would shoot him in the chest with the spear gun.

Jonah's handler, Bill Carson, had dropped by twice. His last visit was just in time to see a submerged and almost invisible Jonah rise from the depths, grab a mannequin's arm, pull it off the raft, and blow a half inch hole straight through its chest. Jonah looked ready.

Bill Carson, who was no stranger to what the world's clandestine services called "wet work" walked out of the pool area and upstairs to his office before calling Deputy Director Batsly's direct line.

"Batsly."

"Carson."

"Well?"

"He's ready."

"Are you sure?"

Bill Carson drew in a long slow breath. Even knowing who the target was...he actually felt bad for the poor bastard.

"Yes, sir."

CHAPTER 34

—〰—

Surf & Turf

Jonah's drive down to the Florida Keys had been, for the most part, relatively uneventful. The official point of the trip, and part he was getting paid per diem for, was to get some actual in ocean practice with all of the gear including the new underwater scooter. He wanted to make sure he had all the bugs worked out and knew every little quirk of the unit that would make the difference between him living through the upcoming mission or dying in the warm shallow waters off the Island of Martinique. The other purpose of his trip was to kidnap, or at least visit, Jimmy Bicksford at his Florida City truck stop and take him down to the Keys for a few days of R&R. The two of them could anchor off the beach at Wisteria Island, camp for a few nights, try out his new gear and recover the stuff he'd left buried in the sand several weeks ago. They would leave when they were done eating grilled fish, grabbing a few lobsters, drinking ice cold beer and talking shit about the good old days.

As Jonah passed Coral Gables, he called Jimmy at the truck stop. If Jimmy had too much time to think about it he would probably say "no." With less than forty-five minutes time from call to pick-up, he was gambling his friend would say "yes." The phone picked up on the third ring.

"Bicksford's!"

"Hey, I'm looking for Jimmy?"

"Hold on."

Jonah really hoped his old friend would make the trip. He needed some guy time. He'd refused all offers of help, counseling and even several trips offered by the "Wounded Warrior Project."

"This is Jimmy, how can I help you?"

"Hey, Patch!"

"Jonah West! As I live and breathe. What's up sir?"

"What are you doing for the next few days, Patch?"

"Same shit, different day...Why?"

"Can you bust loose from the truck stop and come to the Keys with me? I've got some new toys I'd like to check out and we could just chill for a few days."

Patch hesitated. It sounded like fun but something told him something was up. "Why are you really coming?"

Jonah laughed, "to get my phone back."

Patch opened the top drawer of his desk and pulled out Jonah's iPhone. The tiny SIM card had been taped to the phone since Ronnie brought it back from Eugene, Oregon. It had only been back in his office a week.

"Sure, I'll bite, when are you planning to be here?"

"You've got forty-five minutes to be ready."

"You're shittin me!"

"Nope, just passed through Coral Gables."

"Forty-five minutes! You're kidding right?"

"Patch, now you've only got forty-four minutes. Friendly's inbound."

Jonah hit "end" on his phone and laughed for the better part of a mile.

Jonah had already reserved a fishing boat from the Naval Air Station Key West MWR (Morale, Welfare, Recreation) facility called Sigsbee Marina. The two men loaded the boat with two coolers of ice, one cooler of beer, and a smaller cooler with several large T-bone steaks.

It was late afternoon when the two finally shoved out of the marina's boat slip and into the quiet waters east of Dredgers Key. Jonah took them slowly southwest through the slot between Fleming Key and Key West proper. The narrow channel was populated by half a dozen fishing boats taking full advantage of the changing tide and the hungry fish it usually contained.

It was a two mile trip and they were soon anchored on the west side of Wisteria Key, just north of an old shipwreck, in less than twenty minutes.

"So you were out here for how long?" inquired Patch.

"Three months or so. It wasn't like I was being a hermit. I came out and said 'hi' occasionally."

With his prosthetic leg, Patch couldn't walk on the sand worth a damn so Jonah shuttled all the gear back down the familiar path to his former accommodations. Nothing had been vandalized or disturbed that he could tell. He glanced up into the Australian pine tree above his place and saw that the little black warning flag with the message *SEALs Never Sleep*, with the SEAL logo, was still secured high above his shelter.

After some light housekeeping, and unburying a couple of five gallon paint buckets to sit on, they were ready to have a few beers.

Patch did the honors and cracked open a couple Budweiser's. "I love what you've done with the place."

"Thanks, it's not as comfortable as it looks though."

They tipped their beers and both took several long swallows.

"You all right?" asked Jonah.

Patch was quiet but nodded in the affirmative.

"Ready?"

"Yup."

Jonah tossed Patch a second beer.

Patch tugged on some straps and his prosthetic leg came free. He gently set it to one side. "Sir, do you think it's possible that you could, without the benefit of an overload of bullshit...tell me why we're really here?"

Jonah looked around and gestured with his outstretched hand. "How could I keep this place to myself?"

Patch was not amused, but granted the comment a weak smile.

"Alright, here's the thing, I need to practice with this new gear for an upcoming job and I thought you could use a break from the truck stop and be willing to be my spotter while I'm here."

"You mean mission," said Patch as steady and cold as he'd said anything in years.

"Tomata, tomato."

Jonah felt slightly uneasy. Patch was just sitting on the overturned bucket glaring at him.

"Hey, Patch, lighten up buddy."

"Fuck you man. Did you know you're the only one from the teams who still pretends I'm even alive?"

"So you're sore because I've invited you out here to help me do my job safer?"

"MISSION!" bellowed Patch.

"Fine, mission, what's it matter?"

"It's about being honest, sir, no more lying! I'm so tired of being lied to."

"Fine…"

Jonah had not foreseen this turn of events and was beginning to doubt the trip would be helpful…to either of them.

And then, as if nothing had been said between them and with a broad smile on his face, Patch was back to being Patch.

"So, the scooter looks pretty cool!"

—⁂—

It took the two men a bit longer than planned to get organized the next morning, but by eight o'clock they were just over seven miles away at the very private Big Mullet Key. The scooter was on the diving deck on the back of the boat and Jonah was already in the water outfitted in his Lycra dive suit.

"That's just crazy, sir, you're invisible from your face down."

"Good to know. I'll be sure and use some camo face paint tomorrow."

"Check this out Patch. I ordered an integrated GPS interface with the scooter. No matter what, it will bring me back to wherever I launch from."

"That's cool."

"All I need to do is hold on tight."

After a momentary awkward pause, both men laughed nervously.

"Well, let's check this thing out already."

Jonah grabbed the handle and pulled the unit into the water. Smiling like a six year old about to test ride his first two-wheeler, he gently squeezed the trigger and in a moment was underwater and gone from view.

Patch waited patiently, but after two minutes he was standing on the seat of the boat trying to find his old friend.

Suddenly, and completely from a direction Patch wasn't expecting, Jonah broke the surface with a shout less than ten feet from the boat.

"That was AWESOME!"

It happened so fast that Patch had fallen off the boat's seat and barely caught himself from going over the side.

"Dude, I couldn't see you at all!"

"This thing's perfect! Check this out. I can put in up to ten way points."

"Bullshit!"

Jonah laughed, "Well, I'd need the coordinates of course."

"Alright what's next?"

"How about the rebreather rig?"

Although it had great function, the rebreather unit was a bit bulky and getting out of the boat was going to take some practice to get the body mechanics just right. It took four tries, but after figuring out the center of the weight and how far up he had to swing his legs, he had it down to three moves. Jonah practiced getting in and out for about twenty times before it was second nature.

"Ready to try it for real?"

"Sure!"

Jonah turned the unit on and slipped beneath the calm waters. It had the same familiar SCUBA feel but his air didn't leave the mouth piece like it did with normal equipment. He laid on the bottom motionless to get used to the sensation. It was remarkable, the rebreather caused so little disturbance that the local wildlife came in really close. He apparently looked no different than a hunk of reef. The trio of barracuda was a touch alarming but they seemed oblivious to his presence as well. Jonah's confidence in the equipment was increasing with every passing minute, he slowly kicked his fins until he had changed his position from where Patch had last seen him to a couple hundred feet to the west. He surfaced and removed his mask and mouth piece. "Patch."

Once again Patch was caught staring at the wrong part of the bottom. "Damn it, that's amazing!"

Jonah kicked over to the small diving deck and pulled the scooter into the water. "Now, let's try that waypoints feature!"

Jonah entered the coordinates of where the boat was anchored as waypoint one. He gunned the scooter taking him just over a hundred yards away from the boat. He stopped briefly, entered the location where he was currently treading water as waypoint two. He needed to trust his equipment fully and there was no time like the present to get a good warm fuzzy. Jonah hit waypoint one, closed his eyes and held on. He decided to try several of the other options on the return trip including the programmed speed and depth mode as well as a GPS and waypoint "arrival stop" mode. If things went the way he hoped, the unit would take him back to his boat and use just enough power to keep him at that particular location. Jonah estimated the return trip to take between eighteen and twenty seconds. At the twenty second point, the scooter's motor quit and Jonah opened his eyes.

"Holy shit that was awesome!" screamed his enthusiastic friend.

"Did you see me coming?"

"I saw a brief glimmer of gray as you passed over that real sandy part, but with the glare on the water I couldn't reacquire you before you were bumping your fist on the boat."

"Enough for today! Let's do some fishing!"

They had moved back toward the east about four miles where some passing boaters said they grabbed some lobster a few hours earlier. Within thirty minutes Jonah caught six lobsters and thrown the two smallest back. Over the next hour, while calmly drinking a few beers, the two caught enough Yellowtail Snapper to tide even their appetites over for a few meals.

Patch was quietly cleaning the fish at the back of the boat for about fifteen minutes when he put the knife down and looked over at Jonah. "Hey."

"What's up?" Jonah tipped his hat back just far enough to see his friend.

"Sorry about yesterday's blow up."

"Sure," Jonah closed his eyes and pulled the brim of his hat down again. He hoped they weren't going to get into each other's faces again.

"It's just ever since I've been like this," Patch gestured toward his missing leg. "Everybody thinks this," pointing at his head, "is damaged too. That's when they think they can lie to you about anything."

"Like what?"

"Geez, anything man. Doctor's appointments, meds, disability benefits, anything that's relevant when you're like this." Patch motioned toward his prosthetic limb again. "It's just wrong and it screws with your head. I seriously think most people don't really want to off themselves, but when you start to think everyone has it out for you...I'm just sayin."

Jonah lifted both his hat and polarized glasses to look at his friend. Unless you knew Patch was missing a limb and survived a severe trauma you'd never know it by looking at him. Unless, you studied his face. He looked older than he should have. It was out of character with the rest of his athletically fit body. It seemed almost out of place. He wouldn't describe it as sad or stressed, just tired maybe. Very tired. Jonah tipped his glasses back down into place. "Yunno I got your six right?"

"Yes, sir, and I yours."

Jonah saw the mood starting to shift toward a more morose vector and he forcibly switched the conversation to how well all the gadgets and toys had functioned in this morning's test. "Could you believe how fast that scooter pulled me through the water?"

"It was very impressive."

"It's not even that company's most powerful model. I only got this one because I might have to carry it at some point."

"Why don't you give it a try? You haven't forgotten how to swim have you?"

"No, but I tend to swim in a slow arc to the right."

Both men laughed at the obvious self-deprecating dig on Patch's missing right leg.

"Hey, speaking of that, I brought you something."

Jonah reached into his oversized dive bag and pulled out a giant shoe box.

"What the hell is that?"

"Open it."

Patch opened the box and pulled out the largest flipper he'd ever seen. "What the hell?"

"It's a custom flipper to fit over your leg."

"No, way!"

"Yes, way."

"How did you get my size?"

Jonah laughed. "A pretty girl at the Miami VA said she couldn't give me your information because of HIPAA regulations, but she could send your measurements to a vendor without your name attached and it would all be legal. They said even you'd be able to figure it out."

"They did not! Sir, this is awesome!"

"They did mention something about not getting sand in it."

"Can I try it out now?"

"Patch, it's yours, try it whenever you want."

In four moves Patch had the flipper over his stump and secured in place. "See ya!"

Patch was over the side before Jonah could even comment.

Jonah looked over the side in time to see Patch swimming strongly underwater and away from the boat. He'd stayed in great physical shape, but just wasn't comfortable being out in public.

Patch surfaced about two hundred feet from the boat. "This thing's fantastic! Now I curve to the left!"

In his haste, Patch had neglected to put a flipper on his good leg.

Jonah scouted the water below and saw that many fish that had been there only moments ago were no longer there. "Hey, Patch?"

"Sir?"

"Yunno all those fish guts and trimmings you've been dumping in the water?"

"Yeah."

"They worked, stay put."

Using the universal sign for "shark" and hoping he could see his hand signals, Jonah gestured for Patch to move away from the boat.

Jonah pulled the boat's anchor, turned on the trolling motor and slowly and quietly moved toward Patch's location. Glancing behind the boat at the small wake caused by the trolling motor, Jonah saw what he hadn't wanted to…"Change of plan!" he hollered at Patch.

Due to the size of the shark trailing the boat, Jonah opted for a high-speed moving pickup. He turned on the boats gas engine, nudged the throttle forward, stood behind the seat and leaned over the right side of the boat. With his arm extended towards the water, he braced for the deadweight impact of Patch's bodyweight.

Fear is a terrific motivator and when focused can be very effective at getting a task accomplished. Without even a slip or a scrape, Jonah had one handed Patch up and into the rear of the boat.

"You better not be screwing with me, sir!"

Jonah pointed behind the boat.

"Holy Shit!"

Jonah laughed "One leg or not you'd have made a good Hammerhead snack!"

"How big you figure it is, sir?"

"Tape measure's on the console. You can hop back in and tape him."

"Seriously? He looks about twelve feet long!"

Patch hopped back to the chair opposite Jonah and slowly eased himself into place but kept staring behind the boat. He was a funny sight to behold sitting there with the drooping dull blue flipper still secured to his leg. Patch didn't seem to even notice. His mind was obviously elsewhere. "Hey, sir?"

"Yes?"

"Can we get back to dry land and have dinner? Suddenly dry sand under my feet sounds like a great idea."

"I'd have to agree with that assessment. One thing though..."

"What's that?"

"Get that damn thing off your leg."

They laughed almost all the way back to their mooring spot off Wisteria Island. While Patch was showing signs of forgetting the stresses of his past and, at least for a little while, Jonah was putting aside the thoughts and stresses of his future.

Most of the next morning was spent loading up the rented boat with one of the buried weight sets and some other gear Jonah now wanted in D.C. After reaching the marina they repeated the process, only this time they loaded all the gear from the island, the dive gear and scooter and three empty coolers onto the little trailer Jonah had borrowed from Patch's truck stop.

"I gotta tell you, Jonah, I had a great time, we should do it again when you get back from your trip."

Jonah hesitated, not sure he wanted to ruin the mood of the moment. "Hey, Patch, about that. Would you mind watching my ride and stuff while I'm gone?"

He didn't look, but knew that Patch was staring at the side of his head. "Well?"

"I will agree to temporarily watch your ride until you return from your trip."

"Super! I will need a ride up to Miami International tomorrow to catch my flight. Think you're up for that?"

"Sir, after this week I think I'm probably up for almost anything life throws my way!"

Jonah smiled and inwardly chuckled to himself...mission accomplished.

CHAPTER 35

—⚭—

Sunny Side Up

The trip to Dominica was an adventure from the takeoff at Miami International to the overnight stay in San Juan, Puerto Rico. Getting from the airport to the Marriot Resort in Puerto Rico would have been an even more challenging event if the agency hadn't arranged, through the state department of course, overnight storage of his dive gear at the airport. It was secure and had already been screened through customs for the next day's early morning flight to Dominica. That left getting to the hotel in a torrential noon hour downpour with very little clothing options to change into. Jonah ducked into a clothing shop near the hotel for a pair of light-weight linen slacks and a dark navy blue Polo shirt. Destination shopping was becoming something of a habit and it tended to be a touch on the expensive side.

The San Juan Marriot Resort and Stellaris Casino was an amazing property. As Jonah walked through the lobby he made a mental note to perhaps stay a few extra days on the return leg of the trip. Jonah dropped his bags by his room, which didn't have a view of the ocean, but rather the bustling skyline of downtown San Juan. The notes from his travel advisor recommended lunch at a hotel restaurant called the Red Coral Lounge, but

Jonah opted to sample some of the local food and fair.

When Jonah expressed an interest in eating local food at the hotel's front desk, the concierge directed him to take a cab to the Ruta del Lechón. According to the concierge, this part of San Juan was famous for its succulent roast pig and other island specialties. Two hours later, Jonah was not disappointed with his choice of lunch, but felt somewhat glutinous for the amount of food he'd managed to pack into his gut. A run on the beach would be in order, but not until he'd napped for a while and let lunch settle in a bit lower and safer than its present location.

It was almost five when he awoke from his planned quick snooze. With lunch in a much safer location he changed into his running shorts and set off down the beach for a four mile run. The sights and sounds of a strange place were always more enjoyable when someone wasn't shooting at you. He made sure that he ran fast enough to benefit from the exercise, but not too fast to miss the occasional compliments and invites from several ladies sunning themselves on the beach. To avoid the beachside distractions on the return trip he dove into the sea on the way back and swam until he was once again abreast of the Marriot.

More exhilarated than tired, but just as pumped up, he threw a towel around his shoulders and walked back through the lobby to the bank of elevators at the rear of the ground floor. He had the pleasure of riding almost all the way to his floor with six tittering teens that were too shy to talk, but bold enough to take several selfies. He was sure that at some point this evening he would be on at least six girls Snapchat or Facebook pages.

The plain fact that his flight left so damn early necessitated an early wakeup call. Jonah tried to sleep, but wrestled with his new reality. When he had been working with the SEALs, part of the reason they were so successful was due to the team concept, someone always had your back. Starting tomorrow he'd be, for all intents and purposes, on his own. After an hour of tossing and turning he got dressed and headed downstairs. He drifted past the bar and ordered a beer.

"Stella Artois please?"

"Yes, sir."

The beer arrived and Jonah poured it himself. He really didn't care if the beer snobs of the world insisted that a poured beer must have a head on it. At this point in his life, he liked what he liked.

"You are staying for a few days?" It was the bartender.

"Nope, leaving tomorrow."

"You do know that many of the ladies at the bar tonight were talking about you?"

"Really?"

Jonah didn't really care, but didn't want to be an ass either.

"They were surprised you don't have a beautiful woman with you."

Jonah laughed, not because of what the man said, but in what or whose picture flashed before his eyes when the man had said *beautiful woman*. Staring back at him through his mind's eye, with her own beautiful green eyes, was the most beautiful woman Jonah had seen in years. He said her name to himself and it made him smile.

Sunday morning's early flight to Dominica left, as most planes in this part of the world do, late. As the departure time slipped from the planned time to "Soon," Jonah started questioning his plan. The plane looked sturdy enough, but Jonah was glad it was a short hour and fifteen-minute flight. The seats were close together and there was no in-flight service, unless of course you counted the warm Coke. He didn't.

They landed at Canefield Airport, Dominica thirty minutes late, 09:20 local time. Jonah was just about to protest the imagined treatment of his luggage when two very strong individuals approached the aircraft and showed one of the baggage handlers a form of some sort. Within moments, his gear and luggage were both gently placed on a cart and heading in the general direction of baggage claim.

"Dawson?"

It took the man calling his alias name twice before he remembered the name.

"Here."

Jonah tipped the men ten dollars each and they both gave him that look of gratefulness rarely seen anymore back home.

"Can we get you transportation?"

"I've got someone coming thank you just the same."

Almost on cue a large dark blue Ford Explorer pulled up at the curb.

"Dawson?"

This time Jonah didn't hesitate and waived at the man in the Ford.

They loaded the gear and pulled away with Jonah in the back seat behind the driver.

"The apartment?"

"Yes, please."

The "apartment" that the driver referred to, as well as the driver himself, had been supplied by the agency. It was important at this point that his mission not fall victim to something so silly as a greedy driver or unscrupulous landlord.

They drove in silence for the better part of twenty minutes when the driver asked Jonah if he was "squared away."

"Yes, I believe I am. I will need information on the boat's particulars."

"There is a package for you up here, would you like it now?"

Jonah looked at his watch. "How much longer is the drive?"

As the crow flies the airport's distance to the small town with his "apartment" was just over nine miles away. Unfortunately, he wasn't a crow and it would probably be twenty miles of third world bone jarring roads.

"Probably another forty-five minutes."

Jonah laughed and peered out the slightly tinted windows. He'd probably seen everything worthwhile on the island about fifteen minutes ago.

Jonah reached forward over the seat, "I'll take the package."

The driver handed it back, it was far heavier than Jonah expected. He retrieved a small knife from his smaller dive bag and carefully slit the tape on the box. Inside the box was a smaller black plastic case. He opened that case and it contained a small pair of night vision binoculars. The next box was roughly the same size but contained a Berretta 96 .40 caliber semi-auto pistol with a threaded barrel. A smaller box contained a sound suppressor for the Beretta. He practiced with this at the CIA range before he left and all you could hear was a loud click as the slide flew back and forth. Also in the box was a package of eight photos taken from different angles of Atash's compound. Two of the images were obviously taken at night with an infrared or low light camera as everything was in the negative. He could clearly see the security detail at their respective posts and either a roving patrol or replacements. Jonah checked the time the image was taken. Ten seventeen local. That increased the likelihood that it was a roving patrol. For his current plan, this was all good information, but irrelevant to his success.

The other images showed him that, at the time the images were taken, nobody was moored to the northwest of Atash's cove. All favorable information.

At the bottom of the box were the documents for the boat, what he assumed was ten thousand dollars in cash and a tube of sunscreen. A small handwritten note said *Have a good dive* and was signed *the guys you left behind in the office*. Somebody had a very interesting sense of humor...

Jonah tucked all of his new goodies into the small dive bag and handed the envelope with the images back to the driver as the instructions on the envelope indicated.

"Everything in order?"

"Right as rain."

The remainder of the trip was bumpy but otherwise uneventful and they were unloaded and "squared away" in his apartment in less than an hour.

"Fridge is empty," stated Jonah.

"I'm your meal companion while you're here."

"Excellent," said Jonah with an honest grin.

Jonah watched the man walk away toward the car.

"Think you'll be hungry by one?"

"Definitely!" hollered Jonah down to the man now back at the car.

The man held up his index finger and without turning around, got in the car and drove away.

Jonah looked at his watch. He'd have just enough time for some calisthenics and a quick shower.

Looking around the apartment, Jonah quickly realized this probably wasn't a typical residence in the little town of Scotts Head, Dominica. The door, although very traditional and similar in appearance to many of the doors he had already seen on the island, was solid steel and set in a steel frame. It would be a very difficult door to breech. He ran his fingers over the door's locking mechanism. In addition to having a separate locking system for the apartment's occupants, the door had both a horizontal and vertical locking system. He'd have to look at getting one of these in his apartment back home. When the lock was turned from the inside, dead bolts slide into all four steel sides of the door frame. That was awesome.

Although from the outside the windows were the standard three feet off the ground, examination of the inside wall revealed that the window opening between the two foot level and the five foot level was poured concrete.

Jonah had to smile. What, or whoever, the agency expected to visit would not have an easy time getting access to this apartment's occupants.

The shower felt amazing and he was dressed in his very best island shabby when the driver returned just before one o'clock.

"Hey, we never got around to some basic pleasantries earlier, like your name."

"Mr. Dawson, you can pick whatever name you wish for me." The man smiled a thin, stone cold smile.

"Oh," was all Jonah could come up with.

"Do you know anyone named Marcus?"

Jonah thought for a moment. "No, sir, I don't believe so."

"Very well."

The man stuck his tanned hand out and smiled a weathered grin. "Mr. Dawson, Marcus Westerly at your service."

Jonah reached out and shook the man's deceptively strong hand. "Nice to know you Marcus."

The man's voice was now as hard as steel. "You say that only because you don't."

Jonah was rocked back by the man's comment. He attempted to mask his shock but was certain the man had seen his face.

The man was walking back to the car.

"Lock up Mr. Dawson, it's time for lunch."

CHAPTER 36

—⚇—

Hocus Pocus

On Saturday morning, one of the most spectacular water main ruptures in downtown Washington occurred right in front of the BOATSS building. The fact that there was no water main under that section of the road hadn't hampered the FBI and other groups from staging the elaborate hoax on anyone within a line of sight of the project. The building directly across from the BOATSS building and both sides had been closed by the fire marshal for obvious safety reasons. The contractor had been promised a $50,000 bonus to be done by five a.m. Monday morning.

"Done," in this case meant no evidence that they had ever been there. Even the tops of the normally conspicuous stainless steel posts had been custom fitted with cobbles that matched the surrounding sidewalk. Jewels had seen the pictures over the weekend and was unable to discern any abnormality in the sidewalk. As a last precaution a thin layer of dirty sand had been haphazardly strewn across the area from the pile left near the exterior wall of the building. To the casual passerby it appeared to be yet another dirty job site in D.C.

On Monday morning at 11:54, exactly one minute before Maureen's calendar said he would be there, Mr. Ramón Rodriquez showed up with a rather distressed look on his face. He obviously feared the worst when he'd heard the news about the water main break. A job like that could have, and normally would have taken weeks to repair. He seemed relieved and looked around, rather conspicuously, at the area. Maureen walked out to meet him and they had walked away for their lunch.

What was different about the plaza were that several new high tech HD cameras that had been placed in several surrounding buildings by the FBI. Only two of the cameras faced the BOATSS building, the rest were placed to document who, if anyone would come and attempt to film the attack. They were ready, or thought they were, for whatever was coming.

It had been a *long lunch* kind of lunch and Maureen returned to her desk at 1:30. No one ever seemed to notice when she came and left and that was fine with her, especially on a day like today. A new tech guy she hadn't seen before waved at her and smiled. He had a visitor badge and an escort from downstairs. She feigned being friendly and smiled back. Maureen looked down at her calendar, pulled the cap off her red sharpie and put a few more hearts around today's lunch date. Glancing to her right she smiled at the travel brochures pinned to her partition. It won't be long now my love...

What Maureen Templeton didn't know was that the new tech guy was an FBI surveillance expert who had photographed every item on or near her desk as well as her now infamous calendar. Each new doodle would be scrutinized and evaluated for changes or anything notable. They had installed a mirror program on her computers that allowed an FBI agent in the basement to see in real time everything that came across her screen. From this point forward she would be the most watched woman in the District of Columbia.

—m—

Although it would technically be accurate to say the men had physically eaten lunch together, it would be a stretch to say the men enjoyed each other's company. This man took his job very seriously and was all business. He even ate his sandwich with one hand while keeping his right hand low in his lap. While Jonah hadn't seen the man's weapon, he assumed two things right off. It was not only there...but the man would be lethal in its application if the situation arose.

"Can we go past the marina after lunch to check out the boat?"

The man flashed what Jonah now knew was a totally phony smile. "Of course sir, it's only about a mile down the coast. I'm not sure calling it a *marina* will help you get your head wrapped around the boat's location, but we'll call it a *marina* just for shits and giggles."

Jonah shook his head in bewilderment. He would have to remember to quit this job before it consumed him like this guy.

"Terrific, is it all fueled and ready to go?"

"It's all set up with extended range fuel tanks and two week's provisions for your dive trip."

"Good communications gear?"

"About what you'd expect."

The man's coy answer belied Jonah's knowledge that some of the best communications gear had been temporarily affixed for his mission.

"Super! Are we done here?"

Jonah left the table leaving "Marcus" to pay the tab and walked down to the car and waited for Marcus.

Marcus joined him a few moments later. "That was pretty shitty man! You could have at least got the tip."

Jonah laughed. "You are correct, I *could* have. Keep busting my balls and I'll make this a very long afternoon for you."

They were both in the hot car now and safe from prying ears.

Marcus mumbled what Jonah thought was, "Sorry."

Jonah glanced over to his left, but the man didn't meet his gaze. "What?"

"Don't make me say it again."

"What's your beef with me? I piss in your Wheaties or something?"

"Or something...can we leave it at that for now?"

"Sure thing."

They rolled the windows down and drove along the shore road to a point where they were adjacent to where the boat was moored in Soufriere

Bay. The man had been correct, calling this spot a marina was like putting lipstick on a pig. The boat was anchored about one hundred yards off shore and was covered with a large dirty paint splattered tarpaulin.

A young teenage boy ran up to the driver side window and looked suspiciously through the window at Jonah. After holding back his comments until Marcus nodded and said everything was okay, the boy reported that nobody had approached the boat but several people had walked by and made comments.

"Thank you, Jhonny."

The boy walked off toward the water and tried his hand at skipping some stones.

"His name's Jhonny?"

"Oh yeah," the man chuckled, "like I'm Marcus."

Both men laughed and the tension lifted just enough to know the emotion was genuine.

"I've been stationed here for just over three years and I'm here to tell you the boredom and the complacency of this garden spot will get you killed as surely as a bullet in Cape Town or Morocco."

They sat quietly for a few minutes just staring out to sea.

"When's high tide tomorrow?"

Marcus pulled out a local newspaper and dragged his finger across the posted tide chart.

"04:10."

"Ouch," said Jonah.

"The moon sets at 04:30 so we'll plan on being here around 04:45. How long do you figure it will take to get your gear onboard?"

"Assuming we'll be taking a skiff out to the boat..."

"Yeah."

"Then it won't take but ten minutes to load and be a speck on the horizon."

"Are you ready to head back?"

"I need to talk to the boy for a moment."

Marcus walked out to where the boy was still trying to get a stone to skip. Whatever he said to the boy set off a very animated chain of events that had the boy clapping wildly.

"What was that all about?" Jonah asked when he returned to the car.

"I told him I was proud of him for doing such a good job for us today."

"That's it?"

"Well, I might have told him we would use the boat when you were done with it."

Both men laughed and waved at the boy as they drove away. It occurred to Jonah that he now had yet another reason to come back safely. As suddenly as the thought of returning safely crossed his mind so did an image of Jewels, and he smiled all the way back to the "apartment."

—⁓—

Four o'clock came earlier than Jonah expected and he did a quick workout to clear his head then a fast shower. Marcus, as his driver wished to be called, arrived promptly at four twenty and after a quick look around Jonah locked the apartment and they headed down to the boat. The roads were deserted at this time of the morning with only the occasional rat scurrying past a dumpster as they drove down the road that hugged the shoreline. He felt a little bad for some of the people in the small town as their car woke up at least three roosters as they passed by.

The beach was dark as they dragged the gear toward a small skiff near the sea wall. Everything looked different at high tide and his perspective on distances was slightly off. This afternoon there was several hundred feet of sand before the surf line and now at 04:40 he could see the foaming surf a mere fifty feet away.

Marcus knocked on the overturned skiff and whispered, "Jhonny."

"Buenos Dias, senior," whispered a voice that Jonah recognized as the young man from yesterday afternoon.

"Flip the skiff Jhonny while we get the rest of the gear."

While Jonah watched, the young man flipped the small skiff and dragged it single handedly to the waterline.

"What's his story?" asked Jonah.

"He's sort of my unofficially adopted son," whispered Marcus. "He's safer on the streets than with me and our arrangement is mutually beneficial. Are you ready to go?"

The men each had a handhold on the scooter and set it down next to the skiff.

"Slide it out a little farther into the water Jhonny."

"Nice meeting you Jhonny. Thanks for all your help this morning."

The men placed the scooter in the back to offset the weight of the other equipment and Jonah standing at the front of the small boat.

"I'll be back in ten minutes, Jhonny, and we'll go grab breakfast. Push us out buddy and don't tell me the water's cold!"

The sounds of the small trolling motor were indistinguishable from the sounds of the small waves on the sandy shore and the electric motor was more than capable of pushing the boat out through the gentle surf. They were alongside the much larger boat in minutes and with the release of three well placed trucker's hitch knots the tarp had been stripped from the boat, folded and placed onto the starboard bench seat in the dive boat.

Jonah swung his legs over the side of the larger boat and dropped his small dive bag on the seat.

"Alright, Marcus, what do you say we get this party started?"

Marcus handed the bags of gear up to Jonah one at a time with the heavy scooter last. It was a cool piece of equipment, but Jonah was looking forward to not carrying it around for very much longer.

"Try the engine Dawson. Not much point in this exercise if it won't start."

The engine turned over with not so much as a cough and all the gauges indicated all the boat's systems were for the moment functioning.

"Thanks for the help, Marcus, see you when I see you."

Jonah dragged two of the larger bags down into the cabin and as he came back to the rear of the boat he realized he hadn't heard a response from Marcus.

"Marcus?"

Jonah looked over the side of the boat and the small skiff was no longer alongside. The man who Jonah called "Marcus" was already more than half way back to the shore.

—✺—

The trip to Martinique mapped out at just over forty-five miles and would take an hour with the boat's throttle wide open. Showing up in this particular boat that early in the morning would raise eyebrows so Jonah set the cruise control to just over fifteen knots and set about organizing his equipment. He did a communications check with whatever assets were tracking his every move. Jonah would be living off the boat for the next several days and getting his stuff organized to look like he was just a diver, took a bit of work. The boat had lots of the usual bells and whistles for a boat of its kind and those pieces of equipment were out in the open and in plain sight. The more specialized equipment had been installed with Velcro under several out of the way locations. If it came down to it he could simply rip the equipment out and throw it over the side with no trace of its existence remaining behind.

Jonah looked at the plan as it stood at the moment. He would anchor the boat in the bay to the east of Atash's compound, just on the other side of a quarter mile long peninsula of land. He hoped to do two reconnaissance missions of the beach area in front of the compound, by water, to get his approach and departure timing down and to set the waypoints into the scooter's GPS system. On mission day, he would have more than enough on his mind and not want to be messing with inputting coordinates into the scooter.

Jonah brought up the Garmin navigation system and using the ocean current overlay looked for where he would send both Atash and the scooter at the conclusion of the mission. He picked a spot ten miles to the northeast of where he'd have the boat anchored. Jonah carefully transcribed the coordinates into the navigation system on the scooter and hit *set*. If all went according to plan, the scooter would take Atash's body far out to sea and then nature would do the "circle of life" thing. Jonah opened up one of the smaller nondescript boxes that were delivered by Marcus yesterday. The most noticeable feature was a large faced device that looked remarkably similar to his dive watch. The difference, and it was significant, was that attached to the back of this particular watch was a quarter pound lump of plastic explosive. He carefully attached the device right above the serial and model number plate on the scooter. He would start the timer once he returned to the boat.

Although the mission prep was exciting he couldn't help but miss the whole team aspect that he'd grown so accustomed to in the navy. There was no hand off or second chances and he would live or die in the next few days on his own successes or failures.

It would have been difficult to miss the Island of Martinique. It was the only land mass he'd been looking at for the past half hour. He glanced around to make sure all his non diving goodies were stowed out of sight of prying eyes and he slowed the boat to five knots.

Jonah hoped throwing a fishing line in the water would help remove any suspicion from early morning curious eyes. He worked his way into the small cove he'd chosen to drop anchor and dropped his small bow anchor. The line drew taught with about thirty feet of distance between the anchor's location and the cleat on the bow. With the tide still on its way out, the large boat slowly swung around so the bow faced the shoreline. Jonah popped the canopy top to stay out of the morning sun and also block anyone on the ridge from seeing into his boat.

The ridge on the peninsula dividing where he was and Atash's compound was significant if anything were to go wrong. From the small sandy beach, currently off his boat's bow, it was only one tenth of a mile over the small rise to the compound. Of course that short of a distance could just as easily work against him as well. This was a small community, talk of a really nice boat in the next bay just might get him some unwanted attention. Jonah pulled out the paint splattered tarp and draped it over just enough of the boat to break up its silhouette.

Jonah pulled out his nautical charts and saw that at low tide, in his current position, he would only have three feet of water under his propeller. He had tied the anchor line off at the cleat nearest the canopy so with one strong tug he could set himself adrift without exposing himself to view or potentially hostile gunfire. During the mission tomorrow he would have the boat farther from the shore and pointed toward the open sea.

At noon, Jonah decided to do an overland recon and see exactly how far out in the little bay Atash would do his daily float. He brought his binoculars and a big goofy sunhat. On missions like this you wanted to be all things to all people. Today, he was a visiting ornithologist from the United Kingdom studying the habits of the Island's White-breasted Thrasher. He'd come with notes and everything a visiting ornithologist would be expected to have.

The walk up the hill had taken a very short amount of time and Jonah found himself cresting the top sooner than he'd anticipated. It was just approaching one o'clock and as of yet there was no sign of movement in the compound...at all.

CHAPTER 37

—◊—

Kesheh Research Center

Behrouz knew he wasn't supposed to, but he had found a way to access the big world internet and accessed an old email account of the major's from years ago when he was back at University. He didn't have very many messages as his spam filter was set to only accept emails from established contacts. One of those contacts was the dean of his University's College of Computer Science and Engineering. According to the email, some group was looking to make contact with anyone interested in taking on a project which entailed programming industrial machines remotely. He placed it in its own folder he'd named "Later."

Things here were getting a bit sporty and he had already created several digital video loops of himself busily working at his computer or reading something relevant in a software instruction manual. He had several versions that he was cycling through the room's security feeds when he only wanted to appear busy working. He was done with the programming of the aircraft mission and was basically stalling while he looked for an exit strategy from the mess he found himself in.

—◊—

Behrouz knew that he had to stop the madness that emanated from this subterranean fortress but at the moment, the *how* escaped him. He knew all the outbound emails were watched, so getting a message to the Americans that way was a definite no go. In a perfect world, he needed several things to come together in fairly rapid succession. He needed to get word to the Americans that the bomb laden planes would be inbound, and tell them not only where to strike the mountain, but when. He had a reasonably good grasp on almost all of the mission related stuff but the part where *he* didn't die, still eluded him.

He began working on embedding a packet of info in a transmission that he could send in the outgoing data stream. It was a loop and simply gave the GPS coordinates of the facility over and over again. He then called up the PDF file plans of the facility. Behrouz looked for the most critical areas such as air ducts, elevator shafts and entrances. With each page he became more and more impressed with his predecessor's engineering brilliance. It would be very difficult to deal this facility a critical blow with any conventional weapon he was aware of. He did know that the Americans spend untold billions of dollars on weapons' research each year and it was quite possible they would have the right tool for the job. He wasn't a structural engineer by any stretch of the imagination, but he managed to put together five pages of files he thought might help anyone planning an air assault. Behrouz then turned that into an executable file and placed it into a draft message as well.

—⁓—

Jonah had brought two bottles of water and already finished the first bottle when he noticed activity at the compound. First on the beach were two security men with both automatic weapons and binoculars. They walked to the water's edge and scanned several boats that were several hundred feet away and they also spent some time looking at the ocean itself. The only way to see anything under the water would be to have polarized lenses in the binoculars. Even with polarized lenses, they wouldn't be seeing anything clearly out more than maybe twenty feet. Two more men now walked down the beach and positioned themselves approximately half way between the tree line and the water. Jonah shifted his gaze to the big house and the enormous glass window that faced the ocean. It was tough to make out, but he would swear he could see a man standing there in his swim trunks; arms folded watching the ritual on the beach. Eventually a third pair of men walked him from the main house down to the water's edge.

Jonah was low to the ground and placed several tufts of vegetation around his head and shoulders to break up his profile as well as the binoculars. He could see them clearly but didn't read lips so had to infer from his histrionics that the little man was Atash and that he wasn't happy being told something about the ocean. As Jonah watched, the man uncoiled the nylon line they used to tether the raft to a tie down in the sand. Jonah counted the number of times the man took a coil of line of the larger coil resting in his hand. Calculating that every coil of line unwound was three feet, the man had given Atash enough rope to go out fifty or so feet. Jonah glanced back towards the house just as the slightly built man walked to the water's edge. He was a perfect match to the photos they had on file back at Langley. The man splashed some water on himself and sat down backwards on the raft. Jonah watched as the man slowly paddled himself out until the line pulled taught. It was perfect. The water from about twenty-five feet out transitioned to darker shades of blue seemingly with every foot. The most important part to Jonah was this looked like the minimum distance the man ever went out. Jonah smiled, more than half of the coil of rope still sat neatly coiled on top of the small concrete post up by the guards.

—⁂—

Jonah spent the afternoon trying to catch his dinner and finally, after significant effort, had three fish worthy of eating in his bait well. He looked over his menagerie of fish and decided to keep the Grouper and let the others go for another day. It was the largest and he had a pan searing recipe from Patch that he was aching to try out. He checked the boat's cold storage locker and found the white wine and butter. In the dry goods locker, all the seasonings he had asked for were stocked. Dinner would be an adventure either way and whether or not it tasted good, remembered forever.

Everything on the boat was modularized and went together like a very expensive Lego set. Fortunately, all the relevant cooking equipment and its assembly instructions were in the small cabin with the rest of the equipment manuals. It took twenty minutes to set up but was a masterpiece of engineering. The two burner gas stove was connected to a propane tank somewhere below deck by a quick disconnect connection. The whole cooking apparatus was attached to the boat's stern and designed to be rapidly dumped off the boat and into the water in the event of a cooking "emergency."

Jonah cracked his first and last beer at seven o'clock while watching the tropical sunset off the stern of the large boat. If he could set aside the reason he was here in the first place, and the fact that he could never tell anyone why he was here, this place with its beautiful waters and amazing views was flat out one of the prettiest places he'd ever traveled to.

—⚏—

The birds had awakened him to a beautiful morning of calm seas and clear skies. It had taken a while for him to get used to the rocking motion of the boat last night but he had last seen his watch at 10:40. Seven hours was more sleep than he had received in recent memory so he stretched and got on with his day. He turned on the news, boring as usual, same shit different day. He flipped it over to the weather forecast.

"Increasing cloudiness as a low pressure system
works its way through the Lesser Antilles's over the next several days.
Clouds and rain building in intensity with ocean swells at above
normal heights in the next twenty four to thirty six hours."

It took Jonah a full minute to comprehend what he was hearing. As if he'd been struck with a Taser, Jonah suddenly remembered that Martinique, the island he was moored next to, was in the small chain of islands referred to as the Lesser Antilles's. With the storm that close he had either today or tomorrow at the latest to complete his mission. Jonah got on his encrypted satellite phone and texted:

Weather requires accelerated mission profile.
Are assets available between 1700Z-1900Z today or tomorrow?
Standing by...

The response took less than a minute...

Green for the next 48 hours effective receipt of this transmission
Have a safe dive...

Somewhere high above the island was a watchful eye that could no doubt see his every move. Jonah stepped to the rear of the boat and gave two thumbs up accompanied by a great big smile.

Jonah looked at his watch. Nine twenty. He thought about the plan and realized that if he swam around the corner and the currents weren't cooperating causing him to miss his window today, he'd have tomorrow. On the other hand, if he waited until tomorrow and Atash thought the surf was too rough...the mission would be scrubbed. It wouldn't be that difficult to add the missing two waypoints on the way in if he planned ahead. Or maybe he could get them off the boat's Garmin system. Jonah pulled up the map of where he was and then selected a spot just off the peninsula that was twenty feet deep and hit enter. Success! He did it two more times creating a return trip that placed him over a hundred feet from the coastline and kept him in water deep enough that he couldn't be seen from the ridge or a boat moored off the point. He copied the GPS coordinates from the Garmin out to five decimal places and entered them in the GPS module on the scooter.

Starting the engine connected to the generator, Jonah brought the scooter up to full charge. The indicator was already green but five more minutes of power on this dive might make a huge difference.

Jonah began the slightly arduous post mission planning of the disposal of Atash's body. When he was done, he had programmed three mission profiles into the scooter's GPS interface module. The first profile took him to a point three hundred feet from where he had seen Atash on the raft. He would take it in by hand from that point. The second program would enable him to do an emergency return to the boat if necessary. The third and final program would take Atash's lifeless body an hour out to sea at a heading of 040° with gradual increases in depth. Once the battery charge ran out, the scooter would sink to the bottom. Twelve hours, and well after Jonah departed the area, the plastic explosive would create a frenzied feeding event two hundred feet or so below the surface.

At twelve thirty, Jonah placed all his heavy equipment on the diving deck at the rear of the boat. After running his mental checklist one more time, he slipped into the water with as little splash as possible. He'd left the radio on a local French music station in the hopes anyone passing by would steer clear of an occupied boat. With the boat now positioned farther away from the shore, it was unlikely that someone would swim out to the boat uninvited. The rebreather was working beautifully as was the scooter and the first program was bringing him steadily, point to point, around the end of the peninsula and into the bay were Atash lived. It was just over two hundred yards from the point of the peninsula to his planned ambush spot. It would take less than a minute to cover the distance. He paused the scooter. It was ten after one and he was a touch early. Jonah sank to the bottom and watched the amazing variety of tropical fish for five more minutes. It was time. Jonah headed to his predetermined spot, rolled over onto his back… and waited.

He was happy that he'd remembered his drift spike. Without the spike, he would have been rolling uncontrollably back and forth on the sandy bottom.

There, about fifty feet out, he could see the man's hands back paddling the raft out into the bay. For whatever reason, he was coming out farther today and Jonah goosed the throttle of the scooter to back up about fifty feet. Jonah watched the man while readying his spear gun. He thought of the millions of deaths this one man's actions had caused and removed all guilt from himself for his pending actions. He'd modified his original plan so that Atash would experience some of the fear so many of his victims had experienced.

Jonah waited patiently for the man to put his hand in the water one last time. In one blurred motion, Jonah slashed the raft and pulled the helpless man into the water. Jonah brought the panicked man to the bottom and let him live and struggle long enough to know he was being killed by a man before he shot him directly into his heart. With one hand firmly grasping the line to the spear, he reached back and gunned scooter's engine.

From the shoreline, the men couldn't believe what they were seeing. From their vantage point their boss had been jerked off his raft and into the water. Even at this distance they could see the blood in the water. There was nothing they could do but shout at each other.

Jonah's forward speed was being seriously compromised by the added weight of Atash's crooked body. He hit pause and secured Atash's dead bleeding body to the cleat at the rear of the scooter and put a half hitch loop around his neck. This straightened the body out and their progress through the water was much faster. He was glad he'd opted to use the GPS to get back to the boat as it took them on a wide arc around the point.

Jonah had just come alongside the boat when he noticed they had acquired a following, literally. Unfortunately, it was the gray kind with very big teeth. Jonah needed to work quickly because as he watched, two more of the shark's buddies joined the party. First, he used his underwater camera to take a picture of the dead man's face. Atash's eyes were still wide open as if he didn't grasp his current situation. History had proven that someone always wants a picture. With his dive knife, Jonah removed Atash's right index finger and placed it in his small mesh bag. Thankfully, it drew no more additional blood for the now circling future diners. He activated the timer on the explosive charge, entered the third mission profile and hit enter.

As he watched Atash's body being quickly dragged away by the scooter he relished the thought that he would be taken apart piece by piece. Jonah remained motionless until the larger of the sharks made the decision that following the already dead body would be far less work. His friends apparently agreed, and after one more circle of the boat, followed the body out to sea.

Shedding the rebreather and the camouflage suit was paramount to appearing normal as quickly as possible. He moved slowly, but purposefully, wasting no motion getting the boat ready for his trip back to Dominica. He pulled the lines releasing the tarp which he then gathered and folded quickly. He started the engines, backing up slowly until the anchor was free and safely onboard. Lines secured, and hatches locked he started the second engine and nudged the throttle forward. After a few moments, he pulled the throttle back to twenty knots. Jonah was definitely in a hurry but he didn't want to appear in a hurry. The French radar on Martinique probably wouldn't be watching for a speeding boat, but why test that theory?

As he passed the five mile mark he texted in his password and the phrase, "Feet dry in ninety minutes." Jonah reached down and nudged the boat's speed back to thirty knots.

He received his response a moment later, "Dinner's waiting."

On shore, Atash's former security detail got together and agreed on the story they would tell anyone who asked. A large shark had obviously dragged their employer off his raft and taken him out to sea. Of course there were more holes in the story than in Atash's raft but who would say it didn't happen just the way they'd said...

CHAPTER 38

—◆◆◆—

Feet Dry

The thrill of driving the beast of a boat was almost more than Jonah could stand. The roar of the twin engines had his adrenaline started and he was, after all, an adrenaline junkie at heart. Unfortunately, today's situation called for him to keep his speed slow enough not to attract the attention of the French authorities on Martinique...but fast enough to get himself safely back on Dominica.

With the boat's cruise control locked at thirty knots, his Garmin navigation system would have him back in the small marina on Dominica in another forty-five minutes.

Jonah made good use of his time during the first few minutes of his trip by scanning in Atash's finger print on a device the agency had provided for him. It was just slightly larger than one of those credit card gizmo's that attach to smart phones for credit card payments. He'd scanned the finger three times and sent three separate files to a waiting group of technicians. When they were happy with the image they told him so and he quickly tossed the finger overboard. It was easy to imagine that the finger hadn't made it all the way to the bottom. Jonah laughed, he was probably ready to explain almost anything about his trip, but he wasn't yet talented enough to explain what a dead man's finger was doing on his boat.

Jonah looked around at all his gear and thought through his mental checklist. He was returning early from his dive trip because of the approaching storm and had only been able to dive once and take some pictures. Rather than explain why his spear gun had no spear he reloaded it with the extra spear he'd brought for this very purpose. After sending Atash's picture to Langley he threw the used memory card overboard and replaced it with the one that contained the pictures of tropical fish he'd photographed when he'd first arrived in the small bay on Martinique.

Looking in the mirror, Jonah ran his fingers through his long hair one last time. It had taken him just over three years to grow, but it was time. He cut the pony tail first and threw it overboard then gradually took the rest of the hair layer by layer until he finished with a shaved head. It looked nasty.

The Island of Dominica had been in view for some time and he marveled at the Garmin's technology that steered the boat to the west around the half mile peninsula before taking the boat back eastward into the little bay.

Jonah disengaged the auto-pilot and brought the boat to within fifty feet of the shoreline. The small skiff with Marcus aboard was alongside his hull before Jonah even dropped anchor.

"Get in the skiff," said a seemingly irritated Marcus.

"What? No hello or welcome back?" asked Jonah.

"Get in the damn skiff and take nothing with you that you're not wearing. NOW!"

Jonah recognized the tone and complied quickly.

"Go to the sea wall and Jhonny will be along shortly and tell you what to do."

Before Jonah could say another word, the boat, Marcus and all his cool toys were rapidly heading north out of the bay.

Jonah dragged the small skiff up onto the beach, well above the tide mark, and proceeded to the wall where he took a seat.

"Do you want a water mister?"

"Hi, Jhonny."

"Who's Jhonny? I'm Alejo."

"Sure, I'll take a water."

Obviously something wasn't right and he needed to get out of this exposed area...soon.

The boy, who he had previously known as Jhonny, handed him a bottle of water and pointed to a small crumpled up paper lunch sack near Jonah's feet.

"Mister you shouldn't litter."

Jonah protested, "It's not mine kiddo."

"Marcus says differently."

Now intrigued, Jonah looked at the brown paper bag.

"What the hell?" he mumbled as he bent over to pick up the bag. It had some weight to it and as he turned to comment to the boy...he had vanished into thin air.

Jonah opened the bag and looked inside. It contained a passport in his alias's name and a picture to match his current appearance and a ticket to San Juan that left in two hours. It also had a small hand written note.

"Your bag with a change of clothes is under the first seat to your north. Following seas...Marcus."

Jonah found the bag exactly where it was supposed to be and looked for a place to change. There was a small cantina on the other side of the road and he ducked inside to change.

"Eric Dawson" emerged a few moments later looking as island chic as possible including a hat large enough to cover his melon sized pasty white head. He looked leaner and meaner than with the pony tail but at the moment, it fit his demeanor rather well.

At his current location, Jonah was certain he wouldn't get a ride to the airport in time for his six o'clock flight, if he could get a ride at all. He'd been walking north on the beach road when a car pulled up slowly alongside him. Jonah's instinct said run, but he hesitated and the man's window was already down.

"Are dgew Eric?"

Jonah caught his *no* just fast enough.

"Yes!"

"Mr. Marcus say dgew need a ride to the airport. Get in?"

Jonah dropped heavily into the back seat. The car's suspension reminded him of his car back in Florida. He had anticipated a bumpy ride but this car floated on the straight aways and was tight in the turns. In addition, any thoughts of the man's driving skills vanished after three or four turns on the windy road. Twice Jonah caught himself staring out the back window in awe that they hadn't yet killed or maimed a person or animal. His driver was devoid of all feelings of responsibility in his quest to get Jonah to the airport. With adrenaline pumping, Jonah decided to enjoy the ride. It wasn't as if he had a choice.

The man had seen Jonah's initial anxiety and then emotional transformation to enjoyment.

"Meester Marcus sayed you would like this car, yes?" he had shouted over the noise in and around the car.

"Yes, it's like mine at home," Jonah yelled at the man while they rounded yet another turn that a normal car would not have made.

Jonah reached up out of habit and grabbed a handle above the door that he knew for a fact wasn't an original manufacture's part.

Jonah looked at his watch. It read 5:13. "How much longer?"

"Two minutes!"

The man down shifted twice, made a hard left and passed the sign for departing flights.

At exactly five fifteen, Jonah was dropped off at the curb in front of *Air Caribbean*.

"Mr. Marcus sayed five fifteen! Dgew here at five fifteen!"

Despite being at a complete stop, Jonah's heart was still pounding in his chest. He laughed. If time permitted, he would have seriously considered having the man drive him back to town again.

"Adios, my friend. Tell Marcus I enjoyed the ride."

The terminal was far more crowded than it had been only a few days before, with customs and security personnel seemingly overwhelmed with the sheer number of people. Although his Spanish was a touch rusty, he understood the gist of what the weather forecasters on the TV in the terminal were saying about the approaching storm. Apparently the storm, now named "Allan," had turned to a more northerly track, intensified and was projected to start making landfall tomorrow morning as a Category three storm. Anybody who could get out was trying to do just that.

He was waiting in line to check in when he was approached by an older man wearing an *Air Caribbean* uniform. Again, his gut said run, but he played it cool.

"Mr. Dawson?"

"Yes," answered Jonah as calmly as he could given his current circumstances.

"You are already checked in, sir, if you have no baggage to check you may follow me."

Jonah followed closely as the older gentleman made light conversation.

"Did you enjoy your visit with us?"

"Yes." replied Jonah somewhat warily.

"It's unfortunate that the weather has turned ugly."

The man looked up into Jonah's eyes nearly a foot above his. He outstretched his hand, "Mr. Dawson, sometimes the approach of a storm can be a fortunate occurrence. Wouldn't you agree?"

Then the old man did something Jonah hadn't expected... He'd winked.

It took a moment for it to sink in.

"Enjoy your trip home, sir."

"Thank you."

Jonah shook the man's weathered outstretched hand, turned and headed up the stairs to the plane.

The trip to San Juan had taken only ninety minutes due to the already increased winds from the storm.

Jonah was on the ground in San Juan at seven thirty. He'd actually hoped for a longer flight so he could decompress and think about the past forty-eight hours. As he passed through the gate, the flight attendant handed him a baggage tag. At this point Jonah learned not to make a scene, but to just go with the flow. He proceeded down to the baggage level and approached the woman sitting at the desk. He smiled and handed her the slip of paper.

"Good evening, sir."

"Good evening," Jonah replied as cheerfully as he could muster.

"Would you like all of your checked items or just the actual luggage?"

"Could I see how everything looks?"

"Yes, sir! I'll have someone walk you back."

In a moment a middle age man escorted Jonah back to where his items were apparently waiting.

Jonah was speechless. Sitting on the floor of the cargo area was his rebreather rig and two leather bags.

"Sir?"

"I'll take the bags. Can the larger item remain here on courtesy hold?"

Absolutely, sir! Whenever you are ready to either retrieve them or continue to another destination. I see your paper work's done for a ninety-six hour hold in courtesy storage."

Jonah grabbed his bag and headed for the door.

"Enjoy your stay!" shouted the man to Jonah's back. He waved without turning around.

Due in part to the small size of the front desk staff at the Marriot, and the fact that passing himself off under a different name less than forty-eight hours after staying there as "Jonah West," Jonah had been booked at a different hotel for tonight's lay over. After checking into the hotel and getting settled in his room he called the twenty-four hour operations line at Langley to check in.

He showered, came back downstairs after an hour and sat in the lounge area near the pool drinking his now second beer. The eye candy was young and very pretty, but he really only wanted to talk to one person tonight. He finished his second beer in one continuous swallow, looked at his watch and dialed the number.

"Hello."

"Hi Jewels, it's Jonah."

They'd talked for more than an hour about everything and nothing at all. In the end, they both resolved they would keep in touch. At this point in his life, Jonah thought he knew a brush off when he heard it and he was fine with the way the conversation wound down. He'd already said good-bye and had his finger poised above the "END" button when he heard her voice calling his name.

"Jonah?"

"Yes?"

"Good, I caught you. Hey, do you have a ride when you get back to D.C.?"

"Actually, I'm driving back into town."

Jewels was silent for a few seconds while she gathered her thoughts. Well...that certainly sucked...

"Jewels?"

"Well, give me a ring when you're back in town."

"Sure thing," he'd managed before she was gone.

Jonah stared at his phone. "I'll be damned," he whispered to no one in particular.

CHAPTER 39

—m—

It's Complicated

Just over fifteen hundred miles away, Jewels was staring at her phone as well.

Jewels tipped over sideways on her couch and lay still for several moments replaying the conversation with Jonah in her mind.

"That's it; I've lost my damn mind!"

Jewels rolled off her side and leaned forward just enough to put her phone down on the coffee table and pick up her now half full goblet of Merlot. She settled back into her couch exhaling as she slowly let the cushions envelop her. Like she didn't have enough shit to worry about in her chaotic life! Now she was bringing a man into her life she had known for what? Maybe two weeks, three at best. An older man at that! Had he been married? Widowed? Divorced? Crap! The man could have three kids and a mange afflicted dog for God's sake!

Jewels took another large swallow of her wine. She was almost thirty-five and had been in only one semi-serious relationship in her adult life and, as of this evening at eight thirty, it was apparently going nowhere. Perhaps a change would be a good thing. She had a sense Mr. Jonah West wouldn't be playing any head games with her, but would more than likely, unlike her current situation, be playful at all the right times...

At the moment, however, Jewels had some other, more pressing issues and switched over her efforts from the right "creative" side of her brain to the left, and more "logical," side of her brain.

So far, the idea and subsequent plan to track down the source of the signal was going slower than expected. What they'd learned so far was that whoever was behind the data stream that controlled the freighter *Shooting Star* had their computer systems behind some serious fire walls and the system itself was very tightly controlled. What she and the team needed was a break.

They knew their former professor Harem Fallahi, now Major Fallahi was somehow involved, but that was as far as that particular line of logic had gone. Jewels struggled to remember anything she could about the man and couldn't remember anything precise as far as interests or hobbies. The only take away from their relationship in the classroom was the man's incredible ego. He was, in many ways, a classic narcissist. Could it be that simple?

She did remember on several occasions delighting in his abilities when they came to him with a problem.

What the hell, she'd work with Gina and team Katar to contrive an email that would appeal to his inflated ego. At this point? What could it hurt?

—◊—

Across town, Mitch was in that especially dark place many guys go when their love life seems to be drifting sideways. The incredible pressure at work was only made bearable by what he thought was a stable relationship when he clocked out at the end of the day.

"Rick, what the hell happened?"

"Shit, buddy, I thought you guys were solid. Maybe it's like they say that stress either drives you together or apart?"

"But we *were* together," groaned a despondent Mitch.

"Together in your mind or hers?" asked Rick after a brief pause.

"What the hell does that mean?"

"I'm just saying, maybe she wanted more than you were willing to give? Hey, I think we've both had enough beer for the night, agreed?"

"Agreed!"

Rick softly punched his friend in the shoulder, "Bar tab's on me tonight."

Mitch gave his friend a funny look, "Now I know for sure you've had too much beer."

Both men were within ten feet of the door when Beyoncé's song *Should Have Put a Ring On It* came on in the bar.

Both men ducked their heads and said in unison...

"Seriously?"

—⟊—

Two miles away, in a trashy "pay by the week" motel, Ramón wasn't having any trouble with his love life. In fact, he had just finished this evening's adventure with Maureen and although satisfied with the sex, was looking forward to her imminent demise. He knew exactly when, where, and how he was going to do it. The thought of dragging this fat ugly bitch to a secluded beach in Vietnam for the rest of his life almost made him gag.

He had been getting her used to sour blended drinks for several weeks now to better hide the taste of the drugs he'd acquired to place in the drink. When the time came, he would be very ready to do the deed. It was almost ironic, in a way, that the drug Ramón had chosen was designed to relieve long term chronic pain. In the end, the powerful narcotic drug would do as it was designed, for the both of them...

CHAPTER 40

—⚜—

Destiny

Jonah's flight left Puerto Rico at ten in the morning getting him into Miami International just past noon. As arranged, Patch was waiting for him at the arriving flight's curb in Jonah's vehicle. As Jonah approached, he noticed a part of his front right bumper was significantly different then when he'd left it in Patch's care...

Jonah had needed the assistance of a porter to get all his stuff to the curb. Jonah thanked him, giving him a twenty, and stood alone on the curb alternating his gaze between Patch and his front bumper.

Patch stood near the back of the vehicle with the door open. "I've decided not to charge you for the additional body work on your wheels if that's what you're worried about."

Jonah continued to look at the damaged bumper and then at Patch, back to the bumper and then back at Patch. "I gotta tell you...I kinda think it adds something to the overall look of the ride! Did it take long to do or was it the very first night you had it?"

Patch knew he was being jerked around...hard.

He smiled at his friend. "Got enough shit?"

"Now that I've given you some? I've got just enough!"

Laughing, Patch limped over from behind Jonah's car and they shook hands. He gave Jonah a look that quite clearly told Jonah, I'm glad you're back. Patch grabbed the smaller of the bags and held the back door open while Jonah loaded the rest. "Where's the scooter?"

Jonah looked his friend dead in the eye and hoped he'd get the hint. "I didn't need it anymore."

"Oh," was the best Patch could come up with.

Patch tossed Jonah the keys. "I don't think the beast likes me."

They drove back down to Patch's house in Florida City listening to the satellite radio and talking like they hadn't a care in the world.

"I went to one of those damn veteran's meetings while you were gone."

"Bull shit."

"Nope, seriously. I was watching the news the day after you left and they were talking about how many vets were taking their own lives. I'd heard it all before and really had some empathy for a lot of them.

Jonah looked over at his friend.

"And now?"

"Well, I guess it's different since our mini vaca to the Keys."

"How so?"

"Let's just say you put things into perspective for me in a way I don't think anyone else could have."

Traffic was thickening up and they drove on in silence for the better part of ten minutes. Patch waited for a red light.

"Jonah?"

Jonah looked over with a smile. "What's up man?"

"I wanted to tell you something and then we won't talk about it again."

"Okay."

"You saved my life for the second time when you called me to go on that trip to the Keys."

"Bullshit."

"Jonah...I had the gun in my hand."

Jonah almost hit the car in front of him.

"I want to put this damn war behind me and live as full of a life as I possibly can. Some days things will suck and some days things will be great. I realized that life before the navy wasn't perfect. Why was I expecting things after the navy to be perfect? 'Unrealistic expectations' is what the guy at the V.A. had called it."

"That's awesome Patch. The last part, not the first part!"

"Thanks!"

"So, what's next?"

"Well, for starters, I'm selling the truck stop."

"Why? I thought you loved that place?"

"It's become a security blanket and a boat anchor all at the same time. I want to get out and meet new people and maybe save some other vets along the way."

"That takes some serious bank my friend."

"Jonah, do you have any idea how much money I'm getting for that truck stop?"

"Nope."

"Just over 4.3 million dollars, my friend. I'll do just fine. I'm setting up several different accounts so I'll never run out of money and the VA said they'll help me steer the waters with other veterans' groups."

Jonah smiled all the way to Patch's house. It was good that after a career of causing damage he could now do some good. It was sort of karma really. He'd taken one man's life because he'd deserved to die and saved another man's life because he deserved to live.

He'd stayed the night at Patch's talking about his dive trip, grilled some fish, and drank beer well into the night.

After breakfast, and a quick shower to clear his head, it was time to go. As he headed out the door he grabbed his friend by the shoulders, brought his face in close and said, "Three times."

"Three times? What's *three times* mean?" asked a curious Patch.

"I've saved your miserable life not *two* times but *three* times."

"How do you figure that?"

What? Jonah feigned being hurt, "The huge shark in the Keys didn't count?"

"Fine! Three times it is! So, what now? I'm forever in your debt?"

Jonah smiled and gently punched his friend in the chest.

"Yup."

"Whatever!" hollered Patch as Jonah climbed into the truck.

Jonah rolled down the windows in the already warm car. "Come visit me in D.C."

Patch shot him two thumbs up, an exaggerated cheesy smile and a big wave.

Jonah smiled back his very best toothy smile and tore out of Patch's sand and coral driveway leaving his friend in an enormous cloud of choking white corral dust.

He looked back through the cloud of dust at his friend and, deep inside, where his demons currently rested...Jonah knew it would probably never happen.

—◆—

With this week being as physically demanding and mentally challenging as any he'd had in recent memory, he curtailed the evening's activities early, but not before living out every carnal activity they had the energy and enthusiasm to participate in.

Maureen gasped, "Ramón, you were amazing, and from the looks of it you're ready again!"

"Sure thing, babe, but let's have a drink first, I'm parched!"

"What's your poison? Rum and Coke or a Whiskey sour?"

"Oh my goodness, one of the sour things would be wonderful!"

Ramón carefully mixed the powdered drugs and sour mix together, palmed the wrapper, added the liquor, water, and lastly the ice. Not to be rude, he poured himself a Bacardi and Coke with lots of ice.

"Here, babe, drink up!"

He leaned back in the torn leather chair and watched her drink her entire drink without ever taking the glass from her lips.

"How's that taste?"

"Amazing, did you double the shots? It's going straight to my head! Whoo Hooo!"

"Mine's good too, ready to get it on?"

"Always," replied Maureen with a giggle, slightly slurring her words.

Ramón helped her get into bed, centering her there, face up, with her head on the pillow. "Comfy?"

"I'm so sleepy...can't...seem...to get a full breath."

"You're fine, just take a nap and we'll start again after a bit."

Ramón watched her breathing become more and more shallow...until it stopped, completely. Her mouth was moving the same way a fish does when sitting on a dock in the hot sun, its brain trying desperately to get a breath. Her eyes made contact with his and her terror aroused him. He waited for five minutes then took her pulse. It was over. Well almost. Ramón pulled back the sheet and turned her over one last time...

—m—

They agreed to meet at six just to have everything done in the early morning light and with significantly less potential for witnesses. The warehouse was in a rundown section of town, with little, if any traffic, vehicular or pedestrian, was expected. It was one of those delightful areas that cabs didn't drop fares and even the men in blue didn't respond to anymore.

"Ramón, you are impressed with our little project?"

"Yes, sir, it looks like it should do the trick. The last thing Maureen heard at her office was that they were planning to have a staff meeting the day after tomorrow at seven forty-five in the morning."

"How long do these staff meetings last?" inquired the Imam.

"Maureen said they have been sending out reminders to all key personnel all week so I would imagine the bitch will suck up at least an hour of everyone's time."

The Imam glanced around at the men gathered behind him, "We had a thought last night, since this is, for all intents and purposes *your* target, perhaps you would like to do the honors of driving this week?"

Ramón gasped as if he'd won the lottery. "Would I, you bet I would. I don't have a commercial driver's license though."

"Don't you worry about that, JAveed will get you lined up and you just need to back it up. Do you think you could manage that?"

Everyone in the room was laughing. "How hard could it be?" shouted Ramón.

"Indeed." said the Imam as he exchanged a nod with JAveed. "How hard could it possibly be?"

JAveed clapped his hands to get everyone's attention, "Let's do a dry run system's check and then get everything locked up."

Ramón followed the Imam down the hall briefly, "Sir?"

"Yes," the Imam despised Ramón and it took a great deal of control to not show that emotion.

"I'd like to check my account balance before we leave for the mission. Is everything in order?"

"Your money will be in your account tomorrow at midnight Ramón. Now go and help the others check out the systems and familiarize yourself with the truck."

Ramón returned to the others with a smirk on his face that he couldn't get to go away. Seventy-two hours from now he'd either be on a beach or well on his way to a life of pure enjoyment.

—⚉—

Jonah had taken his time coming back up the Florida coast and stopped after only six hours of driving to spend the afternoon in Jacksonville. He visited some retired buddies, drank a few beers, went fishing and of course, told war stories and other lies. The following day, again after six hours of driving, he stopped in Fayetteville, North Carolina and dropped in on some friends at Fort Brag who had left the SEALs a few years back and were now instructors at Fort Bragg's Air Assault School. Even an extended happy hour at the Cadillac Ranch drinking beer and looking at pretty ladies didn't distract him from where he really wanted to be...back home.

They'd dropped him back at his hotel around eleven fifteen. After the required and expected razzing about Jonah calling it an early night, they'd waved and driven off.

He'd walked down the sidewalk, opening the door to his forty-two dollar a night room, and sorely missed his luxury room back in San Juan.

Jonah flopped down on the bed, hopefully not stirring up any indigenous creatures living in the mattress, and stared at the ceiling. It was approaching eleven thirty and he thought as seriously as you can on seven beers about whether he should call her this late. He moved his thumb back and forth over the "Jewels" button in his contact list but decided it was too late to call...but for whatever reason pressed the button anyway.

Jewels answered the phone so quickly he hadn't really gotten his head around what he was going to say.

"Hello, Jonah?"

"Hi Jewels."

"Are you okay?"

Jonah sat up and looked in the mirror. "I suppose. A few too many beers with some buddies tonight, but nothing a shower and a run won't fix. Maybe some food. My room is kinda crappy. It's hot here. Is it hot in D.C.?"

Jewels stifled a laugh. "Jonah, how many beers did you actually have?"

Jonah thought about the question, "Too many apparently."

Jewel smiled. "I had a night like that just a few weeks ago. The tequila demon bit my ass. Maybe we're getting too old to drink?"

"Bullshit!" exclaimed Jonah. "Even my buddies were teasing me tonight about turning in too early!"

"Well, from where I'm sitting it sounds like you came home at just about the right time."

"Hey Jewels, I'm sorry I called so late. Feeling a bit like a jerk but you've been on my mind."

"No, no, no! Don't be silly," Jewels laughed and it felt wonderful. "It's good to know you're not actually perfect!"

"I think I better call you back when I'm sober so I don't embarrass myself more than I probably have tonight."

"No, I'm glad you called Jonah. I've been thinking about you and was worried about you while you were away. Is that weird? I mean, what's that all about?"

Jonah wasn't sure exactly where Jewels was heading so he abruptly changed the subject. "So, I've got one more stop in Richmond tomorrow afternoon."

Jewels laughed, "You're not acting like a man in any hurry to get back to D.C."

"Hey, it's not like that. I'll be getting back to D.C. Tuesday morning."

"What's her name?"

"Who's name?"

"The lucky young lady in Richmond."

"Very funny. There's no lady in Richmond prettier than you."

Oh shit, he thought...he'd said that out loud...

"That was very sweet."

"Hey, anyway, I'm apparently meeting a lawyer to discuss settling a friend's estate."

"Am I missing something?"

"A guy I met when I was in Florida died and his lawyer sent me a letter. It's weird, though...I got the letter the same day my friend died. He actually handed me the letter himself. It was like he knew he was gonna die that day."

"I'm sorry, Jonah. Had you known him for very long?"

"No, but I don't think he had any family left and we sort of hit it off while I was on that island."

"What did the letter say?"

"It just said to call this attorney guy and make an appointment to see him in Richmond."

"He wouldn't tell you anything over the phone?"

"Nope, said I had to come in person."

"Weird."

Jonah looked at the clock. "Man its midnight! I'm so sorry! I'll call you tomorrow?"

"That would be nice Jonah. Why don't you take a shower and get some rest."

"Night Jewels."

"Goodnight Jonah."

Jewels turned the volume down on her phone, turned the screen off, set her alarm clock and lay back gently on her pillow.

She smiled and imagined what Gina would say when she told her about *that* conversation tomorrow. Gina would waggle her finger in her face and say "Girl you've got it baaad." And, of course, she'd be right!

Three hundred and twenty three miles away Jonah West also lay back on his pillow. Fell back would be more accurate. He didn't shower. He didn't set an alarm. He did, however, for the first time in quite some time, fall asleep with a big goofy smile on his face.

CHAPTER 41

—ɷ—

Options

The phone on the small nightstand was ringing and Jonah wasn't sure why. He answered, "What?"

"This is your wakeup call."

He vaguely remembered waking up around three, needing to use the bathroom, and calling the desk requesting a wakeup call. He swung his legs over the bed and launched himself in the direction of the bathroom. Looking in the mirror, he was starting to think the guys were right, he *was* getting too old for this crap.

Jonah looked at his bald head, and the still lighter colored silhouette where his hair used to be. Boy was Jewels in for a surprise. He started the hot water running in the sink and started the process of becoming human again.

With Monday morning traffic, the trip to the lawyer's office would take almost four hours. It was just after seven so with the shower, packing the room, and grabbing a bite to eat he should be there right on time.

—ɷ—

Jonah followed the directions from his car's turn-by-turn program and arrived at the rather ostentatious building, with its fancy marbled facade and client parking, at twelve-forty on the dot. Although the person in the booth did give his car the "what the hell" once over, she still gave him the parking ticket and allowed him to park.

He walked to the combination information/security counter and, reading off the envelope, politely asked for the offices of Henshaw, Black, and Snell.

"First elevator on the right, thirty fourth floor, sir. Have a pleasant afternoon."

A pleasant afternoon? He befriends an old man at a marine dock in the Florida Keys a few months ago and suddenly he's responsible for all the man's worldly affairs? He'd only known Clarence Peabody for just over three months and looking back realized that he actually knew very little about the old man. He'd helped Jonah get set-up on Wisteria Island and handled his mail and then, in the end, given him his little boat. It's not that he wasn't grateful, he was. It was just turning into a time consuming hassle for an old boat.

In reality, he'd only seen the man every few days when Jonah would drop over to get supplies or his mail and they would shoot the shit for a half hour or so but he'd never told Jonah about his life or family. Clarence had mentioned once that he knew who Jonah was because of "that nasty business up in Alaska" as he had referred to it.

"Thirty fourth floor." said the automated voice. The voice made Jonah jump.

He sighed heavily, and walked off the highly polished elevator and got himself a paper cup full of citrus infused water on the credenza directly outside of the offices. These folks didn't mess around and he tried to imagine what their billable hourly rate was.

Even the lobby of the firm was beautifully decorated and Jonah was really trying to connect the dots on how the little old man in the dock office would have any use for the folks at Henshaw, Black, and Snell or vice versa. Jonah walked up to the desk with the enormous golden monogram of H.B.S on the front and waited for the older woman to finish her call.

"May I help you?"

"I sure hope so; I have a one o'clock appointment with Mr. Henshaw?"

"Oh, you must be Mr. West. We were all so upset to hear of the passing of Mr. Peabody. Our condolences."

"Thank you." Jonah turned around so his facial expressions wouldn't be seen. Just who the hell was Clarence Peabody?

Jonah took a few sips of water and turned back around.

"He spoke very highly of you."

Jonah turned around just fast enough that the water he coughed didn't go near the immaculate oak desk.

"He did?"

"Yes, sir."

The woman's intercom buzzed quietly.

"Mr. Henshaw will see you now. It was a pleasure to meet you Mr. West."

To his left, a large polished oak door opened and a man of perhaps twenty extended his hand. "Mr. West?"

"Yes, hi, are you Mr. Henshaw?"

The younger man laughed, but not in a rude way, more in an "I wish" way.

"No, sir, I'm his assistant, Blake. Mr. Henshaw's in the conference room. Would you follow me sir?"

Jonah fell in behind the man and they walked through one room, which Jonah assumed must have been Blake's office, to a much larger room just off to his left.

"Mr. West," boomed a loud voice reminiscent of the way Clarence used to address him.

The man standing at the end of a long conference table came around the table and shook Jonah's hand. The grip was solid and, for a man his age, rather impressive.

"Hello, Mr. Henshaw?"

"Yes. Hi Jonah. May I call you Jonah?"

"Certainly, sir."

"Sorry, I didn't make it to the door to greet you."

"You've met Blake?"

Jonah nodded and smiled. Inside, Jonah felt the whole situation surreal.

"I seem to have forgotten my manners. Would you like something to drink? Blake fixes a mean Martini!"

"No, I'm good sir."

"If you change your mind, just let me know."

The two lawyers exchanged a look and smiled at Jonah.

"Sir? May I ask you a question?"

"Certainly Jonah, what's on your mind?"

"Why am I here?"

The room was dead quiet for about ten seconds.

"Blake, I believe you owe me five dollars."

Blake came around from behind where Jonah was standing and handed Mr. Henshaw a crisp five dollar bill.

"Mr. Henshaw, am I the butt of a bad joke because..."

"No, no, no, not at all Jonah." The older man laughed.

"Please have a seat. Here," the man tapped the corner of the enormous desk, "by me if you don't mind."

The men now sat diagonally across from each other separated only by a small stack of papers.

"No, Jonah, young Blake here lost a bet about Mr. Peabody and I am the beneficiary of his youthful innocence."

"What bet was that, sir?"

"The wager was whether Mr. Peabody would tell you about his last will and testament."

Jonah leaned back in his chair. "Clarence gave me his little fishing boat. Do I need to sign papers for that or what's this all about?"

"Jonah, how much do you know about Clarence?"

"Well, not much really. He looked down on his luck and he smoked way too much. He was very kind to me and we enjoyed talking when I would come and visit him at the dock. We never had a meal together or even had a beer. Is there something about him I should have known?'"

"Jonah, it's said that, as you get older, time becomes more precious than money. Have you heard that expression?"

"Yes, sir."

"Well, let me tell you a little about Mr. Clarence Peabody. Clarence's mom and dad were depression kids, very frugal and looked forward to eventually retiring and spending time with their only son Clarence. Around 1971, Clarence volunteered to go to Vietnam. His parents were very upset as they had hoped he would go to college. During his second tour, he was declared missing in action."

"I do know that story. Isn't that when the SEALs went up the river and rescued him and his buddies?"

"Yes, what was left of them...They were shot up pretty badly."

"Clarence hadn't told me that part."

"Yes, but Clarence recovered and returned to duty back in the states, and as you know, the greeting those men returned to wasn't the best to say the least. He stayed in the army and got married in 1975. 'Sweet Caroline' he called her. Like the song by Neil Diamond. She worked at Wal-Mart as a cashier and then a department head until 1981 when she became pregnant with their daughter. Unfortunately, the daughter was still born and apparently Caroline never really recovered. She died in a car crash in 1986. She left everything in her will to Clarence, but he never touched any of it. For whatever reason, he felt he hadn't earned it."

Jonah looked inquiringly at the two men, but they just shrugged.

Mr. Henshaw continued, "Both of Clarence's parents died within a year of each other in 1988 having never retired, they left all of their worldly possessions to Clarence as well. Clarence was all alone and as we've learned recently was probably suffering with depression and more than likely some level of PTSD. Clarence bummed around for a bit but when he retired from the army in 1993 he took the job at that navy pier in the Florida Keys where you met him. It required very little of him and, as a federal employee, he received a livable salary. His expenses were relatively low and he put most of it aside for a rainy day."

Jonah absentmindedly glanced at his watch.

"Are we holding you up from something, Jonah?"

"No, sir, I just know you guys bill by the hour and if this visit's on me..."

"Jonah, let me put your mind at ease. Today's visit is all taken care of no matter how long it takes."

Jonah relaxed, but honestly wondered where this was all headed.

"So, in 1993, Clarence was here in Richmond for something or another, he actually didn't remember, and he calls our office and says he needs a firm to manage some 'family matters.' We met and he brought a briefcase full of documents and letters as well as the wills of his wife and parents. Everything had been probated years before, but he wanted someone to, as he put it, 'neaten it up.' We agreed and consolidated his holdings and other assets."

"Every year since then we would draft our agreed upon maintenance fee and would let him know where he stood on all matters relevant to his estate. Jonah, as crazy as it sounds, the man never drew a dime out of the estate."

"We sent him a basket of fruit every year, but we never actually spoke again until three months ago when he met you. He said he'd finally found someone worthy of his family's legacy."

Jonah was getting a little uncomfortable and adjusted his position in the chair.

"Well, we drew up the appropriate papers, as he had requested, and sent them to you. We heard from the police the next day that he'd died at his desk."

"Yes, sir, I was there at the time. It was almost as if he knew it was his last day. As a matter of fact he handed me the letter from you maybe five minutes before he died."

"Interesting...But he said nothing to you?"

"No, sir."

"It's sad really, he valued your service to your country and he greatly appreciated the time you spent with him. Apparently everyone else treated him by the way he looked. He said he saw something different in you."

"Well, that was very kind of him, but as I said I just talked to him. It was an honor to be his friend."

"Jonah, I'm not sure how to tell you this but he left you everything he owned."

"That was very nice of him. I'm surprised but, okay. To be honest, I've never done this before and don't know what that means exactly or where we go from here?"

"Well, Mr. West, you'll need to read and sign these documents and that will either conclude our business or open a new chapter. The choice will be entirely up to you."

Jonah looked up in time to see both of the men smiling at each other.

"I think he was right about you Jonah."

Jonah turned to the first page and it was a lot of party of the first agrees that the party of the second part...kind of stuff. He signed his name, printed his name and dated in the appropriate section.

The second package was labeled "Liabilities" and was an accounting of all of Clarence's outstanding debts. It took an entire page to say he was debt free and that even this year's taxes had been paid. Jonah signed the bottom and went on to the final package titled "Assets."

Jonah opened the page and found an attached listing of Clarence's portfolio. It went on, single spaced, for thirty two pages and ended with a number that Jonah just stared at...$11,235,457.82

"That can't be correct!"

"That's today's account balance Jonah."

"Mr. Henshaw? I think, if it's all the same to you, I'll go ahead and take that drink now."

CHAPTER 42

—∽—

Hades

The building security personnel had been on high alert ever since Ken Shortman connected the dots about Ramón. Both local and federal law enforcement had been looking for the man but he was in the wind. It was apparent that their only defense would be the newly installed barrier and that would be tantamount to a "Hail Mary" at best. Guards had been stationed at all the approaches to the building as well as someone specifically monitoring the security cameras that pointed outward from the building. CP1 (Checkpoint One) was within line of sight of CP2 and both were in constant communication with the temporary command post, referred to as "Control" that was set up across from the entrance to BOATSS. It was exhausting work and like most high stress jobs it was important to rotate the personnel frequently to keep everyone sharp.

In the event this attack actually went down, Jewels had her IT team transfer all of their server's data offsite to the CIA annex on the other side of town. It would be some cramped working conditions for a while, but it would be far better than losing all of their files *and* a place to continue their work.

Jewels, Gina and Mitch had gone over yesterday and agreed it was a pretty good set up except for the size. In many ways it reminded them all of how their office had looked back in early March before the proverbial shit hit the fan. The team would be crowded but they would be functional. After conferring with Homeland Security, the FBI and her own building security team two days ago it was established that they were ready for whatever was coming, they would transfer en masse if the situation called for it.

—⁓—

After his lengthy meeting in the offices of Henshaw, Black, and Snell, yesterday afternoon, Jonah had gone to the Wells Fargo Bank in Richmond where Clarence had kept his bank accounts. Technically, the law office had their driver drive them over to the bank in the Lincoln Town car. Mr. Henshaw and Blake insisted on coming along to make sure all the paperwork was done correctly and the accounts and links to the portfolios were established. Jonah looked at the balances in the accounts and transferred $100,000 over to his new account in McLean, Virginia.

They'd driven back to the parking garage at the firm where Jonah stepped out and shook the hands of the two men.

"What now?" asked the normally self-confident Jonah.

"Well Mr. West, enjoy your new life and if you need our assistance please don't hesitate to call."

Blake handed him several of the office's cards. "Mr. West?" whispered Blake after Mr. Henshaw had entered the car. "Do you have a girlfriend?"

"No, not really, why?"

"Because, sir, now would be an excellent time to get one!"

With good reason, Jonah had some trouble sleeping last night after all the excitement with the lawyers, but this morning, at seven thirty, as he headed North on I-95 he felt strangely refreshed and recharged. He should be at the BOATSS office in about thirty minutes depending on traffic.

Jonah wasn't sure why he was going to see her...or what he was going to say...but he now had twenty-nine minutes to figure it out.

—⚏—

Jewels had baited the trap earlier in the week by announcing the upcoming "important meeting" at the Monday staff meeting and stressing the importance of everyone arriving promptly. She arrived early with the rest of the building's department heads at six o'clock. When the rest of the staff began arriving at eight they were directed through the BOATSS building and into the commercial building directly behind their facility. From that point, everyone's cell phone and other electronics were gathered as a security precaution and all employees were essentially placed in lock-down. The FBI determined that if they, whoever "they" was, were attempting a Timothy McVeigh type attack, it would not have been necessary for Ramón to do as many measurements and pictures of the front of the building. Of course, that was only their professional opinion...

The morning seemed to drag on with everyone watching the clock. Maybe today wasn't the day after all. At just past ten the guard on the north corner of the building checked in.

"Control, CP1, heads up! I've got a fuel truck approaching the intersection."

Everybody prepared for what they thought was coming when CP1 radioed back that the truck had passed the intersection and had proceeded up the block.

"Control, CP2."

"Go two."

"That fuel truck made a right turn about two blocks up."

"Roger that."

Jewels looked down into her half-filled cup and saw ripples in the coffee. It took a few moments to realize that they were being caused by her hand shaking.

"Control CP1."

"Go one."

"Either the truck that went past is coming by again or they have numerous trucks on the same route."

Suddenly everyone could hear over the radio the sounds of shots and a man scream.

"Control! Shots fired at CP1! Vehicle has stopped and the driver appears to be dismounting. I'm being engaged by unknown gunmen!"

Ramón ran around from the passenger side, hopped in the driver's seat and threw the massive truck into reverse. The transmission caught on the first attempt. He awkwardly lined the rear of the truck up with the front of the building and hit the gas. In his side mirror he could see the fabricated reinforced discharge pipe unfold and extend from the rear of the truck. It took a moment to get the weight of the truck moving and Ramón checked his mirrors one more time and saw something he couldn't believe. From out of nowhere five enormous stainless steel posts had erupted from the roadway blocking his path. The rear of the fuel truck hit them with such force that his head was thrown rearward into the glass behind the driver's seat. He was at least thirty feet short!

"Mother fuckers!" When the hell had they put these in?

Ramón decided he didn't care, it was time to go! Reaching down he pulled the door handle and although it moved, it was definitely locked.

"Screw this!" he yelled and tried to release his seatbelt but it too was apparently stuck. "No, no, no, this isn't happening!"

He looked across the street and could see one of the men from the warehouse filming the whole thing. Looking at the dash he could see the small timer counting down from thirty seconds. He glanced back and could see the gasoline forcefully spraying at a tremendous rate out the back of the discharge pipe. The entire area in front of the building and the gutter was flooded with gasoline.

Inside the building all personnel ran down the hall closing fire doors as they went and kept on going even after they'd reached the supposed safety of the next building.

"Come on people let's move, move, move!" shouted Ken. "You've got *no* time until your world's gonna get rocked!"

The first explosion ignited all the fuel that had been pumped and broke every window on the front of the building. The heat melted the tires of

260

the truck and distorted the aluminum in the building's window frames, yet remarkably, Ramón was still alive.

He tried pounding on the windows but ended up burning his hands so badly the flesh was already starting to hang off his palms and left forearm.

"Oh my God!" The pain was unimaginable!

The fire on the front left side of the cab exploded the front left tire ripping open the already weakened cab to the fire still swirling beneath the truck. The smoke was choking, blinding and searing hot. Ramón recalled his mother talking about hell being an inferno from which no one escaped. He was there now!

Ramón thought he could hold on for the first responders but they weren't approaching! They were just standing there watching him burn to death!

The gasoline on the ground had burnt itself out in less than a minute and although everything was still technically on fire the flames were less than a foot high.

Ramón knew what was coming next and simply closed his eyes, thinking instead of a beach he would never see.

From across the street a man in a hoodie looked at his watch and started slowly backing away. The small timer on the iPhone ran down to 00:00:00 and an alarm sounded. He looked back just in time to see the secondary explosion go off. What remained of the fuel truck was easily thirty feet in the air and the entire front of the BOATSS building had simply disappeared.

"Allahu Akbar." "Allahu Akbar," the man yelled as he ran up the street.

Jonah, who had finally given up trying to get any closer to the building, lucked out and got a parking spot on the street. No sooner had he chirped his car alarm when he'd heard the first explosion and seen the towering column of black smoke streaming upward. He began to run toward the BOATSS building. Nothing mattered any more except getting to the building. Jonah wasn't fifty yards away when the second explosion hit destroying the remainder of the truck and the front of the building. Less than twenty feet away stood a man filming the whole event. Jonah snapped. He'd simply had enough. The man turned toward him with a crazy look on his face and screamed "Allahu Akbar" twice before Jonah reached out, without slowing down, and in two lightning fast moves broke the man's neck. "Allahu Akbar that!"

—✸—

With all the emergency vehicles in position already, Jonah was getting the feeling that maybe they'd been tipped off before the actual event or at least as it was happening. He flipped up the perimeter tape and made it three steps before he was challenged for his credentials. He'd felt bad for the officer, at five three she was intent on doing her job but he could tell she was scared to death about the whole situation swirling around her.

"It's okay, I'm one of the good guys," said Jonah with a big grin. She politely checked his ID. She looked at the photo, then Jonah's bald head. "Where's all your hair?"

"I had to get it cut off."

She sighed, "Well, that's too bad."

"Where are all the people from this building?" Jonah pointed over her shoulder at the still smoking hulk.

"Everyone's in the building behind it."

Jonah started to walk quickly toward the building.

Second floor, sir!" she shouted as he distanced himself from her.

The officer turned and worked her way down the perimeter. She'd looked back once, shook her head in disbelief and mumbled something again about his hair.

All the personnel that had evacuated to the insurance building behind the BOATSS complex had come through unscathed with the exception of Mary Whitman who was in the middle of a full blown anxiety attack. No one could really blame her. Her husband Kelly had died at the Pentagon when the third plane hit just below his office. EMS was just leaving, opting to take the stairs, because, according to Mary, she was claustrophobic, when a giant bald man rushed past them and into the room.

"Jewels!" the man bellowed.

"Jonah?"

"Freeze big guy!" Ken Shortman had drawn his weapon and scooped Jewels behind his massive body.

At this distance even Jonah wasn't going to make a move.

"It's alright Ken, he's one of us."

Jonah slowly reached into his pocket and presented his credentials.

Ken Shortman holstered his weapon and glanced at the man's ID. It looked legit, but he still looked at the other man warily.

Jewels came around to the front of Ken and placed her hands on her hips. "Where the hell's your hair?" Laughed a shocked Jewels.

"My hair? Where the hell's your building?" was Jonah's quick retort.

They embraced just for a moment.

"Ken Shortman, Jonah West, Jonah West, Ken Shortman head of security and apparently my other body guard." The two men shook hands.

"So you're the guy who saved her out in front of the restaurant?"

"Yes," was all Jonah could muster.

"Any idea who is behind this mess?"

"Well, we know who precipitated the attack but also know he didn't have the chops to pull it off by himself. To me he found someone local and very willing to do the heavy lifting. Fortunately, thanks to Ken, we were as ready for them as we could have been. Unfortunately, we really don't have the luxury of time to even think about that at the moment. We need to get over to the annex on 21st and keep working on several other issues that are currently pressing.

"Need a lift?" asked Jonah.

"Sure."

"Let me let everyone know I'm heading that way and tell them to follow when they can. Ken, you're good here?"

"Yes, Jewels."

Jewels did a double take and looked at Ken. She was all set to scold him when he surprised her by calling her *Jewels*. "See, that wasn't so hard!"

"You have no idea..." mumbled Ken as he turned and got back to securing his now destroyed facility.

They both showed their IDs as they left the building and walked up the street past the front of the building.

"They would have had us dead to rights if Ken hadn't been doing his job."

Jonah smiled. He would have to remember to somehow reward Ken at some point.

Jonah looked ahead to his left and could see the heavy police presence around the terrorist he'd killed on his way to the building. No sense being identified at this point. He'd put it in his report and hoped that Langley could work their "magic" with the local LEOs.

"Let's cross here."

"Where's your car?"

"Well, it's not actually a car per say, it's more like a hybrid."

"Now that's funny, I certainly didn't pick you as being a 'hybrid' kind of guy."

Jonah laughed, "Well, Jewels it's not really *that* kind of hybrid."

"Let's cross back over."

"Did you forget where you parked?"

"No, not exactly." Jonah feigned looking left for traffic as he made sure that they were far enough away from the crowd of people that no one would see him. Jonah pointed his key chain fob up the street. "Chirp, Chirp" went his remote and the beat up looking Blazer roared to life.

"You're kidding right?" Jewels mouth hung open in surprise.

"Just get in." Jonah loved this part. He never got tired of it.

Jewels opened the passenger side door and had the same reaction Rick had just a few weeks before.

"Oh my God this is crazy!"

"Buckle up Jewels. Does your phone have any music on it?"

"Of course!"

"Well, sync it up and play it loud!"

"Seriously?"

Jewels retrieved her phone and synced it to Jonah's audio system. In less than three seconds the very loud and distinctive sounds of *Thunderstruck* by AC/DC completely filled the Blazer.

Jonah's jaw dropped open and he looked to his right.

Jewels smiled and leaned toward Jonah and hollered, "Sometimes I really need to feel alive!"

Traffic moved slowly as they once again passed the spot where the dead man, now covered in a yellow tarp, still lay on the sidewalk.

As they passed the building they muted the music. Jonah rolled down his window and showed the officer at the end of the block their IDs.

Jonah made the left turn, un-muted the music but kept the volume down. "Where to Jewels?"

"We have an emergency annex setup at the corner of 21st and C. The below ground parking is actually before you get to the building. Take your second left and head down 21st NW. We'll cross Virginia Avenue NW and it will be on your left in about three hundred feet.

Jewels reached forward and turned the volume up to a level that almost hurt.

Almost everyone has a way of dealing with their demons in one way or another and Jonah was getting a peek at what Jewels' coping mechanism was...and he liked it!

He hoped it worked.

CHAPTER 43

—◊◊—

"The Gipper"

aptain Briggs watched the battle plan being briefed as it unfolded on the large screen at the end of the briefing room on the *Ronald Reagan* and was in total awe of its complexity. It wasn't the plan itself, but the way it was presented was a technology that he only recently even read about...but had never seen in person.

Because of the very intricate nature of the navy's battle space, the presentation was using a cutting edge holographic projection to depict all three levels of the battle space to include surface vessels, aircraft and submarines. It wasn't quite yet at the level of holographic projection as depicted by Hollywood...Briggs chuckled, but they were getting pretty damn close.

The way it looked at the moment showed his *Connecticut* sliding out through the passage south of the island of Palawan as planned and then heading northeast through the Palawan straight. The water was significantly deeper at the bottom of the straight and due to the amount of other traffic in the area the *Connecticut* would be able to run almost full out without fear of detection by the Chinese.

The first leg of his run would take him almost two hundred and thirty-seven miles to the deep waters on the east side of Leslie bank. At this time of year, the current, although not fast moving, would at least be going in the same direction they were.

In reality, the northern slope of Leslie Bank would be their proverbial go/no go point. With the increase in both Chinese naval traffic and the potential of anti-submarine aircraft, cutting across the path of both inbound and exiting ship traffic from the cluster of atolls occupied by the Chinese would be risky on a good day. They would leave the relative security and depths of the eastside of Leslie Bank at twenty-one hundred hours and begin their thirteen-hour run to the west of Thitu Island.

Briggs looked at the latest intelligence and couldn't believe his eyes. The bastards had been going full out in their dredging operations and now had thousands of acres of new land above sea level. In fact, so much of the area had been dredged that several sections of his navigational charts were no longer valid. Areas that could have been used to avoid contact or beat a hasty retreat had been filled in. These guys were crazy, but very efficient.

"All right gentlemen, so much for our travel arrangements. Let me see where our threats are."

The image changed to the anticipated threats poised to the different platforms in the area and according to the briefer they were becoming more ominous with each passing week. Every time enough coral had been dredged and compacted the Chinese were bringing in either surface to surface weapons or ground to air defense systems. Many were outdated and would be easy enough to spoof with electronic jamming but a few lucky shots and this thing could escalate quickly.

The greatest threat, at the moment, to anyone in the immediate area was the Chinese ballistic missile submarine *Great Wall*. That's where the *Connecticut*'s piece of the puzzle came in. On the morning that they would move, currently four days away, the *Connecticut* would make its run through the area where the *Great Wall* was *not*. As she made her run, the *Connecticut* would send the *Sea Dragons* to their predetermined hold positions and reenter the Palawan straight. Effectively, the *Connecticut* would be circling back to where she started three days prior.

The American Navy had been participating in joint exercises here for just over a year with several countries affected by the heavy handed Chinese presence in the disputed waters and small islands. In an effort to nudge the Chinese to stop their expansion in the area, the navy had done rather "in your face" transits of the area. As of last April when the drilling platforms were placed, it was apparent that "nudging" them wasn't going to get it done. According to both the navigator and recent records, the two hundred and sixty mile crossing back to the East side of the Spratly Islands would take just over eight hours at close to flank speed. At this point, making a little noise wasn't a concern because of the anticipated range from the *Great Wall* to the *Connecticut*. The only spoiler, and it was a real doozy, would be if the Chinese Navy had deployed additional ships with anti-submarine capabilities. Nothing was showing up on the brief but the Intel the briefer was using was over six hours old.

Briggs had gathered all he knew so far just by looking at the presentation up front.

The briefer droned on and switched slides every few minutes. Apparently, once the *Connecticut* was safely back in the trench, the American ambassador to the United Nations was to request again with the support of all the nations affected that the Chinese leave the area or face significant consequences. It was anticipated that the Chinese would say "screw you" in their most polite Mandarin and phase three would begin shortly thereafter.

Briggs perked up. What the hell was this bullshit? He leaned forward and listened intently to the briefer.

"Three Vietnamese light cruisers who are currently on 'routine patrol' will turn east and begin to approach the contested area of the Spratly's the Vietnamese government felt was rightly theirs. They will begin hailing the Chinese on the various islands and request that they evacuate the disputed area until the United Nations could work out a fair resolution. They will add that failure to comply would result in the Chinese possibly being injured."

Captain Briggs just shook his head. The entire plan shot to hell because somebody wants to be touchy feely with arguably the toughest and certainly the most dangerous adversary in the area? Please people, grow a pair.

"Excuse me, can I speak up and interject a comment at this point?"

All eyes in the room turned to Briggs. There were several murmured voices to his left. It was not briefing protocol to interrupt. In Briggs' view it was his life, his crew's lives, and his boat's survival that were in the most jeopardy and he frankly had never cared much for protocol.

"Gentleman, perhaps it's due in part to my recent close encounter with a nuclear weapon but my balls have apparently grown considerably over the past several months. I feel that at this point in the briefing, you've gone plum off the rails. Admiral, sir, with your indulgence I'd like to propose that we just flat out tell them they're surrounded and to leave the islands in a due north procession in order to prevent annihilation."

"That's not the way we do things anymore in the navy...captain." The man had used his crew position on his vessel as opposed to his rank on purpose...and it momentarily stung him.

"So admiral, respectively, you would suggest that we keep doing things the way we did things prior to one third of our navy and untold millions of people being murdered in San Diego by a nuclear weapon that we suspect was placed in position by Chinese surrogates?"

The room was deathly quiet and Briggs knew he had probably pushed it too far.

"Commander Briggs." It was the captain of the *Reagan*.

"A word please?" He motioned for Briggs to leave through the rear of the room.

They walked down the passage and came to a room that was occupied by two sailors having a cup of coffee.

"I need this room!" was all he had said and the two rocketed to their feet and were gone.

Captain Klineman stepped into the small compartment and closed the door behind them.

"Have you lost your damn mind? We've all got our balls on the line here! I, for one, agree with you, but damn it man, in front of Admiral Boozeman?"

"It's a bad plan, sir."

"So your twenty something years trumps some of the guys in that room's thirty years?"

"No, sir."

"Then what's your damn problem with following our battle plan? This is what we train for and now it's time to execute the plan."

Briggs stood at parade rest and was silent.

"Permission to speak, sir?" It wasn't his style but he didn't need any more enemies tonight.

"Speak your mind Commander Briggs."

"The problem with the current plan is that they know what our current plan will be. They've watched us, studied us and have more than likely literally read our books. We're so busy being nice we've forgotten our warrior ethos. Do you think it was an accident that someone sent a civilian vessel to San Diego? They knew we would hesitate. Have you read the full report or the *cliff notes* version?

"The cliff notes, why?"

"So you don't know about the jet propulsion system, anti-submarine radar and the reactive armor! They know our play book better than we do!

"Listen, they nuked us and now they're profiting from that and our inability to do anything about the situation we're facing now."

"What's your suggestion, commander?"

"Let's try something we haven't tried since WWII...an ultimatum with an iron fist to back it up! Once we're in position, have Washington call them and explain that they have four hours to safely evacuate the atolls. Anyone or anything for that matter remaining on the atolls after that time has the potential of being killed or destroyed.

The Captain bowed his head and exhaled slowly. When he brought his head back up he looked Briggs straight in the eye.

"I'd love to see that happen, but we don't orchestrate policy we just carry it out."

Briggs couldn't believe he was hearing this.

"So let me get this straight, Sir. You would advocate giving them a heads up and enough time to reinforce the atolls with even more missile systems that can drop your air wing's aircraft and bring in more surface ships to kill the *Connecticut* and potentially sink the *Reagan* because of an antiquated foreign policy that hasn't yet adapted to the world as it is today?"

"I think we're done here commander." The captain of the *USS Ronald Reagan* and the man in charge of roughly six thousand lives turned and walked out of the compartment. He closed the hatch behind him leaving Briggs staring at the closed gray hatch.

CHAPTER 44

—◊—

Birds of Prey

The five men and one woman had performed their parts as flawlessly as they had in the dress rehearsals and no one on the ground was the wiser. They briefly waved to the cargo ramp personnel as the massive jets started to move toward the runway. Just as they turned onto the active runway, and thought everything was going flawlessly, the aircraft's brakes abruptly engaged and the sudden force threw everyone in the cockpit forward into their seatbelts. The impact had been so severe, the shoulder straps left red marks everywhere they made contact with their bodies. Since nobody could even reach the brakes, and all had been given strict instructions not to touch any of the controls, it was assumed, without comment, that the computer program running this charade had simply "burped." All three hoped such burps were now out of the way and wouldn't occur at altitude traveling at 445 miles per hour.

Tengku had done as he was told and been in awe of both the power and the amazing view as his assigned 747 began its slow climb out of Kuala Lumpur International Airport. As if by magic, the enormous plane started a slow left turn to the west thirty seconds after takeoff and stayed in that turn for almost five minutes. He could see the beautiful mountainsides of

Sumatra and for a short time the oddly circular shape of Lake Toba. As the aircraft's turn passed 110° it began a slow roll out of that turn and was wings level on a northeast bound course. Tengku watched as the digital compass' numbers slowed, 090, 089, 088, 087, 086 and finally stopped at 085°.

Although five minutes behind the lead aircraft, Siti, the only woman on either of the aircraft, could see the first plane's contrails high above them and just slightly to their right. They would be at the same altitude shortly and level off for the long flight to America. Remarkably this was her first trip on an airplane and it would, sadly, be her last. She had been chosen for her part of the plan because she and the others of her party looked similar to crew member's documents the group had created or stolen last week. Her family had put up a decent fight but once they shot her eldest son in the face...her fight evaporated. Like many families in the Philippines, Siti had a large family and the thought of them all being murdered was unbearable. It was only two days later that she and the others had learned that the people they replaced were dead. They hadn't actually been told that but they had accidentally seen six sets of legs wrapped in a tarp leave the warehouse in the back of an old pickup truck. It had been an ominous sign, but she remained hopeful the men that had seized her from their home would keep their word. They hadn't...

Two other people sat in the cockpit with her and judging by their facial expressions they were having the same or very similar thoughts. All three realized they would be dead in about fourteen hours, but it would be quick, or so they had been told, and each would finally see America...briefly. They engaged each other in conversation and talked of what they thought their children would do without them. They were not sad or frightened for they had been told that all of this was the will of Allah...

They had been flying for just over an hour, and although desperate to stay awake, the toll of the previous week's events had sapped all of their emotional energy and apparently, all of their physical strength as well. One by one each of them had reclined their seats and gone to sleep.

—ɯ—

Behrouz was very busy at his workstation and had been for several hours now. The flight control systems were performing amazingly well and had only had one hiccup at the very beginning when the brakes on the second aircraft had been forcefully applied in error. He hoped everyone had been buckled up for that one.

He was running each flight control package on its own screen and could see at a glance everything was proceeding as planned. Eleven minutes ago for the first aircraft and one minute ago on the plane with the brake "issue," the amount of oxygen in the cabins dropped to the point where its occupants were either drowsy or fast asleep. For the first aircraft, the effects of the induced hypoxia would be permanent in about five more minutes and for the other crew, about twenty minutes more.

Unknown, of course, to the individuals on the two planes, the computer program had been bleeding oxygen from each respective aircraft five minutes after each aircraft had leveled off at cruising altitude.

In the end, it had been the only failsafe method in which they could ensure that no one on the two aircraft would have the opportunity to play hero and tamper with the aircraft or its cargo. It wasn't necessarily a bad way to go and at the end of the day, dead was dead.

Behrouz sat very still for a moment and gathered his thoughts...It was time. With several well practiced moves that made everything appear normal he reached forward and with only a few wayward keystrokes started the recording. He had practiced this several times now and only the other day realized that if someone was in fact watching carefully from the cameras mounted on the wall behind him they would be able to see that the mission clock didn't match the real time. Not one to worry, he simply redesigned his program's operating program to display the mission clocks at the very bottom of the screens and out of sight of a particular snooping colonel. He needed at least one solid hour of recording with two being optimum, for his backup plan to work.

—⁂—

After only thirteen hours into the flight and just passing south of the Aleutian Islands and Anchorage Alaska, the first aircraft began its turn to the southeast toward America's west coast. Both aircraft had just over three hours before they reached the Seattle-Tacoma area and were making their required calls and course corrections as they passed through the airspace controlled by Anchorage control.

"Are we on schedule?" inquired a crazy eyed General Tehrani.

Behrouz jumped. The sound of the man's voice scared him as much as the realization that he hadn't seen the man enter the room.

The plan had been to have both aircraft hit their designated targets at approximately 02:00 p.m. and 02:10 p.m. PST. At this particular time of the day, only one of the locations would have the maximum number of personnel out in the open and thereby cause the most amount of collateral damage.

"General, it's just eleven a.m. pacific standard time and both aircraft are just over three hours from their programmed destinations. We'll be home free once they clear the outer air traffic control markers and are on final approach to Seattle.

"Excellent!"

"By the way, sir, if you're interested, the CenturyLink stadium is sold out and the Seahawks are favored by only three points."

Tehrani spun Behrouz's chair around and shouted in the young man's face, "Do you honestly think I care about the point spread of the American football game?"

Behrouz had to think quickly because the man was literally hissing mad.

"No, general, of course not! It's just when the game is anticipated to be that close nobody will be leaving at halftime."

General Tehrani got a funny look on his face and just like Hollywood's B movie villains began wringing his hands and smiled ear to ear.

"Stay on it, Behrouz!"

—⚹—

Behrouz looked at the clock and realized he needed to go within the next few minutes or be caught in the mountain like a rat on a sinking ship, that was on fire. He'd already hacked the cameras and the codes for the outside doors. He just needed to gather his wits and go. He started the timer for the cameras to point ten degrees off their programmed converging arcs, gathered a few personal items and jammed them into his pockets. He quickly scanned his console, checking his settings to ensure everything he needed to run undisturbed would run in the background, from the server, locked out the servers and stood up.

"Going somewhere?"

The nasally and very distinct voice of General Tehrani was indistinguishable from anyone else's voice he had ever heard.

"No, sir, just stretching my back and then hitting the restroom."

Behrouz feigned stretching his lower back and did some hamstring stretches just to keep it real.

"We've got thirty minutes before we hit the outside ADIZ (Air Defense Zone) and I don't wish to have a full bladder when that happens." He laughed as genuinely as he could and quickly glanced at the wall above the general's head. He now had less than eight minutes before he would be locked inside the mountain with everyone else.

"If you can bear with me, sir, I'll be right back. You can track the mission's progress on the monitor to your right.

General Tehrani glanced up at the large plasma TV displaying the mission tracking program and sat down in the large office chair. He glanced at his watch. "Don't be too long Behrouz."

"I won't sir."

Behrouz rounded the corner to the hall the restroom was located on and looked at his watch. He was behind, but not so far as to imperil his escape plan. He glanced up and could see the cameras moving away from the wall he was walking along and he slowly increased his speed.

His plan had been rather complex to put together, but with access both granted and "appropriated" his plan didn't involve any physical confrontations and would get him out of the mountain fortress way ahead of whatever the Americans decided to do.

He was at the exterior door and entered his special contrived combination. Once entered, the door would only open one more time before a computer time lock would secure the building for thirty-six hours. These doors were heavy blast doors and nothing that was currently inside the building would be strong enough to break the doors down.

Behrouz typed in the numbers corresponding to the text *THATS*FOR* MAJOR*FALLAHI.* The system would randomly change the code, rendering it uncrackable, until he or someone else sent the unlocking code. Hopefully, it would be the Americans...

The massive door opened with a hiss. He stepped through into the blazing sunlight and heat of a central Iranian afternoon. He hadn't been outside in over eight weeks and it was, for a moment, a bit overwhelming.

He walked quickly to a small security truck and true to form the keys were in the ignition. Heading down the road he looked at the timer on his watch counting down. He'd been gone for just over five minutes. The general wouldn't have been notified of a small locking issue with the doors right away. That would bring his legendary wrath down on the messenger. The general should be getting notified of the exterior doors being locked and the elevators being inoperative in about...three, two, one. Behrouz smiled broadly for several miles and it dawned on him that he had spent all his time planning to get out of the mountain and very little time on actually surviving his freedom.

—◊◊◊—

"What do you mean the exterior doors are locked closed!" raged General Tehrani. "BEHROUZ!!!"

General Tehrani looked at the flight controls on the desk in front of him and saw that he still had at least limited control of the two enormous aircraft. Very well, if he wants to run away that's fine. He would be caught and put to death slowly and painfully for his cowardice. It won't change today's outcome.

He switched to the camera feed from inside the two 747s. There were three views available; forward, out the front windows, and both a left and right view.

The front view was clear with some light clouds below the aircraft. He looked at the view coming from the camera mounted on the right facing camera. Dead guy: Right where he was supposed to be. He checked the left facing camera and could see the top of the head of the other dead guy, right where he was supposed to be. Both of the bodies had begun to form ice crystals on their skin as the bodies had cooled to the unheated cabin temperatures which were now well below freezing at cruising altitude.

Although still furious that Behrouz had abandoned his post, the general decided to test the controls of the aircraft scheduled to cross into American airspace first. He carefully moved the joystick to the right and watched the scene before him change before he slowly moved it back to the left. He repeated the same moves to the left, but for the most part, the scenery was the same. Perhaps descending would be more interesting? The general pushed the game stick forward but in just a few seconds a light and audible alarm told him to return to flight level 37,000. It was amusing, but no more than a cheap video game. He yawned; overall it was a boring process and would be over in just under an hour.

Placed carefully on the desk in front of him were the questions and appropriate responses to air traffic controllers that he may receive on his approach to Seattle's airport. They weren't very difficult and he'd seen Behrouz practice them several times. It wasn't as if he needed to know how to land the damn thing. The general turned and faced the large screen again. He examined the track and chosen trajectory of his aircraft. Although it did cross his mind briefly that in less than an hour he would be murdering hundreds if not thousands of innocent infidels, his reaction was not what most people would have expected. A passerby glancing in the observation windows would have seen a grown man...giggling hysterically. It would have been quite clear that the man had completely lost his mind.

"Sea-Tac control, this is Hunan 673 heavy passing approach marker Indigo Mike 23."

"Roger Hunan 673, come right to 017° and descend to ten thousand, change to frequency 119.9 and confirm your approach as runway16L."

General Tehrani slid the cursor over the list of frequencies and selected 119.9.

"Confirm SeaTac control, coming right to heading 017° and descending to ten thousand for a landing on runway 16L. Have a pleasant day."

General Tehrani smiled. This was going to be so easy. In less than five minutes he would declare a missed approach for a "bird strike" and push the key which entered the new waypoint for the navy submarine facility at Kitsap. He slid his chair down to the next monitor and replicated what he had just done with the first aircraft ten minutes earlier. A voice modulator changed his voice from his regular voice dropping it on one aircraft and raising it on another. The same software also synthesized his voice so he sounded more western.

—ɯ—

It was late Sunday afternoon and both Jonah and Jewels were mentally, physically and emotionally wiped out. For Jonah, the events of Thursday and Friday had been the ultimate combination of bittersweet. On Monday he'd found out he was a millionaire many times over and the very next morning had almost lost the one person he wanted to share the rest of his life with. For Jewels, the destruction of everything she had worked on for over a year and the disruption of so many people's lives had taken its toll emotionally.

They had both slept most of Saturday and agreed to meet for a late Sunday brunch at the *Madhatter* restaurant. Its location between Connecticut and 18th made it only a few minutes' drive from Jewels' apartment.

After a leisurely brunch, they arrived at the CIA annex building across town. They had shown their IDs at the parking lot security checkpoint and were pleased to see that security had been kicked up a notch. They had been politely asked to step out of the truck while security conducted their newest line of defense, a visual search of the car which included a cursory walk around by an FBI canine and his handler. It had only been a short delay and soon Jonah was waved through the checkpoint. He proceeded down the restricted ramp and into the garage. He parked his "ride" in the reserved spot for visitors and they'd gone inside where Jewels had signed him in as her visitor and got him a badge.

Being Sunday, Jewels had expected to find only a skeleton crew on their floor but was surprised to see almost the entire staff working on tasks such as organizing their desks to setting up a new coffee area.

"Hi Jewels!"

"Hi Mitch..."

Mitch looked at Jonah. "Mr. West."

"Mitch."

Jonah had extended his hand but Mitch left him hanging.

Mitch turned to face Jewels, "Jewels we just got a call from Rick over at Langley and from my dear old friends at the NSA. Everyone says they're tracking a satellite feed very similar to the one used on the rouge freighter last March."

"Can we link with Rick at the Operations Center?"

"We were just about to patch us into their feeds."

On the enormous LED screen on the far wall appeared two images, one of Rick, who at the moment was *way* too close to the camera and a shot of the NSA Operations Center.

Jewels found operations center relatively calm considering the gravity of the current situation.

"Hey Rick what's going on?"

"Hi Jewels. Well, we're tracking two unidentified but familiar satellite downlinks at the moment. Both seem to be taking turns linking to two east-bound 747s. FAA says that they are manifested correctly as computer parts for various manufacturing plants in the Seattle area.

This one's a bit different. For one thing, the primary data stream is coming in burst transmissions and the second thing is that it also contains a separate package of data. We're working on cracking the primary feed but the second is very clear cut.

"What's the smaller feed say?"

"You're not going to believe this. You BOATSS folks were dead on. It reads as follows:"

My name is Behrouz Yavari and my physical location is 29°58'55.08"N ~ 57°26'49.06"E in the Kesheh Research Center. The two aircraft you are tracking are heading either to the submarine pens at Kitsap or the CenturyLink stadium. You must destroy both the aircraft and my facility. I have locked the exterior blast doors of the facility in the closed position until 09:00 Zulu time and will then lock them in the open position until 10:00 Zulu time tomorrow. Do not be late. Once the blast doors to the facility close, the facility will once again be impenetrable.

If I do not survive, it is important that the world know that Major Harem Fallahi did not know that his research was being used to attack San Diego or anywhere else. He was murdered the minute he figured it out. Good luck.

"Holy Shit, Rick! That means Fallahi's been dead for several months!"

"Jewels, at this point just sit back and watch. Nothing we can do now."

Although the conversations were getting louder, the tone remained professional. Jewels soon lost track of who was speaking, so while very unusual, she did what she was told and just watched the chaotic event unfold on the large monitor:

"Are you into the feed or not?"

"Has all air traffic been diverted to McCord AFB?"

"We've got this as under control as we can at the moment."

"Shit, I can see the instrument's read outs but can't get access to the control system!"

"Hold on," shouted a woman in the back left of the Operations Center. "More code coming in...Try it now!"

"Folks, I'm at five thousand feet and damn near out of gas. If these babies have barometric triggers or something in the gear position assembly that will detonate this on landing we should put it in the water ASAP."

"Can you zero out the current GPS destination coordinates?"

"Standby three seconds...done! Aircraft one is my aircraft! Where do you want it?"

"Do you have the gas to get it out to sea?"

"Gas? Yes, but keep in mind that somewhere there is probably a guy on the other end of this system trying to wrest control of his bird back from me. What do you want to do?"

"Can you bring it left ten degrees and put it into the water?"

"Coming left to 330° and descending rapidly."

"Get the gear down!"

"Gear is down! Angle of attack is forty-five degrees. Speed is increasing to 425 knots!"

"Shit, this is gonna make a mess!"

"One thousand feet!"

"Impact!"

The 747 hit the water at 437 knots and detonated almost immediately on impact. The explosion was so loud and the shock wave so intense that the fans in the Superdome heard it almost seven miles away. Play continued with most fans believing it had been nothing more than a loud clap of thunder.

"Sea-Tac control just reported another aircraft from the same company with an almost identical manifest requesting approach vectors to Sea-Tac. Do you see any signal out there remaining?"

"No way! Here comes another one!"

"Codes are slightly different on this one! Did you get any more passwords from your guy?"

"Here, sorry, he wasn't sure which aircraft had which code."

"Well, if that one was heading for the arena this one's supposed to dive right in on the navy sub pens at Kitsap. Damn it! Somebody's flying this plane remotely as we speak. I can lock them out of vertical control but I'm afraid the course is not up to me."

"Can you time the drop to put it in the water as well?"

"It's gonna be close!"

"Impact should be twenty miles to the north in the center of the channel! Get coast guard and navy assets headed up there now!"

"How long?"

"Impact's in about thirty seconds unless they get control back!"

"What are our chances?"

The younger man smiled. "Well, let's put it this way, all those hours of playing video games that my mom said I had been wasting all those years?"

The young man's hands were flying over the keyboard.

"Yeah?"

"Well...Mom...I..."

"Impact!" shouted an unseen analyst.

"Just...saved...Seattle!"

In a small box on the left side of the still split screen, all the various government agencies that were tied to the link had seen the huge aircraft flash briefly across the screen before impacting the water with an enormous explosion.

With the excitement over for the moment and catastrophe averted, the crowd of people that had congregated over the past twenty minutes began to thin out. Jewels stared at the screen and realized that without these extremely talented people, thousands would have died.

"Hey, does anyone know how to switch this to a regular TV?"

A young guy Jewels didn't even recognize, came over and with a few button clicks had the screen connected to network TV. Jewels checked her TV guide app for what channel the Seattle Seahawks Game was being televised.

"Stand here for a minute and when I nod at you switch it to channel 37."

"Yes, ma'am."

God she hated being "ma'amed."

"Can I have everyone's attention please?"

Everyone in the room reformed in front of her.

"I'm sure everyone here would agree that this week has been much longer than any of us originally thought it would be when we started last

Monday. I wanted everyone to step back and consider something. A man, who many of you never even say hello to, saved many, if not all, of your lives on Friday and another man, in a faraway country, helped save several thousand people in the Seattle area today. We work hard here and I just wanted to show you why."

Jewels nodded at the young man and, as by pure dumb luck, the network was showing the Goodyear Blimp's view of CenturyLink stadium. "All of those people will go home tonight and never know that we saved them. How great does that make you feel?"

A loud cheer went up from the group.

"Alright, let's lockup and go home."

Jewels scanned the room looking for Mitch. She expected that he'd be happy they'd scored a point against the bad guys and even found their hidden lair, but he was nowhere to be found.

She found Jonah talking to Gina on the far side of the room.

"Congrats sista." Gina gave Jewels a double high five.

"Pretty hairy there for a bit."

"Jonah, are you busy?"

"Not really, I was going to run over to the office and file my after action report and some other paperwork, why?"

"I could sure use a lift. Don't you go past my place?"

Hearing that, Gina rolled her eyes and with a brief wave, walked away.

Jonah caught the eye roll and smiled at Gina. "No problem, Jewels, I'd just have to take the bridge up by your place instead of down here...no problem at all. Are you ready now?"

"After that little adventure? Very!"

"Your friends were talking about getting together later for a drink." Jonah grinned at her but she just laughed.

"What's so funny?"

Jewels covered her mouth trying to get a grip. "Your absence of hair!"

Jonah reached up and stroked his bald head and just smiled. "So that's a 'no' on getting together with your friends?"

"Yes, that's a no. I've got a few things that I need to do tonight."

Jonah gave Jewels a smirk. "Alright, let's go for a ride in your favorite car."

The two walked to Jonah's Blazer without speaking. Occasionally, Jewels would step a little too far to her left and brush her hand against his. How clumsy of her...

—⁂—

It had taken almost fifteen minutes with the evening traffic to go the mile due north to Jewels' apartment.

"Thanks for the lift."

"Anytime Jewels."

"How long does it take to file your after action whatever report?"

Jonah laughed. "It used to take about thirty minutes, but this is a new company to me." He winked. "So, probably an hour or so."

"Have fun." Jewels closed the door and Jonah rolled down her window.

"How long is your stuff going to take?"

"About the same, why?"

"Just curious, night."

"Night, Jonah."

Jonah rolled up the window and waited for her to get inside before he pulled away from the curb and headed over to the Theodore Roosevelt Bridge. He had a good fifteen-minute drive ahead of him and after the past two days? He just wanted to get home and "chill."

Jewels threw her coat onto the chair by the door and went straight over to the book on her shelf labeled "Travel Adventures." It had a hollowed out center and was sold at most office supply stores. Most people she knew kept cash or other valuables in theirs, but hers only contained one item...a small 16gb flash drive that would change the world.

Jewels took a minute to make sure everything was in place just as she had planned. Everything was, with the exception that she hadn't plugged in her electromagnet science project. That would have sucked.

She logged onto her GNUnet server and, after insuring she had partitioned her system against what was on the flash drive, inserted the small drive.

Jewels took a look around her apartment and realized that within two days everything in the world would be forever changed.

With a few keystrokes Jewels opened what the drive had been labeled "Triton Special" in homage to all the students and faculty that had been killed in last March's attack. The file opened and she began the process of moving it onto the Darknet. Due to the slight complication of the Air Force or somebody blowing the crap out of the research facility, she inserted a delay that would activate the bug one minute before the 10:00 Zulu deadline. That way, if for some reason the bombs didn't make it into the compound, the bug could slip in and upload on the servers of the facility. Jewels typed in the password that she'd been given and hit enter.

Suddenly, **DO YOU WISH TO CONTINUE?** popped up and her heart skipped a beat. Jewels typed in "Yes."

In less than two seconds a message came up with music playing in the background.

Thank you for what you have done.

~ The Alumni of UC San Diego both living and passed.

The background music made Jewels eye's well up with tears...it was the fight song of the UC San Diego Tritons:

Fight on,
with mighty Triton spirit,
Hail to, the Triton name.
Men and women
march victorious,
On to fame.
Fight on,
the Triton host prevails,
March on, in unity —
Bold and strong we fight
for Triton victory.
U-C-S-D! Fight! Fight! Fight!

Jewels decided she needed more wine...

—◊—

Six miles to the north Jonah had just finished his various reports and, as predicted, it had taken just over ninety minutes. How could one government have so many different forms, documents, and regulations all designed for the same purpose.

Jonah got into his truck and just sat there. He reclined his seat and turned on the sound system with the remote. He surfed for a solid three minutes before he found what he was looking for. He hit play and listened to Thunderstruck by AC/DC.

The song ended and he watched the clock on his dash change from 9:45 to 9:46. He was tired, but knew he wouldn't fall asleep if he went home. He closed his eyes. 9:48.

He picked up his phone scrolled through his rather short contact list and tapped the seventh number down. It rang five times...

"Hello."

"Hi Jewels."

"Hi Jonah, did you get your reports finished?"

"As a matter of fact, I just finished. I'm sitting in my truck too wired to sleep and was wondering what you were doing?"

"Drinking wine and trying to put some parts of today behind me."

"Oh, okay."

"Why?"

Jonah was boxed in now. Nothing ventured, nothing gained.

"I was wondering if you would be interested in seeing my new place. I'm not big on decorating and thought maybe you could give me a few pointers?" Jonah cracked himself in the head with his phone. Man, that sounded so cheesy.

"Tonight?" Jewels had goose bumps.

"Yeah, sorry probably a dumb idea."

Jewels laughed, "What time will you be here?"

Thirty minutes later they were back at his place walking from empty room to empty room.

"Well?"

"Well, the good news is that it's a blank canvas except for the box spring, a mattress and two pillows."

"Hey, now that's not fair. I've got sheets and everything."

Jewels fluffed the pillows on the bed. "You know they come in colors now, right?"

Jewels walked down the hall closely followed by Jonah and into the empty kitchen. Jewels opened the fridge.

"Beer?" Jewels giggled.

"But it's a great beer." Jonah was so out of practice it was embarrassing.

Jewels pulled two bottles out of the fridge. "I see they were made in May of this year. Was this a good year for beer?"

They both laughed at *that* thought.

Jonah walked into the kitchen with a bottle opener.

"Are you going to stand there holding those beers or let me open them for us?"

Jewels put the two bottles on the counter and walked out of the kitchen. Jonah opened the two beers wrapped them both in paper towels.

"Hey, I charge for delivery!"

"I'll pay up, I promise!"

Jonah followed the sound of her voice and found her sitting on the side of his bed. He sat down beside her.

"You're a class act Jonah West!" Jewels laughed as they awkwardly clinked their bottles together. She smiled as she adjusted the paper towel around her beer.

"Jewels, one day we'll look back on tonight and smile."

Jewels took a few long pulls from her bottle and set it down on the floor. She moved across the bed closer to Jonah and placed his beer on the floor as well.

Jewels leaned over and put her arms around Jonah's waist. "If indeed that's the case, I would suggest we have something more to smile about besides the beer."

CHAPTER 45

—ɯ—

Game Time

As Farid boarded the first class flight to New York's Kennedy airport a lovely brunette helped place his garment bag in the small coat closet. He double checked its position to make sure his magnificent vest wasn't in danger of being wrinkled by someone else's garment bag. Once confident it was safely stowed, Farid sat down heavily in his seat. It had been months since booking his flight and glancing around at the cabin crew, he was, at this point, very happy with his seat selection. Farid always chose this particular group of seats so he could watch all the different people board. He remembered when flying used to be fun. Now, the parade of ill fitting spandex, flip flops and crying children made the experience no different than taking a Greyhound bus.

Farid found it interesting watching the dull, dim witted American populous go about their business without a care in the world. The fact that only seven months earlier, way over on the west coast, 2.3 million people had been incinerated by a terrorist seemed to have either never entered their consciousness or had been so fleeting a thought it had been quickly replaced by concerns of what was happening in the next episode of "Game of Thrones" or what level of "Candy Crush" they were working on. The nation had lost its mojo for sure.

Just last week a government office building in D.C., rumored in his circles to be CIA, had been destroyed by a terrorist attack, and two enormous 747's had crashed and exploded in the waters near Seattle, Washington. Nobody was even discussing the recent current events.

It had been a brief run, but the nationalism that had existed in the 80's and 90's had long faded away with the past several years of an apathetic government. They even dressed like they didn't care.

Occasionally a military or former military person would meet his gaze and give him the quick once over, but he noticed that even those incidents seemed to be on the decline as well. America had, as the country's right wing conservatives always said, "Lost its soul."

Of course, the other reason to sit in this particular seat was that he was closer to the flight attendants. He hoped that on this flight the attendant was a pretty girl instead of a pretty boy. He got lucky, the thirty something flight attendant was saying something. He removed his Bose sound cancelling headphones. She repeated her question.

"Sir, can I get you a beverage?"

"Dewar's," was his curt reply. He preferred Chivas but it wasn't served on Delta's domestic flights.

She was indeed a looker. And Farid was certainly looking. "She had legs all the way up to her ass." He laughed to himself thinking of the first time he had heard that, so many years ago now. She turned and feigned a weak smile. He knew that look well, he should, he'd received it often enough. He stopped staring and drank his scotch. It felt warm as it slid down his throat. It had been a very busy few weeks and he closed his eyes and walked himself back through it. Loose ends were not something his superiors found amusing.

The flight had been relatively uneventful. Some cretin close to the first-class section had decided to fly with a child. It wasn't the child's fault, but it had cried all the way up to cruising altitude and all the way back down. Of course, the child didn't know about swallowing to get his ears to pop and the parents hadn't brought anything to assist him so he screamed...a lot.

First class had its limits, of course, in that the child couldn't actually be sick *on* him or actually kick *his* seat but the unhappy sounds had wafted through the "privacy curtain" without even slowing down. And, since it's idiot parents hadn't brought anything for him to play with, he had fussed for the entire flight. The entire situation became much more tolerable once the pretty first class flight attendant with the long legs finally figured out the gently shaking of his empty glass meant he wanted more Scotch. He'd finished four before the young lady cut him off.

It was a good thing too because, as it was, not only had he not known they'd landed, he'd walked right past his driver at the baggage claim, sign and all...twice.

The driver grabbed his bags off the carousel for him and loaded them into the back of a stretched Lincoln Town Car. After cautiously getting him situated in the back seat of the luxurious car, the driver began their trip into the borough of Manhattan.

"And you're still going to the Ritz-Carlton, sir?"

"Yes," replied a somewhat inebriated Farid. Being an overweight alcoholic had very few perks but a high tolerance for the effects of alcohol was definitely one of them.

"How's traffic tonight, how long until...?" his voice had trailed off.

"We'll be there in 45-50 minutes, sir, Chivas Regal is in the rack as you requested. Hit the white buzzer if you need anything, sir." If that son of a bitch threw up in his car, he was adding $150 tip to the fare.

The driver closed the smoked glass partition and Farid was alone. He poured himself three fingers of his favorite Scotch and stared out the window at the passing cars. Three more days. Farid took a large mouthful of the cool liquid and pulled some air into his mouth. It was wonderful. He would make the most of the three days. After retrieving his iPhone from his left breast pocket and pulling out his little black book from the other, he smiled as he dialed.

"Hello."

"Cynthia!"

"Hello, Farid." responded a voice as smooth as his 25-year-old scotch.

"Are we still on for dinner at seven?" he slurred slightly.

"Oh course, my dear, I'll meet you in the bar at 6:45."

Farid hit *End* on his phone. He was almost shaking with anticipation of tonight's events. The entire night's activities would run him close to $2000 dollars, but he didn't really care. It wasn't his money and less than a week from now...it really wouldn't matter.

Twenty-two miles away, on Manhattans' lower west side, Cynthia Kazensky felt nauseous. As she looked at herself in the mirror she readily understood why these creeps always called her. At five foot eight, shiny blond hair, blue eyes, and phony hourglass figure, it was what all the men dreamed about but had either never found or were unable to keep. She had made enough over the years to retire and move to Boca. Just the thought of spending the night with a man like Farid made bile rise in her throat. He had a kinky streak a mile wide and enough prescription drugs to keep going all night long. She gargled, twice. Granted, twelve hundred dollars was a lot of money, but come on. As she finished readying herself to go uptown she glanced in the mirror one last time. She was perfect...and this was her last week. She called her car service and poured herself a stiff drink...

CHAPTER 46

—⚭—

Into the Trench

They'd traveled almost eight hundred miles since Briggs had left the deck of the *USS Ronald Reagan* just over twenty-nine hours ago and were now cruising at minimal speed near the bottom of the Palawan Trench just sixty miles from the southern tip of Palawan Island.

"Sir, we'll have a good long break in the surface traffic in about five minutes if you'd care to come to communications mast depth."

"Thanks, chief."

Briggs looked at his watch. It was the nineteenth of November already and he had planned all year for this to be his family's first Thanksgiving at the Idaho ranch. He'd managed to call home and video chat from the *Reagan's* communication suite just prior to his disastrous mission briefing appearance. Everyone was fine and although he'd only been gone a few weeks it looked to a father's eye that his little family had grown again. His lovely wife Stacy had been her usual sweet self and then after everyone had said their own particular greetings she had told the kids to go feed the horses. Alone, Stacy's demeanor changed.

"Trent, I know damn well why you're there and you had better keep yourself and your crew safe."

"Honey, you know me! Safety first!" Briggs had smiled in the camera attempting to reassure his wife of over fifteen years.

Stacy was having none of it.

"Trent...I do know you and that's what both scares me and keeps me sane. All I'm saying is that I support you and know you'll do the right thing. You always have. Do you remember the story you told the kids about never following a bear into a cave?"

"Yes."

"Good, tell the story to yourself and come home safe."

As if to emphasize her comments his black Lab Boomer let out one big, "woof."

"I need to run honey. Give everyone a hug and say hi to your folks for me."

She waved and sweetly blew him a kiss.

Briggs brought his brain back into the present. "Bring us to mast depth chief!"

The bow of the sleek boat pitched up ever so slightly and after a few minutes they were at a depth whereby the *Connecticut's* communication mast was just clearing the surface.

The mast would be breaking the surface for less than a minute to get any updates on orders.

"Negative message traffic sir."

"Alright folks let's take her down and get this party started." He'd added a horrible impression of a dance move his kids had taught him.

The crew on the bridge laughed. This is why they loved him and would follow him to the very end if needed.

In the *Connecticut's* forward torpedo room Chief Thomas was reading the operating instructions for the *Sea Dragon* torpedo system again and making sure he knew what he was supposed to do when the time came. According to the instructions, all communication with the weapon was through a tiny antenna that sat in its own little dent near the rear of the unit.

"I'll be damned."

"And, I'll be double damned!"

"What're you guys reading? Hi Chief Long! What brings you three decks down?"

"Just a little light reading with Chief Thomas," the man chuckled.

Torpedo man second class John Isaacs was getting curious.

Chief Long was the first to break the silence.

"I've read this OI (Operating Instruction) three times and still can't believe that this thing lets you program it to kill a particular ship."

Chief Thomas opened what looked like a hardened iPad and waited a few seconds for the screen to illuminate.

"See the red banner? It's in test mode now so it's safe to practice. Watch this. First you select the name of the ship or select from tracking interface."

"What's the tracking interface they're referring to chief?"

"According to this, it can tie into our ship's sonar system and record the acoustic signature we tell it to and either track and kill that particular signature or log it for the future. And get this, since we got that latest update from the commander's girlfriend in D.C..."

"The captain has a girlfriend in D.C.?"

Both of the older men laughed.

"Son, if I tried to explain it to you now...your head would probably explode. Good story, but for a different day."

"Anyway, this new software can tell us not only where the ship is, but where it's been in the past several months!"

"That's so freaking cool."

"Yes it is," remarked the sonar chief with a smile.

"How long can these things stay on the bottom?"

"All that stuff's in a classified addendum that only the senior staff has access to."

"So when do we start plugging in the signatures?"

"When the skipper makes the decision on who lives...and who dies..."

CHAPTER 47

—⟋⟍—

Subterfuge

Most experienced diplomats understood early in their careers that the UN was nothing more than a large international front for big business interests and an even bigger front for corruption. In the fifteen years that his associates had worked here they had done nothing that translated, in any form, to a benefit to their homeland. On the contrary, they had lined their own pockets with investment funds and aid money that had been intended for everything from water projects to the building of schools. Some of the money, sometimes as little as twenty percent, had made it to the various agencies back home, but the amount wasn't usually enough to even break ground.

What he was going to do on this particular Monday wouldn't alter the daily business and corruption practices at the United Nations one bit. All he was doing was making a point. He chuckled to himself, a subtle point. Subtle...like a large brick.

On today's schedule of events were several briefings regarding the nuclear weapon attack on the city of San Diego last March. The UN assigned an investigative team to determine who, if anyone, was to blame for the attack.

Everyone on the planet knew an investigation done by the UN wasn't going to go anywhere except perhaps for the sanctimonious self-important bastards currently seated in the great room. Those meetings had wrapped up earlier in the day with the expected outcome...accusations and feigned outrage and denial.

Farid was here today, because as the old American expression goes, "Even a blind squirrel finds a nut now and again." He needed to stop any progress in the investigation whether real or imagined.

He arrived in the underground parking garage below the United Nations facility early enough not to feel rushed, but late enough to not appear without purpose and generate undesired attention. He had shaken the hand of his driver, exchanged seasonal pleasantries, and had said goodbye.

The unseasonably inclement weather, so different from his departure city of Palm Beach, had necessitated he wear a heavy coat. He slowly removed it as he approached the security checkpoint for UN personnel. New procedures were in place and, similar to the airport, he placed everything on the small conveyor. He elected for a wand scan and, as anticipated, the wand made its annoying high pitched beep as it passed over his decorative metal vest. He carefully removed it. The guard rescanned him and as expected, the wand had emitted its shrill tone again as the wand passed over the upper part of his left chest. Upon hearing the second loud tone, one of security officers had taken a step back and placed his hand on his gun. The second officer's eyes and Farid's met briefly, "Pacemaker, the stress of this job will kill you!" laughed Farid.

"So I hear," said the officer with a laugh himself as he waved Farid on through.

Recovering his vest, coat, and other items, Farid walked from the garage elevator out into the lobby.

Several people commented on his attire. He had to admit, for someone trying not to garner attention; he was getting quite a few compliments on his shiny new vest. He checked his coat with the pretty Asian girl at the coat check, took his claim ticket, casually crumpled it up, and dropped it in the small waste can a few feet away. He glanced back at the coat check girl and smiled. She returned his smile gently parting her lips as she smiled. She was rather alluring. As he moved away and proceeded down the hall he chuckled to himself quietly and wagered that her social calendar was always rather full.

The United Nations General Assembly building, in its 1980's renovated form, was designed to have a maximum seating capacity of 1,800. Attendance at meetings wasn't mandatory and rarely was the room fully occupied. Due in some part to the fact that today's meeting of the general assembly wasn't scheduled to accomplish anything earth shattering and, without incident, would probably not be recorded in anyone's diary except perhaps a tourist or two, coupled with the fact that the weather in New York City this afternoon was a particularly nasty and damp thirty-five degrees, with a stiff breeze off the East River, he anticipated attendance at this afternoon's meeting to be light. In reality, it didn't matter in the slightest. It wasn't the *number* of people in the room that Farid cared about, it was *who*. Farid watched the monitors as he moved slowly down the long corridor. According to his most recent information, the Israeli ambassador's speech was scheduled to run for at least another five minutes.

The enormous room itself was 165 feet long by 115 feet wide, and was the largest room in the United Nations New York complex. At the front of the chamber, and what most people think of when they describe the room, was the rostrum containing the green marble desk for the President of the General Assembly, Secretary-General and Under-Secretary-General for General Assembly Affairs and Services and matching lectern for speakers. Unnoticed by many visitors and rarely portrayed in the news or in Hollywood movies, were the less conspicuous two murals on each side of the room by the French artist Fernand Léger. Farid had always thought they reminded him of his days in high school Biology class where they had looked at stained samples of pond water under a microscope. He mused that the print looked to him like a group of single cell organisms squirming and struggling to survive in a hostile environment. Perhaps Léger had metaphorically captured the essence of mankind's struggle. He looked briefly at the prints again. Farid smiled. As he had been told on several occasions, by friends and strangers alike, it was probably best that he pursued paths unrelated to art.

Behind the rostrum was the United Nations emblem on a gold background that extended from the floor to the ceiling seventy-five feet above. This enormous golden wall was the image everyone recalled after a tour of the building. Flanking the rostrum is a paneled semi-circular wall that tapers as it nears the ceiling and surrounds the front portion of the chamber. In front of the paneled walls were the seating areas for guests and above them, within the wall itself, large windows which allow translators to watch the proceedings as they work. On the floor itself, each of the 192 delegations had six seats with three at the delegation's assigned desk and three alternate seats behind them.

Farid imagined the overall enormity of the setting was imposing to the casual visitor. He knew better. He knew that the majority of the people who frequented this room, and the supposed importance of their work, the endless perks and diplomatic immunity, all lent itself to the narcissistic behaviors exhibited by the majority of the United Nations' body.

Almost to the door now, Farid double-checked his seating chart. As plans go, this was certainly not the most complicated he had ever undertaken. Timing from this point forward was essential. Although he didn't want to dawdle getting down to his delegation's seats he also didn't want it to be perceived that he was walking quickly. Walking too quickly might draw unwanted attention to his arrival. Farid entered through the left set of double doors, placing him between gallery sections **BB** and **CC**. From here he would walk forward between these sections then cross over to his right two sections to get to the Iranian consulate's table.

Farid casually glanced to his right. He noticed another man enter through the set of doors at the other side of the rear doors. They exchanged cursory nods and although having never practiced this operation together, simultaneously proceeded to the Iranian consulate table. This pass by the delegation's table was the last chance to step back from the mission, the ultimate failsafe point. They arrived at the table within a second of each other. If they were to abort the mission, they would be invited to dinner.

After a brief smile in greeting, an exchange of "Allah Akbar" and the "go" signal, he would then cross back across the massive room and proceed down the gently sloped floor towards the front of the hall. He glanced briefly to his right and could see his partner looking in his direction. They had not received an invitation to dinner...

The men left the table, split up, and when they reached the top of their assigned aisles they began moving quickly down the aisle to the front of the General Assembly.

The American Ambassador to Israel, Aaron Shapiro, and the Israeli ambassador to the United Nations, Yousef Adelson, were just shaking hands after concluding their joint speeches on continued cooperation in resolving the recent uprisings in Gaza...again.

Farid was halfway down the ramp when a member of the UN security detail noticed his fast pace toward the dais. Some countries' representatives were shouting and pointing. He tuned out their shouts of alarm and increased his pace to a run.

He remembered hearing somewhere that in the fleeting moments before you die or approach death, your mind slows everything down and you relive your life in the blink of an eye. He desperately needed to focus now, but the past year's extensive planning, personal pain he had endured flowed through his mind like a fast turbulent river. He glanced quickly to his right at his partner and screamed, "Allahu Akbar." From behind him he heard several of his colleagues yell, "Allahu Akbar!" back at him.

Farid was rapidly closing the distance to the left dais and ambassador Adelson. At this point, it wouldn't have mattered if a squad of US Marines were between he and his target, he would be unstoppable. He glanced quickly to his right at his partner and mouthed, "Allahu Akbar." As he rapidly approached the left dais and experienced the compression of time caused by the massive amount of adrenaline coursing through his veins, he looked up into the somehow knowing eyes of the Israeli ambassador. Something was very wrong! It wasn't the look of fear or anger he had longed for and hoped to see for so very, very long. What he saw instead, and what would be forever recorded on the video archives of the UN and broadcast around the world, was an image of two Jewish men's strength of character and courage in the face of certain death. The bastard Jews had smiled briefly, raised their heads to the heavens, moved their lips as if praying and slowly closed their eyes.

Farid's very last thought, the instant before he died, was that *it just wasn't fair!*

CHAPTER 48

—ᴍ—

Panic

Exploding a mere quarter second apart, the resulting effects of the dual explosions were catastrophic. The first ten rows of seats were now missing with the exception of their base plates and bolts. The entire front half of the vast hall, including the two daises, and where only moments before the ambassadors had been standing, was completely obliterated.

The very shape of the domed ceiling, seventy-five feet above, had worked against the people in the room as it had focused the initial blast wave like a lens and projected a secondary wave back downward into the member's seating areas throughout the hall. The repetitive sounds of wailings, that only death or medical help would curtail, rose above the din of the moans and shouts for help. Far in the back corner of the room three men emerged from beneath the Iranian consulate's table. They had ducked just before the blast, and, other than an incredible ringing in their ears, were uninjured. On the floor several feet away from the men was a briefcase. It was pock marked and looked damp. One of the men scurried on all fours over to the case and retrieved it.

Knowing with certainty that the two bombers brief stop at their table had been captured on the closed circuit camera system the men feigned injury and left the destroyed hall. Prior to the detonation, two levels of enclosed glass suites, where interpreters and guests had been seating, were now windowless voids of pain and death. The glass had blown in on the people seated there at a speed of over 1600 feet per second. Those not immediately killed were bleeding out in a futile wait for aid to arrive. The blast radius of shrapnel had exceeded the first ten rows of the hall and had lethal effects on delegates of both the United States and the United Kingdom.

Due in part to human nature and natural patterns of movement, every person who could move under their own power had tried to exit out the back of the enormous hall putting them in direct conflict with the torrent of New York police and fire department personnel now pouring into the hall from the same four sets of doors. Police and fire on scene commanders were using megaphones to direct people out the side doors. If they could see the carnage and death that was what used to be the front of the once magnificent hall...they would have surely understood why the people were attempting to exit through the rear doors.

—◊◊◊—

It had only taken four minutes for the networks to get wind of the "Explosion at the United Nations" and, depending on what network you turned to, greatly affected the story you initially heard. As was the norm in the press these days, the reports varied widely from CBS New York's reporting that they had received word that it had been a gas leak with several people injured to FOX news reports of hundreds dead and injured. News crews were being kept back to the extent that you can keep cameras back these days, but with the portability of digital cameras it soon became clear, due to the horrific nature of some of the injured, that this clearly had not been a gas leak.

It took the Iranian men almost fifteen minutes to go the three city blocks west to the Iranian Mission. Although none of the men were visibly injured the tremendous pressure of the bomb in the enclosed space had caused small veins in their eyes to rupture. Although all three had placed ear plugs in their ears just prior to the explosion, they had only been marginally effective. All three men's inner ears had been compromised leading to both disorientation and balance issues. They proceeded directly to their offices where they had been met by a member of the mission's communication's office.

HesAm BeNum was the public relations expert for the Iranian embassy in New York and he was overjoyed that they had made it out alive and were now standing in front of him with the briefcase.

"I'll take that."

The case was removed from their custody, with little ceremony or words of gratitude. They would have been wasted anyway. As it was, none of the men were going to be alive in ten minutes time anyway. That was hardly enough time to even start feeling bad about someone's poor manners. Two of the mission medical team and three members of the mission's security detail escorted the men out of his office. The last man out the door gestured to HesAm both the "thumbs up" and the "thumbs down" sign with his outstretched arm.

HesAm saw the man gesture and hesitated but a moment...thumbs down. With an acknowledging nod, the man was gone.

HesAm carefully unlocked the case. Inside, were mounted two HD GoPro digital cameras that had been focused at different focal points in the room. Both survived the blasts and he removed them from their respective protective cases. After attaching their USB cords he plugged the first one into his computer. They were color coded with masking tape with the blue tape signifying the intermediate focal point and the red tape being the close up of the front of the assembly hall and the large dais from which the two Jews had been speaking.

As much as he wanted to see the carnage wrought in the front of the hall he chose the blue camera first. The technician skillfully fast forwarded the recording to the part where Farid and Tamal were leaving the consul table and walking down their respective aisles to the front of the room. He could hear the shouts of warning and the slow reactions of the security just prior to the detonations. Even at this range, the camera picked out a tremendous amount of detail before being swept off the table by the blast. His hands perspiring, he removed the first camera's USB cord and plugged in the second camera. On this camera, the two men's journey down the aisle was a bit blurry, but they came into clear focus as they approached the fourth row of seats. He slowed the video down so he could savor every moment. He watched in slow motion as the men approached the rostrum and detonated their bombs. He backed up the video and watched the reaction of the two Jews at the podium.

Something wasn't right. They were not terrified! Neither man even ducked below the perceived safety of the rostrum. They looked upward as if praying! He watched again. Their lips were moving! They were definitely praying to their God! He watched it three more times before he called someone above his pay grade. This would ruin everything! He dialed the number he'd memorized so long ago and had only used twice.

The phone began to ring....

He couldn't put this version out!

"Hello."

"I need to speak to Mansoor."

"And whom should I say is calling?"

"It's HesAm! You must hurry!"

"Greetings, HesAm! I see we are on the news again! Allahu Akbar! Do you have the video?"

"Yes, I do, and there's a problem that you need to see."

"I'm sure it's nothing to worry about. I'll be down shortly."

"No, you need to come down quickly!"

The man was only two floors up and talking like he would have to make travel arrangements!

HesAm knew the dangers the video in his position presented. They might be able to write off the official UN video as propaganda but their own video? This was a major problem. In its current format, the video depicted the two dead Jews as brave heroes! Martyrs even!

He had a very short amount of time to alter the reality to fit the narrative...a very short time indeed.

CHAPTER 49

—ww—

Marco Polo

The *Connecticut* was coming shallow, as the sub crews called it, in order to get any message traffic. Several packets of messages were received and the submarine slipped silently down to her hold depth at four hundred and fifty feet.

"Captain flash message from COMSUBPAC (Commander, Submarine Force, U.S. Pacific Fleet)."

"Read it!"

"United Nations General Assembly attacked by Muslim extremists. Hundreds are known dead including the United States Ambassador to Israel and the Israeli Ambassador to the United States. Negotiated withdrawal of Chinese forces by United Nations efforts alone no longer deemed viable."

"The UN! Is nothing sacred anymore? That's the end of the message? No further instructions?"

His communications officer looked down at the message again.

"No, sir."

"That sucks! Religion of peace my ass!" growled Briggs.

Kirkpatrick walked over to Briggs on the far side of the command center. "What's the play, sir?"

"Well, Steve, we could go home and forget all about these assholes."

"Hell no! That's not even an option!"

"All righty then! Looks to me like we're doing it the *Connecticut* way!"

"Well, it's about damn time, sir!"

"Helm, bring us around *Reed Bank* at our best maneuvering speed. I'm wagging that distance at about two hundred and fifty miles?"

"Two seventy, sir! But I'm not one to hug the inside of a track like you."

Most everyone in the command center laughed. Briggs had a reputation of cutting the corners off tracks whether he was being pursued or doing the pursuing.

Briggs had moved over to the digital mission planning board. "Can you zoom in on this spot here?"

Briggs pointed at the center of the atolls they would be travelling through.

"Perfect. I want to deploy four of the Sea Dragons in this general area. Put the first one here after we pass by. The next two, here by *Livock Reef* and a pair on each side of *Eldad Reef*. Put them in water that the *Great Wall* would try to use as cover. Deploy them at a point where they will use minimum power getting into position. Preprogram all four of them with the signature of the *Great Wall*. Listen up real close on this, according to what I've read, we can program the *Dragons* to engage at different ranges and intercept angles.

"No freakin way!"

Briggs laughed. "Not only that, but the *Sea Dragons* can apparently talk to each other *and* to the new ASSASIN (Automated Sub Surface Attack Signal Identification Node) system. "I want as much control over this situation as possible and don't want to worry about sending destruct signals to these things. I would prefer to shoot her in the belly as far forward of her reactors as possible. Everybody clear on this?"

"Yes, sir!"

"Phase one, assuming we're not recalled, will take roughly ten hours. We'll drive down a hundred and fourteen miles, or so."

He looked at his navigator Kenny McBride and winked.

"Any deep spot will do Kenny."

"Phase two will take about five hours."

Briggs leaned forward and placed his finger on the screen.

"And phase three another six hours putting us right here. And let's leave one of our *Dragons* right about here before the turn west."

The weapons officer had been placing coded marks representing the *Sea Dragons* at each of the locations the captain had indicated and added one more.

"Isn't the *Great Wall* sitting in the trench on the east side of Fiery Cross, sir?"

"You're absolutely correct so you all need to get your heads together and figure out how to get her up in this area to the northwest in twenty one hours. I need her at least three hours away before we're south of Fiery Cross. How many *Sea Dragons* do we have left?"

"Three, sir."

"I'll want them here, here, and here."

"But isn't that where we'll be sir?"

"No, Lieutenant. If everything goes according to plan...that's where we *will* have been."

The navigators and other components of the mission planning team worked for the next two hours on cementing together a plan that resembled the captain's.

"Evening, sir," the combat coordinator tipped his coffee cup at Kirkpatrick.

"Captain around?"

Kirkpatrick indicated that Briggs was in the head.

"What have you come up with Mr. Connelly?"

"Did you know that we could get to this point almost six hours sooner if we went through these slots at a higher speed?"

"Yes, I knew. But did you know that he knows that there's no moon after two a.m. tomorrow night and that the SEALs are inserting a team to shut down that gas plant at two thirty a.m.?"

"Damn, he's good."

"He's why we're all still alive, remember?"

"Yes, sir."

"Did you figure out a way to draw the *Great Wall* to the northwest?"

"Yes, sir!" he said with a broad smile. "I think we've got that part all figured out."

"Oh, do tell Mr. Connelly, do tell." Briggs was back from the head.

"Well, sir, the Vietnamese military has already agreed to help have they not?"

"Yes."

"Then I think they need to be right about here," Connelly pointed to the northwest, "causing trouble about three hours before we're here." Connelly drew a circle around the *Fiery Cross Reef*.

"Where are they now Mr. Connelly?"

"If they stayed on course they should be about one hundred and sixty or so miles away from where we need them right about now. They'd need to start getting in position pretty soon."

"Drag the wire and send the message to the Reagan. Give them a GPS box and tell them to stay in it. Be sure they understand that they must stay in that box."

"Trent, won't Admiral Boozeman try and stop you?"

"No, not today." smiled Briggs.

"Shit Trent! For all intents and purposes you bitch slapped him, in front of his command staff, on his own flag ship! Why not today? What do you know that I don't?"

Briggs reached up with a smile and put his hands on his executive officer's shoulders.

"Two reasons Kirk. One, the reason he didn't like my plan is that, right or wrong, he really believed in his heart and soul that the United Nations was a good organization. Do you know what his favorite quote is?"

"No."

Briggs cocked his head to one side. "The soldier above all others prays for peace, for it is the soldier who must suffer and bear the deepest wounds and scars of war."

"That sounds familiar."

"It should, it was said by Douglas MacArthur."

"That's it?"

"No, two, did you know that the admiral is Jewish? The bad guys took two things he loved from him today. He's so pissed right now that I bet he wishes he could turn the whole battle group loose."

"Geez...How do you always know the crap that nobody else even *cares* about?"

Briggs laughed and released the grip on his executive officer.

"I read books by authors that inspire my imagination and fill my mind with limitless possibilities. You should really try it sometime instead of trying to beat your daughter's score in Candy Crush!"

Both men laughed and left the *Connecticut's* command center and headed downstairs.

"You know, I am getting pretty close to her score."

"Sure you are, Kirkpatrick, sure you are!"

CHAPTER 50

—⟋⟍—

Ashes to Ashes

The lumbering B-52s from the 96th Bomb Squadron at Barksdale, Louisiana had been TDY (Temporary Duty) at the small British controlled island of Diego Garcia for just under a month and were very ready to go home. Their hosts for their month long vacation to nowhere? The Air Force's 36th Combat Support Wing.

For the past three weeks, each aircraft, using alternating crews and two support tankers, had left the small island every day at 06:45, flown north-northwest for approximately 1925 miles toward the garden spot of Iran, then turned to a south southwest heading of 235° and flown up the Gulf of Aden toward Djibouti. One at a time, the B-52s would take on a few thousand pounds of gas, change altitude, practice emergency procedures and other emergency scenarios. It was in reality just as much training for the tanker crews as the bombers themselves.

Last night when they returned from their flight they found themselves parked next to two B-52s from their sister squadron, the 11th Bomb Squadron out of Barksdale. Their gold striped tails shimmered eerily in the heat. It was good to see friends from home, but they were almost a week early for their rotation to what the aircrews referred to as "the rock."

The debrief was a bit off in that the commander was a touch more intense than usual and was very quick to get the maintenance reports processed and the aircraft, all four of them, cleared of any issues and mission ready.

As the mission debrief wrapped up, it was announced that the crews, both old and newly arrived, were not to communicate with anyone from home. It was no big deal. It was pretty standard to practice mission dark status.

What was off, was that it had been customary for as long as anyone could remember that the crews rotating in would bring letters, a goody bag or two and beer. The crews and personnel from the 11th? They'd brought nothing.

Majors MacLean and Jackson, both navigators from the 96th, spotted a fellow navigator from the 11th at the Post Exchange.

"Hey Chuck! Why'd you guys screw us over? Y'all freakin too lazy to get some shit thrown in a box for us?

Captain Gleason put his fingers to his lips and motioned the two other men to follow him.

At the end of the hall, with his back against the wall where he could see anyone approaching, he whispered to the men. "We're not even "here" guys. Everybody thinks we went to Eielson to do the northern track training."

"Wait, you're not even our replacements?"

"Nope. All I can say is we're not here and I am the most junior officer on my crew. No more here okay? Just please don't let anyone else in your squadron give anyone else in mine any shit."

The men had shaken hands and got together as a large group for an early dinner.

As the dinner got under way, as orderly and coordinated as a meal in a mess hall can be, the executive officer of the 36th rapped his spoon on the side of his water glass and both toasted the second bomb wing and instructed them that tonight was "dry" and to get some rest. Crew briefing's at 0430 with a 0600 takeoff.

For many that would mean going to bed in about an hour from now. It wasn't a big change, but everybody likes to bitch about something. As the crews, some members still grumbling, moved out to their respective quarters, many could be heard commenting on the evening's change of plans.

—⁂—

Every crew briefing covered essentially the same things whether it was a training mission or a no shit gonna get shot at combat mission. Today's mission had been different from the moment the crews had been put into crew rest last night. Like everything else that's done to the point of muscle memory, the slightest change is noticed by anyone paying attention. In the entire time they'd been deployed, the aircraft commanders had never told them to stay out of the pub and get a good night's rest.

As they rolled into the briefing, they saw the four crew chiefs and two maintenance supervisors, as well as the armament guys, sitting in chairs along the wall. They all looked like hell!

"You guys did get the word that there wasn't to be any drinking last night?"

Without even making eye contact the master sergeant said with a dead pan voice." Yes sir, we've all been up babysitting the birds all night."

"Maintenance issues?" inquired the colonel.

"No, sir, orders."

The senior pilot was just about to push it when the room was called to order.

"Sit down and shut up, we've got a busy morning ahead of us."

An airman was quickly passing out red briefing binders.

"In front of you are the plans for today's mission. I will guarantee that by this time tomorrow every man and woman's life in this room will be forever changed."

The room was dead quiet.

"Open your binders please, and no talking until I ask for comments. Let me start by saying unequivocally that today's mission is not a drill. We will, in fact, be releasing two nuclear armed AGM-86B cruise missiles deep into Iranian territory."

The sound of crewmembers sharply sucking in air was surprisingly loud.

"The Pentagon has identified the hardened facility that guided that freighter into San Diego this past March, as well as the almost successful drone attack on the Seattle Superdome, and the Bangor Trident base just west of downtown Seattle. The Joint Chiefs think it's time to take this place down...permanently!"

Cheers went up briefly, but then the reality of what was potentially coming in the weeks and months ahead tempered their celebratory spirit.

"Here's our plan, and please save your questions until the end unless it's a flight safety issue. Major Ricketts will brief the Intel portion of the brief. Major?"

"Thank you, sir. The success of our little ruse, if you will, is that we've been flying this route with four aircraft every day for almost three weeks. Today we will also be flying four aircraft except they will be four bombers instead of the normal pairings of tankers and bombers. Your flight plans will be almost identical to what you've been flying except we'll top you off about two hours out of here and out of their radar range. I don't have a personal preference for who's on top..."

Several people snickered at that...

"But, it must appear at all times that two of you are tankers. You'll be receiving your call signs and maintenance is prepared to swap out your transponder codes as soon as you decide...who will be on top."

The commander paused knowing that it would get laughs again...

Ricketts smirked, "Who's playing whom?"

The crews laughed even harder.

Ricketts continued his briefing, discussing Iranian coastal defense systems as well as suggested ditching and egress directions and locations. The survival guys did their thing and handed out the usual safe haven destinations, call signs and pickup locations. It was strongly suggested that no one eject in any area that may carry them into Iranian airspace.

"Ejection at low altitude is a bit sportier, but your chances of being back for chow, as bad as it is, are significantly better. Winds will be coming from the southeast at fourteen knots so if you do need to eject at altitude, head up the slot."

Ricketts motioned to the back of the overcrowded room.

"Boom."

The man of the hour worked his way to the front of the briefing room. Weapons Officer Keenan Boomarski, AKA "Boom," looked around the room and smiled at a couple of the more familiar faces.

"Alright, everybody settle down. Here's the breakout that we've decided to do to cover our bets. One of you, and don't get all worked up again, that is playing the tanker's role will be carrying one of the 86 Bravos. Everything we have will be launched simultaneously to confuse the piss out of their Russian tracking equipment. Our hard target, that we simply cannot miss, is located over here in the base of this mountain." "Boom" used a laser pointer to show the projected path of the two nuclear equipped 86 Bravos.

"Into the side of a mountain?" somebody in the back of the rooms enthusiasm for the mission plan was clearly waning a bit.

"Listen, you launch the missiles and let us worry about the targets. Fair enough? The 86 Bravos aren't what I'd like to drop on these bastards and the mountain complex isn't where I'd place them. Having said that...for the target we've been assigned, the Bravos will make the intended impression. Agreed?"

Once the whistling, cheering and chaos of his comments had subsided, he moved everyone forward to the next section of the briefing.

"Major Ricketts?"

Ricketts walked back to the center of the room and rapped a hunk of rock on the lectern.

"Alright break out into the usual groups of hooligans and thugs and get this thing planned out. I'm told the weather, etcetera is in your binders."

The brief had run slightly longer than planned, but that wouldn't affect their intended take off time. Strategic Air Command may not be around anymore, but their legacy and long history of on time takeoffs was still very much the template that drove every mission.

—ᴍ—

As it stood at briefing time, the four aircraft would take off at 0600 and rendezvous with two real KC-10 tankers that had left thirty minutes sooner. By 0700 all four bombers would be inbound to their first waypoint, approximately four hours later, just short of the opening of the Gulf of Oman, in two race track patterns, they would make it appear that they were taking turns refueling. In actuality, they would be waiting for the mission go/no go call.

It was just after 1300 and they were on the last northwestern leg of their last run when they received the encrypted code they'd been waiting for. It reached all four aircraft simultaneously and all four began their "descent for landing" procedures at AL Udeid Air base in Qatar three hundred and sixty two miles to their west.

"Control this is Exxon 56 requesting control and vectors to Al Udeid."

"Roger, Exxon 56 come to new heading 271° and begin your descent, maintain 25,000 feet."

"Roger, control, Exxon 56 descending and holding at 25,000 feet."

The first bomber with the tanker call sign tipped its nose over and began its descent.

The other three aircraft had made the similar calls and began their descents to the altitudes requested by the air traffic controller. Each aircraft would be conducting the exact bomb run checklists. Throughout the years it had been emphasized in years of training and in recent combat over the sands of Southeast Asia that the only difference in an aircraft checklist from plane to plane better be the accent of the crew.

"Everybody ready?"

"Oxygen masks on?"

From around the aircraft came the familiar double click on the mic switch indicating, "Yes."

"Crew position report and status."

"Radar Navigator, Green."

"Defensive Navigator, Green."

"EWO, Green."

"Co-pilot, Green."

"Pilot, Green."

They were currently at 37,000 feet and the descent would take each aircraft just under five minutes to make it appear as a normal descent.

Lt. Colonel Landon's stomach had some knots. He keyed his mic three times and said nothing.

He'd trained his whole adult life for the next three minutes and it was harder than he ever imagined. He keyed the mic again. "Confirm mission and weapons release code."

The co-pilot and the EWO opened their respective cards.

"Challenge color, blue."

The navigator looked at his card and replied, "Parrot."

"Code confirmed."

Lt. Colonel Landon keyed his mic, "Ping home one more time please."

"Home plate authenticates with code phrase Manta347\890#632."

"Mission confirmed."

"Open secure SATCOM link."

"Linked."

"EWO, this is your ballgame now...I got us here and I'll try and get us home."

"Roger that, sir. All aircraft...weapons release on my mark."

Captain Mitchell looked at his screen one last time and waited for the pixels to line up..."Mark!"

The airframes of all four massive aircraft shook as six cruise missiles left each aircraft.

"All aircraft reporting weapons free."

"Roger that, weapons free."

"Al Udeid control, Exxon 56, were gonna need that new heading and call sign change right about...now!"

"Roger that."

The colonel waited a few moments for Al Udeid control to make the changes in their flight profile.

"Grave Dancer 32, please come to new heading of 268° descend your best speed to 10,000 feet, contact Riyadh approach control for further instructions."

"Thank you for the assistance Al Udeid."

"Oh no, sir...thank you!"

CHAPTER 51

—ɯ—

Eclipse

The information that Behrouz had supplied the CIA needed to work or the world would be both angry and laughing at the prowess of the United States military and that chain of either "hero" or "goat" status would affect the entire chain of command starting with the four US Air Force B-52s, the twenty-two conventional cruise missiles and two nuclear armed cruise missiles it had just sent into the sovereign airspace of Iran. At the end of the day they would effectively be at war. It was an easy bet that the war would last the one day. Once the United States played its ultimate trump card and let the nuclear genie out of the bottle, pushing into a second day would be viewed as foolish even to the Mullahs.

The conventional cruise missiles were launched at targets such as power grids and the half dozen known tracking sites along the Iranian coast. All of these targets would be hit within eleven minutes of launch. It was hoped that in the complete pandemonium that ensued, the two terrain hugging missiles would get through unnoticed and find their targets.

Whether they actually reached their targets or not was of little or no consequence. They would either be shot down or detonate a conventional payload on a military target. If, and it was a real if, the Iranians were able to determine the direction and potential target of the second pair they wouldn't even give them a second thought. The mountain was hundreds of feet thick and deemed impenetrable by the engineers who had designed it and confirmed unintentionally by a veteran senator from New Jersey who, while exiting a Senate Armed Services Committee meeting a few years earlier, had lamented at the complex's impressive strength, design and impenetrability. Once again it would appear that the Americans had been cowards and tried to simply "send a message."

Of course, that all changed quickly when after thirty-six hours of trying to open a door of the hardened Kesheh Research facility, any door, to the outside, the facility's staff suddenly found itself, at 1300 local time, with not only its two front doors locked open, but every fire door and internal blast door locked open as well.

The two missiles, which had been guided for most of their trip by GPS coordinates had made it past all of the known Iranian missile defensive systems and were well on their respective ways to their targets. The nuclear equipped AGM-86B version of the weapon would be using its TERCOM (terrain contour-matching) guidance system to fly to its assigned target. Several recently uploaded pictures of the entrances insured that the missiles would find their intended targets.

Flying close to the ground at just over five hundred and fifty miles per hour each twenty foot missile had traveled just over 637 miles and taken just over the estimated seventy two minutes to reach their assigned targets.

Both missiles, traveling with less than one hundred meters separation, had flown a forty-five minute zigzag pattern through the valleys leading to the small town of Kesheh. For a moment, the little regional airport on the hilltop in nearby Esfahan thought they'd seen something on their approach radar, but at five hundred and fifty miles an hour? It hadn't really mattered.

Many of the workers who had been locked in the complex for over a day were still streaming out when the two missiles, at just over seven feet off the ground, screamed past them and into the enormous facility's door openings, normally protected by the massive blast doors.

With both the main and various internal blast doors and other defensive systems so eloquently designed by Major Fallahi removed, both missiles made it more than one hundred feet into their respective tunnels before each detonated its 200 kiloton warhead.

Satellite photos taken during and after the attack would later show that, for all intents and purposes, the mountain, formally named "Karkas Mountain," simply no longer existed. The air blast kill radius of the attack was just under a half mile and the fire ball had engulfed everything flammable within 575 feet.

From the city of Tehran, almost one hundred and fifty miles away, the people as well as the government bureaucrats and the Imams, stood in the streets and watched as the enormous pillar of super-heated rock, sand, and air streamed almost straight up. The winds were light this afternoon and were coming out of the north. That fact alone would spare most of the more densely populated areas from the impending deadly radioactive fallout.

It was, in many ways, a beautiful thing to behold. Many of the poorly educated simply didn't know what it was and began shouting, "Allahu Akbar."

CHAPTER 52

—◊—

Day of the Dragon

Everyone got their coffee and sat around the largest table they could find like they'd done for the past few months and listened to and watched the morning briefing. It wasn't the same coffee and it wasn't the same table. As a matter of fact, nothing this week, was anything like last week...except the people. They were all here and everyone was really no worse for wear except that they had been rather rudely reminded that they lived in a dangerous world. Everyone was delighted to find that Ken and the other members of the security team had collected all of their personal items off their desks and brought them over to the annex over the weekend.

Rick Wagner, in his position as liaison to the BOATSS group, had been assigned the morning briefing.

"As many of you have heard through the various news sources there was a tremendous nuclear explosion at the Kesheh Research and Special Projects Facility in south central Iran. Let me remove any speculation from your minds. We blew the living hell out of their little shop of horrors."

Jewels sat quietly at the side of the room taking it all in.

"Our next briefer is Major Textron from Cyber Command, Ma'am?"

"At approximately 1005 Zulu on the afternoon of the explosion we noticed what we at first thought was an after effect of the weapon strike. Whole sections of the Iranian infrastructure began to collapse and fail. As I said, we originally thought it was perhaps an EMP affect. Our sources both in country and others have said that the entire country's computer and communication networks have been disabled."

"Everything?"

"Disabled isn't exactly accurate. Fried would be more accurate. At the present time there are no operating computers in the country of Iran. Not in the government or in the private sector. Even cell service has been shut down."

Mitch couldn't resist the urge to ask a question. "What the heck could do all that?"

"Well, that's a very good question. Nobody over in our shop has been able to figure it out."

"Any indications it was a virus?"

"Whatever this thing was, it did what everyone always hears about a really bad virus doing on the internet, except eat their lunch. This "Virus," for lack of a better term at the moment, destroyed the computers they accessed. It wasn't after files or doing malicious damage, it just flat out destroyed the computer."

"Ms. Folk? You're being uncharacteristically quiet this morning. No 'big ideas' from the genius from MIT?"

Jewels smiled her best crocodile smile. "No major, I'm just trying to wrap my head around the fact that my building is gone and until we can get back to work our mission here is being compromised. The UN's been attacked by crazy Muslims and Iran's been attacked by America. My team and I would like to see if we can avoid a full blown war with the Chinese if you could let us get back to our primary mission."

Several people around the small room clapped.

"Cyber command will get to the bottom of this eventually."

"I have a question major." It was Chris Sutterfield.

"What's your question?"

"You came in here this morning almost threatening us over something

GOOD that's happened in the *War on Terror* and then tell us you're going to expend resources to find out who, what, where and why this was done? Why don't you go back to your office and concentrate on your core responsibilities of keeping our nation's secrets safe and while you're at it, the records of all the people who have put their lives into keeping this country great."

With the sound of applause at her back, Major Marcia Textron left the briefing.

"Way to go Chris!"

Jewels walked up to the front, sat down and looked at her "crew" as she referred to them. "Well that was fun!"

Everyone laughed.

Gina looked at her friend and could see something was different. Suddenly she connected the dots!

Jewels took a swallow of cold coffee and met Gina's gaze from across the table. "A few things before we dive back into our new and hopefully temporary normal. I hope that the next week slows down some, but right now we have a submarine captain and what's left of the pacific fleet sailing into a potential shit storm unless we pull up our britches and help them out. Any questions?"

Susan Atwater waved her hand. "Hi Jewels, this team was assembled to find out who was behind the attack on San Diego and I believe we should know how long you think we will have jobs?"

"Excellent question, Susan. It is my belief that our hunt is not quite over. I read some Intel last week that leads me and others to believe that the Chinese government is in this mess up to their necks. It is for that reason, and my personal admiration for the guys out in the South Pacific, that we need to get back into this game as quickly as possible."

Jewels looked over at Gina and caught the wink. "That's it for now people. Get back to whatever it is you get paid for."

Gina mouthed, "Good job."

Mitch stood up and worked his way around the table.

"Hey!"

"Hey yourself. What's up?" Jewels pushed back her chair without making eye contact.

"You did a nice job in here today."

"Thank you, Mitch."

"Seriously, you seemed very confident in yourself, very self-assured. Jewels, I..."

Jewels put up her hand and cut him off. "Not here Mitch, walk me upstairs to my office?"

"Sure!" Mitch responded enthusiastically.

Jewels did not respond and simply left the conference room. In the background, she could hear Gina telling everyone to top off their cups with coffee and get upstairs and get back to work.

She smiled to herself. There would be lots of changes this week.

Well, she might as well get this over with...

After everyone else had headed upstairs, Jewels headed for the elevator. "So Mitch, about us..."

—⁂—

The *Connecticut,* now safely on the far west side of the Spratly's, was once again, after two days of quick but silent maneuvering, coming shallow for final instructions and message traffic.

"Captain flash message from COMSUBPAC."

"What the hell is going on in the world?" I used to be submerged for a month and the only major news event would be Chief Black's wife having another kid!"

"This one's not funny sir! The country of Iran is saying we attacked it with a nuclear strike and the White House *isn't* denying it."

"Don't editorialize it lieutenant, just read the damn message!"

"B-52 strike against the Iranian facility that coordinated the attack on San Diego, successful. Fallout confined to within the Iranian borders. Unknown cyber-attack has crippled the entire Iranian infrastructure. That's the end of that message."

"Anything else?"

"Yes, sir."

"Well?"

"Sir, apparently, there was an attack on the BOATSS complex just prior to that."

Briggs shot out of his chair. "Anyone hurt?"

"Just the bad guys, but the BOATSS facility is a complete loss."

"Shit! Any more good news for me tonight lieutenant?"

"Well, sir, I wouldn't call it great news, but after their building blew up the BOATSS people helped destroy two drone 747's that were headed for the sub pens at Kitsap and the CenturyLink stadium.

"Anyone hurt?"

"Two fishermen were hospitalized for exposure when their boat capsized."

"I'm afraid to ask, anything else?"

"Yes, sir, but its marked 'Captain's Eyes Only.'"

"Give it here."

"Thank you lieutenant. Kirkpatrick, you're with me. Let's see what the United States Navy wants us to do for them today."

—⧟—

Briggs opened the documents and read his orders.

"Well?" asked his anxious executive officer.

"Here, what do you think they're saying?"

Kirkpatrick read the orders. He was always fun to watch because even at the ripe old age of twenty-nine...he still moved his lips when he read.

"What do *you* make of this?" Kirkpatrick handed the documents back to Briggs.

"I honestly don't see where our current battle plan needs to change at all. They want to be sure that we are aware of the potential complications the attack on Iran could lead to.

"Such as?"

Briggs leaned as far back in his chair as he could and exhaled for what seemed like fifteen seconds before drawing a deep breath.

"Well, for one thing the Chinese are now damn sure we're pissed off about the San Diego situation as well as the drone aircraft. By using the nukes in Iran, we've announced to the world that we're going with our 'A game.'"

Kirkpatrick leaned forward in his chair. "Why do I sense that there's a part of this that's not good news for our particular situation?"

"If the Chinese get too panicky they could decide it would be better to strike us first. While I'm not sure whether the other boats in our little pond here have nukes on board, you can be damn sure that the *Great Wall* does."

"Skipper, I don't see this ending any other way than with us, or somebody else, sinking that submarine."

"Kirk, old buddy, I don't either, but that's why I keep the company of as many smart people as I do. What time is it in D.C.?"

Kirkpatrick checked his watch. "It's just coming up on 08:45. Why?"

"I need to be at communication depth in fifteen minutes please."

"And, pray tell why is that, sir?"

"Because, young man, I've got a video date with a very pretty lady in D.C."

CHAPTER 53

—✦—

BOATSS Annex

Jewels was just starting her second cup of coffee for the morning when the geek from the day before stuck his head into her cubicle and said she had a call on the secure line. Jewels, at least for the immediate future, didn't have the luxury of a crypto secure phone on her desk, but every time she asked she was told to be patient, it was "in the works."

"Any idea who it is?"

"He said his name was Briggs. Not the best connection..."

She was already in motion before he had finished his sentence.

"Where!"

"Third cubicle to your left!"

She grabbed the phone, "Julie Folk!"

"Hey good looking! This is a very long distance call. At least you could have some music or something when you put me on hold."

Jewels laughed. "If you're calling me it's not to complain about my phones..."

Briggs laughed. "No, not today."

"Good, what's up sir?"

"From what I hear we're both having interesting weeks. I take it you're not set up to video conference yet?"

"Standby, sir."

Jewels waved the geek over. "Can we video conference to this number from downstairs?"

"Yeah sure, why?"

Jewels hissed at him. "Write the number down and get ready to make it happen, NOW! MOVE!"

"Captain Briggs, can I call you back in five minutes? We're still surrounded by a significant level of chaos here."

"I'll be right here." The line went dead.

Jewels went to the center of the room and cupped her hands to her mouth.

"I need my team of geeks in the basement conference room right now!"

With a flurry of movement, fifteen people with pads of paper and cups of coffee hurried down the two flights of stairs into the conference room.

"You!" Jewels pointed at the tech guy. "Make the call to Captain Briggs."

"Yes, ma'am!"

"It's connecting, ma'am."

"Thank you."

There was a loud click.

"*Connecticut* Communications Officer, Lieutenant Clifton, I show us secure."

"Good evening lieutenant, Captain Briggs had requested a video link?"

"Yes, ma'am."

Damn it, three times in five minutes she'd been "ma'amed."

Suddenly the large briefing screen was filled with an image of men trying to get around a table.

"Hi Jewels!"

"Hi Captain, what can my 'boat' do for yours?"

"Hey, kiddo, we're in a bit of a jam here. The attack on the Iranian facility has everyone over here spooked that the Chinese might panic and go nuclear before we can gently convince them that they need to leave the area. I really don't want to sink their big missile boat and was wondering if perhaps you might have a suggestion..."

"Let me ask the brains of my outfit. Standby, sir, I'm going to mute us for a minute or so."

That was okay with the crew of the *Connecticut*. Most of the officers in the room hadn't come to hear the pretty lady talk.

"Well, you heard the man. Can we do anything from here to help him win without shooting?"

"Can submarines really talk to each other, or is that just in the movies?"

"Good question, why?"

"Well, if they start talking digitally we could maybe piggyback a virus and shut the Chinese sub down."

"Don't they look for that?"

"Yes, the trick would be to not look like what they're looking for."

"Un-mute us please."

"Sir, is it possible that you could communicate with the other sub or is that just in the movies?"

Briggs looked around at his staff. "Mute us please."

Lieutenant Clifton leaned forward. "Sir, I'm not sure I'm comfortable discussing our comm. system with these folks."

"Would you rather become a giant smoking hole in the seafloor lieutenant? We came close to that back in March. If I recall you weren't very comfortable with that either."

Several men around the table chuckled.

"Your concerns are duly noted lieutenant, but please answer the pretty lady's question."

"Yes, sir, we could, but I'm not sure what we would talk about? As soon as we made contact they would...Holy shit, sir...they'd come to *us* at flank speed..."

He stood up and looked at the chart superimposed on the table. "Right over the *Sea Dragons!*"

Briggs smiled. "Un-mute us please."

"Hi there, apparently real life has finally caught up with Hollywood. The easy answer is, 'yes' we can contact them."

"Well, that's good, right?"

"The problem is that we'll need to ask them something or tell them something they want to hear in order for them to engage us in conversation. Compounding that is the fact that his orders may be to destroy me and he'll be doing everything he can to lock onto my position."

"Standby, sir."

"Clemson, how much time do you need?"

"Three hours on the outside, maybe two and a half."

"Sir, we'll be ready in two and half hours. Do you want us to call you?"

"I'll need to surface and I..."

Jewels interrupted him. "Respectfully, sir, no you won't. Go find a safe place to hide and look for us to call you on...standby sir."

Jewels looked at her acoustic whiz Tom Sperry. "And what frequency would you like to call them on?"

"Sorry, calculating...ahhh...0.023 Hz."

"You're sure about that?"

The young man gave her a smile and two thumbs up. "Sir, we'll initiate contact with you, on frequency 0.023 Hz, in just less than three hours for some final coordination."

"Roger that, Jewels! Thanks for the help."

Briggs made a slashing sound across his throat and the connection to BOATSS was terminated.

Briggs turned to the sound of his torpedo man and his sonar man chuckling together in the corner of the room. "Gentlemen, did I miss something funny?"

"No, sir. We were just trying to decide if she was as smart as she was pretty or vice versa."

"And?"

Briggs walked over to the two men.

"And as crazy at it seems, she is smarter than she looks!"

Kirkpatrick, whose sense of humor was not engaged at the moment, said, "Enough, the captain asked you a question!"

Briggs held up his hand. "Would you care to explain to us dummies what's so funny?"

"Sorry, sir! Do you remember when you saw us reading the operations manual for the *Sea Dragons*?"

"Yes."

"Do you remember when she said that if we needed her, she could communicate with the *Sea Dragons* from her end?

"Yes."

"Sir, she's gonna use their BOATSS underwater hydrophone system to communicate with the Chinese sub!"

"Oh My God, that's brilliant! They'll never get a fix on us because we won't actually be in direct contact."

"Until, or unless, we *want* to be," piped in the young communications officer.

Briggs was smiling ear to ear. He loved having options.

"Alright, although it appears that we will end this without a major catastrophe, I want all departments ready for battle stations if our little plan doesn't work. I want status reports every thirty minutes."

—⚓—

Jewels looked at her group of amazing minds assembled in front of her at the table.

"I'm reasonably sure that if you guys can pull this off...you'll all keep your jobs."

"Ms. Folk, are we legally allowed to do this?"

"What? Stop World War III? I'll go out on a limb and say that I'm reasonably sure that the legalities will be brushed aside. That being said, if you just muck it up..." Jewels shrugged her shoulders and lifted her hands as if to say who knows?

Gina pulled her aside. "Was that your idea of a pep talk?"

"Yeah why?"

"You're such a nerd!"

"Chris, you've got this right?"

"At the moment I'm just wasting time standing here gabbin with y'all."

"Go, go, go." Gina shooed him out the door.

Jewels looked at her watch. "I've got us at two hours and twenty minutes before we call Briggs back with an answer. Have you seen Ken around today?"

"He's setting up our new visitor desk, why?"

"I've got a job that's right up his alley."

"Is it legal?"

"Probably not."

"I'm in!"

"Alright, here's what I need him to do..."

—∽—

"Hi, Rick."

"Don't you 'hi' me! You broke Mitch's heart. I should hang up on you."

"Hey, listen I need you to go secure with me right now!"

"Whatever." After a brief pause he was back, "I show us secure. What's the fire this time?"

"Can you get your hands on the debrief from the former captain of the Chinese submarine *Great Wall*?"

"Probably, why?"

"I'm trying to avert WWIII and my solution will require that debrief and your boss, Mr. Batsly, over here to the annex pronto."

"Jewels, I don't have any control over that man's schedule. He's the Deputy Director of the CIA for God's sake."

"Rick, you've got to try. I have, two hours and twenty minutes before two bad things will happen. The first is I will make contact with an uncooperative foreign government's ballistic missile submarine and then Cyber Command is going to swoop in here and shut me down. I need a heavy hitter here ASAP."

"I'll see what I can do. No promises."

She placed the phone down. That sounded kinda sketchy. Maybe Jonah could help? She dialed the number.

"You've reached the desk of Clayton Beewater, please leave a message."

"Shit!"

She waited five minutes and tried again...

"Hello...I mean West!"

"You're there!"

"That's your greeting?" Jonah laughed.

"I'll greet you later, right now I'm trying to save the world and at the same time not get arrested doing it!"

Jonah sensed she wasn't kidding. "What can I do?"

"Get Roger Batsly over to my office ASAP!"

"Can I ask what for?"

"You need to trust me!" Jewels hung up the phone.

Jewels looked at her watch, somehow hoping that by looking at it, it would slow down.

CHAPTER 54

Ace of Spades

Jewels walked to the lower floor where Ken had set up their new visitor desk. They couldn't shut down the building because it technically wasn't all their space, but they were certainly within their rights to restrict access to their floors. "Are we all set Ken?"

"Yes ma'am. Security teams have been briefed and nobody's coming through that door unless *you* say it's okay."

She continued to walk briskly through the various areas of the annex making sure everything and everyone knew what they had to do.

At 11:45, only fifteen minutes shy of their deadline, Chris came up to her at a fast walk. "Gina built the firewall like you suggested, but their systems saw it right away. We got what we needed done, but they'll be here in fifteen minutes to shut us down. By 'shut us down' I mean everything from phones to computer and probably even our cable feed from Time Warner. How far out is your guy?"

"I'd hoped we wouldn't be cutting it quite so close."

Another of her team trotted up. "Jewels, Ken needs you at the visitor desk, something about you expecting two visitors and seven people are there."

Jewels walked down the hallway to where she could see a group of people milling around the desk and two of the BOATSS security team were blocking the hall.

"Jonah?"

"Hi Jewels! You sounded frightened so I brought who I could. The group of men parted and in the center of the group was Ken Shortman shaking the hand of Roger Batsly, Deputy Director of the CIA.

"It's been a long-time sir." Jewels extended her hand, but he gently brushed it aside and gave her a big hug. He leaned in close and whispered in her ear. "I got you into this mess and I'm going to get you out." He released his embrace. "What can we do?"

"I need a few guys for security and, if you brought that debrief, you can follow me. We're in a bit of a time crunch so we need to talk and walk down to the conference room."

"Yes ma'am." said the deputy director with as much sarcasm as he could muster.

"Here's the plan sir, we're going to attempt to contact the Chinese ballistic missile submarine *Great Wall*. Technically it's the *Great Wall II*, but I digress. Anyway, Captain Briggs is on the bottom of this canyon right here." Jewels pointed to the area on a map someone had found of the South China Sea. "He's already deployed the new *Sea Dragon* weapons, but would really not like to sink the Chinese sub in such shallow water. The risk of radioactive contamination is enormous and would defeat the entire point of reclaiming this area for the surrounding countries."

"Good thinking, so far so good."

"We want to tell the new commander of the *Great Wall* that the old commander has defected and that we know all the weaknesses of his submarine. Of course this is a complete head fake because what we're really doing is uploading a crippling virus onto his boat while we talk to him."

"We can do that?"

"Can you ask me again in an hour?"

Roger Batsly slowly shook his head and smiled. "Why do I even ask? What can I do?"

"You can talk to the President and keep Cyber Command off our backs, sir."

"Well, Jewels, you certainly know how to show a guy a good time!"

Roger Batsly walked over to the far corner and asked his aid for his phone. The aid reached into his breast pocket and pulled out a secure satellite phone and punched in a few numbers. "Roger Batsly for the President. Yes? Really? Golfing? Really? Well, maybe you could get ahold of his Secret Service detail for me and tell them that he better either call me or sit in the golf cart with the nuclear launch codes because some of us are trying to prevent WWIII." He hung up the phone.

"Jewels, Cyber Command's at the door."

Roger Batsly looked at Jewels with a warm smile.

"Are you going to be alright, sir?"

"I'll be fine...I put in my retirement papers last week. Get me upstairs so I can speak to these bureaucratic blowhards."

He turned one last time to give everyone a thumbs up.

Jewels turned back to her team, "Your name's Bruce, correct?"

"Yes, ma'am."

Could you please place our call to the *Connecticut*, Bruce?"

"It'll just be a second."

"Everybody ready?"

The whole team gathered around and wished her luck.

A loud click led to a hollow sounding Captain Briggs, but it was working.

"Right on time, Ms. Folk."

"Unfortunately, sir, not without the usual drama."

Briggs laughed.

"Hey, I'm going to step back and let the geeks work this, sound good?"

"I'm doing the same here. Let me quickly tell you the plan. Your voice will pass through this link and then we'll re-direct through our system and send it to him from several directions at once. We're affixing a virus to disable his boat. Are we good with the plan?"

"Let's Rock and Roll."

"Clemson, you're up. Do us proud!"

"Submarine *Great Wall* this is the attack submarine *USS Connecticut* hailing the *Great Wall* do you copy?"

It took several attempts, but eventually the communications officer responded.

"*USS Connecticut* please state your intentions please."

Crap! This guy spoke better English than half his crew!

"Greetings! This is Captain Briggs of the *Connecticut,* is your captain available?"

"I'm here, Captain Briggs, please state your intentions. In fairness, I will tell you that we are triangulating your position as we speak."

Briggs chuckled, "Ah, yes, about that. Well, we're using some new technology so I wouldn't put any fish in the water just yet. Listen, we were going to work all this stuff out with the United Nations, but that doesn't look like that's going to happen anytime soon. So, here's *our* plan…"

"I don't have time for this right now, captain. I'm in the process of dealing with the Vietnamese, but I assume you know that."

"It won't take me thirty seconds, captain…"

"You have thirty seconds, Captain Briggs."

"Fair enough, we need you to call all your ships and people in the area and tell them they need to head north within the next hour."

"Or what? You will nuke us like you did the Iranians?"

"Captain, with all due respect, your options are actually very limited."

Jewels looked over at Chris and got the thumbs up. The virus was loaded.

Briggs smiled over at Kirkpatrick and winked. "Captain, your Lt. Colonel Chung was very helpful as well as thorough in his debrief. He sends his regards and hopes you will make a reasonable decision."

"Captain Briggs, you're wasting time. I am an experienced card player and I say you're bluffing."

"Fair enough. I'll let you go but not before I pass on one last message from Colonel Chung.

"And what farcical story would you wish to tell me now, Captain Briggs?"

"He said, and I quote, 'Please tell him it would be a family tragedy for your mother to lose both her children to the sea.' That's it! Good speaking with you."

Chris cut the feed to the *Great Wall* and reestablished the voice connection with the captain of the *Connecticut*. He placed the captain on speaker phone.

Briggs thought for a moment and stared into space. "Sonar, what have you got for me?"

"High speed screw sounds being relayed through the BOATSS network."

"Which direction?"

"Southbound, sir!"

Briggs looked at the electronic map. "Anything near a *Sea Dragon*?"

"Sir, at her current course and speed the Chinese destroyer *Kunming* will pass over *Sea Dragon* position two in just less than three minutes. Standby, sir. Sonar now indicates she's making max revolutions. If you want to hit her you've got about thirty seconds to commit.

"Damn it! I'd really hoped a strong message would suffice. It's not my call to turn this into a shooting match."

"No, actually it's the President's call and he says sink her if you have to!" Roger Batsly had quietly re-entered the room and observed the last several minutes of interaction.

Briggs looked at his communications officer and nodded. "Can you folks send the launch code for that *Sea Dragon* to get the *Kunming*?"

"Sir, we've been waiting for your word to launch."

"Captain, sonar says ten seconds sir!"

"Thank you, Mr. Kirkpatrick, sink that son of a bitch! Repeat, sink the *Kunming*!"

From thousands of miles away Jewels could almost sense the snarl on Briggs' face.

"Launch codes sent."

"Sir, sonar reports an odd track...very high speed screws transiting from 735 feet and ascending rapidly. No speed or course corrections for the *Kunming*."

"Kirkpatrick, why isn't the *Kunming* taking evasive maneuvers?"

"Sir, the *Kunming's* own engine speed will blind her at her current speed. She can't hear anything except herself."

"Sonar reports, five seconds sir."

"Impact and detonation!"

Briggs walked over to Kirkpatrick and the chief, giving both men high fives. "Drag the wire and see if we can pick up any chatter."

"Sir, sonar reports massive secondary explosions. The *Kunming's* breaking up and sinking rapidly at the bow. One Mayday was transmitted and her distress beacon has been activated."

Everyone on the bridge agreed that there was probably nothing like 650 pounds of high explosive going off under your keel to ruin your day.

Briggs leaned toward Kirkpatrick and whispered, "Can you even imagine the devastation on that ship? With her forward speed of close to 45 knots and instantaneously losing the front third of your ship?"

Kirkpatrick shook his head. "At least it would have been quick."

After five minutes, sonar reported negative chatter.

Briggs addressed the crew over the ships communication system. "Alright people we still have the *Great Wall* to deal with and I'd imagine her captain is none too pleased with recent events."

Kirkpatrick casually pulled the captain aside. "Now what boss?"

Briggs just smiled a big toothy smile and whispered, "Magic time."

"Jewels are you guys ready to do your magic?"

"Yes sir!"

"Well, you and your folks have done a marvelous job so far, but the *Great Wall* is in shallower water than she was five minutes ago and isn't showing any signs of backing down. So it's time, my dear, to do the voo-do, you do, so very well."

Every head in the room looked at the Deputy Director. He nodded once to Jewels who in turn, nodded once to Chris. Chris hit a series of keys on his keyboard and the room waited for some kind of sign that it had worked.

Everyone watched the second hand on the large wall clock as two minutes turned into four. Jewels could hear the ring tone of a phone coming from the director's aid's pocket. The man was so engrossed that he didn't hear the telephone in his own pocket. She hand signaled him that it was ringing.

The man answered, then quickly handed the director the phone.

"Batsly here. Really? Well, that's good news! Thank you! Goodbye!"

"Your attention please," the room was dead silent. "My sources tell me that the Chinese submarine *Great Wall* was spotted doing an emergency ascent and is now dead in the water. Other sources indicate that other surface combatants are slowly leaving the area in a northerly direction.

Jewels gently nudged some of her team to one side. "Move over so Mr. Batsly can speak to Captain Briggs."

"Captain Briggs, Roger Batsly, CIA, here. How're them apples, captain?"

"Sir, that's the best news I've heard in a long time."

"Safe voyage home, captain. Kudos to your crew on a job well done!" Roger laughed, "Again!"

"Thank you, sir."

"Trent, it's Jewels, we're signing off here, sir. Christmas at the ranch this year?"

"Absolutely! Just give Stacy a call for me and let her know how many. Briggs out."

—⁂—

Mitch smiled at Jewels briefly and headed upstairs first, followed by Roger Batsly and his detail. As Jewels approached the top of the stairs she could hear Roger Batsly really laying into someone. Jewels felt bad for whoever it was until she got a bit closer. It was that bitch Textron from Cyber Command.

For an old man he had one hell of a voice!

"And, Major Textron if I ever hear of you messing with or threatening my people again I'll have your entire chain of command fired. AM I CLEAR!?"

The Deputy Director was in the middle of turning away when he abruptly paused. He turned slowly and gestured for Jonah and Jewels to follow him.

In plain sight, and probably with total understanding of the message he was sending, he put his arm around Jewels as they walked out.

"Kids, we need to take a little ride."

—◦—

It was right in the middle of lunch hour and for that reason many of the offices were empty. Roger Batsly told his secretary to hold his calls and they went into his office and closed the door.

"Jonah, I've got a confession to make."

"Excuse me, sir?"

"Although I pretended at our first meeting to not know you, I knew everything about you. Perhaps more than I should have. I'm retiring in two weeks. I needed to stay just long enough to fulfill a promise to my son. You understand loyalty Jonah so I don't think you'll be angry with me. Jewels could you hand this picture to Jonah?"

"Certainly, sir."

Jonah took the picture and looked at it. It was five or so marines sitting on the hood and roof of a Humvee.

"Sir?"

"Turn it over please."

Jonah turned the picture over and read the note on the back that Roger Batsly had read every day for over ten years:

"Hi Dad, we're on our way to Ramadi this week to extract some SEALS!! 10/18/05 Love you! Skip"

Jonah felt the blood drain from his face.

"JONAH!" Jewels looked at his face. "Are you okay?"

Jonah raised his hand and waved her off. "I'm fine."

"Jewels if you please?"

Roger handed Jewels the second picture from his desk and Jewels handed it to Jonah. He gazed at the picture and read what it said...twice.

It was a picture of a tombstone in Arlington Cemetery. The epitaph simply read:

Roger "Skip" Batsly II
Loving son,
Outstanding Marine
2/1/1980 - 11/10/05

"Jonah, I'm sorry it took so long to thank you."

Jonah tried to speak, but his throat was as tight as it had ever been at any point in his life. "He fought so hard to make it back to you. I fought so hard to save him. I've always wondered who he was, but never had the courage to ask."

"Hey, Jonah, how about a drink for my son and my new 'family?'"

Jonah took his glass and raised it to the ceiling promptly swallowing the entire contents of the glass in one gulp.

"Semper Fi Marine! Semper Fi."

CHAPTER 55

—◠◠—

Respite

It had been just over eight months since Jewels and Jonah made the decision to leave the rigors and stress of a life in Washington D.C. Their new lives brought many changes to them personally and professionally. Despite the cold of an Idaho winter, they had so enjoyed their trip to the Briggs' ranch at Christmas that Jonah bought almost one hundred acres of ranchland adjacent to the Briggs' property. Stacy Brigg's mom still didn't understand what Jewels did for a living and would still introduce her as one of those computer techie people.

With the new enormous home built to Jonah's slightly paranoid specifications and Jewels attention to detail, the home's construction had seen several delays. As a result, the two were still shopping for furniture and other items to fill it. The untrained eye wouldn't have noticed that several of the last groups of contractors were from the McLean, Virginia area and that they were putting some very special final touches on a room they designed especially for Jewels. It was underground and constructed completely of poured concrete and had several other unique features that most home offices didn't need. It was similar to the room Jonah had built at the other end of the basement but different in one major way. Jewels' room had been designed, constructed, and paid for by the Central Intelligence Agency. It was sort of their way of saying "thank you" without making a big deal about it.

Upstairs, halfway down the hall, an artist who now went by the name "Kenneth" in his new circle, was busily filling an entire room, floor to ceiling, with fanciful pictures of enormous butterflies so detailed it appeared they could fly away at a moment's notice.

"Ohhh Kenneth! A quick reminder...Although I love the job you're doing, these babies will be delivered on time, sixty-one days from today! We will come home from the hospital with the babies to this room and it will be set-up and ready for them!"

The woman waddled her way down to the unfinished nursery. "Are we clear about this or do I need to fly Ms. Gina out here to supervise?"

The enormous man, with vibrant colored paint covering most places on his clothes, slowly turned around and looked at his former boss and smiled. "Yes, ma'am."

Jewels turned without saying a word. As she slowly waddled down the hall and out on the front porch where two old friends were sitting having a beer, she could still hear the big man laughing.

Jonah looked up at her and smiled. His blond hair had grown back to a point where he could actually put it in a ponytail.

"What's the big guy laughing about now, sweetie?"

"Damn it, Jonah, he ma'amed me *AGAIN*!!!"

Acknowledgments

Setting out on the journey to be an author is always exciting, but not without its challenges. Each book, or adventure, may require different motivations than a previous work. Unlike my first endeavor, Checkmate, I had a source with Archer's Paradox that I never imagined, fans. When people, other than family, ask when they're going to get their hands on your next book, it adds something to the effort. In some ways, you feel energized to give them a better story.

I would like to thank the usual cast of characters that help me with my writing such as my family and friends. Of special note, my friend Arnie Patterson, USN (ret) who helps an Air Force guy write stories about the Navy as well as my good friend and SCUBA Instructor Eric Dhabliwala who made sure my characters didn't drown…accidentally.

Also, an especially loud shout out to my beta readers, particularly Ashley Thomas whose wit and keen eye made my final edit far less painful.
~ JP

www.ingramcontent.com/pod-product-compliance
Lightning Source LLC
Chambersburg PA
CBHW020243200626
46816CB00001BA/97